Haunted Stars

Albert Wendland

D G STAR
BOOKS

Haunted Stars © 2023
by Albert Wendland

Published by Dog Star Books
Bowie, MD

First Edition

Cover Image: Bradley Sharp
Book Design: Jennifer Barnes

Printed in the United States of America

ISBN: 978-1-947879-58-4

Library of Congress Control Number: 2023931488

Contents

Foreword.. 7

Chapter 1: In a Lonely Bar on a Lonely World 9

Chapter 2: The Raid.. 21

Chapter 3: Politics and Money 31

Chapter 4: The Mountain Seekers 40

Chapter 5: The Blood Star.................................... 50

Chapter 6: Rimport 3.. 61

Chapter 7: In the Hangar 71

Chapter 8: Shadows Past 80

Chapter 9: 82A 91

Chapter 10: The Fixer 101

Chapter 11: In Flight 114

Chapter 12: Cloud Forest................................... 122

Chapter 13: On the Plateau 131

Chapter 14: Basecamp.. 139

Chapter 15: The Interrogator 148

Chapter 16: Long Night...................................... 165

Chapter 17: Eye 181

Chapter 18: The Obligation 190

The events in this story occur after *In a Suspect Universe* but before *The Man Who Loved Alien Landscapes*.

Foreword

Heidi Ruby Miller

I met Albert (Al to his friends) Wendland when I became a graduate student in Seton Hill University's Writing Popular Fiction program back in 2005. A few years later, he became my boss when I started teaching at SHU. A few more years later, I became his editor at Dog Star Books when I acquired his critically acclaimed novel, *The Man Who Loved Alien Landscapes*, the first book in his Mykol Ranglen series. Somehow, our friendship was only enhanced by those constant dynamic shifts because they all revolved around our mutual obsession with science fiction. (Oh, and Al is a really nice person.)

Be it his Ranglen books, his short stories, or the ingenious poetry collection as told to him by Mykol Ranglen himself, *Temporary Planets for Transitory Days*, I've always been easily immersed in Al's writing. It's how he turns mystery into hope and awe, his ability to tame the sublime, and the way he can use story to show us the value and excitement of ideas that are far from what we can imagine in this time and this space. Al says it best in *Haunted Stars* when the no nonsense character of Hatch explains to Ranglen why Ranglen's on-again, off-again lover Anne is so successful in her business dealings:

> "Think about it, Mykol. The whole point of her business, the foundation of what she wants to import and sell, is not based on material value. She sells instead the *story* behind the object. There's potential here—diamonds found in space, broken free from the heart of a star. Some white dwarves might even be *made* of diamond—though you'd never be able to chip off a piece, the gravity would kill you. But what a great tale you could spin—how it symbolizes the vastness of the stars, how it speaks of interstellar cataclysms squeezed down into glittering trinkets. *That* has value,

the glint of off-world exoticism—not what it *is*, but what it *represents*."

As writers, we try to show readers our ideas through our words. The implication is ours, of course, but the inference can only come from outside ourselves, so we choose carefully how to tell the story in order to give it the value we hope others will see. Al reminded me of why I love science fiction in *Haunted Stars*. For a genre fan, *that* has value. Indeed, that has the glint of off-world exoticism and what it *represents*.

—Heidi Ruby Miller, author of the Ambasadora series
   November 10, 2022

Chapter 1: In a Lonely Bar on a Lonely World

The old man didn't like where he was. Not the room, not the town, and certainly not the planet.

The planet was Ventroni, where the distinction between criminals and law-enforcement was never clear. Haphazardly colonized and not fully "settled," it was run by power-broking clans more than any legal government.

And the town was only the outskirt rim of a spaceport, a circle of taverns, warehouses and dorms made for transients. Since it was walled off from the rest of the city, which glowed like darkened crystal beyond, you would not be questioned and your ship not inspected as long as you didn't cross that wall (which was good for the old man, since his ship would never pass such review).

And the room was a mixture of "gangster nostalgia" and high-tech subtlety, its dark mood that of a classic noir saloon, with wooden tables inlaid with gargoyles, dim lights in hanging frames, and waiters prowling like ghosts of long-forgotten crimes. Behind a wide serving bar and racks of bottles, a neon display hissed and flickered in tubes of green, purple, and pink.

But the old man knew that even with its theatrical look, the room was designed for up-to-date security. While the frames between booths discouraged spying, the shady patrons—from loose accountants to grubby thugs—could talk and scheme while yet knowing that voices were cloaked, visuals blurred, and DNA tracers quickly removed. The room was *made* for socially-mixed face-to-face dealing, where body language could be flaunted, asserted, challenged, and feared.

Maybe it was the best place to meet after all.

The man's name was Lihandro, and he had come here to confer with a possible investor for a personal project. But he wished the backer had not insisted on meeting here instead of on Earth, his own home planet. He *knew* Earth.

Still, the man felt he had all the advantages, that, even on this world, he could negotiate a bright future.

At least he hoped so.

When a man crossed the portal from the darkness outside (you couldn't see the people at the tables, but anyone entering was fully displayed—a safety precaution), he felt immediately this was his contact.

The visitor didn't look suspicious. He was not very tall, his clothes outdoorsy for a spaceport as if he had just left a hunting party. The short white beard was well-tended. His silver-rimmed glasses shone dark and, thus, maybe hid surveillance screens. He wore a peaked worker's cap, a worn and many-pocketed jacket (the "hunter" image), baggy slacks, and heavy gym-shoes. He looked like someone's gruff uncle or a local guide for nature excursions.

Lihandro wasn't fooled. If the recommendations about this man were accurate (and they should be—they came from a friend who, like Lihandro, was also a member of the Seekers of the Mountain) he should be exactly what the old man needed. And his not looking the part was an advantage.

The visitor found Lihandro easily—he had told him which table to take. He approached, sat, stared at the man, and made no move to greet him.

Lihandro could see now the visitor's scars and broken nose, likely the result of old fights. This made him more distinguished than scruffy, even handsome, and he had a strange scent of copper about him, which was almost appealing.

The man removed his glasses and set them on the table, a possible gesture of equality. His dark and assured gray eyes probed Lihandro, not like those of an interrogator but more like an engineer examining a machine.

"Mr. Muletti?" Lihandro said.

"Aarov is fine."

Lihandro asked, too quickly, "Why are we meeting here and not on Earth?"

Muletti hardly smiled. "Because you claimed your discovery was momentous, maybe dangerous. In that case, I wouldn't want Earth."

"But still, why?"

"Earth has become too high-handed. If what you found is valuable, they'd take it from you. If it's dangerous, they'd blame you for finding it and put you in prison. I'd avoid Earth."

The old man silently disagreed. Earth had many places now where illegal cargo could be unloaded, abandoned ground with broken surveillance, especially after the recent disasters. He waved his hand about the room. "But then why here?"

"We're not really 'on' Ventroni if that's your worry. We're in a buffer zone where no one shows interest in what anyone does. Instead of meeting in some wasteland on Earth or on a dead moon, I prefer the ambiguity of this place, the feel of impermanence, of 'fly by night.' It appeals to me. I'm like that."

Lihandro was surprised by the man's chattiness. He had expected a cold reserve.

"Ventroni might as well be in another universe. We're isolated, and no one can hear us. So, don't be concerned. Or did you want your friend from Earth to be included, too? Is that why you suggested we meet there?"

"No, I was just told you visit Earth often, so I assumed...."

Muletti sighed. "Look, maybe we should get started. What have you found that's so important? I don't usually do these kinds of 'interviews,' but your friend is also *my* friend, and she vouched for you. And—I think you know—it would be hard for you to get someone else you can trust."

Yes, he knew. Thank the Mountain for his connection to the Seekers.

Muletti leaned forward. "So, what do you have for me, old man? Tell me your story, and I'll let you know if I'm interested or not. Take your time. I want the feel of it. I make a lot of decisions based on that. And I was told by our friend that a 'gut response' is important for understanding what you've found."

Again, Lihandro was surprised. He had expected a "just the facts" approach—which he knew would make his task harder. The "facts" in his story weren't very clear.

So, he began. "I was exploring near a red-giant star…."

And he had tired of the sun's ruddy stain. Such color was all relative, of course—though called a "red giant," it had only an orange tint in its fierce white light, and it glowed intensely from even a light-year away.

The system seemed to be the result of a cataclysmic break-up or collision, with no large planets left, only planetoids in drifting debris and profitless dust. Nothing about it looked appealing from where he scanned it beneath the ecliptic, and it seemed almost too crowded with wreckage. The star was somewhat variable, too, so maybe unstable.

He had come there pursuing an old dream, desperate to find something of worth—though he was aware such dreams were much too common now. The discovery of the first Airafane Clip and its light-space drive provided cheap and easy transportation, which quickly gave humanity the stars. The finding of the second Clip brought gravity-plates, allowing another means of propulsion more short-range but widely applicable. Given such stimuli, entrepreneurs built easily-purchased spaceships. If you raised enough money, you could head off into the universe—in family vehicles, business cruisers, enormous and crowded colony transports, or tight little two-seater roustabouts.

Like Lihandro's.

The old man's ship started as a small efficient spacer but its overuse, the lack of good maintenance, and the weary drag of many light-years had taken their toll. And, though he named it "Airafane City"—written in large letters on the side—to bring him good luck, he never made much of a strike.

Yet, in this first-time-visited star system, he read on his instruments something… peculiar. And unless his scanners worked incorrectly (which would not be surprising) it was worth a look.

A large circular area, almost an eighth of the system's radius and halfway in from the rim to the sun, seemed remarkably clear. Any floating material—of which there was less than in the rest of the disk—moved in independent orbits about a small object in the center. That object was apparently an asteroid, but it had a shape, based on the radar beams bounced from the surface, almost perfectly round. The thing was too large to be a spaceship but too small to exert enough gravity to pull it into such a flawless globe.

"What the eyes...." (The old man's expression came from the Mountain Seekers, referring to their belief in, as they called it, a 'Mountain with Eyes.' It conveyed the same perplexity as "What in God's name," or "What the hell.")

He didn't debate before moving his ship closer, and he tried to reign in his eager hopes—they had been demolished too often before.

He crossed the system below the ecliptic but then ascended and entered the freer circle around the object, which registered a gravity larger than it should—almost 90% of Earth's—though it was only a few hundred kilometers across. It was not reflective in the way that polished metal would be. Indeed, according to his instruments, the outside was almost porous, and to a fractal extent (meaning that the algorithms approximating the surface used fractal patterns). Openings contained smaller openings, and those too were made of smaller ones yet, as if the globe was covered with a sheet of deep froth.

Also, the rock material that swept around it moved oddly, the angular velocities all the same. The debris was aligned in permanent spokes that swung about the planetoid like parts of a wheel.

Much too strange.

But Lihandro lived for moments like this. His whole life in space was a search for enigmas. And though he wanted to use such discoveries to get rich, the *secrets* behind them appealed to him more.

Like every prospector, he knew the stories of how the galaxy once reverberated with the wars of the Airafane and Moyocks, the extinct races from millions of years ago. And he knew that treasures were left in the buried Airafane Clips that later races could discover and use, as humanity had done. There were ruins, too, and hints of vanished interstellar cultures whose traces haunted the present stars. Everyone in space looked for such things—derelicts or "Flying Dutchmen," disappearances in "Bermuda Triangles," ships lost in "Sargassos of Space." Legends that originated on Earth spread outward and permeated the galaxy.

You *lived* for them. But then, in your lifetime, you found nothing.

Until maybe now.

The old man and his spaceship moved gradually forward. He took in what he saw and what his instruments told him, muttering as he did so, "Keep working, little ship. Do your job and then we go home." He knew the vessel was not in great shape.

The rocks floating around the globe passed close enough for observation. They looked like typical dark meteors, nothing artificial, and yet the orbits were too unlikely. They suggested, quietly, "We don't behave in the way you expect, there's something about us you can't understand."

His imagination stirred, which wasn't always good.

The orbits grew dense as irregular lumps shuffled by. Through magnification, he could see they were jagged with whitened edges, hardly worn down—like dirty teeth or filed claws.

He did spectrographic analysis, reflection comparisons, radiation scans. But his instruments were old and in need of updates, his tests inconclusive.

"Keep moving, little ship. Stay loyal…to me."

Proceeding with lack of data was unwise. But this didn't stop him. He even shifted his orbit to capture one of the rocks.

His ship didn't have grappling arms or mechanical waldos so, it wasn't easy. He had to match orbits and catch a stone in the tiny airlock without smashing the interior, making his ship into an open mouth trying to swallow a floating piece of candy. It took a while. His data-feeds broke, and his thrusters grew spotty. He became too tense.

But, finally, the rock drifted safely inside. He restarted the airlock's gravity plate and shut the outer hatch.

After pressurizing the chamber, he opened the inner door. With calipers and gloves, he lifted the rock and brought it inside.

It was heavy in the artificial gravity of the ship, the size of a small loaf of bread. He had no facilities for sterilization or protocols against infection. He just took the thing in and placed it on his one table and stared at it.

An ugly black rock with sharp white edges.

He was disappointed. It looked uninteresting.

He'd run composition tests later. He didn't have time now, being more interested in the bigger object, the centerpiece of the weird orbits.

He returned to his pilot's seat and watched the central object grow near.

It was perfectly round—frightening for such a small body even with its larger than usual gravity. It had to be artificial. But instead of looking metallic, the illuminated crescent was patterned with yellow, soft and blurry, while a circle of mist outlined the globe.

Then, as he got closer, the detail grew. The surface resembled a smooth carpet, pale yellow-ochre with curves of brown, red, light gray, all stained by the orange-tinted light of the star.

It suddenly struck him—these were the tops of trees!

A forest blanketed the planetoid. No wonder the algorithms used fractals to imitate the exterior. Gaps between the trees repeated and grew smaller the closer the scans, the distance between the trunks shrinking to that between the leaves—or whatever the equivalent of "leaves" existed here. Maybe the mist that encircled the globe really was an oxygen-CO_2 atmosphere.

Why hadn't his instruments shown this? The analysis should have identified the gases, the presence of plant life, the density of growth. But he only got readings on basic topographic structures, and the branching into an infinite number of more intricate and miniature shapes.

Did something protect the world from observation, shield it from chemical and biological scans?

None of the Airafane finds in space had showed any life. The Clips were always self-contained, packaged in their palm-sized tetrahedron stasis-field "fluorite" crystals, and buried in worlds with plate tectonics—this was consistent for all three Clips found so far. And the Airafane ruins scattered on different worlds were exactly alike—impossibly so, incredibly old—not just dead but "outside time," maybe not even part of our universe, like visitations from another reality stationed here for no known purpose.

But this find was different, an asteroid likely transformed to make it look artificial, then given a covering of plant life in its own atmosphere.

The old man grew too excited. It frightened him. This was the greatest discovery of his life, maybe of the century. Like the first Clip all over again!

Should he turn around? Get out while he could?

Of course, he went on.

He entered an orbit that would bring him close to the asteroid's surface. He lowered his ship over the night-side as the wide orangey crescent of day shrunk behind him. He approached his desired attitude when he passed around to the illuminated half. He didn't think it smart to get too close to the surface—but an insane indulgence pushed him yet downward.

He thought he saw hints of luminescence in the darkness below, yet the gleams flickered and quickly vanished. If anything really glowed down there, it was hidden between plants and lay close to the ground—if there *was* a ground.

Then dawn came. A gingery light in an arc of brightness spread outward from the rising sun.

He tried to control his amazement at what he saw.

Billowing tree growth passed below, vast waves of tawny boughs that tossed in air which shouldn't be thick enough for wind. The trees were not terrestrial. Pale trunks with rings of joints rose into staggered tiers, breaking into plumes that shook like feathers. The world's surface seemed alive, like the flank of a breathing animal whose hair tossed as its body stirred. Other types of trees made agate patterns of red, umber, sienna, ivory-blue, their growth in varied and elaborate swirls of palms, ferns, cups, scales, bouquets, whips, tentacles, hands—hands that waved in long fingers.

Waved at *him*.

He checked his gauges, desperate for dry scientific data. But the readings for gravity still disturbed him, and he wondered how many plates—it must be astronomical—had to be used to produce such an effect. Did the Airafane have more than one method for producing an equivalent of gravity?

His instruments showed nothing conclusive.

At one time he would have lavished in this uncertainty, thrilled with yet another wonder in his universe. But he was old now and felt himself becoming too frightened.

He couldn't afford good medical care and knew his body couldn't tolerate shocks.

Yet he wanted to land.

He brought his craft down closer yet.

Now he had glimpses of the actual ground. It was covered with a light undergrowth that looked soft as ferns. The colors were different, pale green or salmon. And he could see that the land was not perfectly flat. It had a slight rolling topography that seemed artificial, as if following a landform-producing algorithm, like early attempts at virtual reproduction or 4-D printing.

But if you have the ability to transform a planet—or to *build* one—shouldn't you be good enough to make it perfect? Why leave hints that the place is fake?

When he tried for closer views through his scopes the images distorted. The stronger he magnified, the more undefined the scenes became, like a visual equivalent of an uncertainty principle, the phenomenon similar to the camouflage effect above Airafane ruins on other worlds.

The Airafane!

This *had* to be an Airafane product—something every space-explorer wanted. Near the end of his life, he was finding a miracle.

But his ship was so old. *He* was so old.

He saw no structures, no houses, no people. He thought he saw paths but wasn't sure. No animals either.

Then a narrow canyon rose over the horizon and widened before him. Like an arrowhead aimed at his ship—a wedge or "V" of two high cliffs spreading apart and making a flat valley between.

It was too symmetric, too vaguely artificial. He didn't want to fly over it.

Then he laughed—the *whole planet* was artificial! Why should he be scared?

He hadn't seen this canyon from space. Most of the surface he saw then was in shadow.

The two cliffs spread apart at a constant rate, opening, inviting. The floor looked made of white crystal, glittering but not brightly, like translucent rock catching glints of sunlight. Nothing grew there even in the scattered areas of dirt, and nothing grew on the cliff-sides either. The walls seemed made of only soil and stone, smooth, high, but too straight and unnaturally alike. They drew apart at a pace too constant and thus too strange—too uncanny.

He tried to gauge the height of the walls, the angles of the cliffs. But, at that moment, his scanners stopped working.

More fear. His hands shook, and he felt weak.

Something came up over the horizon.

A structure sat in the middle of the canyon. It stretched several kilometers between the two cliffs and touched both sides, a curved wall rising with a gentle inward slope. The edifice appeared circular though Lihandro could see only one side of it. The middle curve lay closest to his ship while the outer flanks banked away as they reached the earth walls.

The construction was smooth, clearly unnatural, a gray solid like metal or concrete. Sitting on top of it was a low hemisphere that came to the edge, made of a slick and dampened-looking glassy substance. The flattish dome rose in two parts, the bottom dark-brown and filled with complicated pipes or branches while the top was a darker circle of black. The intricacy of the bottom half with its forking lines shown vivid in the orange light, as if illuminated from within.

It was clearly built by aesthetic intelligence, like the asteroid itself and the modified orbits of the stones around it.

Then, before he passed over the structure, he saw what appeared to be a door in its side. A high rectangular entranceway, open.

And he suddenly knew—he promised himself—one day he would enter that door.

It fell behind as he flew across the top. No detail could be seen in the black central circle.

The round structure drew to the rear. The walls of the canyon came together, closing at the same rate they had opened before. Both valleys thus stretched equally from the two sides of the dome.

After several more kilometers, he passed over trees again.

The sun lowered. The yellow landscape became red, dark.

He took the ship higher, staying in orbit around the world but distancing himself.

He knew he couldn't land now. The discovery was too big. He would be foolish to take this on alone. He needed help.

But a necessary calm settled over him. His instruments now worked again.

He had to think clearly. He'd profit from this discovery, of course. He'd have a new and wealthy life. But such a find was above self-indulgence. It belonged to everyone.

From his higher orbit, he wanted to see the structure again, to take more readings though they probably wouldn't work. Photographs neither. Other Airafane ruins discouraged such efforts. The canyon would be small on the face of the globe but still noticeable.

He returned to the rock he picked up earlier, if only for something to divert his attention. He took it from the table and set it in the passenger's chair beside him. With a knife, he scraped off some of its dark material and exposed the white stone beneath.

It reminded him of the crystal at the base of the canyon.

He suddenly froze. "No, impossible!"

He believed he knew the composition of the rock.

He feared a heart attack. He told himself to breathe, to remain calm.

And he had to turn away. He looked through the port to settle his nerves. The sun peeked over the edge of the asteroid, made a crescent that widened into dawn.

A dawn for *him!* For an affluence and power he had never known—a new existence so dramatically different he feared it would kill him.

The face of the planetoid filled with majestic yellow light.

And in the middle of it…

The elliptical canyon, the round object, the black center—

And now—*NOW!*—

A *pale blue* ring around it, no longer brown—

It was a monstrous eye!

And it stared at *him!*

The color in the "iris" had changed. It was now blue. Impossibly blue in this orange light.

Like *his* eyes.

A spike of horror punctured his chest. His throat closed, and he felt dizzy, as if passing out. He was a member of the Mountain Seekers, and they believed in a mountain—with *eyes*!

It sees me!

He slammed the thrusters. He had to get away.

Breathe, old man! You stupid old man!

He rose from the plane of the stellar system. He couldn't stop shaking.

Soon—as soon as possible—he plotted a light-space jump to Earth, entered the coordinates and left the star.

He'd have two days now to settle himself, to reach a state he desperately needed. To think. To plan.

He prayed the vision would somehow leave him. It filled him with too much terror and shock. But he reminded himself, the discovery was his. There was no going back now. All of human history might change.

Did the Airafane have eyes?

And why—*why?*—did the color adjust to match his own?

He wanted to pray but he didn't know which god to choose. Earth's humanized elderly father? Or the Seekers' "Mountain"—with its now significant connection to reality?

And, of course, his life would change, drastically. He now could make amends, correct mistakes. "To be good for someone. Just to be good." He had read that somewhere and now the thought appealed to him.

But would his discovery destroy the Seekers?—or give it influence beyond its dreams?

Take your time, old man. Think for yourself as much as for others.

And what would he find beyond that door? The structure, the whole planetoid, called for attention. Something had to wait there that wanted to be found. Would it be wonderful?—or terrible?

Tears leaked from his eyes.

Of course, he'd need help. But the discovery would always be *his*.

The old man finished.

Muletti hadn't moved throughout the story, his eyes hardly blinking and his lips slightly parted. Lihandro knew he had kept his attention.

With the old man silent now, Muletti stared at him and said nothing for a time. Then he glanced about the room and offered casually, "What do you need from me?"

Lihandro gave out a breath of relief. His listener wouldn't ask this if he wasn't interested.

"I want to go back," he said, "but I need a new spaceship. I don't trust mine to last for as long as I'll need to stay there. And I need a bigger cargo hold. I want to get more samples. I also need to carry better equipment for recording, scans, analysis. Especially, I want to land and explore the structure that makes up the 'eye.' It's obviously important and can only be a product of the Airafane. And I think you know what I expect to find there."

Muletti softened his expression. "Yes, I do know. If it really is an Airafane structure, and if it *is* calling attention to itself."

"What else could it be doing? The whole world was redone somehow. *We* can't do that. The Moyocks left nothing behind them after destroying the Airafane. And, even if it is a Moyock construction, that too would be significant. It's a call—and maybe a call directly to *us*—the ones with eyes. It has to be Airafane."

Muletti leaned forward, as if wanting to stick to business. "Let's not speculate on what we don't know. And tell me what's special about the floating rock you found. You didn't say."

Instead of answering, Lihandro opened a cloth bag that sat on the bench beside him. He pulled out an object wrapped in a towel and handed it over.

Muletti first checked the controls on the table's wall-screen, making sure all outside surveillance was blocked.

He opened the towel and stared at the ugly black rock. He turned it till he came to the spot where the coating had been scraped away. He pulled from his pocket a jeweler's loupe and examined the white substance through the lens.

His expression didn't change.

Then he took a palm-sized instrument from his pocket and flipped a switch on it. A ready light came on. He removed a plastic cover from a metal needle's tip, which he held against the clean area of the stone.

Lihandro asked, "Thermal conductivity?"

Muletti was too focused to nod. But when he got a full-bar reading on his device, which Lihandro could see, he looked satisfied. He recapped the needle and put the instrument away.

Then he wrapped the rock back into its towel and left it before him on the table.

He did not give it back to Lihandro.

He looked thoughtful, but his eyes were brighter than before.

Lihandro didn't flinch. The two days in light-space had built in him a strong resolve, and he'd left many of his fears behind. He was determined—he would be the first to enter that dome.

"Okay," Muletti said. He pointed to the rock in its wrapping. "I can find a buyer for this. And the sell will supply us with enough funds."

Lihandro nodded, said nothing.

"You realize it has no *intrinsic* worth. Stuff like this has been discovered before."

"But, as you say, you can find a buyer."

"Yes. There's value, just of another kind."

Lihandro waited. "And the 'eye'?"

Muletti looked wistful—or maybe possessed, touched with a near transcendent emotion. "Yes…'the eye'…That's quite a story."

Lihandro kept quiet. He had talked enough.

"Look," Muletti said, "I don't believe in your Seekers, even if they do worship the Airafane. And what you found doesn't change my feelings. But…you're a member. How do you think this will change things for them?"

Lihandro felt sad. "It will either destroy them or make them more powerful than they ever should be. Either result could be a disaster."

Muletti stared at the glowing neon behind the bar, but his attention seemed elsewhere. "Yes…I agree. It all comes down to power, doesn't it? This will have vast repercussions."

"That's why I'm asking for help."

"Which is another question. Why didn't you go straight to the Confederation authorities, or at least to the government on Earth since you're from there? This discovery needs a party of scientists, investigators, even the military, not a rogue prospector and his…'fixer.'"

Lihandro straightened his back, said precisely, "I'm not telling anyone because it's *mine!* You know what'll happen if a government gets aware of this. None of us will see it again. Only *they* will. And they won't share a bit of it. People like us, we'll learn nothing."

Muletti didn't comment, as if his question had been more a test. He sat back and tried to look relaxed. "Well, old man, I have to say…you've impressed me. This is giving me a lot to think about."

Neither of them spoke, words maybe too much for the moment.

Then Muletti leaned forward and became practical again. "All right, I'll get the spaceship. And this little thing,"—he indicated the rock—"will pay for it, and more. I promise you, we'll get back there."

" *We?* "

"Yes. I'm coming with you. I want to see this object, too."

Lihandro peered back at him. "I expected that, but I want you to know…*I* will be the first to walk through that door."

19

Muletti laughed. "Are you kidding? I wouldn't have it any other way. I won't say I'm frightened, but I *am* careful. You can be the foolhardy one."

Lihandro just stared.

"For now," Muletti said, "you go back to Earth. I'll contact you when I've made all the arrangements. It should take about two weeks. We'll then go to your system, but we won't stay long—or at least I hope not. We just want to get more confirmation and data. We'll see about that doorway then, how far it leads in and where it goes. But we're not an exploration team. We're just lighting the way—and taking what we find, of course, whatever that might be, to our advantage. We'll also get more of your 'rocks.'"

Lihandro nodded. He knew not to be too demanding. He was glad to put preparation into someone else's hands.

But he kept the coordinates of the system to himself. He'd give those to *no one*. And he appreciated that Muletti knew enough not to ask for them.

"All right," Muletti repeated, with mild detachment that again seemed feigned. "This has been most satisfying. Not just a good business proposition, but...hell, I think you and I will become part of history. It's all very strange and yet *so* appealing. I understand why you're excited."

The old man nodded again.

"Don't worry about looking for me," Muletti said. "I'll find you through our mutual friend."

Then he stood up and quickly left, with no signifying flourish or "good-bye."

Lihandro noticed that he left the room through a different exit than the front door—as if he followed a habit of never using the same entrance twice.

The old man stayed a while longer, enjoying this new sense of satisfaction, of secrets kept and growing protections. He was wary, of course. He knew he couldn't allow himself to trust Muletti fully. And the discovery was almost too enormous, bigger than the life of a simple old man who knew he was neglectful and often self-indulgent.

But he now had the chance to become different—to atone, right wrongs, help people he had hurt. All good things. All back on Earth.

He relaxed and had a quiet meal.

And he recalled to himself how, from his story, he had left out one significant point. Well, *two* points.

When he gathered the rock into his airlock, he captured more than one. And those others were hidden safely away.

The other point was far more drastic...he intended to go back to the planetoid one more time, alone, in secret, *before* Muletti got him a fancy new ship. His old craft could take it. He had done some repairs since getting back.

He thought of all this while he ate his meal, which was quite satisfying.

When he left the bar, he noticed that even in the floodlights of the nearby landing field, he could still see the stars.

He had read somewhere another line he remembered, "In a lonely bar on a lonely world with a star-crowded but lonely sky."

His seeing the stars was reassuring. He had something to live for.

Two weeks later, the old man was dead.

Chapter 2: The Raid

Not dying! she wanted to scream.

But there was no point in yelling. The ship had been attacked, and Braya had little time—food, water, air, or life—to wonder why.

She was a refugee, a "displaced person," kept inside a huge compartment on a cargo ship taking her and other migrants to a colony in space.

All of them had lost their homes on Earth because of environmental disasters, and the government there found it best to send the victims to corporate-run interstellar settlements instead of re-locating them on Earth. It was a good financial and political move—but not so good for the victims, who still had to pay transport fees, clearance charges, and down payments for land rights on the new world, the cost of which the corporations took out of their first earnings. This often amounted to years of bond-debt. Some people never managed to pay it off and became company "property" for the rest of their lives.

But, to Braya and the other migrants onboard, anything was better than the flooded and storm-tossed cities of Earth.

They were kept in a big cargo container that was surprisingly comfortable—with beds, food, showers, entertainment. But the place was crowded, and they were not free to roam the ship. This unit would be deposited on the undeveloped world to which they'd be taken, to provide early shelter and working space, temporary but immediately useful. The people didn't like being confined to it while onboard the ship, but they all believed their indentured servitude would be temporary and the promise of freedom soon fulfilled.

Braya knew better but she said nothing.

Indeed, she kept quiet about most of her opinions, though people assumed they were strong. Her small body moved in spastic energetic fits, as if stirred by deep locked-up emotions. Her eyes darted and took in everything. Even her short hair, black and jagged, and her tight-lipped scowling mouth appeared defiant. She said nothing until threatened, but then she'd break forth in loud tirades. People, uncomfortable, turned away and left her to herself.

One person did try to get close to her but failed. Her name was Krin, and to Braya she was crazy—because of her outlandish dress, clownish face in wild make-up, and hair like a nest of pink steel-wool. She was a loud and talkative member of the Mountain Seekers, who worshipped Airafane Clips because of the influence they had over society, and she pestered Braya constantly. She first approached her on Earth while they waited in crowds before disembarking, telling foolish stories about a "mountain with eyes," a "beast in a cave," "deep time," and coming rebellions from an "underworld." She clung to Braya as they filed on board, and in the narrow space of the cargo container she hovered too close to her.

Braya pushed her away, even tried to kick her.

"Why can't you *believe*?" Krin persisted.

And off Braya went. "Because you're stupid and irrational. You're not the type to have privileged information. Everything you know you've swallowed whole with no *thinking* at all. You just want to gain power and justify yourself—to others first and then to yourself. It's all pettiness. You say nothing new. You're just a foolish old woman who wants someone to be your convert or servant—so you can feel important!"

Krin looked shocked but unfazed. "Well, goodness, and you've been so quiet up until now. But such a great fire you have—my little flame, that's what I'll call you. And you'd be perfect for the Seekers. Let me share with you what they believe. We're bringing new ways to get out of our holes. You can be one of us. You—"

On and on.

Braya, fed up, shoved her aside and hurried away from her.

But then, when the raiders attacked the ship, the old woman was the first to stand up to them, stand right in their way and face them down.

She also was first to maybe get killed.

The attack came with a loud thud, a reverberation through the hull. People sat up from their beds and looked warily about.

Then came a loud cracking scream like metal sheets ripping apart.

The artificial weight from the gravity-plates switched off. The refugees glided up from the deck, swinging their arms and shouting in fear—then they fell back down, heavier, some of them lucky enough to land on their beds. The plates had restarted and returned the gravity but now it was stronger. People tumbled to the floor. Confused noises of shock and pain filled the room.

The door to the rest of the ship blew inward—an explosion of debris. People in light spacesuits followed, carrying energy weapons hooked to backpacks.

Krin grabbed Braya and pushed her away, stepped between the refugees and the invaders, yelled hysterical curses at them—"You beasts out of time! You Moyocks of hate!"

One raider, with an orange stripe on his arm and carrying a handgun instead of a large firearm, struck her in the face. She fell to the deck.

He hit her again.

The rest of the invaders aimed at the refugees and shot electro-laser beams. People fell, burning, screaming.

Braya, after Krin pushed her, tumbled into a small alcove. It was not much of a hiding place, but she stayed behind its partial wall. As the invaders rushed by, they didn't see her.

The refugees tried to run for safety but they found few places where they could hide. With their backs against the far wall, they could only watch as the raiders moved in and fired at them red-white beams.

Shouts and cries, thumps of falling bodies, smells of burning.

The invaders shoved before them anyone still alive and herded people into a corner.

In front of Braya, the man beating Krin lifted the visor of his spacesuit. He pulled the woman erect till her bleeding face hung before the helmet's opening. A male voice shouted at the near-lifeless figure, but Braya couldn't make out what was said.

The other raiders moved away from the exploded door-frame. They gathered the refugees on the other side of the room which now left the opening clear. Braya stood close enough to run through and maybe get away.

This was her chance.

She leapt from her hiding place, felt the heavy pull of gravity.

The man holding Krin threw her to the floor, turned, and saw Braya. He had a white beard.

He shot at her with his handgun. A bullet impacted the bulkhead behind her.

She ran into the corridor and hurried to her right, still hearing the chaos of shouting and killing. The gun fired again and struck near her. She knew that bullets should not be used on board a spaceship. They could puncture the hull.

She rushed around a corner and saw no one. She was in the restricted part of the ship—any place outside the cargo container—and she ran in a direction she thought would take her to the superstructure at the stern of the craft, which she knew contained crew's quarters, the bridge, possible help.

Three people entered the passageway in front of her and charged toward her, not in spacesuits but jerseys and slacks. They must be crew.

Two of them grabbed her while the third ran on. "Move," the woman said to her, "Get back to the container."

Braya fought them. "They're being killed or taken away! People broke in and started firing!"

The man who continued down the hallway suddenly fell.

The two women holding Braya stared at him, then released her and ran to his body lying on the deck.

The man in the spacesuit with the orange stripe came around the corner. He shot at both women, and they fell too.

Braya ran through a nearby doorway into another stretch of corridor. She glanced back but could not see the man with the handgun.

If the crew had been trying to repel the boarders, then why weren't they armed? And why did they grab her, who was not in a suit and clearly a passenger, and then try to take her back to where the shooting occurred?

She once had worked in a spaceport on Earth—until accused of thievery and sent to jail. Though no cargo ship this large ever came down the gravity well, she knew there should be lifeboats on board as well as individual escape pods. But she wouldn't know how to work a lifeboat, and if the raiders were also killing the crew, they probably destroyed the boats already. And the escape pods did not have the power to get her away from the slaughter—they were just airtight balloons that floated in space and flashed lights for rescuers to find them. Or to make perfect targets for attackers.

She wanted a spacesuit with thrusters instead. She could maneuver it and thus get out of reach, at least she assumed. She had seen such suits at the port where she worked and had snuck into several—another occasion that got her in trouble.

She hurried while fighting the heavy weight. The air stirred menacingly around her, as if moved by a growing breeze—being siphoned out? It wasn't explosive decompression yet but just a gradual leakage instead, as if controlled.

Slow death.

She entered another compartment—and stopped in shock.

It was filled with bodies. Proof the killing was not limited to the refugees.

Gravity ceased again. The bodies—crew, passengers, officers—rose into the currents of jostling air, their faces stark, their entrails exposed, burned open or ripped apart. She could smell the charred flesh, the stench of stomach acid and vomit, half-digested food, piss.

They weren't people anymore. Just the dead.

She fought being sick as she rose from the floor too.

She also saw, on the other side of the room, a line of lockers with doors thrown open—and inside them hung what looked to be spacesuits. People must have rushed here to don them but were butchered instead.

She'd have to glide across the room, now filled with floating corpses. She was horrified—they'd bounce against her, the gargoyle faces in front of her own, blood and fluids soaking her clothes.

Gravity returned. Everything slapped down to the deck, splattered her with blood.

Back on her feet now, and before the gravity could vanish once more, she rushed across the room. She tried to avoid stepping on corpses but this was impossible. She didn't look down.

She reached the lockers and glanced inside the first that was open. A hanging spacesuit!

She pulled out its rack and backed into the front opening. She didn't remove her shoes and jacket because the suit was too large for her. She closed the connections, pulled on the helmet and tightened the seals. Then she followed the symbols in the wrist-booklet for powering the suit and pressurization. She assumed—she had to—the backpack was fully charged and held new oxygen tanks. Of course the suit was different from the ones she had worn back on Earth but the principles had to be the same.

She moved too fast. Her hands shook.

Clean air hissed around her face. The smells diminished but still leaked in. She didn't dare let herself be sick.

The gravity gave out again. The bodies rose.

But she herself didn't have to float now. The bottoms of the boots had suction grips and magnets. She stuck to the deck and was able to walk if she moved slowly. It made crossing through the drifting corpses easier, but it took longer.

She bumped into them. They careened away, dense with inertia, sent other bodies spinning about, causing more to strike against her. Dark liquids stained her faceplate.

She tried to stay calm, look straight ahead, and let her side vision remain blocked by the helmet.

She finally reached the other side of the room and quickly entered the passageway. She pulled her feet up from the deck and grabbed handholds to pull herself forward in a weightless glide. It was faster but more difficult, yet she soon learned how to control her flight.

She believed she was in the superstructure now, the accommodation block. The large room with its spacesuits was likely a part of it.

But that implied everyone might be dead. The crew of the ship would not be large and that room had been crowded. Who'd want to kill or kidnap refugees and then slaughter everyone else? Why did the ship's alarms give no warning, no call to action, no counter response?

Her helmet gauge said the air in the ship was almost gone. Any weightless objects that had floated with the currents now wandered chaotically.

She passed blue lights on the wall. She assumed they indicated escape pods. She still didn't want them. She wouldn't die floating powerless in space. And no one had been shown how to use them anyway—refugees were just cargo, human traffic. Safety procedures didn't extend to them.

But she could hide in her spacesuit now, "play dead," remain quiet till everyone left and then wait for rescuers. And a suit had thrusters. Maybe she could avoid being killed.

25

Not dying! Not yet!

She encountered no one. Was she the last person alive?

The gravity returned.

She fell, tumbled, lay prone on the deck. The spacesuit made it difficult to stand up. But if someone still manipulated gravity then the raiders had not yet left.

Reverberations shook the floor. It lurched and tilted. She stood up awkwardly, then righted herself and raced on, hoping for a way to get outside or at least see what was happening.

From a nearby doorway, a figure in a spacesuit appeared, holding a handgun. The sleeve did not have an orange stripe.

But before noticing Braya, the person was suddenly riddled with bullets. The body hit the deck, the suit punctured and leaking air.

Another person in a spacesuit ran from the doorway, also holding a gun, stopped and leaned over the body.

Then that person too was shot.

More arrived, but Braya ducked into another passageway and ran off before she could be seen, at least she hoped.

Were the raiders now killing each other?

She found a ladder leading upward, possibly a way to reach the bridge, though she had little hope now of finding people who could help her. The freighter was large but the cargo components self-contained with no need of upkeep—hence a small crew.

More thuds and tremors through the floor. The higher she climbed the better chance she had to view outside.

After three levels, she reached an observation chamber with a wide wall of rectangular ports. She must be on the lowest of the control decks, a lounge or casual meeting spot that could double as a station for observing the ship.

No one followed her. In the absence of air, she'd hear no one anyway.

She looked outside.

The layout of the cargo carrier was familiar, though she had seen only smaller versions at the spaceports where she worked. Built around a long central spine, it ran from the tapered hood at the bow to the engines in the stern with the big superstructure rising up before them. The base of that structure encircled the hub and held crew accommodations, officers' quarters, storage rooms, support systems. She stood in the area above those compartments but beneath the bridge, called the "wheelhouse," with its navigation deck and extended observation wings. Above that would rise the nest of aerials, radar equipment, scanning dishes, and communication gear.

From her high position, she could see the racks of cargo containers, in varying sizes but fitting together for maximum use of space. They encircled the core spine. Two derricks, rising from the nested containers, could move forward, aft, and laterally around the core, to load or unload the cargo. If the containers were removed, the only parts of the ship remaining would be the stern engines, the superstructure standing before them, the wedge-like bow, and the long connecting backbone running down the center—which held the corridors where Braya had been chased. But when loaded, the ship became a wide cylindrical array of boxes, tubes, and crescents surrounding the hub, to be transported to and deposited at various ports in space.

But what she saw now was a ship being destroyed.

Debris and wreckage, drifting containers blown apart, holes cut open in the central frame, damage leaking from the forward hood—and floating bodies. The colonists' unit was easily identified—the largest container, contoured and smoothed for descent into atmosphere. Though still clamped to the central shaft, a large side of it had been blown away. And what looked like a type-3 troop carrier, ex-military and cheaply refitted, gathered people from the breaks in quickly inflated passenger pods.

She didn't want to think where they'd be taken.

Another small trooper siphoned objects from torn-open containers—which shocked her. Pirates would make more money if they took the containers intact and then commandeered the ship, removed all identifiers, altered the appearance and sold it illegally. But these raiders were destroying it.

The two carriers fired no weapons and were not involved in the destruction.

But then she saw the real killer.

A ship appeared above her, close, in full view, smaller than the troopers and more unique. Its flat plate of delta wing tapered out to down-curving and claw-like tips. The fuselage swelled forward where, on its bottom, a slanted opening held the mouths of missile-ejection tubes. On top of the fuselage, a flattish dome resembled a beetle's carapace, where the pilot and sensory arrays would be held. The slim tail had a high fin, and from the ship's bottom protruded stabilizing prods that could be used for either horizontal or vertical landings.

The craft looked hawkish, feral, deadly, and it was streamlined for atmosphere as well as space. It could only be a military attack fighter, but it had no identifier of home planet or port registration.

On both sides of the missile launcher, large torpedo-like bombs bulged beneath the delta wing, fat and heavy, ready to be fired. Four of them, and each looked big enough to break and destroy most of the ship.

Missiles flashed from the forward tubes, struck at the base of the superstructure. The deck shook beneath Braya. She almost lost her footing as pieces of hull flew out before her into space.

The attack craft made wide passes and slashed at the spine, broke off containers, struck at the engines, methodically dismantled the craft. The feel of the strikes ran through the decks.

Just a matter of time before everything would be gone—herself included.

It made no sense. They were destroying their profit.

Then two other ships joined the fray.

One looked to be a standard 4-seater, commonly used for interstellar travel, lozenge-shaped, with an observation bridge in front and narrow type-2 engines in back, wingless but with stabilizer prods. It had additional carrier racks on its sides that held the same missiles like those in the fuselage of the fighter. They rained destruction.

The last ship was smaller, a two-person roustabout, old and in need of repair. It also had carrier racks but with fewer weapons, and this ship stayed further out, as if watching over the procedure, keeping a "look-out." Yet it too shot off rockets.

The attack had been planned—it was precise, meticulous, almost military and professional. Identifiers had been removed from the two other craft also.

No wonder the crew had been killed so quickly—to remove witnesses. Any refugees left alive would be gathered in the larger troop ship and sold to corporations needing workers.

A deep hysteria rose inside her. She faced death and knew she couldn't survive, but a fierceness, a brutal fury ignited within her, a focus stronger than any she had felt before. It overwhelmed her.

The hawk-like fighter—the "*Killer*" she called it—dived at the bridge. Several missiles flew toward her.

She jumped back.

Everything crashed. The bulkheads cracked and the windows blew open. She tumbled outward into space as chunks of wreckage banged against her.

She spun out of control in a cloud of dust and sharp-edged metal fragments that struck against her, terrifying her.

But the wreckage swirled away and dispersed. The life-support gauges inside her helmet indicated no breaks in the suit, no loss of air. She tapped emergency controls with her chin, flipped through data on orientation, stabilization, propulsion dynamics.

The spin gave her vertigo. Her mind grew sluggish, her field of vision seemed to narrow.

She tried to consult the wrist booklet as she tumbled, but light and shadow alternated too fast. Her visor was still stained with blood, and it was hard to find anything in the book, much less read it.

She accessed the codes for gyro controls and entered them desperately, hoping the in-suit computer would take charge, read the data and compensate.

Something worked. The low thump of a thruster reaction pressed against her and applied drag.

Chaos still whirled around her in flashing lights and quick explosions, but the spin slowed, grew almost gentle, a drawn-out and lethargic revolution.

She drifted away from the wreck. It still spun around her but at a slower pace. She could read a name on the side, "*Lochner*," and the registration symbol for Earth.

The raiders had broken the long mid-section, the backbone severed and the containers adrift. Wreckage spread away in different directions with the gaps between them widening. The small troop carrier flew about and picked up pieces of the wreck.

Then either the fuel in her spacesuit's thrusters ran out or her computer was damaged, for she still spun at an unchanging rate. Or maybe the machine decided she'd be safer in a slow revolution to distribute the heat from the nearby sun. Possibly the coolant was malfunctioning and it was necessary to modulate the heat.

Her instruments told her nothing.

The sun passed in front of her as she turned. It sat in a wide, hazy, apron-like disk of sparkles and gleams. A star apparently newly born and still wrapped in its left-over gossamer creation. Slightly visible plasma plumes ejected from both poles.

Then something else came into view.

She whispered, "Annulus."

Even she had heard of this world, seen pictures of it. Even Krin, the woman who annoyed her, had talked about it, praising it, bragging she knew Seekers there who lived "under the ring."

The form of the artificial habitat was a vast circle, like the outer rim of a dish from which the center had been removed, leaving the wide, sloping edge. The top surface of this broad ribbon was illuminated by the sun—except for a third of it left in light shadow—and vivid with color. A thin band of red formed the outer edge, a wider trail of yellow lay inside, then much green and blue filled the inside rim. Six spokes led away from there at the same sloping angle and converged at the center in a small circular cradle of gray.

The view was spectacular, the place well-known, the result of the third Airafane Clip. No wonder a Seeker would speak of it with reverence. It was a major product of the Airafane legacy.

Had this been the ship's destination? Were the refugees intended to be a work force here? They had been told nothing by the Earth officials. But Annulus had a reputation for fair working rules and equitable labor. Braya had assumed a more primitive destination—dangerous and undeveloped, where they'd need to struggle to survive.

The *Lochner* came into sight again, now farther away and badly broken, like a shattered toy. The stern engines had been severed away, the funnels of the exhaust ports stared at her and were torn apart. The superstructure had been sliced into pieces. Cargo containers drifted everywhere, most ripped open, some in fragments.

And the destruction continued. Lances and trails of raining missiles ended in sharp starburst explosions.

All silent. All growing distant.

The sun passed before her again, its swollen mass with its smog-like disk of comets and asteroids wheeling around it.

Then Annulus once more.

But this time it was bigger.

She was drawing toward it. *Falling* toward it.

More fear gripped her. Would she pass through the center and continue on into space—die there alone, gradually and painfully? Or would she strike against the surface, plummet onto that brightly colored loop which curved over onto itself?

She almost laughed—to be flung at a circular target in space. Then killed by it, by a great work of art.

Her mouth located a plastic tube and she sucked warm water.

She saw the cargo ship again, or what was left of it, the explosions even bigger now, the large bombs from the *Killer* destroying all evidence. She even thought she saw the big troop carrier blown apart. If true, then the refugees taken inside it also wouldn't survive.

More profit lost. Why? Why?

Again the blinding sun.

Then Annulus, nearer yet.

She had to do *something*.

She leafed through the wrist booklet but it was still too hard to read, the light shifting, the sun competing with reflections from the habitat. "Emergency approach," "Gradient thrust," "Focused alignment." Nothing helped.

The ring grew larger. It spread both above and beneath her, the curved surface rich with detail. Mountains near the outside rim, then plains and rivers, then forests and lakes toward the inside edge. An impossible but grand vista.

More explosions in the area of the ship. Everything there being "disappeared."

Then Annulus, engulfing her. She would land in the reddish outer rim. It looked barren, hilly, hard.

A boiling fury rose up in her, just as before. She remembered the three destructive ships. She wanted to find them so she could destroy them. Get the pilots. Learn why they did this and then kill them, too.

The jets kicked in, shocking her. Then they stopped.

Her roll ceased. She faced only Annulus.

How nice! She could watch it now as it rose up and struck her—smashed her in the face!

But why did the jets ignite? They didn't prevent her from moving toward the surface. She instead moved faster, the gravity-plates of Annulus affecting her.

Haze of atmosphere, small clouds, red desert with a crinkled edge. Like crafted and pristine jewelry. The detail precise, extensive, deadly.

Flashes of light ignited around her, other falling debris exploding. Meteor defenses from the habitat. The place would need safeguards—it lay open to a dangerous sky.

Bitter laughter again. "I might be killed *before* I get killed."

But if she survived she'd *do* something! Nurse the anger! Use it! Apply it!

When she hit, would she blow a hole through the habitat's surface? Blemish the artwork and stain its perfection?

She felt the acceleration more now.

"Dammit! Dammit!"

Then the jets again. What was going on?

More small flashes, destroyed pieces tumbling past her. She felt warmth, friction from entering the thin frame of air.

She saw rocks on the surface, like fists punching up at her.

She approached at an angle. Maybe she'd roll—bounce back into space. Was that the reason for the thrusters?

The ground flew up at her. She closed her eyes in terror—

Then struck.

Chapter 3: Politics and Money

Anne Montgomery no longer came to Mykol Ranglen for love and pleasure.

Especially at 4:55 in the morning.

Ranglen's on-again off-again romance with her had ended in one more dramatic break. After he returned from Alchera and felt his memories of that planet slipping, he kick-started his old relation with her in maybe too-obvious desperation to blanket his emotional loss—and the fear of his brain malfunctioning as memories of Alchera deteriorated. The heat between the two of them ignited, blossomed, then paled, as predictably as it had in the past. But it did help him to control his post-traumatic slump. And once he felt like himself again, they quickly entered their "impatience phase"—interests conflicted, world-views clashed, and a once-superb physical intensity dissolved into dry ritual. Fiery debates led to departures.

She didn't return. He didn't ask her to.

"Don't pretend I awakened you," she said, through the tiny extension of his cellpad that tried to ergo-shape to his ear. "I know how early you get up."

"What's wrong?"

"I have a problem. Can I come over?"

"Personal or business?"

"Both, and I'm hoping you can help."

"Okay. You want breakfast?"

"I'll pick something up."

Anne arrived twenty minutes later with egg-and-cheese sandwiches and cinnamon scones, his favorites (the accuracy of her recollection impressed him), bought at the local red-eye pass-through. He had coffee ready.

She was not dressed casually. A black vest covered a white full-sleeved blouse. Snugly fitting black slacks tapered down to stockinged ankles and black heels. He was surprised at how business-chic she could be at this early hour, then guessed she'd go straight to work after leaving him. She never looked casual while on the job.

Yet her long black hair still lay on her shoulders in a seeming careless abandon. It shadowed her darkly textured face with even darker provocation. Awaking memories in him of wonder and pain.

"Don't look at me like that. This is serious."

He had not intended his face to be revealing.

They sat at the small table—he was in a hotel again, for no good reason except his obsession to feel "on the go." The hotel was part of a transport complex set up for the electric shuttle-trains that ran on loops around the vast ring of Annulus. You could hear the trains in his room—like the whining of midnight, he said to himself. He loved the sound.

They opened the wrappers about their food and he asked once more what was wrong.

"Since the last time we talked, I've finally started my import business."

Ranglen nodded, focused on his sandwich and not her dangerous raven eyes.

"I just commissioned a special shipment from a private source. A cargo ship was supposed to pass here twelve hours ago and send my cargo pod to Rimport 3. But the ship was destroyed just before it arrived, apparently by an explosion caused by an asteroid that struck the craft and made the reactors blow. There were no survivors. Some pieces of wreckage crashed into Annulus a few hours before I called you."

"That doesn't sound right," Ranglen said. "Any ship in our system should be prepared for asteroids. And wreckage falling toward Annulus would be destroyed by the meteor defenses." Even ships from outside the system would know the region to be dangerously rife with star-birth rubble. The Airafane Clip that constructed Annulus had required material from a recently formed star—the reason why Annulus was built here in the first place. Even though the structure sat above the ecliptic, ships approaching knew they might encounter trouble.

"For the pieces falling on Annulus, the defenses stopped most of them, but not everything. Some smaller fragments did get through."

"Was anyone hurt?"

"Everything fell in the rim mountains or the desert so no one was hit. The ground cover got tore up in spots, but the under deck was only bruised. It might show from space but it's purely cosmetic. As for the ship, everything was destroyed. There's hardly any evidence of it left."

"I heard nothing about this."

"Sorry, Mykol, but that proves how much they're keeping you out of the loop. I was only informed because I had cargo that was supposed to reach me. The news outlets won't detail the incident because the authorities want to prevent any reaction from Homeworld. They don't want hysteria about faulty meteorite screens—though the shields did work. Anything really dangerous was stopped. The large number of small pieces must have been too hard to track."

Ranglen was irritated by the current government which told him nothing. Though he liked his isolation, he did not appreciate it forced on him. Annulus itself would not exist if he hadn't made his discovery—finding the third Airafane Clip that brought the habitat into existence. But both Annulus and Homeworld authorities wanted nothing to do with him now. This neglect made him brood in anger.

He said, "I know all the safeguards aren't finalized yet, but they still should work. This'll be a wake-up call for those responsible."

"Never mind that now. It's not why I'm here."

Ranglen still didn't like knowing Annulus could be hurt. "So you lost your cargo?"

"I assume. Nothing substantial has been found of the wreckage."

"You're asking me to look for it?"

"No, but if you do find any traces, I'd be grateful. I don't think you'll have any more luck than Annulus Security. They're searching the site of the wreck now, and if anything turns up, it will be returned to me. What I really need from you is to find a person."

Ranglen kept his expression blank. It wasn't like Anne to request such a task.

"The man's name is Aarov Muletti. He set up the transaction that got me my cargo. I tried to reach him after hearing about the wreck but I had no luck. I was told he's been gone for weeks and that no one seems to know where he is. He was supposed to make sure my shipment was dropped at Rimport 3 and not at any other port, where he was to get it himself and bring it to me. He was not supposed to be on the ship, though now I'm worried he might have been."

Ranglen's suspicions grew. "So you didn't set up the transaction yourself?"

"It was too complicated. It involved off-world contacts only he had connections with."

"That's not the way you usually work."

"He and I had a close agreement. I knew him and trusted him. I've used him for several deals before, and he was a big help in setting up this one."

"What was the cargo?"

She shook her head. "I can't tell you that."

"You 'can't,' or you won't?"

"It doesn't matter. Respect me on this. I have my reasons."

"Was it insured?"

She looked both insulted and embarrassed. "No, it wasn't. And I understand you don't approve. My cargo was arriving in a sealed pod that only I had the codes for opening. If I insured it then I'd have to identify the contents. I chose not to."

"Anne, you can't do this."

"Don't lecture me, Mykol."

"Then where off-world *was* this deal?"

She seemed more uncomfortable with this question than the one about insurance. "It was on Earth."

Ranglen set the last of his sandwich onto the table and briefly stared at the cinnamon scone, knowing now he wouldn't enjoy it. "Dammit, Anne. I thought you were trying to *start* a business, not finish one."

"I'll start it in any way I like. It's *my* business, not yours."

Guilt always made her stubborn. "You realize a private, unspecified product coming from Earth, especially one in a sealed pod and delivered to the shadiest of the six rimports, might be viewed by Homeworld customs as attempted smuggling?"

"Annulus wouldn't see it that way, and there's no reason for Homeworld to know about it. That's why I used Muletti."

"But they might learn of it now because of the wreck. And this Muletti obviously bribed agents back on Earth."

"But he assured me Annulus would not be concerned and not report anything to Homeworld. He's employed by the Import Regulations Commission. He guaranteed me that all the relevant authorities on Annulus would remain tolerant if they learned of the deal. Other people on the Board would even be happy I was working with Earth—some of them told me that."

"But Annulus doesn't write its own laws. *Homeworld* does. We're not a free colony, remember?"

"And why should they care about my dealing with Earth?"

"Because they don't get along with Earth, especially now. And anything coming from there to Annulus without their approval suggests they are weak."

"Which is all nonsense."

"Not to them. If they notice your operation—and now they could—Annulus will have to deny knowing of it to stay in good graces with Homeworld, our 'benefactors,' our 'loving parents.' So any stated support for you from Annulus means nothing. They'll give you up if they want someone to punish—and not Muletti if he does have connections to the Commission. Even if Homeworld doesn't take you to court, they could stop you from working with your dealers both there and on Earth. *Then* how will you get your precious imports?"

She looked angry but also shaken.

"Homeworld isn't our friend, Anne. You have to accept that."

"They never were."

But he could tell she was scared. Anne was a brilliant planner and negotiator, but she also took too many chances. She was probably right that Annulus secretly supported her dealing with Earth. They had been trying to ally themselves with Earth against the restrictions of Homeworld for years. But recent politics among the three worlds had become intense, close to a crisis.

Even war.

When Ranglen discovered the third Clip, which contained the blueprint for how to build Annulus, he shared it with all the worlds of the Confederation. But Earth and its one-time colony Homeworld, now independent and strutting its prestige, had the most power in that loose group of planets. For reasons he never understood, Earth agreed to let Homeworld oversee the building and populating of Annulus—maybe because of Earth's environmental problems at the time, their ongoing political upheavals, and the uncontrollable emigration that occurred after finding the first and second Clips, which opened up the universe to cheap travel. Whatever the cause, Earth gave up a source of income to its one-time subject colony.

Homeworld did little more than allow the Airafane Clip to do its job, which was to generate a horde of nanotech "workers" to remake the debris from a new stellar system into the ring of Annulus, whose curving surface humans soon inhabited, enjoyed and loved. The people who lived there were a hearty and self-reliant breed, and they adored their world, whose rainbow arc displayed so beautifully in their lower sky.

But soon exploitation came, mostly from Homeworld. Corporate groups sent investors who favored the growth of their own planet more than Annulus. Homeworld saw the Ring as easy income, a flourishing market and source of revenue, from which they could reap profit or enlist soldiers and spaceship crews. To them, Annulus was just a commodity, a means to an end and not an end in itself—something consumed, not savored.

It made him angry. Annulus was *his* world, after all.

Anne said, "We should be happy Earth's taking more notice of Homeworld's influence. They don't like an ex-colony with too much power."

"Their ex-colony is now a recognized force in the Confederation, where their speeches have become more anti-Earth. Insults fly."

"Have any treaties been broken?"

"Earth claims that Homeworld deals secretly with unlicensed buyers and gives favors to privileged markets. Earth still has the most wealth and trade outlets, but they feel threatened, and justifiably so."

Anne grumbled. "That's why we have all these damned tariffs."

"And it's getting worse. Earth sets tariffs on products that Homeworld sends to them, then Homeworld (which Earth originally called 'Homestead,' by the way, but the colonists found the name demeaning and quickly changed it) responds with their own tariffs against Earth's imports. Earth goes further. They establish a 'paper blockade' against Homeworld. It's not enforced militarily, but Earth authorities look the other way at any independent Earth ships stopping and boarding Homeworld transport—to reject, or confiscate, Homeworld products. It's close to privateering, but not quite. It's still sporadic and half-hearted. But some Homeworld crews have resisted anyone boarding their ships, and they then threaten armed retaliation. Earth ignores Homeworld's protests. Threats fly. And poor Annulus, 'owned' by Homeworld but desired by Earth, gets caught in the middle."

"For saying you're uninformed, you seem to keep up."

"It's become a habit, and I do it on my own."

Anne grumbled. "It infuriates me, Mykol. Annulus should be *respected*. It's a direct product of an Airafane Clip, a unique creation. Doesn't that allow us special treatment? But if our products get through to Earth, Homeworld says we're disloyal. They pressure us to follow their rules. I've had my orders intercepted and almost stopped. That's why I used Muletti this time, to do his magic and avoid all this. Our exports to Homeworld are threatened too, with tariffs levied even against *us*—their own colony. What's next? Unrestricted piracy?"

Ranglen said nothing.

"Or is that what just happened?"

He only shrugged, but he wondered too.

"Now I know why everyone wants this quiet."

Ranglen saw a chance to enforce his point. "And in the middle of this, *you* come along with your undisclosed and bribed cargo from an already arrogant Earth, trying to sneak it past Homeworld's envious eyes through somewhat shady Rimport 3 and onto supposedly innocent Annulus. And if you're exposed, I can imagine people taking advantage—like your economic rivals obviously, but also Annulus politicians to prove they're doing a good policing job, and finally Homeworld, to defend itself from being accused of government-sponsored piracy that became too destructive. And, by the way, Homeworld loves to put people in jail. I've been there. I know."

She cursed slowly but looked serious. "Am I really in trouble?"

"Well, I can't believe Homeworld would allow the destruction of an entire ship. That's a level I don't think even they could tolerate. And independent pirates are difficult to imagine. Space isn't an ocean. You don't know where ships will emerge from light-space and the distances are too big for planned encounters. Finding something to raid would be extremely lucky. Of course, Earth or Homeworld might have methods of tracking they've kept to themselves, and I'm sure Homeworld has informants on both Annulus and Earth. It might be easy for spies to gather shipping schedules and thus to calculate exit points. But I still find it hard to accept."

Anne took a deep breath but looked determined.

"Let's get back to what you're asking me to do. And please note I haven't agreed yet."

"Just find Muletti," she said. "I need to learn why he didn't fulfill his part of our agreement and why he disappeared, why he didn't get in touch with me after all this happened and why he vanished before it took place."

"Are you certain he wasn't in the ship that was destroyed? It's the easiest explanation."

"He said he wouldn't be, and I don't see why he'd lie about it. He wouldn't be able to pick up the cargo if he had to enter through a passenger port. And why then should he use a cargo ship at all? He could have flown the stuff himself."

"If he knew the transaction might be exposed as illegal, the crash could have scared him and sent him into hiding."

"Then I especially need to find him. If this leads to danger for me or my business, I have to know more. He owes me that. The return on my investment was supposed to be the big start of my company. And if there's to be a war between Homeworld and Earth, I need to know about that too. We *all* do."

"Then tell me what your cargo was."

"Not yet. Not if I lost it. You wouldn't approve. And, don't forget, you've helped me yourself in ventures that were not fully legal. If I'm taken to court, you might be implicated."

"That might be true, but my reputation is different from yours, Anne, and much harder to smear. I'm the founder of Annulus, remember?"

"But my being on trial would still compromise you. Annulus likes to see itself as not following many rules, even when we do. But indiscretions by its founder? If even *you* can get away with things, then maybe more laws should be imposed. Many people wouldn't like that."

Sadly, she was right. He *had* supplied her with off-world trinkets in the past, and they certainly would raise questions at customs.

"I can't change what was done, Mykol. And I'm not responsible for any spaceship getting wrecked. I don't intend for it to stop me or hold me back. I need to learn what happened so I can be prepared for my next move. I have to find Muletti. Can you do that for me? That's all I'm asking."

He still hesitated, maybe because of deeper contentions between him and Anne, which always arose when they grew too close. In their long-suffering relationship, he wanted less "business" from her and she wanted more "presence" from him. She didn't like his habit of suddenly wandering off into space. What right did he have to such freedom when it was the same freedom she wanted? But they sought their freedom for different reasons—he to explore, she to "expand." She claimed she could never be as exotic to him as one of his alien planets, and he claimed he could never be to her just one more "product" in her line.

"And if you *can* find my cargo," she added, "I'd appreciate that too."

"Naturally," he answered, with very light irony. "Look, I believe Annulus will support any cover story that Homeworld, in its authority position, will spin about the cargo ship.

We don't have enough clout yet to challenge them. I don't believe the 'asteroid' explanation, but it can be made acceptable. Whatever summary becomes official, just go along with it no matter what you lost. And try not to call attention to yourself."

Anne nodded.

"Also, if Muletti did a good job getting pre-shipment clearance taken care of on Earth—in other words, if no trace of bribery is found—then you shouldn't have to worry *too* much about blame. Of the three worlds, Annulus will keep this quiet the most, so they won't suggest to Homeworld that customs procedures on Earth be investigated. They want to stay friendly with Earth. I can't promise that nothing will happen to you, but at first glance, I don't think it will."

Anne looked comfortable with these assurances. But the silence that then grew between them felt a bit sinister. The food sat on the table forgotten.

And he still hadn't agreed to what she wanted.

"Mykol, you don't have to probe what actually happened. You might get into trouble if you do. People in Annulus Security can be tight after something like this. I've heard they look out for themselves, especially if they feel blame is coming. So, for your sake, don't go any further than just finding Muletti."

Ranglen tried to look impressed. "You sound worried about me."

"I always worry about you. I know what *I'm* doing, but I'm never sure about you. Still, I'm convinced you can handle this. You can even use your reputation as founder of Annulus to protect you."

Ranglen grunted. "Why am I called the 'founder' of Annulus? I'd prefer being its 'father.'"

"Because you don't look old or wise enough. You're too scruffy, too 'bad boy.' And good fathers don't run from their child as often as you do."

"My reputation means nothing anyway. It allows me to see people without making appointments, or to get the better tables at restaurants. That's about it."

"Don't lie to me. You know exactly how to use your notoriety."

He didn't argue.

Then the room grew quiet again, and this time the silence lasted. Ranglen's thoughts went far away—because her accusation of abandonment, of children or otherwise, touched a nerve.

Everyone knew he found the third Clip, a miracle in itself. But he hadn't told anyone of another incident, very recent, that would be seen as even more miraculous.

He had found a *fourth* Clip.

And it had been so dangerous, he destroyed it.

The memory of that act was gradually leaving him, whether he wanted it to or not. Some peculiar physics concerning how he found the Clip weakened the memory and, in time, would erase it. But if the rest of humanity knew he destroyed one, they would despise and vilify him, even torture him, to find the secret of how he alone was able to discover *two* Clips.

And—a revelation that would shock everyone—he *did* have a secret method. The thought of which always tormented him. For it, unlike memory, would never go away. And if discovered that he had such a secret, hatred and torture certainly would follow.

This responsibility weighed on him in devious and uncontrollable ways. It was one reason—as well as his destroying the Clip—why he came to Anne after returning from Alchera. He wanted to lose himself in her, to avoid guilt, though he knew that the Clip's termination had been the right thing for him to do.

"And besides," Anne said. "You *need* this mission."

"Excuse me?"

"You've been strange since you returned from your last trip. Your mind's been elsewhere. I even thought the two of us might stay together, at least longer than usual, because you had more need than you usually do. But it didn't work. You'll still always jaunt into space, though you never seem to find what you're looking for. So, maybe this job could be good for you, get you back to where you were…or to what you want to be."

Ranglen was surprised. He seldom gave Anne's perception enough credit, even when knowing his neglect of it was a defense mechanism, a way to remain hidden from her and unrestricted. But he hadn't realized how much she understood him.

"I doubt that," he emphasized.

"I'm not interfering with your precious solitude. But I'm worried about this situation between Homeworld and Earth. Based on what you said, it's worse than what we think."

"Bad for business?" Again, the irony.

"Bad for life, for anyone's life. And you wouldn't be doing this just for me but for Annulus. *Your* world."

Not mine anymore. Mine got away.

But then, after brooding for a bit, he finally said, "Okay, Anne. I'll do it. And, like you told me, I won't go overboard. I'll just speak with my contacts, visit Rimport 3, look around and ask some questions. If I can, I'll find your Muletti. I'll first talk to Hatch."

Her eyes widened. "Hatch? *No!*"

The reaction shocked him. "But why not?"

"He and I aren't getting along. I owe him some money."

"Does that involve this recent venture with your unrevealed cargo?"

"No. Not really. But I'd rather you didn't ask about it."

"Do you want me finding Muletti or not?"

"Of course I do, and you can follow any leads you like. I'm not making restrictions. Hatch just doesn't have a high opinion of me right now. I'd rather he didn't cloud your judgment."

"Hatch doesn't think highly of anyone. Besides, he's been busy with his new spaceport. It doesn't leave him much time for sympathy."

"I know," she said drily, as if this irritated an old wound.

"And I always keep my ship with him, so I'll have to see him in order to get it."

"All right. I understand. I'm just saying…."

He let the matter drop, which made a poor start for his "mission."

And he was certain, though he didn't know why, he'd get no clear answer to his next question either, an important one. "Can you tell me more about this Aarov Muletti?"

And he was right.

Chapter 4: The Mountain Seekers

Braya swam up out of darkness, fighting to reach a dim light that soon grew brighter. Her eyes blinked, steadied, focused. She forced her listless mind to work, to take in details, to make conclusions.

Fabric hung above her, brown and grim. She lay inside a make-shift shelter of bent metal rods draped with cloth, hung with beads and home-made chimes that made a slight tingling noise. Big metal girders thrust up around her with fabric laid over them, like drapes on angled ribs, a crude tent. A dirty lamp hung above her, no brighter than a candle. The air was stuffy, ripe with the smell of burnt meat, disinfectant, and sweaty garments. Several blankets had been propped beneath her on a hard floor. Boxes, pails, stacks of clothes and old shoes surrounded her.

A woman sat near, said to her, "Alive again, my little flame?"

She had a face like a mask. The grooved network of wrinkles in the skin was expectable for how old she must be, if exaggerated and deep, but not the red rims around the eyes, the blackish marks across her cheeks and beneath her mouth, the coiling out-of-control hair whose pure white looked almost purplish, artificial, like spun wires or a stiff wig on a cheap doll. She wore big-fitting work-clothes, with bands or suspenders tied behind her shoulders over a heavy and patterned shirt. The clothes displayed all kinds of decorations—pins, badges, handkerchiefs, paint-marks, flags, string—wildly flung about. Small feet in dirty white socks were tucked into strapped and ancient sandals. She looked like a retired mechanic who, in a fit of wayward enthusiasm, remade herself into a street-theater performer.

She reminded Braya immediately of Krin, back on the *Lochner*, but this version was more extreme. If Krin had been a first draft, this one had all the fine detail.

Braya muttered, "Where am I?" her mouth dry and her lips chapped. She could tell she hadn't spoken for a while.

The woman watched her. "You're under the Ring, behind the façade, one among many who lurk down here."

"The Ring...Annulus?" Braya remembered falling into it.

"Yes, little flame. Very perceptive. You were lucky."

Her spastic phrases were also like Krin's.

"Was I...?

"Were you hurt? Yes. Could have been worse. Your spacesuit helped. Its jets must have kicked in before you struck. Softened your fall. Amazing you have no broken bones. You should be crippled. You had a concussion and were out for hours. Very confused when you awoke. You'll be sore—a lot of bruises. But you make a tough little survivor. You impress the hell out of me."

Braya sat up, but her world spun. She lay back again. She didn't like the woman or the words she spoke.

"Easy there, flame. Lie still. Save energy."

"I want to get up."

"Not yet. Not advised."

"How did I come here? And who are you?"

The woman's smile showed yellow but firm teeth. "My name's Hideki. I found you. You plowed up a furrow while landing. It reached down to the basement, which is Airafane. Not much is left of your spacesuit."

Braya still wore her own clothes. Whoever had worked on her must have removed them and then dressed her again. She felt bandages on her arms and legs.

"You landed not far from a doorway, leading from the surface down to here—down to me and all of us together. I happened to see you. We brought you to my hut."

"You rescued me?"

"If bringing you here 'rescues' you, that's up to you."

Braya found the line darkly ambiguous. "Is anyone coming for me?"

"We didn't report you, if that's what you mean. We don't do that to people here, not under the Ring. Wreckage fell with you. We left it alone. We believe you're the only survivor. People nosed around. Security, agents from the defense shield. But we don't call attention to ourselves. We won't do that to you, either. They know we're here, but we make sure they don't care. We assumed you'd want that. If you stay with us, we'll require it."

41

Braya didn't like that last statement either. "You have doctors here?" She wanted to know how well she'd been "rescued."

"We have a portable examination suite. We lifted it from a spaceship years ago. With some care, we've kept it working. That's how we learned you weren't seriously hurt."

Lifted? So, they were scavengers and thieves, which might be good, or bad.

"You didn't have an ID. We assumed you were part of a colony ship. Those companies always keep personal documents and passports—to maintain control of you, make sure you don't leave. I've seen that."

Braya still acknowledged nothing. "Why are you here, 'under the Ring'? Are you some kind of resistance movement?"

"No. We keep to ourselves. Don't want to change things. Annulus is tolerant. They accept us, though they don't believe in us. We stay out of their way. Keep our heads down. We've got places to go. You can come too. We won't push you."

Braya remembered Krin again, who had tried to tell her about Annulus and a group living on its underside. Krin argued a connection between them and the Seekers—and thus with all refugees from Earth. She preached a grand unification, that Braya would "like" them, find them "similar," see they were like refugees too.

"Are all of you Seekers of the Mountain then?"

"Not everyone here. *I* am, and most people I know. We believe in the 'Mountain with Eyes.' We believe it will take us to the Airafane and set us free. Everyone on Annulus should rightly be a Seeker—Annulus itself is a result of the Airafane. We live on their construction. We are closest to their glory."

Braya cringed at the near religious enthusiasm.

Hideki persisted, "Non-believers are ruining the Ring. They don't pay attention. They're too busy. They don't have the necessary respect."

"And *you* do?"

"We all do."

Braya tuned out.

"Try sitting up now."

She managed to do so, felt more confident.

"Do you remember much?"

"Nothing after I hit the Ring."

"The concussion gave you brief amnesia. When you first awoke you asked the same questions over and over. You're coherent now."

She gave Braya herbal tea and a can of grain-and-fruit mush—soft, wet, easy to get down.

But all this time Hideki watched her with her dodgy predator eyes. Braya felt she was being evaluated for some secret task. She didn't like it.

"You want to try walking? I'll show you around. Bring you to where you fell. You'll like us here."

Braya wanted to reconnoiter, but on her own if she could manage it.

Hideki helped her up. Her legs felt weak but she pushed herself forward.

"Easy now."

"Please let go of me."

"Stubborn, aren't you? Hot little flame."

"And stop calling me that!"

Krin had used that phrase too, so it must have some Seeker significance. But Hideki annoyed her more than Krin. The two women resembled each other but Hideki seemed more affected, more intentionally outlandish—as if playing the part of "eccentric" to cover a hidden side of her. Except for her moments of Seeker religiosity and "little flame" silliness, she spoke with basic sense and reason. And yet to look at her you'd never expect it.

They passed through the shelter's opening.

Braya was overwhelmed.

Surrounding the tent was a vast repeating network of girders—struts, trusses, racks, latticework—all very big and powerful-looking, stretching away in both directions and curving up over the horizon formed by the ceiling, the parts getting smaller into the distance, producing long infinity-shots of shrinking repetition that moved off in upward-bending trails.

Braya assumed this huge interlocked stabilizing structure made up the undersurface of Annulus and stretched around the entire circle. In the thousands of angles, she could see several nested shelters like Hideki's. Fragile, scattered, partially hidden. They made up an "underground" of small dwellings in the countless roots of this metal forest.

"Do you like our homes?" Hideki sounded proud. "The labyrinth is worthy and serves us well. A great place to hide…if you need to hide."

"Is that why you came here?"

"We don't need to conceal ourselves yet. Surveillance will come. It always does. But no one here is a fugitive. We stay low and keep our heads covered—literally, under a roof." She laughed with an unpleasant cackle. "We're all well-behaved."

Hideki might claim not to be political but she sounded too guarded, too suspicious. "How many people live here?"

"Not many. Enough. Nobody keeps track. We don't force anyone to stay. You can go when you please."

Braya didn't believe her but she didn't argue. "Are there gravity-plates beneath us?" The curved underside of the ring above was made of the layered myriad vanes that secured objects to the surface on top.

"Just a few, at the ends of the longer struts. The Airafane must have included them for maintenance workers. If you walk far, you'll lose their influence, then have to float to a different area. There's breathable air, which is good. The atmosphere above extends below. Airafane efficiency. They provided for people working and even living down here."

Braya guessed what Hideki would imply next.

"Maybe they even intended for those like us to be here, to make our version of an underworld. We like to believe so, that they knew we'd be needed. Typical of the Airafane. They knew so much already, so much *about* us, more than we do. You can't help admiring them."

Braya didn't answer.

Hideki led her to a set of spiral stairs, then up a ladder ascending a shaft, finally to a hatch in the endless ceiling.

"Where are you taking me?"

"You'll see. You're feeling all right now? You're not straining? You can handle all this?"

Braya felt she was being taunted. She grew more distrustful and almost turned back.

The woman opened the hatch with a lock-tool she kept on a lanyard around her neck. "Come on up. You'll want this."

She coaxed Braya through the opening but told her not to rush. "Heavy perception about to hit you, knock you over. You'll soon feel it." Her grin was witchy and very annoying.

Braya, too curious, stepped after her—and onto the upper surface of Annulus.

She had seen the habitat as she plunged into it after the wreck, but her view then was through the narrow and dirty window of a spacesuit and she had been too focused on her upcoming death. Now she could look fully about with no suit filtering what she saw.

The sensory input was overpowering. She felt vertigo, like standing on the edge of a precipice and fighting a dizziness that pulled her outward and upward into the scene. Everything spread before her—too exposed. The arc of Annulus rose to either side and then bent over to merge together in the lower sky. The wide rainbow-like structure was especially vivid since she stood in the shadow that crept around the Ring, caused by the invisible Airafane "lampshade" that, she remembered, no one could find or understand but now darkened the ground around her. This made the smooth handle-like sweep of the opposite side well-lit and vibrantly tinted—soft red at the top, pale yellow beneath, a wide and complex mottling of dark green and bright blue at the bottom.

It was too unreal, too different, too varied and too inclusive, like the surface of a planet twisted through a space-warp and then flattened and pulled across the sky. Her perception threatened to lose control, to become too lost with nowhere to settle. She could even see from the small knoll on which she and Hideki stood the fringe of delicate blue aurora lining the inner edge of the Ring, and the six spokes that continued down to the central mechanized disk.

It was too much. She stepped back, almost in fear.

"Overwhelming, isn't it?"

Braya couldn't answer. In the silence of the surrounding desert she heard and smelled the almond scent of the waving grasses in the plains, felt the cool and earthy whiffs that slid and tickled across her skin. She sensed the mists creeping through the distant forests, their thin humidity and subtle flavors riding the changing directions of air. She caught the delicate calls of birds, saw them in gliding far-away clouds. She spied towns and small motions on the veins of roads and transport lines that ran between them. She thought she even heard voices.

"You learn to live with it," Hideki said. "You don't notice after a while. It's just a big dish with its center missing. But it *is* rather magnificent, is it not?"

Braya was overcome, but she felt her current physical weakness maybe contributed to the reaction. It was a good defense, anyway.

"Take deep breaths. You can see now why the Airafane deserve our worship, why we give them reverence and honor."

This sudden evangelizing ruined the mood.

"Let the Airafane touch you," Hideki continued, "warm you, reach you, and then caress you. Humanity might own the future, but the Airafane still rule the past, and we're meant to join together in the present, the two cultures made into one. You'll see this on the Mountain—with its 'Eyes.'"

All of Braya's doubts returned. Did Hideki bring her here just to gain an advantage, take control of her while her mind stumbled from what she saw? "Leave me alone."

"You can't reject it. Earth or Homeworld would die for this. It's more than just a new world—it's transcendence. We live in their creation. Maybe we're becoming Airafane already."

"Stop it. Don't preach to me."

"You have to open yourself, relate to the world in other ways than anger. We can help you, guide you."

"I don't want your help. And I especially don't want your 'guidance.' You're just trying to control me. It's meant for *you* and not me. It's defined by you—*for* you."

"No, little fire. It's the Airafane. I didn't believe in them till I saw the Ring. Then everything changed. The Mountain talked to me. You can be part of it."

The glory Braya had felt for the view now evaporated. Anger returned. "If you love this so much then why don't you live up here? You could always see it. Why hide underneath it like rats in cages?"

"Because we're *free*. Surface people become preoccupied and forget what's around them. If you're under the Ring, you savor it more. Your eyes open every time you come up here. If the Mountain has 'Eyes,' then the Ring *is* an Eye, an enormous Eye, the biggest of all."

Hideki moved too close to her now, and Braya pushed her off. But the thrust brought to her a wave of dizziness—which made her angrier.

Hideki croaked, "Feeling it, eh? You're still hurt. Too much splendor, aesthetic overload."

"Please shut up."

"It's like being present at the galactic dawn. The Airafane saw it. Cuts into the brain."

"I'm not joining your group, your Seekers." Braya felt sick now. She had to get away from Hideki.

"All right, let's go back. You do need rest. But take another look before we go. This is what the universe is supposed to be. A house of grandeur."

Braya ignored her, moved toward the hatch.

"You landed over there, by the way. See the dark spots in the desert?"

She stopped for that, looked closely. It brought back memories of her approach.

"You almost missed the surface. You would have died. You were lucky to land close to this entrance. They're scattered along the outside rim. Few people live here. You're lucky we came, that we take in vagrants."

Again Hideki's words unsettled her. She hurried down the ladder.

She privately questioned what Hideki said. Based on what she'd heard back on Earth, Annulus was too young and too tolerant for a "drop-out" society to exist already. Settlers here should still be too busy establishing their world, with plenty of jobs and goals to occupy them. Maybe the Airafane did intend for a group to live under the Ring—to provide variety, an alternative viewpoint to the "top" culture. But, to Braya, that would make everyone only the result of ancient social engineering, and thus hardly original—predictable, petty, uninteresting.

Hideki followed her off the ladder and onto the stairs, then back between the girders. "You never told me your name."

"Braya. Just Braya."

"And you saw the cargo-ship being destroyed?"

Braya stopped, stared at her. "What do you know about that?"

"Oh, we know things. We pick up a lot. We're good spies—good 'Eyes,' all of us. We heard the announcement that a cargo-ship was destroyed. But we also saw the falling wreckage with you in the middle of it. You came from it then? What did you see?"

"So *that's* why you saved me. You want to know what happened. You want to *use* me."

"No, just help you."

Braya walked faster toward the hut. She felt sick again, muttering as she went, "You're just like Krin, both of you, the same."

"What? You knew *Krin*?"

This surprised her—did everyone in the Seekers know each other? "She was on the cargo-ship. She wanted me to join your group too. Is that why you're alike?"

"She resembles me because she *imitated* me. I showed her all the ways to the Mountain and coaxed her to become a Seeker. But you say she was on the ship? Did she talk to you?"

"She tried. I didn't listen."

"Did she say anything about me or Annulus? Give you any message?"

"No. Why should she? She just told me the Seekers were present here."

"She was one of us, a good member—a true 'Eye.' I can understand her wanting to talk to you. She would have looked out for you."

Then a memory struck Braya.

When the raiders broke into the refugee container, Krin pushed her away from them and into a protective alcove—from where Braya was able to escape.

Did Krin do that on purpose? Did she take the brunt of the invaders' attack just so Braya could maybe survive?

The idea disturbed her, troubled the resolve that had grown so strong in her, which was the only thing she relied on now, the personal fierceness that sustained her. "Let's get back. I don't feel well."

"I said you needed rest. Afterward, you can tell me about Krin. She can be a bit crazy. And then we can help you. We offer it freely."

"I said I don't want your help."

"You don't like owing people, do you?"

Braya didn't listen, walked faster.

The area under the Ring didn't impress her now. It reminded her too much of deprivations on Earth, of needing to find a private space where one could cling to a small bit of life—until killed by floods, wars, storms. She had intended to leave all that behind, yet here it was. Weren't the stars supposed to be better than this? Why should people travel light-years to find more poverty, ignorance, delusion? Was this the dream behind Airafane Clips?

She reached Hideki's tent and grabbed her jacket. She checked the pockets and found they were emptied. "You searched my clothes?"

"Of course. We attract spies from above."

She had to get away but she didn't know where.

Hideki wouldn't stop. "You're after something, aren't you? It's easy to tell. You're too much like us. We have our networks around the Ring. We *see* things. And the people above don't watch us when we do."

"Every 'underground' feels that way. You're lying to yourself. I'm sure the police know all about you."

"They only think they do."

"They know everything! They *allow* you to exist. You're easier to track when you believe you're free, and they leave you alone because they're certain you're harmless. You're caught in a prison where you've put yourselves. That's not what *I* want."

"But, by the eyes, what *do* you want?"

That question stopped her. It echoed emptily in her head.

But she then remembered, shocking herself, the decision she made during her long perilous glide toward Annulus. Its clarity, its tight, well-defined goal. Something to believe in.

"I want," she said, "to find who destroyed that cargo ship. I want to learn why it happened. And then I want to punish those responsible."

The idea had been there since she woke up. Her accepting it now just made it definite, gave her purpose, simplicity of direction. "And you can't help me."

"But we *can!* We watch the spaceports. We know the ships and when they arrive, even where they sometimes go."

"What are you getting at?"

"It's easy to reach the ports from under the Ring. We keep an eye on them—an 'Eye,' understand? Like those on the Mountain's. Near to us is Rimport 3. It handles small craft and a few container pods brought in by shuttles. The other ports are more specialized and have greater security, where the big ships go. But not this one. We can take you. It's not far."

Maybe she *could* learn something. The pieces from the wreck had landed nearby so this rimport might have information. "Can you tell me what ships arrived after the carrier was destroyed?"

"We have two observers who alternate a watch there, and one of them told me that soon after you hit the Ring, a ship landed with no identification or registry. And because its hull was dirty, you could see the outline of a cradle on both sides of it that had been removed. It could have held weapons."

The correlation was too coincidental. "What kind of ship?"

"Mid-size, type 2 engine, probably a 4-seater, though it looked like it had a refurbished cargo hold."

The description fit that of the second ship—which she now called the *Prowler*. (And the last one, the small one, she had named the *Spy*, just to have titles for what she was after.) "How far is the port?"

"Just over an hour by walking under the Ring. And I can show you a hangar there devoted to only Homeworld ships. Their insignia is above the doors. They believe they own Annulus. And—I'm sure you'll be interested in this—the ship went into *that* hangar and stayed there."

Braya knew of the current tensions between Earth and Homeworld. The cargo ship that had been destroyed, the *Lochner*—she remembered the name—had come from Earth.

She relented. Maybe it was just from weakness and pain, or maybe from a new determination that the wreck had brought to her, a focus for a life that, without it, would become even more random and lost. "All right, you can take me there. But once we arrive I'm on my own."

"Braya, *think!* You have no ID, no papers, no passport. I'm aware of all that because I searched you. If you're caught, they'll make you a dependent of Annulus, or, worse, send you back to Earth. And if they learn you survived that crash, you'll be interrogated, used by people on Annulus who want to score points against Homeworld or Earth. You might even be given up to Homeworld. They'll grill you, torture you, dump you on some colony world and bury you—if they don't kill you first, which would be safest for them."

Again the contradiction in Hideki, the outlandish clown making serious points, talking sensibly when before she didn't. Braya couldn't trust her, but she wanted to know more about the ship that came into the port. "Okay. Take me there."

"You're not going alone. If you want to sneak in to look the place over, and maybe get inside that hangar, you'll need help. I can bring people with us, the two observers and maybe more to cause a distraction."

Braya didn't like that. The fewer people she depended on the better. And she certainly didn't want Hideki.

"Don't worry, little flame. We're used to being secretive. No one I bring will ask questions of you. I'll make sure of that."

Braya finally, bitterly, agreed. "All right, they can come. But I want to talk to the observers now, to hear what they saw."

"You can hardly stand, Braya. You need to rest."

"*Now!* I want to know if they can help me, if *any* of you can, whether you're sincere." Her headache grew worse the more she yelled. "Afterward, I'll rest."

"Okay. I'll find them."

Hideki led her away, between the struts of the vast labyrinth, muttering as she did so a gushing admiration that Braya knew had to be phony, "Oh, you are so much a genuine flame. You burn and shine."

Braya hated this fawning. The old woman knew nothing about her.

Nothing. *Nothing.* Nothing at all.

Braya was abandoned by her parents, and then lost her home when Florida on Earth was half drowned by a hurricane. She worked at the remnants of the spaceport there, then drifted inland and joined a group of labor conscripts. This took her to Ecuador, to a lift-off facility high in the mountains where she worked again. But she was put in jail for trespassing and theft, and then a military coup displaced her. She landed in a refugee camp halfway down the side of a mountain. But the locals hated outsiders so they set fire to the makeshift shelters. Storms came, rain, mud, then a big landslide. New shacks were built (by the refugees themselves, under the order of brutal guards), which then were surrounded with barbed wire—to keep people in and not others out. She saw children playing in the wire, skillful enough not to get hurt, most of them also abandoned by parents who were either impoverished or went hunting for Clips. They had no schooling, and no hope of returning "home." Home didn't exist.

When corporation agents came to the camp to enlist for colony workers, she took a chance and volunteered, though she guessed it was no life-saver. At the spaceport in Brazil, amid forced crowding that seemed intended to humiliate them, a madman attacked her, a Seeker who forced a brochure on her and yelled in her face, "You will see the Airafane!" He got yanked away by a security officer and probably was beaten to death. Soon afterward, she met Krin, who drove her crazy with her tales of underworlds, "forces out of time," and mountains with eyes. By the time Braya entered the cargo ship, she believed even less in her future. But at least it was a future.

Then the ship was destroyed.

And *that's* why she wanted to find who was responsible—they had taken away the rest of her life. She knew a fire burned inside her but not in the way that Hideki thought. It came from a depth that *no one* knew. And no Seeker religious fanatics would distract her from her goal, no glorious rainbow in space, and no indulgence in Airafane dreams.

"I'm thirsty," she said.

Hideki handed her a sealed metal cup she carried in her work clothes. "Water for all that heat. I understand."

Braya drank from it. Crudely printed on its side were the faded words, "Airafane City." The cup was obviously stolen. "Where did you get this?"

"From a wrecked spaceship, a real disaster."

"More scavenging?"

"Here and there. We pick up things."

"Did you steal any weapons I could borrow?"

"We don't use guns. It's one of our rules."

Braya was disappointed.

"But we do have explosives. Would those be good enough?"

Chapter 5: The Blood Star

Hatch Banner was angry.

Ranglen's friend was trying to get the central disk of Annulus, the 20-kilometer wide shield in the center of the ring, transformed into a spaceport. The opposite side of that disk, facing out into space, would make an ideal landing platform, centrally located for the entire habitat.

But cargo moving inward from the Ring to the disk, or outward from the landed ships, would have to be conducted along the six transport tubes that connected to the Ring equidistantly around the circle. And they looked at first too narrow and fragile to be accommodating.

"I can't believe this," Hatch griped. "You'd think the Airafane would know what they were doing."

But, of course, the Airafane *did* know, and every Clip left by them and discovered so far led to well-constructed and highly useful practical products. Annulus, even with its skimpy-looking transport tubes that resembled threads when seen from space, was no exception.

The tubes were as wide as two land-vehicle freeways and could accommodate heavy traffic. The shield at the center allowed for, on its inward side, plenty of space for warehouses, storage depots, customs offices, repair shops, transport hangars, outfitters, container gantries, each with its own gravity plate for sure-to-come shipping companies. On the outer side, many spaceships could land and depart, dock or aim outward to the stars. The use of both surfaces was thus maximized—warehouses on the bottom, spaceships on the top ("bottom" and "top" being relative, of course).

But space still would be at a premium. And Hatch, as much as Ranglen and the more long-range admirers of Annulus, did not want the areas where the tubes connected to the Ring to become cluttered with exchange facilities. The price of success worried them all.

"Look at this crap!" Hatch waved his arm at the construction material accumulating before the wide entrance to the nearest tube. He often placed blame, and he was eager to do so today. "All of it will be taken down to the disk but then more will just pile up here. What a mess! I'm sure this isn't what *you* wanted, Mykol."

No, it wasn't. Mykol believed in the purity of the original Annulus. But if progress, change, and growth had to come, and they did, the habitat could not stay as pristine as it still was. Ranglen didn't like the compromise. He debated, and often wrote about, just how much development should be allowed.

The example of Earth haunted everyone.

"We could send it to the rimports," he said to Hatch—in jest.

Hatch growled. He didn't believe in the worth of the six rimports, though the protruding shelves that curved outward from the far edge of the Ring, opposite where the transport tubes touched the inner edge, obviously had been meant by the Airafane for space docks, if only temporary. And they already were busy, cluttered, mismanaged—one reason why Hatch wanted to rework the central shield as soon as he could in order to funnel most traffic through it. This new location would be neatly separate from the Ring proper, keeping all the necessary build-up to itself. The rim docks would still exist but just for overflow.

It also would provide majority control of most transport in and out of Annulus to Hatch—an obviously plum position.

But Ranglen knew Hatch was the best choice for the job. The tall, gangling, ultra-busy man had a wild past, and Ranglen had been part of it. They "grew up" together, if not literally. Hatch had a natural energetic appeal, and he was lean and handsome and filled with vitality. He loomed over others with his waving gray hair and etched black skin, that looked assaulted by a long history of close work on dangerous machines, the spaceship engines at times exploding when he stood near them. He didn't care. He loved the job. He could have had restorative surgery but he wore his wounds like badges of honor, a storyboard of his past. "I've *been* there," the marks declared.

He and Ranglen didn't share politics and often disagreed, but their friendship prevailed.

"Come on," Hatch said. "We can talk as we're riding down the tube. You need something, don't you?"

Mykol nodded.

Trees around the entranceway, planted in the proper furrows encouraged by the Airafane blueprint, had been cleared. The azure mists that crept about, often present here at the Ring's inner rim, hid some of the untidy chaos around the large opening to the tube, a jumbled mess of crates and containers. "Bad engineering," Hatch said. "Why did the Airafane allow trees here? All this area should have been clear for build-up and then hidden from view."

"Maybe when the trees grow full we'll have that."

Hatch grumbled.

They entered the large opening to the tube that allowed heavy streams of traffic, mostly carriers on tracks, public shuttles, transport pods. The place was busy, and much of the material loaded onto flatbeds was for Hatch's spaceport, coming from specialist suppliers on Annulus. Cargo from other planets was still on the way, but that would be dropped on the central disk.

The two men boarded a shuttle, sat together in a small sectioned-off compartment used for private meetings, and waited for departure.

"I've got your spaceship ready if that's what you need." Hatch always teased Ranglen about his solitary trips into space, the destinations of which Mykol kept to himself. "Why does the celebrated founder of Annulus need to leave it so often?"

Ranglen didn't answer.

He closed the door to the compartment to shut out the other people on the car.

Hatch noticed. "And you say *I'm* paranoid."

"I do need my ship, but only to fly out to Rimport 3."

"Why not take the train?"

"I'm arriving in style, as if I'm important."

Hatch shook his head but acceded to Ranglen's self-indulgence.

Then Ranglen asked, "You heard about the cargo ship that was destroyed?"

"Sure, but everyone stopped talking about it when the official word came down—all was an accident and all's been taken care of."

"It was supposed to leave a cargo pod at Rimport 3."

Hatch shrugged. "I didn't know that, but so what?"

"The cargo was Anne's."

Hatch stared at Ranglen for a moment. "There can't be any connection. If someone wanted to stop her cargo, why blow up a whole ship? It could be confiscated on delivery at the port, buried in a warehouse or dumped into space 'accidentally.' And Rimport 3 is the least efficient of the six ports, so doing something like that would be easy."

"Is the port that bad?"

"Not really, but intentional gaps are sometimes left. It's good to have one port that's a little 'sloppy'—if that's the right word—so that secret imports, private or official, can be passed through without ceremony. Like undercover business agents or government spies. It's the necessary hole in a well-built wall, and perfect for Anne's borderline deals. Did she tell you what she was transporting?"

"No. Does she ever?"

"Was it insured?"

"She claims that would compromise her trade secrets."

"Well, she better not use *my* port once it's up and running. I won't pass anything I don't know about."

"Can she avoid cargo being examined when it comes through?"

"As long as it's seal-locked at the source and all legal fees and requirements have been already handled. Annulus uses Homeworld's agents on Earth and other worlds as customs representatives and to charge all tariffs—we don't have much choice. But they're open to bribery. With the shipwreck, people will inquire, and depending on how far they want to go—like if they always *wanted* to accuse Anne of smuggling, or if a politician is heavily financed by a rival importer—then life for her could get unpleasant. Anne's tough. But if she loses the support of the Regulations Board, she'll never be able to work in imports again."

Ranglen sighed.

The carrier moved, quickly sped up.

He said, "Do you know an Aarov Muletti?"

Hatch shook his head.

"Anne used him to set up the transaction on Earth, and I assume he would have handled any bribes. She didn't tell me much about him, only that he once did investigative work for Annulus customs and that now he's associated with the Import Regulations Commission. But I did some investigating myself—I know people on the Board, too. He's used by them as a kind of 'fixer,' to get things done that are difficult or just over the edge of the law. He's retrieved Annulus spaceships for them that had been impounded for unpaid fees or insurance claims by either Homeworld or Earth. He'd go to the port, sneak on board, ignore the restraints and blast out of there all on his own, right under their eyes. The Board doesn't know quite how he does that—and they don't *want* to know. But they always appreciate it."

Hatch frowned. "Sounds like a bad person for Anne, or maybe a good one. He must know his way around, and the Board won't mind him cheating a little—but for *them*, not for Anne. And why should he bother with her anyway? Negotiating uninsured specialty imports, especially in locked pods, which I assume she used, is hardly difficult and not very profitable. Anne doesn't have enough money—not *yet*—to be overly generous to him."

"A person on the Board said that Muletti once had a big run-in with the courts on Homeworld and that he now hates the planet—and he doesn't like Earth either. I asked why the Board still employed him since relations with Homeworld have become so sensitive. She laughed, as if that *explained* why. She said his bias against Homeworld didn't matter because his work was undercover anyway. Anne claimed her cargo wasn't illegal but that Muletti treated it as if it were, which thus helped her in getting it through."

"It still sounds fishy. I don't see why he'd work for her, especially if she was just trying to avoid Homeworld's tariffs."

"It's a problem she's encountered before. Her imports are so specialized no one knows how much to charge for them, so the tariffs are made unreasonably high."

"None of this explains why a big cargo ship was destroyed—*if* an asteroid didn't do it."

They both kept their concerns to themselves.

The carrier reverberated at maximum speed, the track flipping over to follow the new direction of gravity at the shield. The trip was short and they braced themselves for deceleration. The craft slowed, slid into a dock.

The busy activity of unloading surrounded them. They entered an open-view elevator, rode up through the growing support structures for Hatch's spaceport till they emerged onto the outside surface of the shield, the convex side that faced outward into space.

This area was still fairly open, though gantries, frames, transport rails, communication towers, guidance equipment, and observation domes rose around them. The place would soon become the largest spaceport on Annulus. Now, just a few hangars held ships for special owners.

Like Ranglen.

"Let's go to my office," Hatch said. "It's private there."

His "office" was a self-contained living unit that sat under the strong illumination needed by the construction crews (the sun shone only on the opposite side of the shield). It was cluttered with dirty terminals, traces of past meals, empty cartons, discarded clothing, work boots, and several red-and-white bandannas.

Hatch checked his computers—for security updates, Ranglen assumed. Hatch was the more paranoid of the two, which said a lot given Ranglen's attitudes.

"You brought me here for an important reason, I assume?"

"About two weeks ago," Hatch said, "Anne came to see me. She asked me about, of all things, *carbon stars*. It surprised the hell out of me."

"I've heard the term. Exactly what are they?"

"Red giant stars with large carbon content. They're slightly higher on the Hertsprung-Russell diagram, above the normal path for stellar evolution."

"Why do they have more carbon?"

"A slightly different kind of aging. In normal stars, red giants result when the hydrogen fusing into helium runs out. The star swells, the surface cools and gets redder. But the pressure and temperature become higher, to the point where the helium itself in the core begins to fuse—into oxygen and carbon. In carbon stars, more carbon than oxygen is produced. It comes up into the outer layers and forms a kind of soot, tinting the surface even more orange. The stars are also variable, with periods ranging from years to days, so I wouldn't recommend a settlement near one."

"Are they the so-called *blood* stars? Or crimson, or 'vampire' stars?"

"Ah, there speaks the galactic poet. Yes to 'blood' and 'crimson stars,' and 'ginger stars' too. But 'vampire stars' can be something else, like a black hole or a neutron star sucking in the material of another sun."

"Why was Anne interested in them?"

"A carbon star would be approaching the end of its life, the outer layers expanding because of the changing nuclear reactions. This allows the carbon and other molecules to seep into space and form a planetary nebula—leaving behind only the core of the star to become a white dwarf. That's how carbon gets into the stellar medium, and then into other stars that give rise to planets and eventually life. We're all made of carbon, of course. And that's where it comes from."

"So, what's the point?"

Hatch looked embarrassed. "Well, carbon also forms diamonds."

The realization hit Ranglen, and he became both disappointed and angry. "You have to be kidding! *That's* why Anne wanted to go to a carbon star?"

"I didn't say she wanted to go. She was just interested. I told her that diamonds on Earth formed in a different way, which is what makes them so rare. But diamonds present in the stellar medium are common. You can find them in meteorites. They're just too small to be useful, a few molecules at best. You can't make salable gems out of that. Yet, she was still curious."

"So…why?"

"Think about it, Mykol. The whole point of her business, the foundation of what she wants to import and sell, is not based on material value. She sells instead the *story* behind the object. There's potential here—diamonds found in space, broken free from the heart of a star. Some white dwarves might even be *made* of diamond—though you'd never be able to chip off a piece, the gravity would kill you. But what a great tale you could spin—how it symbolizes the vastness of the stars, how it speaks of interstellar cataclysms squeezed down into glittering trinkets. *That* has value, the glint of off-world exoticism—not what it *is*, but what it *represents*. Hell, Mykol, you're the poet. You could write the ad-copy for her."

Ranglen fumed, but he agreed that the notion of interstellar diamonds would excite Anne.

Hatch continued. "Remember that long needle-like thorn you once gave her? You said it came from some killer plant on another world, that it was part of a bush which shot them out like knives at people. She didn't tell you, but she sold that thorn for quite a lot of money."

"What? She *sold* it? It was my gift to her!"

"You think that would stop her? And, another thing, did you ever see the pallasite she has?"

"What's a pallasite?"

"An iron-nickel meteorite with peridots in it, brownish-green crystals of olivine, gemstones. She showed it to me, and then she asked me if, in my 'dealings,' I ever found any to send them her way. She could make money from them. Did she get that meteor from you?"

"No!" Ranglen snapped. Jealousy awoke in him. Just who did she get it from? Maybe Muletti?

"Are they valuable?"

"No, but she can *make* them valuable, again because of the story she tells. She checked out their origin. Olivine forms only in the interiors of planets, not on the surface. So the crystals mixing with the iron and nickel must have come from colliding worlds, or—another means—volcanoes spewing liquid iron. All interesting stuff, and she can play that background if she gets the right buyer. Isn't it true for famous gems that the material value is jacked up by the *story* behind them—the legend, the curse, the deaths involved, especially the murders? And with stellar diamonds, in order to get to them, you'd need exploding planets, crashing stars, whole systems torn apart. What more could you want?"

It still annoyed Ranglen. He supplied Anne the very story which allowed her to sell the thorn he had given her. It made him feel used, and petty. "All right, what are you saying?"

"A day later she came to me again. She rented a spaceship. Not too large, 4 cabins, about the size of yours. But she required a sizable cargo hold, and she gave no reason why she wanted it, just that the ship needed carrying potential—I pulled out one of the passenger cabins and substituted cargo space. But she didn't pick it up herself. She had me deliver it to Rimport 3, where, she implied, someone else would get it. I found all this a little surprising. Anne never leaves Annulus herself. And she never starts her own ventures, like searching for diamonds. She always depends on other people to bring stuff to her. Like you, and at times even me. She keeps it all loose and random, not renting ships for personal missions."

"Has she returned it yet?"

"No. The contract was for an unspecified length, with the possibility of purchase at the end."

"Purchase?"

"I wondered the same thing. Was she planning some recurring mission?"

But Anne seldom financed people's ventures. She liked to see and feel what she was buying, not speculate on possibilities. Was Muletti behind it? Did he ask Anne to get him a spaceship? But then why didn't he rent it on his own? And why did Anne want it delivered to Rimport 3? Renting the ship in her name meant she could claim its value if Muletti tried to steal it, but it also involved her in any shady import deal. And why had her cargo been put on the destroyed carrier if Muletti had a ship that might be able to deliver it?

"There's more. Anne asked for a special item to be added on the outside of the ship."

Ranglen waited. He didn't like Hatch dragging this out.

"She wanted strong carrier braces, one for each side. They manage heavy loads that won't fit on board."

"You mean she needed even more cargo space?"

"That's one possibility. But if she was picking up stellar diamonds—if that story ties into this—they'd make no sense. Where could she find such bulk diamonds? And a load that big would not only destroy the market for them, but even her *specialty* market, too. You can't tell that many stories. Even worse—and this one's serious—the diamond cartels, all of which were once centered on Earth, are now run by clans on Ventroni. They set the prices, they regulate the markets, and they'd thoroughly squeeze her out of business. Plus, Ventroni being Ventroni, they might well go further than that."

Ranglen now knew where Hatch was going. "Like blowing up the ship that carried her merchandise?"

"Well, I find that hard to believe, but you never know. Ventroni gangsters usually go after just other Ventroni gangsters. They don't like off-world attention. Yet something like this would send an awfully powerful message to small just-getting-into-the-business Anne."

Ranglen couldn't believe it either, but he was deeply worried. "Anne would never call such attention to herself. She knows about markets—and she knows who's in charge of them. She'd be careful to keep her products valuable, even if she had them stockpiled. As you said, Ventroni interests are on Ventroni. How would they know of her?"

"Good question. But there's something else here, something about those carrier racks. You're not seeing it yet. Think a little."

Ranglen at first was annoyed with Hatch for not telling him. But then he suddenly had the insight. "They can house weapons."

"Yes," said Hatch. "In fact, they can house *big* weapons. Big enough to do a lot of damage even to a sizable cargo ship."

Ranglen looked out the small window to the well-lit activity outside, where a whole new spaceport was coming into being. He saw none of it.

Hatch added, "Braces like that can hold and stabilize exterior racks that launch rockets. They provide a small craft the means of delivering heavy destruction, almost military in scope."

"That's why you wanted me here, in your secure office, before you told me."

"I don't like the 'official' asteroid story. I think the ship was deliberately blown apart."

A thin nausea grew in Ranglen. "I wondered, too, but…I can't believe it involves Anne."

"I don't think so either. At least not directly. But if the spaceship she rented was used, unknown to her—as well as the braces *she* required—then she could be in big trouble, especially if Annulus wanted to avoid unpleasantries with Homeworld, or if Homeworld wanted to cleanse itself of any association with the incident. She'd make an easy scapegoat. A small smuggling charge is one thing, but accessory to murder is something else."

All this intensified Ranglen's fears. "Has anyone in authority questioned you?"

"No. And that might be odd, or hopeful. Annulus probably wants no part of this, and for good reason. Destroying a ship of that size would require more firepower than even could be carried on Anne's rental. You'd need an actual military ship with high-grade bombs. And who would supply it? Not Annulus, they don't have any. Not Earth, for it's their own cargo ship. Ventroni maybe, but we agreed this is out of their territory. Then what about…Homeworld? Well, perhaps. Could they be getting a little nervous about how friendly Earth and Annulus have become lately? They might think, 'Let's blow up an Earth ship in Annulus space. That'll stop them, make them suspicious of each other.' And no one saying anything in response might support that notion."

Ranglen was silent for a moment, then asked, "Since it was your rental, did it have your standard tracking programs?"

"I always have them, but I can't read them remotely. If I can board the ship, I can tell where it's been. That record is part of the 'black box' data, and it's recorded even if the box is turned off—which renters often do, by the way, though it's illegal. I make it look as if it *can* be done, but I've put in overrides so the data's not destroyed, just moved to other files which only I know how to access."

"Can I read that information if I get on board?"

"I can give you the code. It's different for each vessel. But if someone is monitoring the craft remotely, they'll know you're doing it. You can't keep it secret."

Ranglen headed for the door. "I need my ship."

"Wait. You're going to Rimport 3 to find what happened, right?"

"Anne asked me to track down this Aarov Muletti. He's disappeared."

"Do you always do exactly what she asks of you?"

"She doesn't ask much, Hatch. And I owe her. We haven't always been good to each other. And I'm worried. I need to know what happened." The simple "mission" Anne had given him had become more involved—and dangerous.

"But there's another point I have to share with you. Anne hasn't paid me for the ship. That's not like her. I had to reduce the first installment just so she could take it, and the braces she couldn't cover at all. She now owes me a second installment on the total charge, but I haven't got it yet. That's surprising. Anne might live on the edge but she's always paid her debts."

Ranglen remembered Anne's embarrassment when he mentioned Hatch. She didn't want Ranglen to hear about this—about the rental, the shortage of payment, and Muletti's possible connection to it.

"Who can I talk to at Rimport 3 who's trustworthy? I need information."

"The person in charge of security there is also a member of Annulus Security." Hatch meant the small armed force that Annulus substituted for an army or navy. He thus suggested the person's credentials extended beyond just rimport policing. "And he's dependable as far as I know. Not so strict that he won't open up to you. He doesn't have enough people under him to do a great job, but I think I'd trust him. Ilya Petrovich Tarakov—I remember names like that."

"Let's get my ship."

Hatch followed him outside to a set of hangars. He opened the bay doors and displayed Ranglen's personal craft, a type-2 "luxury" ship whose extras had been modified for deep-space exploration.

"I still think you should take the train."

"I want to impress. And I need a quick way to get out of there, just in case something happens."

Before Ranglen stepped on board, Hatch stopped him with a hand on his shoulder. The tall, gangly figure tilted over him. "Since you're doing a favor for Anne, maybe you could do one for me."

Hatch never asked Ranglen for help.

"There's been talk of a possible war between Homeworld and Earth. I don't care much for either planet, but I worry for Annulus getting caught between them."

"I understand. So?"

"You and I have talked about how people on Annulus see themselves as tough pioneers—proud individualists. But it's all a bit silly. This is no primitive wilderness. We live in a showplace open to the sky, a boutique world, artificial and already perfected. We have no environments that need to be tamed. Yet we pride ourselves on being practical, goal-focused, charging ahead—we want to keep busy and build."

Ranglen grew impatient. "What are you getting at?"

"People here are too sure of themselves. They don't need a frontier mentality. Both you and I know the unchecked growth that's bound to occur."

Ranglen remembered the clutter at the end of the transport tube and Hatch's annoyance with it—even though he was its major cause. Was he talking this way to avoid his own guilt? "Your point being?"

"This cargo-ship disaster, I'm afraid of Annulus taking advantage of it, of blaming Homeworld and trying to throw them out, rebelling against them before we're ready for it. We'll seek full independence someday, which I'll cheer and support, and we *will* get it. But I know how much power we really have now, and it's not much. Homeworld has a fleet and an army. We have only Annulus Security, which is not well-funded, not too unified, and which sometimes follows its own agendas. Look at how much we don't care about import customs. I believe totally in independence, as I know you do too. But we need to win it on our own, enforce it on *our* terms—the only terms we should work for."

"I know all that. I fully agree."

"So if rebellion occurs, if it just 'accidentally happens' because of this incident, we'd probably have to ally with *Earth* because of our lack of strength. And then, if we succeed in gaining independence from Homeworld, we'd just pick up *another* dependence. And *that* grip would be more difficult to lose. We'd become Earth's patsy, live under their massive military rule. I believe in rebellion against Homeworld. But not if we have to depend on Earth. Living under them would be worse than what we live under now. We'd lose everything."

Ranglen, having grown too suspicious lately, remembered that Hatch was about to open a new spaceport. "Bad for business? Like Anne would say?"

"Bad for *Annulus*. For *your* world. The home you return to after all your travels. I don't think even you want that."

Ranglen grew testy, especially after Anne had said something annoyingly similar, a reminder of his devotion to Annulus as if maybe he had forgotten it. "You think I'd feel otherwise?"

"All I'm saying is, whatever you're doing and whatever you find, don't do it as just a personal favor for Anne. Do it for *all* of us, for Annulus itself. I want us to get through this current mess."

"You don't need to be my conscience, Hatch."

"I know. But just remember what I said."

Ranglen nodded, if still irritated.

"That's all I have to say. You can leave now. Take care and good luck. I've got work to do."

Hatch marched away and didn't look back—as if the conversation never occurred.

The fast cut-off was standard for him. But the words leading up to it had been very different.

Ranglen brooded. What the hell was everyone seeing in him? And why was he treated like some lost cause that needed encouragement?

He entered his spaceship and prepped for take-off.

Chapter 6: Rimport 3

Ranglen generally loved spaceports. But not this one.

The six docks on the outside rim of Annulus sat on shelves at the base of the "mountains," jutting out on cantilevers but also opening back into topography that had been left clear by the Airafane blueprint. Rimport 3 angled down at fifteen degrees from the surface of the Ring and thus was level with the other similarly angled spaceports, so no traffic had to fly over the Ring proper.

A long and narrow elliptical platform, it housed berths, moorings, docks that jutted out into space where mid-size ships could continue to float (the Ring did not rotate so there was no need to match angular velocity). Cranes stood along the edge, then a relatively open area lay behind them for smaller ships making vertical landings, and all that space was backed by a line of hangars, storage facilities, repair shops, supply depots, and offices.

It struck Ranglen as cramped and dull. Not many ships lined the docks now, and activity was slow. A number of smaller craft sat in the back of the cleared area, business transport or privately-owned pleasure yachts. Other vessels could be seen inside the hangars whose doors stood open.

One large hangar had glowing above its entrance the insignia of Homeworld, and it apparently was used for just their vehicles.

Not too many dockhands milled about. Maybe the place was restricted to minimal service until Hatch's bigger harbor was completed. The six small rimports were not adequate for the growing commerce of Annulus, and Ranglen suspected that after Hatch's facility was operational, these ports would become even better for smugglers. A sense of pending closing-down tainted the air.

Braya generally hated spaceports. But not this one.

They usually brought back too many memories of bad jobs, bad pay, random abuse, humiliation, imprisonment, severe neglect, and dreams of escape that never became real.

But this one was quiet, almost orderly, open to a constant star-filled sky that nearly sang with invitation. Small and manageable, did it have no exploitation of labor? Were the positive stories about Annulus correct?

She wasn't here to enjoy herself, though. And her view of the port was privileged at the moment. She stood in the slopes behind the hangars, lofty and removed, and looked down on the less-than-busy landing field below. But Hideki stood too near to her, becoming a problem, so this contemplation would soon end and return Braya to her goal, supported by the regrettably useful Seekers.

An unannounced ship approached. It looked a bit similar to the *Prowler* but it was more expensive and outfitted well. The person on board must be rich or important, and whoever was responsible for the care of the craft struck her as competent and knowledgeable. Her trained eye could see the additions.

Such admiration, though, would not change her plans.

Ranglen landed and disembarked with no fanfare or special introduction. He normally didn't hide who he was but he didn't call attention to it and often tried to sneak in unnoticed. He maybe should have taken the train instead since it was a more secretive mode. But his ship, which looked standard if bolstered by Hatch's engineering, he was proud of, and it gave him a great sense of independence. As long as he had it around, he felt he could be more "himself," or whatever self he chose to be at the time.

Ranglen had called ahead to meet with Tarakov. To the security officer's digital double he had asked questions and received pre-set responses, like that from a good protective secretary. But once he said who he was, he got an appointment.

He walked across the flat surface—the deck had its own gravity-plates—toward the offices that lined the low "mountains" of the outer Ring (just corrugations in the Airafane sheet-like base material). From here, given the tilt of the deck, he couldn't see the opposite half of Annulus, so no colored arc swept across the sky.

Small ships were being unloaded. The larger freighters—like the one destroyed—parked at a distance and portable shuttles ferried the containers across to the port. It was a slow and inefficient process, again underlining the need for Hatch's facility.

As he walked toward the main offices, he saw two people standing at the edge of the deck against the background hills—the farthest they could be from the spaceport and yet still remain a "part" of it. Security wouldn't allow them to get any closer, and Ranglen wondered why they were here. They seemed to be openly observing the port but waiting in an area that didn't encourage bystanders. They were obviously visitors (not dressed in the semi-pressurization suits of the dockhands), maybe tourists out to see the spaceships. But they'd have a better view up in the hills and be safer there.

They seemed almost too blatant, not caring about being noticed. And they made him feel they were watching *him*.

Two other people higher on the slope also seemed to observe him. One was short in dark clothes and the other had strangely violet-white hair—he could see it from even this distance.

If they were local, they had to be from under the Ring, for no villages sat close on the upper surface. He'd ask about this when he got inside.

After entering the complex and telling the reception console of his needs, he filled out a digital form, entered his request and then waited. No human receptionist was available.

He saw two other people waiting. Young, unkempt, and oddly gloomy with penetrating eyes. They seemed both submissive and arrogant, like angry, yet powerless, youth—withdrawn, separate, and proudly not caring about their surroundings. They could have been mindless religious converts or blunted perpetrators of brutality.

They stared at him with unsettling directness.

Instructions were downloaded into his cellpad on how to find Tarakov's office, and he followed them to a designated compartment, glad to leave the two people behind—who watched him leave like spies in training, their eyes following him without their heads moving, the attempt to be subtle just made more obvious.

Tarakov met him at his office door. Though a bit heavyset for a police officer, he moved athletically and his size made him impressive. He had a wheat-colored fringe of hair around a balding head, a huge expanse of heavy face, a blunt nose, and the average cross-race brown skin of Annulus. His uniform—plain, khaki—was heavily wrinkled and a little frayed, but it fit him well, and he carried his badge, shoulder-com, holstered weapon, and open cellpad with an assured formality. And his eyes, a chilly and pale gray-blue, were vigilant and lively—unlike the heavy-lidded ponderous look of the two people in reception. Indeed, he appeared solidly dependable. At an emergency, he'd radiate the feeling that "you're in safe hands."

And if chasing a crook, he'd be relentless.

The officer held out his hand in greeting. "It's a pleasure to meet you, Mr. Ranglen. I've read some of your essays."

"The poems are better."

"I'll give those a try. What can I do for you?" He indicated the chair across from his, and Ranglen and he sat down.

"I need some background for a novel I'm writing."

"Glad to help."

They usually were. The request complimented their authority while allowing them to discuss their work in a safe context. All for entertainment, they felt—names changed, events exaggerated beyond believability, and no harm done.

"You're an officer of Annulus Security, correct?"

He nodded, pointed to the circle insignia on his badge. "The head of safety at any rimport is required to be."

"Then, as both an A.S. officer and the working head of this port, do you see much smuggling?" It was a typical writer's question, blunt, naive, but he also asked it for Anne's sake.

"Formally, no. Informally, yes. It's a thorny point of definition. Satellite surveillance and the meteor defense shield are good in preventing—or at least in keeping track of—unauthorized landings. But the economy on Annulus is still developing, so customs is open to more imports than expected. What might be unwanted because of economic instability on a more populated or regimented planet, like Earth or Homeworld, could be welcomed here. So, there's a certain amount of 'looking the other way.'"

"How do you handle that?"

"We do no customs clearance at this port—it occurs at the other stations which deal with passengers. All our cargos are cleared through agents we send to the points of departure on other worlds, to screen the products ahead of time, to certify the contents and to lock the containers, so we don't need to examine things here. But those agents are unofficially told to be flexible. Annulus is lucky not to have drug cartels, gambling syndicates, human traffickers, arms peddlers, traders in illegal animals or animal parts, or importers of invasive plants, so fierce oversight is not necessary. Of course, someday that all might change."

Anne would be reassured, at least for now when markets were open. But the more complex the society became, the more restrictions would be established.

"There *is* a growing interest in specialty items, rare finds, exclusive crafts, alien exotica, because they help the economy stay unique. And you can't flood a market that hardly exists. We're not a 'collector' culture yet—we don't build museums, as you pointed out in one of your essays—we're still too busy and future-oriented. So, such imports are not openly denounced, and a few loopholes are left open."

Anne would be even happier. It also meant that the customs agents on other planets, all trained by Homeworld but assigned by Annulus, might be open to bribery—which Ranglen *wasn't* happy about.

Tarakov seemed to enjoy talking, probably a release from drudge work and a chance to show-off his knowledge. "It could become an issue if other worlds complain about it. No one's defined yet who owns the artifacts of alien races that no longer exist—the finder, or the finder's home planet? Governments, or research institutes? The many disagreements have yet to be resolved, and until they are, a lot of money will keep changing hands, and the amounts will rise. The tariff war between Homeworld and Earth doesn't help. They're both too eager to get a cut of everything that flows between them, maybe more to hurt each other than to make a gain for themselves. For us on Annulus, we'll continue to prevent the obvious offenses from coming in—untested pharmaceuticals, harmful drugs, faulty commercial products, unlicensed weapons, illegal plants or animals, things like that."

"What about crime in high space? How much of it is real?" Ranglen meant raids on cargo liners but he didn't specify.

"There's more than you think. Annulus avoids much of it, but Earth and Homeworld are susceptible, as well as the less powerful worlds in the Confederation— just not Ventroni, since they quietly support a lot of it. Planetary laws don't extend far into space. A home planet can board and search only ships registered to its own ports and not to anyone else's, though it does happen. The Confederation is trying to change this—the old idea of a 'Space Patrol' that has authority everywhere, with actual interstellar laws to support it—but too many worlds are playing politics, jostling for position and power. They write laws but then don't follow them, though they expect everyone else to do so. And interstellar distance is self-defeating. How can such a vast area of space ever be patrolled? You can't do much about what occurs."

"But what *does* occur? Can you give me examples?"

"Ships can fake their registry, change designated home ports—if it's to their advantage to avoid tariffs or to find docks with more lenient laws. Some ships have no registry at all—'ghost ships,' they're called. A number become rogue and then genuine pirates. And capturing such ships isn't easy because the changed registrations muddy who's responsible for impounding them—though sometimes you find the original registrations through surprising means, like a jacket or onboard stationary, once even someone's pajamas. On top of that, a few planets even support privateering—not publicly, of course, yet both Earth and Homeworld are said to be guilty. The tariff craze encourages it. Private or corporate merchant ships are captured and stripped by fast and well-armed raiders. Victims either die or vanish—space, as said, is so big that any saving 'cavalry' is hampered. Even respectable and planet-based entrepreneurs get involved. They raise money, establish a syndicate, buy a ship, and one good strike returns the entire investment with profit. It might take a long time to make that strike, to find a 'treasure' ship, but once you do, you can retire. Basically, the laws to stop all this either don't exist yet, or the enforcement of those that do exist just isn't politically expedient."

Ranglen assumed Tarakov was exaggerating, which often happened when a researching writer asked for input. Still, the details were disturbing.

"The big distress for me," Tarakov said, "is not the financial but the *human* cost, the loss of freedom and life. Off-world colonization, as pushed by Earth and other worlds, has become a means of not just inhabiting space but of ridding home planets of disenfranchised populations. It's a subtle form of human trafficking because there's a thin line between volunteering and being conscripted. If you're a suffering displaced refugee, you'll sign up for anything—you have little choice. People *are* legitimately needed on new planets for terraforming, construction, farming, mining, or just sustaining the gene pool, and many people have been able to build new homes and make new starts, which is a fine outcome. But there's so much abuse."

Tarakov's tone was strong enough that Ranglen wondered if he was personally involved, that victims of such crimes were close to him.

"Sometimes the colonists are not even taken to other planets but sold as crew to black-market vessels, blockade runners, pirate ships. Some are traded among those ships and they basically become slaves—'floaters,' they're called. They have no rights because when they signed their original contracts with the corporations they were required to waive all of them. They become cargo, not people anymore. Some are told they'll be granted citizenship on a new planet, but only an established legal government can bestow citizenship—not corporations. Contracts are written to support the company and not the person. But people still sign them because they're desperate. Some ships are raided not for merchandise but just the passengers. The captain of one colony ship, to save his life, sold off everyone on board—it was a latter-day slave auction. And he made quite a profit until he was caught, though the refugees themselves were never found. There are even flying armories run by independent investors, who supply the lone-wolf raiders with weapons and supplies—so they don't have to come into any port. And they're much too clever and efficient to be caught."

"How much do you, as an officer on Annulus, deal with this?"

"Thankfully, not much, especially at this port. We get little traffic. We're all waiting for Hatch Banner to take over. At his bigger place, customs and imports will be handled more effectively. The six rimports now specialize. Two of them get passenger liners, one is just for Annulus Security, we here at 3 handle small independent cargo, and the last two get the larger corporate traffic. Problems I encounter are fairly manageable—lost or damaged goods, insurance fraud, impounded craft, ship inspections, overbillings, fraudulent certification, inflated costs, fictitious repairs. It's quite a gamut, but, to be honest, it's petty compared to the larger things that happen in space."

"What about *near* space, in our own system?"

"You're worried about Annulus?"

By saying this, Tarakov acknowledged Ranglen's role as "founder" of the habitat. It was both a recognition and a compliment. "I'm always worried. I have a personal stake, of course. But is shipping in danger even this close to home?" The wreck of the cargo ship loomed behind his words.

Tarakov caught the drift. "Did you come here because of the *Lochner* then, the ship that was destroyed?"

"I didn't know its name. And it's not the only reason I'm here. But, naturally, I was curious." Ranglen did know the name. He had scanned recent news for whatever he could find, but he didn't admit to this.

And he was glad he didn't, for Tarakov now seemed a little suspicious. "As far as a direct threat to Annulus, the meteor shield stopped any large pieces of wreckage from hitting the surface. A few small things did get through, but they're already rewriting the algorithms to prevent that. The ground cover was disturbed but you can't even tell now where it happened."

"They say the ship struck an asteroid."

"Yes, that's the story."

This was Tarakov's shortest response yet. Ranglen assumed more was left unsaid. "Do you believe it?"

"I'm an official. I have to believe it."

Ranglen's attention sharpened even more. Was the response a screen, or an open invitation to probe further? He remembered Hatch saying that Annulus Security had different internal agendas, and he wondered if Tarakov demonstrated one—an opposing view about the accident. Ranglen assured the officer, "I'm not an investigative reporter. I'm writing only fiction, and what I put into my stories will certainly go far beyond the truth."

Tarakov made a careful smile. "I understand."

"So...do you believe the story or not?"

"Well, like I said, my opinion is not part of my job. I enforce what I'm told. If I wonder about anything, I do it privately. But, to answer your question, I'm comfortable with the asteroid premise. It makes sense."

"But you've thought of other scenarios, right? Can you speculate on any?"

Tarakov looked over Ranglen's shoulder as if to confirm that the office door was shut.

Ranglen knew the look. The man wanted to be frank, but he wouldn't put his job on the line.

"Later today there was supposed to be a formal briefing about the accident, but it's been canceled. Reporters were told they've already been given the fullest extent of the story, and that nothing else will be added for now. The blame's on the ship's guidance system, on a failure to negotiate in-system debris, and an incorrect tracking of planetary objects. Bad course plotting. Inquiry will continue, but they'll add to the public story only if new discoveries are made."

"So...let me get a little creative here, do you suspect some kind of cover-up?"

Tarakov laughed. "No. Not a bit. The shield did the job it was supposed to do. No one's responsibility on Annulus is questioned. And any more critical interpretations could be a problem for our relationships with Homeworld and Earth. Speculation's been curtailed and public interest mostly restrained. I agree with that. The basic attitude is to stay out of the way and let Homeworld and Earth fight it out."

"*Fight* it out?"

"Sorry. Bad word choice. 'Work' it out."

Ranglen tried to sound disappointed. "All this is fascinating, and I really appreciate everything you're telling me, but I'm still in search of a useful plot."

Tarakov smiled, but then said, in a serious if maybe sad tone, "There's no evidence for other explanations. The path through the system *was* poorly chosen. The ship was supposed to drop a small cargo pod here at this rimport, though we don't know what the cargo was and it doesn't seem relevant, since the ship wasn't taking the best approach path. It really had to be pilot error or a fault in the ship's navigation system."

"The *Lochner* came from Earth, correct?"

At that point, Tarakov showed a little impatience. "What are you getting at, Mr. Ranglen?"

The reaction surprised him. "Well, as you implied, there's much tension lately between Earth and Homeworld, and many attempts to avoid the tariffs. Could pirates then, taking advantage of the situation, be responsible?"

"I seriously doubt piracy was involved. They would have *taken* the ship, not destroyed it. And it then would have been sold, as well as the cargo. Note that Earth, the ultimate victim of the wreck, has not said a word in protest. Wouldn't it be to their advantage to shout about this incident to the whole Confederation? So, a natural cause seems the only answer, and Earth doesn't want to admit their pilots made a mistake. All parties are wise not to give the event too much attention."

"If not pirates, then maybe privateers?"

"But what government would subsidize such a thing?"

"Well, maybe Homeworld. I got that idea while listening to you talk of crimes in space."

Tarakov cleared his throat. "I seriously doubt that Homeworld could be involved. And I'd be very careful with what's assumed here. That kind of story would be devastating to our relations with Homeworld. It's the worst that could happen."

"But…why?"

"Because, and I don't think I'm being too revealing here, Earth regrets its decision to give up Annulus and allow Homeworld to 'possess' it. Annulus has grown. I, among others, think Earth wants to become more allied with us. Homeworld knows this. Maybe that's why the tariffs between them are just short of economic blockades. If an Earth ship coming here is destroyed, people will wonder—just as you did—if Homeworld was responsible, even though I'm certain that's unlikely. It wouldn't be a simple act of provocation. It could start a war. Homeworld would never go that far."

"But all useful evidence seems destroyed. Isn't that too convenient?"

Tarakov shook his head, implying Ranglen was gullible. "It's no surprise. If the reactor core of an Earth ship is breached, it will automatically self-destruct. It's a safety precaution started after a big liner in Earth orbit broke in half and dropped reactor material onto a city. They don't want that happening again. Surely you'd agree."

"Yes, but—"

"Please, Mr. Ranglen, you can imagine any scenario you want. But, formally, you'll hear less about the incident. Annulus doesn't want a lot of speculation on whether it's true or not. So, you'll get nothing more from them, nothing from Homeworld, and probably not much from Earth."

But Tarakov said this too declaratively. Ranglen drew back a little. And his wariness was soon justified.

"Frankly, Mr. Ranglen, I'm getting a little uncomfortable with your questioning. You don't seem a fiction writer anymore but someone digging for signs of corruption, or bad faith from places like Homeworld."

The officer checked his cellpad, as if Ranglen's allotted time had run out.

"I'm sorry," Ranglen said. "I'll stop taking your time. Just one more question, and it's off the topic we were discussing. Do you know a man named Aarov Muletti?"

Tarakov's expression changed, hardened. He was no longer a writer's "friend" but a fully involved police official. "Why do you ask?"

"I know someone who tried to reach him, and he seems to have disappeared." Ranglen was aware that saying this was dangerous—he wanted no connection leading back to Anne.

The officer gave Ranglen a long stare before he responded. "He's worked for the government but now he's more a mid-level negotiator for import deals. He's seen regularly at all the rimports. He sets up clearance requirements and import duties for both suppliers and buyers. He has a number of clients, and a few have already asked about him. Did your friend want to start a formal inquiry?"

"No. When I said I was coming here, I was just asked to check. It didn't seem important."

"He's not labeled as missing, and he often travels to Earth and Homeworld. At times, he's not easy to find. His clients have told me that."

"I'll pass that along."

"You also might mention that Muletti has been the subject of legal inquiries. No formal charges have been brought against him, but anyone working with him should be told that. He had a serious legal fight on Homeworld some time ago, but he's apparently taken care of it. I don't know the details. I'd advise anyone having dealings with him to be mindful of such history."

"I'll say that, too." Ranglen was surprised Tarakov was so open about Muletti's transgressions. Was it personal? He took one more chance. "Did Muletti have a ship based here?"

"Actually, yes."

"Registered to Annulus?"

"No, to Homeworld, but its last port of call was Earth. I checked when people asked about his absence."

"Registered to Homeworld and not Annulus? Isn't that odd?"

"No. Our port here is becoming more a storage facility than a port-of-entry. A lot of private ships are housed here. One hangar is reserved especially for Homeworld, where special privileges are maintained—I'm not allowed to review the transponders of the ships that are stored there. Homeworld's like that. They submit their logs and destinations, but we get no corroboration from their instruments—we have to take them at their word. The other ports have more control because of their higher flow of imports and passengers, but not us."

Ranglen heard a note of bitterness. "Is Muletti's ship here now?"

"Yes, in the Homeworld hangar."

Ranglen wanted to inspect the ship but he had no good justification for it, and Tarakov probably didn't have the jurisdiction to authorize such an inspection anyway—which likely rankled him.

He also seemed done now with answering questions, stirring in his chair as if wanting to get to work. "Anything else, Mr. Ranglen?"

Ranglen shook his head. He knew to back off.

"Very good, then. I wish you well in writing your fiction."

Ranglen thanked him. But as he rose to leave, he added, "Just one more thing, and it's really trivial. Those two people in the waiting room outside—who are they? They looked like they were held for questioning and didn't like it."

"They're people from the Mountain Seekers." Tarakov sounded dismissive of them. "A group lives under the Ring nearby. We bring them in for questioning now and then—they're willing, though they always look sour. These two claim they speak a different language but they understand us and know when to respond. We don't coerce them. Since the Seekers worship the Airafane, they have a strong affection for Annulus."

"And they live under the Ring?"

"Yes, but they're not the same as the few who lived there already. We keep a watch in case the Seekers infiltrate them and try to convert them. We don't see evidence of that, though. They appear harmless. We question them periodically to keep tabs on them—and to show we know of them."

Ranglen thought they might not look as harmless as Tarakov claimed. "So, they're not drop-outs like the others under the Ring?" He made the tone a bit derisive.

"Hard to say. Maybe they are, but they're more focused. They don't label themselves as disadvantaged, as some other people do who stay down there. They don't seem political at all. There's no leader, and they apparently don't want one. That's fine with us."

Ranglen sensed a light intolerance to both the Seekers and the people under the Ring, but he wasn't sure.

Or maybe Tarakov was just getting irritated the longer Ranglen stayed around. He couldn't help asking another question, though, one of personal interest after hearing about the group. "Did the Seekers originate here on Annulus, since they worship the Airafane?"

"That would seem logical, but there's evidence it started first on an alien world and then spread to Earth before it came here, the ideas carried by spaceship crews."

Ranglen laughed. "They do love to spin tall tales, don't they."

"They say the jumps in light-space put them in contact with other realities, which help them to understand more deeply."

Ranglen nodded, not knowing if Tarakov was serious or not. "Anyway, thanks again."

Just as Ranglen stood up to leave, a red light beeped on Tarakov's desk.

Tarakov picked up an earplug to take the message privately.

Then a knock sounded at his door, and a woman in the same khaki uniform as Tarakov's said only, "You're needed, sir."

He raised his hand to acknowledge her, listened a bit longer on the plug, then dropped it and hurried out, saying nothing to Ranglen as he passed him.

Ranglen followed.

In the hallway, another security officer pursued Tarakov. Then one more alarm sounded. All of them drew their weapons.

Ranglen followed but stayed behind as they emerged onto the open deck.

A fire blazed to their right, near the docks themselves. Banners of flame swirled up from a small ship that had either exploded or been set on fire. The blackened wreckage in its nest of flames sent tall plumes of smoke into the night.

Ranglen knew now he had guessed right. The Seekers were not harmless after all.

Chapter 7: In the Hangar

Braya was fed up with Hideki. The woman had insisted on the diversionary explosion that set a ship ablaze, which Braya thought was extravagant and foolish.

Hideki argued back, "I'm telling you we'll need it. We have to clear people out of that hangar."

"It's crazy! We'll gain just a few minutes and then everyone will ask what started the fire and they'll see it's been planted. They'll comb the port for who's responsible." She had seen that procedure where she worked.

"But it's easy to get away from here. We're up against the mountains. No one pays attention to the Seekers."

"They will *now*. This will bring all of them down on you. You'll never be left alone again."

"Well, it's time we took some steps, moved forward, showed our strength. And if you can identify those killer ships, as you claimed you could, it'll be an important gain for us here on Annulus, the beginning of something. You're the catalyst."

"I won't be part of your foolish plans."

"We help you as you help us. Mutual benefit. Just like we said."

Braya stopped listening. She was too focused now on what they might find. They scrambled on the trail that led between the artificial slopes of the "mountains" and the back of the hangars.

She thought back over how their path of getting to the rimport had been torturous. Braya conceded she needed Hideki's help but she hated being dependent on her. She was ready to drop her when she got there, but the woman never let go.

And Braya didn't like the people Hideki brought with her. By the time they reached the port, five other Seekers tagged along, all of them weirdly quiet and subservient, with creepy eyes that were morose and judging. Hideki said that two of them were needed to set up the explosion while another two would sit in the security office—where they had been called in for standard questioning—to keep watch on the officers. And the last was a so-called "satellite" who had an undefined role.

But then, when they reached the port, they were surprised by a potential danger. An unscheduled visitor arrived in his own spaceship. And he must have been important because the head security officer met with him privately for some time—all of this reported back to Hideki by the two Seekers waiting in the office.

So, Hideki tried to delay the break-in, which infuriated Braya, who threatened to go off on her own and would have done so except that Hideki finally agreed to get started. The woman led Braya along the hidden path behind the hangars so they could sneak into the Homeworld facility through a back entrance.

The walk was not easy. Many places required detours over the slopes that Hideki supposedly knew. "We've been inside every hangar," she said, "sometimes stealing things and taking them to the huts. I know my way around."

Braya found such easy theft unbelievable. At the ports where she worked, perpetrators would be found quickly and ruthlessly punished.

"Okay. We're here." They approached a door in the back of a large hangar. "We made perfect time. I'll send the go-ahead signal." Hideki didn't believe in radio silence, another point of dispute with Braya. But Braya was too close to what she wanted now.

"The explosion will occur in just a few moments." They stood beside the hangar's door, which Hideki said would be unlocked.

A loud crack, then a fast stirring of heated air they could feel even where they stood. They heard fragments hitting the dock. A trail of smoke rose above the hangar and sooty waves crept around the sides.

"Perfect! Wonderful!" Hideki sounded like a chortling witch—and looked like one as she wrung her hands. Braya found it more pathetic than funny.

Hideki insisted on being first to try the door. It was unlocked. "I told you. They don't even bother."

She drew the door slightly open, peered inside.

"Excellent," she crowed. "Everyone ran out to help with the fire. See, we *needed* that diversion. I knew what I was talking about."

From behind Hideki, Braya looked in and saw no one moving among the vessels.

Hideki opened the door wider. "Recognize anything?"

The large hangar held several ships of different sizes but nothing large, mostly roustabouts and business craft, the varied types similar except for small details.

Then Braya saw one that was like the *Prowler*, the mid-sized of the three attack ships. Though many other craft there resembled it—it was a popular make—this one had the stain of recently removed braces still on its hull. It had to be the ship the Seeker spies, or "Eyes," saw arrive here—the one she wanted.

"That's it!" she said. She added, generously, "Your people were right," and pushed past Hideki into the room.

Hideki grabbed her. "Wait! Someone's coming!"

Braya looked to the large opening at the front of the hangar where they could see a glimpse of the fire beyond. There, a person entering.

"Get back! Get back!"

She returned to Hideki who pulled her through the doorway and made her stand outside. They waited together beyond the door, which they left open just enough so they could see in.

Hideki was disturbed. "It's the guy we saw landing, the one who met with security. What the hell is he doing here?"

"He's heading for that ship with the brace stains." Braya inched forward.

"Wait! Wait! Let's see what he's doing."

"I have to get in there."

"Just wait a minute."

Braya seethed.

They watched him closely.

After Ranglen had followed the officers to find the small ship on fire, he stayed behind while Tarakov hurried and organized his crew to fight the blaze.

Ranglen's own ship was parked on the other side of the landing deck so he wasn't worried about the fire reaching it. And since he was left alone and ignored—Tarakov worked his team to keep the fire from spreading, though the ship was obviously lost—Ranglen wandered away to the left and, casually, moved in the direction of the Homeworld hangar.

All storage areas were wide open, and no one worked inside. The crew had run out to help with the fire. It was the perfect diversion for Ranglen, allowing him to move in and investigate Homeworld's privileged space.

He slipped through the open bay doors and walked blithely along, in case anyone observed him, trying to appear he was just wandering. He saw mostly small ships, one- or two-seaters for short jaunts, four-seaters like his own, then one larger carrier for small cargos. He assumed these were either privately owned or kept by businesses for short trips. They all had the official insignia of Homeworld—an ochre-green wedge with a comet slashed across it.

Then one vessel caught his attention. Type-2 engines, "family" size, a common shape and design. It looked a little beat-up and stained, as if it had gone through a fire or explosions.

Long parallel streaks on its sides suggested that a large carrier rack, or some other addition, had been added to it and then removed.

And, unlike the other ships, it had no identifier for the world of its registry.

Ranglen walked toward it.

As he neared, he could see signs that an insignia had been removed. A few traces of color were still left, and he wondered why the change hadn't been more thorough. Instead of the symbol being painted over or replaced with a new hull plate, the old sign had been treated with acid or paint remover and scratched out. You could still see hints suggesting the original—a green-and-ochre wedge with a comet.

Had the removal been hurried, slipshod?

Then he noticed one other interesting detail.

The making of spaceships was still fairly standardized. They hadn't developed yet into competing "brands," though that was coming. The designs were similar because still dependent on the Airafane Type-1-to-3 engines provided by the first Clip.

But Ranglen noticed a small additional band of metal on a landing strut. It seemed no more than a reinforcing loop for the rod, but Ranglen knew it was significant.

It normally held an identifier code labeling it as a vessel rented by Hatch Banner. All his ships had them. But that code, too, had been removed.

Yet, the band wouldn't be there if this wasn't a Hatch ship, which also meant that the original *Annulus* insignia—which came on all of Hatch's vessels—had been erased first, and very thoroughly, before the Homeworld insignia had been added. And then that had been removed, just less completely.

Ranglen remembered what Tarakov had said, that hiding the original registry was often done to take advantage of different port protocols. A supposedly Homeworld ship would get better attention from a port on Homeworld than a ship from Annulus—or, worse yet, one from Earth.

Could this be the vessel that Anne rented? Had it been changed so it could be kept in this hangar, a spot of privilege—and thus relatively "unseen" by Annulus?

But then why was *that* insignia erased also?

Ranglen walked to the other side. The entrance ramp had been lowered, and the access door at the top of it stood open.

This was not too surprising. Most ships in the hangar had been left accessible for repair work, supply deliveries, computer updates, and general maintenance. Enough people would have been about to prevent any unauthorized entrances.

But it still seemed too much an open invitation.

Was someone inside?

He looked beyond the front of the hangar to the still smoldering fire on the landing deck. It was under control, but people there were still busy, making sure other ships hadn't been damaged and searching through the wreckage for signs of the fire's cause. He assumed they'd be occupied a while longer.

Feeling foolish, and terribly conspicuous, he walked up the ramp and looked inside.

Darkness. No internal lights.

"Anyone in here?"

No answer.

He inched his way forward. A musty smell hung in the gloom, of old clothes and unwashed bodies, and something metallic, coppery or iron.

He didn't touch a light switch—a paranoia about fingerprints. He pulled out his cellpad and used its torch.

He saw nothing suspicious. The interior had the familiar look of a Hatch rental, but a thousand other ships would appear the same.

He moved his way forward to the two flight-chairs (there was room for four but two had been removed).

He remembered what Hatch had said about accessing the flight-recorder data. He attached a lead from his cellpad to the control board. He hurried, which made him more nervous. He knew he was crossing a dangerous line, actively interfering now and not just "wandering."

He brought up Hatch's special file that copied the black-box data whether the recorders had been turned off or not. He used Hatch's private code, then downloaded the figures into his cellpad.

This took a while.

He turned off his torch. He was getting too tense.

After he finished, he closed up his cellpad and put it in a pocket inside his jacket. He turned to go.

But he heard a noise from the back of the ship. A kind of moaning.

"Hello?" he said, again feeling foolish.

No response.

An odd wheezing or stirring from in back. He couldn't make it out.

He moved slowly to the rear.

A cargo room had replaced one of the passenger cabins beside the entrance to the main hold. The door that led to the small area stood partially open. Ranglen hadn't noticed it when he first entered the ship. The faint noises came from there.

Ranglen crept closer. Beyond the open door lay darkness.

He reached the entrance and peered inside. Enough light entered through the door frame at the top of the ramp to let him see.

A woman sat on the floor, her back to the wall. She tilted slowly forward and back, as if in mild repeating spasms, moaning while doing so.

What he could see of her baffled him. She had a wild set of hair, a silver-pink halo that was visible in the light, frazzled and neglected. He caught the hint of a marked face and a wildly embellished worker's outfit. She didn't move except for her continued rocking, as if she were drugged or intoxicated.

He repeated his greeting.

She paid no attention to him.

Was the door to this room left open to attract someone? Had the ship's entrance at the top of the ramp remained clear for the same reason? Was all this a trap?

From outside, he heard voices.

"Wait! For god's sake, will you be careful?"

Hideki's caution couldn't stop Braya, who moved farther into the hangar to get a better look at what was happening.

They had watched the intruder examine the ship and walk around to the far side, but from where they stood they couldn't see what he did there. So Braya stepped into the hangar—which led to Hideki's sudden hysteria.

"I don't like this!" the woman almost screeched. "He shouldn't be here!"

Braya ignored her.

Taking advantage of the cover of other ships, she stalked to the craft from the side opposite the access ramp. She, too, could see that the insignia had been removed—which tallied with the three attack craft having none. She also knew from her spaceport experience that registrations were often changed.

She focused instead on the stain-trails where the outside racks had been attached. It was slim evidence but good enough for her.

She imagined—maybe not too hopelessly—of planting inside this very ship one of the Seekers' incendiary bombs (which they had taken from another source, Hideki said, undisclosed, and the explosives had been carried exclusively by her grim companions).

But she also knew if that were done, satisfaction would not be complete. She wanted the pilot, the person responsible.

She crept behind the ship. From there she could see the access ramp—and a slightly ajar door at the top.

She moved toward the ramp, placed a foot on it.

Hideki ran up to her. "Are you crazy? You can't go in there! That other guy might still be around."

Hideki could be right but Braya was too determined now. Besides, Hideki had spoken loud enough that anyone inside could hear her.

Then a harder voice came, solid and flat, and not from the ship but from behind them. "Stay right there. Don't move any farther."

Braya and Hideki turned around, saw a man with a short white beard and a peaked cap. He held a gun on them.

Braya recognized him. The man who attacked Krin on the *Lochner*. And she had seen the same gun before.

He stared at Braya, obviously remembering her, too.

Rage possessed her. "I saw what you did! I was on the cargo ship! You shot at me and tried to kill me!"

A smile of interest grew on his face. "You were hiding in an alcove, right? Then you ran out through the door. That was very resourceful."

"You missed me because you were beating a woman."

The smile went away. "Why are you here?"

"To find who piloted this ship. Was it you?"

"So *you're* the one who went into my backup files. I was checking remotely. Clever again. But you didn't know it would get my attention. Did you find what you wanted?"

"What are you talking about?"

Hideki stood off to the side, closely watching the two of them while their attention focused on each other.

The man said to Braya, "How long were you in there?"

"I *haven't* gone in yet. But I intend to."

"You won't find any clue to the registration."

"There are more ways to identify a ship—the instrument panel, the engine block."

"Ah, I see. You think you know your stuff. You're not the average refugee."

She ignored the insult. "Answer me! Did you pilot this ship when the carrier was attacked—when you raided the colonists' hold?"

He didn't respond. He gazed at her but then looked up at the ship—and saw the door partially closed. His voice darkened. "That hatch was left open. Did you close it?"

Braya remembered the furtive man they had seen earlier. Had he gone inside? "No," she said.

The man looked worried.

Hideki spoke, "Aarov, please," her voice no longer shrill or hysterical but calmly concerned.

The man didn't look at her. "Shut up, you witch."

Hideki walked slowly toward him. "You can't—"

The man lifted his gun and fired at her.

Hideki spun backward and fell to the deck.

Ranglen listened inside the entranceway, behind the door which he had nearly shut but left open. On hearing the name "Aarov," he realized the man had to be Muletti and that his own raid on the files had been detected.

In a fit of irrational courage—an impulse familiar to him but not always appreciated—he considered walking out and shaking up the meeting, relying on just foolish surprise. But he also held now a heavy wrench he had found, which he hoped he could use as a weapon.

Then he heard the gunshot.

He glanced outside. A woman with silver-violet hair lay on the ground. She held her arm against her side and cried in pain. He thought it might be the woman he saw earlier staring down from the hills behind the base.

A man with a well-tended white beard leaned over her—he held the gun that probably had just fired.

Was this Muletti? Short, athletic, cheap cap, not too impressive except for the gun.

And a young woman with jagged black hair stood at the bottom of the ramp—and she, surprising him, looked directly at Ranglen.

They stared at each other, locked in a mutual evaluation—her face too intense for her smallish frame, her dark eyes burning into him. She looked ready to leap and attack him.

Muletti barked at the woman on the ground, "Stop whining! You were barely hurt. I didn't shoot to kill you."

She moaned back, "You're out of control, Aarov. You have to stop."

But Ranglen saw people entering the hangar. They must have heard the shot.

Muletti hurried to the ship's ramp and the second woman at the bottom of it. He aimed his gun at her. "You're coming with me."

Another explosion from outside the hangar.

Everyone turned to see what it was. The reflection of a fireball glowed on the ships beside them.

Ranglen saw his chance. He leapt through the doorway over the side of the ramp, in the opposite direction from everyone's attention. He landed running and jumped into another nearby ship. From inside it, he looked back through the open door to see if he had been noticed.

Muletti was preoccupied, angrily yelling at the wounded woman still lying on the deck. "Another diversion? Up to your tricks?"

But the second woman, the dark-haired one, must have seen Ranglen's every step. She stared right at him.

She said nothing.

He looked to the fire outside. Flames blossomed around a wrecked small craft—another intended blow-up like before. The people who ran into the hangar had rushed back to fight the flames.

But Ranglen wanted their attention. Inside this second ship, he hit a fire alarm.

A klaxon wailed throughout the hangar. People ran back in.

Ranglen saw Muletti grab the second woman. He held his gun to her head and dragged her on board the ship from which Ranglen had jumped. She resisted—but Ranglen felt it might be an act, that she allowed Muletti to take her instead.

The hatch closed behind them.

Ranglen, in a fit of frustration, ran from his ship and threw his wrench at Muletti's vessel, aiming for a navigation rack above the forward viewport—if any part of it was broken, the ship's liftoff would be compromised.

The wrench bounced off, made no harm.

The engines fired. Vernier jets shot thin blue flames.

Ranglen backed away. People rushed around them now but they also retreated from the guidance jets.

The gravity thrusters kicked in. The ship rose and plunged forward, picking up speed. People ducked or ran to the sides.

The craft howled out of the hangar, flew over the second conflagration and disappeared into the dark sky.

Ranglen ran to the woman on the ground. He joined the others who had arrived. She lay on her back, keeping her left arm tight to her side where blood flowed.

He stared at the splotched face and wiry hair. She was a near copy of the half-unconscious person he had seen on Muletti's ship.

Workers and security officers huddled about, called for medical support.

Tarakov arrived. He looked firmly in command and yet disturbed.

The woman muttered, "I'm all right. The bullet grazed my side and arm."

Tarakov looked at Ranglen. "Did you set off that alarm?"

Ranglen nodded. "A man with a white beard shot this woman, then assaulted another woman and pulled her onboard the ship that just left."

Tarakov's face grew stony.

A dockhand rushed in and spoke quietly in Tarakov's ear. Tarakov looked at Ranglen. "You better see to your ship. But don't leave."

Fear swept through him as he hurried through the entrance of the hangar.

This second fire raged beside his craft. He hadn't noticed its closeness when the explosion occurred.

He ran by the burning ship to his own.

It was charred but only lightly damaged by the flying debris—the viewports intact, the hull not breached.

But before he could feel any relief, he saw that a message had been scrawled on the side in hastily painted red letters.

THE MOUNTAIN HAS EYES. AND IT WATCHES <u>YOU</u>.

Chapter 8: Shadows Past

Ranglen should have been fiercely working his brain to interpret this desecration of his ship or at his brain working to decipher what happened.

But instead, his reaction was purely visceral—heart-racing, nauseating. He felt he might faint.

A nearby fire-fighter asked him politely, "Are you all right, sir? That painted message can be easily removed."

He insisted, "I'm fine."

Even Tarakov came over and said to him, "You don't look well, Mr. Ranglen. Go back to my office and sit there a while."

"I'm all right!"

Tarakov waved to one of his people, and she came to his side. He said to her, "Accompany Mr. Ranglen to my office and let him stay there. Make sure he's comfortable."

Tarakov left and went back into the hangar.

The guard moved close to Ranglen and stayed there. "Follow me, sir."

"I'm telling you I'm fine!"

"You can't leave the port yet anyway, sir. You'll need to be questioned, so you might as well be comfortable. Please come with me."

Ranglen had no choice.

The guard led him to the office and sat him inside, asked if he wanted anything. He shook his head.

"If you do, I'll be out here beside the door."

Tarakov's "Make sure he's comfortable" was surely a code for "Keep him confined."

Ranglen didn't care. He took a deep breath, tried to relax.

The near nausea wanted to return. He fought it down and stayed very still.

Not long ago, on the planet Alchera, from where he had come just a few months before, he had seen a *real* mountain with eyes.

At least that's what he believed. Others saw different things, though sights just as threatening.

He had abandoned all those memories, burying the past events of that world—or was it more the past burying him? For it wasn't just *him* erasing recollections but the nature of the universe itself. The phenomena he encountered took away certain memories of experience. And, for a while, he had been safely free of all unpleasant associations.

Then, suddenly, in this brutal way, it hit him in the face.

"The Mountain has Eyes."

Ranglen had heard about the Mountain Seekers when he returned to Annulus. But somehow their talk of mountains and eyes seemed irrelevant to him, part of some imagined stellar folklore and not a result of real experience—not connected to his adventures on a far planet unreached yet by present civilization. There could be no tie.

But now he wondered. Had he, in some peculiar psychological way that used repression and unknown avoidance, buried any thought of a real connection? Was his failure to find a similarity between *his* mountain and *their* "Mountain" not based on reason but just an elaborate defense mechanism? And was this internal shuffling of emotions similar to how, and why, his memories had faded? Maybe no physics was involved at all.

And why would the Seekers hit him with it now? How did *they* know it would affect him?

Maybe the message was just coincidence, put on his ship because it was sitting there close to the burning wreckage?

Or maybe the extinct Airafane were at work after all, tinkering with the present from their deep past. Manipulating humans—as many feared they had done. Or, as the Seekers believed, bestowing gifts by nurturing and mothering humanity forward. Or was their alien influence wider than what anyone thought—deeper, more personal, and thus more intimate, more undermining and problematic?

But you can't question the Airafane. They were all gone.

He pulled out his cellpad. The guard might watch him, but he doubted his call would be monitored.

He brought up Hatch, said to him, "I need another ship."

"Another? Already?"

"Mine was sitting beside an explosion so I want you to give it a full inspection. And there's writing on the side I want removed. Pick it up here at Rimport 3."

"How soon do you need the new one?"

Ranglen didn't want to say in case the guard was listening. "Soon as you can," which should indicate to Hatch he couldn't speak.

"Understood. I can do it today, but it won't be fancy—I won't have time to add all the extras. I'll call you when it's ready."

"I might be busy," meaning he might be detained by the police.

"I'll scramble the message."

Ranglen didn't know if he was joking or not. He signed off.

Tarakov came in soon after, asked how he was feeling.

Ranglen said fine. "How's the woman who was shot?"

"She'll be okay. The bullet just grazed her, no bones were hit."

"And those two explosions, did they come from the Mountain Seekers?"

"Most likely. Their people were around, like the two you saw in my office. They're gone now, but we'll track them."

"What about the ship that flew out of the hangar?"

"It, too, is being tracked. No destination yet."

"If it goes into light-space, you'll obviously lose it."

Tarakov sighed. "That's the bane of interstellar law enforcement."

Then, having allowed Ranglen to ask his questions and delay the inevitable, the professional security officer took over. "Tell me what happened in that hangar. What did you see?"

Ranglen gave a shortened but detailed version. He admitted to wandering into the Homeworld space to satisfy a personal curiosity about independent installations on Annulus. When he noted the insignia had been removed from the one ship (he did not say it was a Hatch Banner rental), he went inside it just to check it out. He said he found nothing. He did not speak of the woman on board, nor of his downloading its black-box records. He described the two other women and the man who arrived with the gun, though he didn't admit to knowing it was Muletti—he did this to protect Anne, feeling she still might be seen as involved. He said the gunshot made him jump from the ship and stay concealed. All of this made sense.

He assumed surveillance cameras recorded everything that occurred in the hangar, so he gave accurate descriptions of all three people and what they did, to make sure his story would agree. But he said nothing of the woman saying "Aarov." He hoped the audio records would be compromised from the noise outside the hangar. And he also was sure no cameras would have picked up the rocking woman on board Muletti's ship.

Tarakov was eager for all the details and kept probing, so much so that Ranglen wondered whether the port's security was not allowed to place cameras in a Homeworld structure.

Maybe he could have said less.

But he didn't want Tarakov suspicious of him either. He believed the law enforcer could cause much trouble if he thought Ranglen was lying. And Tarakov had made no comment yet about his unauthorized wandering into the hangar. To delay such comments, Ranglen asked, "Does the man taking the woman qualify as kidnapping?"

"Depends on Homeworld. It occurred on their territory—*they* have to make the call." His displeasure with that was obvious.

Then he looked keenly at Ranglen. "Your behavior is a little suspect, Mr. Ranglen. Let me speculate, just so you know where I'm going. You went into that hangar hoping you'd find the reason why the *Lochner* was destroyed, since that's what we were talking about and you seemed suspicious of Homeworld. Then you boarded the ship whose insignia had been removed, also because you felt it might have a tie to the destruction. Is all that correct?" But he didn't give Ranglen a chance to answer, as if he only wanted him to hear the question and to leave it hovering over him. "I understand you might not want to answer now, and you're not required to at this point, but I do have to ask the question just so you're aware. And know that, in time, you might have to justify your actions in more precise, more forthcoming, and more *convincing* detail."

Ranglen took advantage of the subtle warning and said nothing.

The officer looked smug, as if almost getting the response he wanted—which was only silence, no response at all. Then he shocked Ranglen by saying, "Okay. You can go now. I have some other inquiries to make that can't be delayed, and I need to consider the nature of your involvement. Know that we'll certainly talk again. I'll appreciate your not leaving Annulus."

Ranglen had *every* intention of leaving Annulus, and very soon. But he said instead, "You have all I know. And if you need more just leave word with me." He even added, in the method of confessing to a lighter sin, "You don't seem angry that I strolled on my own into a place where I probably shouldn't have."

Tarakov said dryly, "It was Homeworld's hangar. Not mine. They can worry about it. That's another thing I have to consider. Besides, if this is any consolation to you, I don't intend to be the officer who suspects, holds, or has to arrest the founder of Annulus. Not on just a pretense, at least at this time. But know that after consultation, I still might have to. And if I find *more* than a pretense, your notoriety will not stop me. Indeed, it won't stop anyone."

He wasn't smiling when he said this.

But Ranglen was suddenly grateful for his "founder of Annulus" standing. He quickly threw in, to take advantage of the moment and to prevent any silence from swelling too large, "Are you concerned about those explosions?"

"No, except for the loss of the two vehicles. Only the person in the hangar was hurt, and that's a different issue, as is the other woman's abduction, both of which are more for Homeworld to consider. The fires seemed intended not to harm anyone. But if the Seekers did this, they made a big mistake. We can be more forceful with them now. And we won't let any of them get close to a port again. The incident will be more damaging to them than it was to us."

Ranglen understood. The "peaceful" group had just lost its harmless status and "credit rating." They'd be watched and restricted now. The move had been stupid.

So then, why do it?

Ranglen quickly said good-bye. He wanted to be gone before Tarakov changed his mind.

He felt many eyes, or "Eyes," if imaginary, on him as he left.

He took a shuttle through the mountains and exited at a transport station where he boarded the train.

He needed to see Anne.

He called to make sure a representative from Hatch was picking up his ship. He didn't want to see the writing on its side again—he didn't trust his own reactions.

And he'd wait until after talking with Anne before he examined the downloaded information from Muletti's craft. He didn't want to know yet what it might say.

Ranglen soon reached Anne's new building. She had moved into it though it wasn't finished yet. She invested in its construction just so she could have the top floor—to be in the stream of clouds that came up a valley from the edge of the Ring, something she had long desired.

She was only in a temporary office on the bottom floor now.

It was late when he arrived, but she still was working at a portable desk, in the same clothes she wore that morning. Open crates and miscellaneous objects sat around her, products that eventually would be displayed in whatever showroom she'd have built—objects from space, exotic meteors, alien carvings, artifacts, creations from beings long dead and not around anymore to claim ownership. As Tarakov had said, the laws for stellar archaeological finds had yet to be written, and she'd take advantage of that lapse for as long as she could.

Ranglen skipped preliminaries. "I need the whole story about Muletti."

"Did you see him? Is he alive?"

"Yes, he's alive." But he added with sarcasm, "I saw him shoot someone and then kidnap somebody else."

"No! He wouldn't do that. There's some mistake."

"Short white beard? Not very tall? Name of Aarov?"

She looked away.

"I know about the diamonds too."

"You mean you found my cargo?"

Ranglen hated her sudden enthusiasm. "No, I did not. And you should be more interested in the other things Muletti did. The ship you rented for him—I know about that, too—just might have been used for piracy and to destroy that cargo ship we talked about. I'm not sure, but I believe it's true."

Confidence drained from her face.

"Anne, the time's come. You need to talk to me. You told me almost nothing about your 'friend' before. I can't help you unless I know everything."

"You sound like my lawyer."

"That's better than a judge. And, by the way, I might be called as a witness against you based on what I've been discovering. Annulus Security has me involved, and it probably won't be long before you are, too." He wasn't certain about that but he'd use the possibility to his advantage.

She sat in her chair as if she had been thrown there.

Ranglen waited.

"I told you," she said, "I met him while dealing with the Regulations Commission. I asked him all my questions about ancient artifacts. He assured me the laws concerning such finds were still open. We got to know each other. He even became a supplier himself. Many of my items came from him. We…" She stopped, looked down.

"Go on."

"We saw each other a lot. We became lovers….What can I say?"

Ranglen expected this. He'd decided it was the reason for her reluctance to talk of him. But he still had to fight down a nagging jealousy, and he didn't want her to think he was interrogating her for emotional reasons. "When did all this happen?"

"A few months ago."

Now he couldn't help himself. "You mean when you and I were *together*, after I came back to Annulus? You saw him at the same time you were seeing me?"

"Just briefly, and…I'm sorry….You and I were never that close."

Ranglen glared at her but said nothing. He didn't have time for these reactions now.

"And you said you weren't the jealous type," she added. "You claimed you didn't believe in possessing, in restricting anyone. You told me that."

"Maybe I lied! But let's not talk about that now. We have other problems. So…he must have spoken to you often then, during your times together, while—" Dammit! Anything he said took on a sexual overtone.

Anne missed the subtleties. "It took him a long while to reveal himself or his past. He's been through a lot. He doesn't say much, but you can tell he has secrets. He's like you."

Ranglen ignored the hint of accusation. "Could he destroy a whole cargo ship?"

"No! That's absurd. But there *is* something dark in his past. He doesn't like Homeworld. Or Earth for that matter."

"Did he say why?"

"Not directly, but there is one story that I remember he told me. It was drastic, and it affected me. It might explain a lot about him."

"Go on."

"He talked about a small interstellar freighter that carried freelance cargo. The ship had gone through a number of shady transactions and it was close to being impounded. The captain made a deal with an Earth-based company to take a cargo of refugees from Earth to another planet where a farming operation, supported by the company, was developing into a colony. The people—about forty of them—were desperate to get away from Earth."

Then Anne hesitated. She obviously didn't like telling the story—at least that's how she made it seem. "The ship didn't have the facilities for so many passengers, and conditions got bad. On top of that, the captain was abusive. He did whatever he wanted with them, and this encouraged the crew to do the same. The ship was to meet another vessel in space from the farming colony, which would take the workers down to the planet. But the ship with the refugees didn't arrive, and it was never heard from again. For years, no one knew what happened. There was little inquiry made into the case since the company on Earth knew the freighter's captain was corrupt, and they didn't want repercussions falling on them."

Anne paused, took a breath. "But Aarov told me what occurred on the ship. The refugees became fed up with how they were treated, so they rebelled against the captain and his crew. It wasn't easy. A lot of them were killed. But eventually the whole crew was captured and most of them thrown into space. They kept the captain alive long enough so that he could see what each of his people went through when they were blown through the airlock. He was the last one killed."

Ranglen guessed who was responsible. "Muletti was part of the crew, right? But he joined the refugees and led the rebellion."

"Yes. I guessed the same thing before he told me. It's interesting that neither you nor I thought he was one of the refugees, and yet we knew he became their leader. His turning against the captain says a lot for him. I was impressed, and sympathetic. His body is covered with scars and a skin condition from that time. The medication gives him that coppery smell. The captain himself might have abused him, too."

"What did he do afterward?"

"They abandoned the ship. He didn't say where. The few who survived, and the few crewmembers who were loyal to the refugees, went their own ways and tried to make new lives for themselves, in places where identification was not needed. Most of them failed. Muletti succeeded—at least he believed so, though at night, he sometimes screamed from his nightmares and became someone else, though never for long. And there were periods when he wouldn't talk for hours. He's normally easy-going and very in control, but that's a façade. He doesn't share much of himself. He impresses by how much you know he's dealing with."

Ranglen waited for more.

"I trusted him, Mykol. I believed in him. He set his own boundaries, but I didn't think he would ever cheat me, if that's what happened with this last cargo. All the stuff he brought, and he brought me a lot, he didn't treat like toys or trinkets. They were important to him, like tiny gifts just for me and not products I'd only sell."

"Maybe he didn't cheat you but just became interested in something bigger."

"I don't know. It's possible, I guess. But he was very excited when he told me about the diamonds. Big chunks of them, as big as bricks and boulders, he said. But I'd have to be careful. And I understood. The market's controlled, mostly by Ventroni. If I didn't get greedy, though, I could sell small bits for years. Just not much as jewelry, which would only call attention to me and make my buyers and sellers get scared."

"But the people on Ventroni aren't rational, Anne. They'd come after you just because they felt challenged. You'd be an insult to them."

"Aarov had connections with Ventroni. He said he knew someone who was very influential there. I felt he could handle them."

Ranglen snorted, not so confident about Muletti's authority. "That story tells me why he might hate Earth, but what about Homeworld?"

"The ship he rebelled against…it was a Homeworld ship with a Homeworld captain."

Ranglen understood. The details confirmed what Tarakov had hinted.

While trying to concentrate, Ranglen let his eyes wander over the items scattered about the room—carvings, jewelry, minerals, scrolls.

Something caught his eye. "Anne, what's that?"

It looked like a shrunken head, hanging on a ragged piece of twine—the skin charred, the mouth sewn shut, the eyes closed in a fierce kind of pain.

"It's not human," Anne insisted. "It's the preserved head of a small animal. It does look like a person, I know. There's a group on Ventroni that uses them as a kind of good-luck charm or holy relic."

Ranglen was disgusted. "Since when do you dabble in such grizzly items?"

"Don't be patronizing. The objects sell."

"Did Muletti get *these* for you, too?"

"Yes," she admitted, and now a bit proudly.

"At least the items I got for you could be cleared through customs."

"Not always, Mykol. You brought me a few illegalities yourself."

Ranglen was too furious to argue. "The ship which Muletti used to kidnap someone…I think it's the rental you acquired for him. It had its Annulus insignia removed, then another added for Homeworld, which *also* was removed, yet it was done hurriedly enough that it wasn't perfect. The ship was stationed at Rimport 3 in a Homeworld hangar. Do you know why any of that was done?"

She looked astounded. "No! Not the slightest. Maybe Aarov went into hiding and was trying to cover his tracks. Wouldn't a Homeworld ship in a Homeworld hangar be outside Annulus jurisdiction?"

"Maybe. But if *he's* tied to the wreck, then you are too, through the ship you rented for him."

Anne gave back only a brooding silence.

"Also, for that matter, why do you still owe money to Hatch for the ship? That's not like you."

She grunted, admitting, "For all our closeness, I wasn't sure about Aarov, not when it came to money. And I knew Hatch would let me delay a little. He'd grumble and squawk, but by not paying immediately, I could hold on to my investment a bit longer. I liked Aarov but…something…."

"Ah, I get it. 'Keep your heart free but your money close.' Is that what you mean?"

"Stop it, Mykol! I can't indulge myself like you can. I worry about money. I have to be practical."

"Never mind. Do you have any idea where that ship might have gone?"

She hesitated. "No….But there was a place where he wanted to take me once—for a visit, he said. I wasn't interested in any 'vacation' with him. What we had together didn't extend to long trips by ourselves. So I said no."

"Where is this place?"

"It's some kind of unique asteroid. He once gave me a pallasite, a kind of meteor with gems in it. He wanted to show me where he got it. He said I'd find all kinds of pieces there I'd want to sell, that the geology was incredible and I could have free pick of everything. But I don't do collecting on my own. He never offered again, even when I suggested he get me more. By then, he seemed preoccupied with other matters."

"Did he give you coordinates for the asteroid?"

"Well, I did manage to get something. We were on board the spaceship I had gotten for him—for a going-away dinner. I didn't want to be there, but we had made our cargo deal, so we were celebrating. We talked briefly about the asteroid, and he said the location was set in the instrument panel already, just waiting to take us if I wanted to go. But I still declined. And then, when he wasn't looking, I recorded the coordinates, just to have them. I made a good deal on that pallasite. If what he said was true, I thought I'd get the location, and then if I lost touch with Aarov, I might ask *you* someday to go there and check it out for me." She seemed embarrassed and yet pleased with herself.

"For god's sake, Anne."

"Don't lecture me."

"Not now, but maybe later. Give me the coordinates."

She transferred them from her cellpad over to his through a secure connection.

He read them and said. "This is out on the edge of the Annulus system. Why didn't you tell me of this place when you asked if I could find him?"

"I honestly forgot I had the coordinates, and he mentioned he hadn't been there for a while. Besides, he's like you. He does a lot of traveling. He could just as likely have been on Earth since he goes there often. Or even Ventroni. I didn't think of the asteroid."

Ranglen almost believed her though he was not sure why.

She asked, "How did you know my cargo was diamonds?"

"Hatch told me of your interest in carbon stars."

She quietly swore. "I need to be more careful with what I say. I got the idea from Aarov. He talked about carbon stars when he first mentioned diamonds."

"Yes, you do need to be more careful, but with what you *do*, not what you say."

"How bad is this, Mykol? Have you learned anything more?"

"According to the head of security at Rimport 3, Annulus will not want to make any waves concerning Homeworld. The official story about what happened to the cargo-ship is still accepted, and other possible explanations have not been made public or are not being pursued. Unless another disaster occurs, you might be okay."

But Ranglen was getting tired of relating scenarios to make Anne feel safe. He didn't always believe them and he didn't like the danger growing around the two of them as well as around Annulus. He didn't want to worry her, but he had no intention of lying to her either.

So he thought it best to leave then, to keep pursuing answers, now with gained knowledge about Muletti. "Listen to me, Anne. Please be careful. I feel there's a lot more at stake here than what meets the eye." *Dammit!* Eyes. He couldn't escape them.

Then, as he reached the door, Anne said, "I'm sorry, Mykol."

He only nodded. He needed to go.

"Wait. I have something to tell you, something that Hatch once told me."

Mykol was impatient. "Is it related to all this?"

"In a way, at least for me—and you. Hatch always tries to be a cynic, you know. But it's all bluster. He accuses you of that also, that you play the Romantic, the little Byron. But he said to me once—and you'll like this, Mykol—that if the Airafane somehow showed up tomorrow and wanted to know what humans were like, *real* humans (and not the 'phonies,' he said, not the 'very-good or very-bad'), that, if asked, he'd send them you, that you'd be his choice for the representative of the entire race....I thought that was nice, coming from a sarcastic guy like him."

Ranglen, at another time, might have been touched. But he felt too many people talking about him lately, heaping him with too many expectations. "Why are you saying this?"

"To show I'm careful in choosing the people who help me. I believe in you."

"You also believed in Muletti."

She closed her eyes and took a deep breath, as if fighting the need to counter what he said. "But it's still quite a statement coming from Hatch. Meeting the Airafane and that you should be the one. Do you think it'll ever happen?"

"No! Not a chance!" But he said this more strongly than intended, and he quickly left. *Why bother with the impossible?*

He went to a different hotel room than the one he had been in—he seldom stayed in one place long. He opened his cellpad and accessed the file he copied from Hatch's rental, the ship that held Muletti and Anne at their celebration dinner, and whatever else they did.

Reading the data, he found that the ship had visited Earth soon after it was rented. Then it came back to Annulus, and then it went to an asteroid on the outer fringe of the Annulus system. He checked Anne's coordinates for comparison.

The same place.

But after the information for the asteroid, there was no more data in the ship's records.

The location for the ship in the last four days, including the time when the *Lochner* was destroyed, had been erased or not copied at all.

Hatch claimed this data was "untouchable."

If Muletti erased it, then he had more expertise than assumed. It wasn't easy to counter Hatch's abilities.

Ranglen considered all of this. He didn't like any of it.

Then he received a message from Hatch that his other ship was ready.

It was very late now, but he gathered supplies, ate a quick meal, and left for Hatch's spaceport. He didn't care about Tarakov's warning not to leave Annulus, which he wasn't convinced was sincere anyway. The man could have done a lot more to hold Ranglen.

By the time he reached the center of the Ring, Hatch already had left for home.

Ranglen went to his new ship and quickly departed. He entered the coordinates given to him by Anne and confirmed by the download from Muletti's craft, a set of differential equations into which present time had to be inserted in order to work out the approximate location. The light-space jump would take, internally, the standard 2.14 days. Even within the planetary system most people still used such jumps.

By the time he entered light-space, he was exhausted. He knew, from habit, that his tiredness would put him to sleep immediately, but once he woke up, no matter how long he had been out, he would not be able to get back to sleep.

That's what happened.

He thought about a mountain with eyes.

He pulled out his notebook and found the spurious unedited poems he had written after returning from Alchera: "The Touch," "The Branch Line Stop," "Ice People," "As It Fell," "Manifest Station," "A Temporary Planet for a Transitory Day." He had written some of these while on Alchera and others afterward when he still had recollections of what occurred.

But those memories vanished quickly, and now he had only the poems, and the name of the planet to hang onto. The poems had become research data, a means of creating *a* past instead of preserving *the* past. Reading them was like trying to put together a person shattered into fragments.

Or, worse, they seemed written by someone else.

His solitude, usually so cherished, now seemed empty. He couldn't go to Anne anymore, though he never shared any of this with her anyway.

He wondered if she and Muletti had done the same. Evading talk instead of welcoming it.

Ranglen tried to get back to sleep, but it was even harder now.

Chapter 9: 82A

Braya was thrown into a locked compartment, a newly constructed and small cargo room, dark and cold. She didn't have a chance to find her way around it before the ship powered up and charged forward—flying out of the hangar, she assumed. She fell on the floor and slid against the wall, inertia forcing her from place to place as the ship used its thrusters in what she guessed were evasive maneuvers.

All motion became gentle when the plates kicked in, and it stopped entirely when they entered light-space, the sense of acceleration gone.

Would she stay locked in here for the entire jump?

She tried to find her way about the dark room.

But she bumped into a person sitting on the deck against the wall, hunched forward.

Braya stepped back till she found a light switch. The glow was pale, showing a cramped cargo hold apparently converted from a passenger cabin. And the woman who sat on the floor was Krin from the refugees on the destroyed *Lochner*. Braya had assumed she'd been killed.

The woman moaned, rocked forward and back. She kept her face tilted and ignored Braya, seemed sluggish and maybe sedated. But her appearance, what Braya could see of it, was unmistakable—just like Hideki's but dumpier and worn, more disheveled and "lost."

More authentic?

"Krin! Can you hear me?"

The woman moved in short arcs back and forth, muttering incomprehensibly. Her face looked worse—the age lines, the murky eyes, a new map of sustained agony.

"Talk to me! Are you okay?"

Krin stopped swaying and glanced at Braya, eyes weary and unsteady. "You're the one from the ship, right? The *Lochner*? You're the little flame."

Braya nodded.

Krin didn't seem interested. She whispered, "He almost had me. But not yet, not this time. Maybe the next."

"*Who* had you? The man with the white beard?"

"Yes. Muletti. My one-time friend. Aarov. But he hurt me. He hit me and then took me from the *Lochner*, just me alone."

"Then you're the only one. Everyone else I think was killed."

"They planned to sell the refugees, but I think eventually they just disposed of them. Muletti wanted something else, something he thought *I* had. But I didn't have it. That's why he beat me when he broke in. Then, afterward, he saved me from getting killed. He's like that. Back and forth. So, you really are from the *Lochner*, eh? I do remember you. You survived. You had such a fire. My little flame."

"*Why the hell does everyone call me that?*"

"It's what you are. It's also a secret. A type of code. The Seekers have their lingo, and I let them know about you."

"What do you mean? You told them about me?"

She laughed, a dry ugly sound. "I said you were more than you think. And you can be that. I know you're tough. That was obvious. You can be a Seeker like us, a true 'Eye,' in search of the Mountain.

This reminded Braya of Krin's preaching aboard the ship, of Hideki, too. It made her angry and frustrated.

The woman rocked, humming as she did so.

"Krin, stop that!"

"You didn't want to talk back on the ship and now you do?" She said this with brittle self-righteousness. "But maybe now *I* don't want to talk. I've been through too much. I don't care anymore."

"What's Muletti after? Come on, *tell me?*"

"He's after his secret. Lihandro's secret. *Everyone's* secret."

"Wait, who's Lihandro?"

"Another friend of mine. I led him to Muletti. They met, talked. Made some plan. I didn't know about it, not the details. Lihandro was supposed to give me something to take for him to the Seekers, to give to Hideki to support their search for the Airafane and the Mountain. But he never did. It's gone now. In the graveyard of the lost, or the depot of the dead. That's where we're going."

"*Talk sense!* We're locked away in here and we might be killed."

"He won't kill us. Don't you worry. Or, well, maybe he will. But I don't think so. He's still my friend." She rocked once more, now side to side, even smiled as she did so. Off in her world, seeming to forget Braya was there.

"Krin, *listen* to me. I think this ship we're on attacked the cargo carrier, that Muletti was the pilot."

"He was flying it when he took me away in it. He left the others and saved me. Kept me here. But I think he drugged me. Or maybe I was sick. I don't know. Leave me alone."

"I saw him shoot a woman when he pulled me on board."

"Really?" This fact caught her attention. "Who was she?"

"Her name was Hideki. She looked like you and said she knew you. She was from the Seekers."

"*Hideki!* She was *here*? Well, that's interesting…but, you know, when you think of it, it does make sense. I told her you were coming. 'Little flame' was the code, that the Seekers would want you. A carrier of fire to light the way. They recognize such things. But I'm sure Aarov didn't kill her. He knows her. Not as well as me, of course. She looks like me because she imitated me. But she didn't get it right."

"Are all of you part of the Seekers, then?"

"Not Aarov. He hates them, calls it a cult. But he uses them. He used *me*. I didn't mind until he hit me. I kept watch for him and did all his dirty work. I was his 'Eye.' And look how he treated me. I don't deserve this. Will you help me?"

"Krin, please! Do you mean the cargo ship was intended to go to Annulus? You didn't see me till right before we boarded it. How did you know I'd wind up there?"

"I didn't know. I didn't know anything. I just watched you. I wanted to stay near you, wanted you to become a Seeker. I knew right away that you'd fit. You were abandoned, pushed close to the edge, with no sense of place or connection—I could see that. No beliefs either, no family, nothing. But I could give that to you and make you important. I didn't realize you'd meet Hideki but I knew you'd get to us someday. How did you find her? You said she was shot? I hope she's all right. She always wanted to be me, you know."

That's not what she *said.*

"You have to realize…I became a Seeker because of the stories, not because of politics. I loved their stories—the 'Creature with Eyes Inside a Mountain,' the 'Graveyard of Lost Ships,' the 'World Called Little Redemption,' even the sad 'Depot of the Dead'—that last is on a planet called Highland, which is Hell, and it's a legend among refugees. It's where none of us want to go. And—the best—the story of the 'Avenging Soul,' the soul of one who's been sacrificed, beaten, hurt, thrown out, and discarded. That's you, flame, what you've always been meant to become. Avenging soul. I think you can do it. Will you? Can you?"

Braya didn't answer. She couldn't decide if Krin knew what she was talking about or she was babbling, or if everything she said had some latent significance. "What secret were you to give to Hideki—the thing Muletti wanted from you, why he beat you?"

"'Lihandro's Bane.' That's what Aarov called it. He could laugh when he wanted to—I loved him then. Lihandro was supposed to give it to me but he never did. I think he was killed. Then I got worried that people would expect that *I* had it, when all along I had nothing. That's why I came to you at the spaceport in Brazil and followed you on board the *Lochner*. You would be my gift to the Seekers. You would reach Hideki someday. Maybe not for years but eventually you'd join them. Then I'd be thanked. Even Muletti would be grateful by then."

"Grateful for *what*?"

"For you, of course. Listen to me. The Seekers aren't brainwashed. You can come and go. There are no restrictions, no initiation—no 'conversion.' They're more a club that accepts everyone. We're a community, a haven for the lost. Everyone now traveling throughout space is a refugee. We've all been abandoned by those in search of something out of reach. That's how Homeworld got its name—because a sense of home has become so lost they thought they could get it back in a title. Clips too, they're no accidents. They're taking us home, home to the Airafane. We'll meet them someday. *You'll* meet them. And then we'll become them. There's a reason behind everything they've done—but there's no reason behind humans and what they do. Each one of us is our own little reign of terror. 'Blood stars,' that's what we are—Aarov called us that. Haunted stars. Or pieces of night. But because we don't know what we are, then we *need* the Airafane. We *have* to find them."

Braya could make no sense of it.

The door then opened and Muletti appeared. He yelled at Krin, "I told you not to talk to her! Get up! I need you."

"Is it true you shot Hideki? She's not—"

"*Be quiet!*" He grabbed her arm and dragged her to the door, not caring as he did so that she banged her shoulder against the bulkhead. "You're staying with me and away from her."

Muletti pulled her through and shut the door behind her.

For the next two days, Braya stayed in the refurbished cargo hold. Food was given to her by Muletti through the door but only if she stood on the far side of the room. A dirty pad lay on the deck, where she slept. A toilet and sink sat in a corner, part of the original passenger's cabin. The place was dark and stuffy and cold, filled with supply boxes. It smelled of oil and disinfectant.

Sometimes Muletti brought Krin back to her, let her stay for a while and then pulled her out again, for no clear reason. This continued throughout the jump, as if he debated whether to keep them together. Any talk between them was broken and frustrating.

During her solitude, Braya thought about the Seekers, Krin, Muletti, Hideki, the *Lochner*, the three killer ships, and finally, somewhere, a man named Lihandro.

She also thought of the person she had seen run out of the vessel, *this* vessel, back on Rimport 3 when Muletti arrived. For some reason, she felt she had seen him before.

After the required two days in light-space, she felt the ship emerge back in time-space, their own universe. She could sense the ship's movement again.

They soon landed, for which Braya received no warning. She could feel the touchdown, the engines whining into silence.

All was still.

But soon, a tremor disturbed the stillness, as if the ground wasn't steady.

On gravity drive, Ranglen approached the coordinates he had taken from Anne and the ship's files.

The asteroid looked smooth. Too smooth for such a world's age. Its surface normally would be pocked from meteorites and churned-up regolith. But this place had a metallic sheen.

Most large asteroids were iron silicates, the same composition as planetary mantle or the outer layers of a larger planet. But this seemed more like metallic core. Maybe it came from some long-ago and bigger planetesimal, where the heavier metals had sunk inward and then somehow were exposed to space.

From his instruments, he could tell that the density of the world was high, a rich find for asteroid miners in search of valuable mineral resources. It was maybe a solid globe of metals.

Then, as he got closer, he noticed volcanoes.

Large fissures and reddish pores spewed forth melted rock that glowed and crept across the flatlands. The surface then was newly formed, covered in shiny metallic blankets that overlapped, explaining the uniform smooth appearance.

Ferro-volcanism, or iron volcanoes.

He reasoned out the chemistry behind it. The asteroid's core, still hot enough to be liquid, was probably hardening from the outside in. And if sulfur was present in the nickel-iron mix, pockets with greater sulfur content would remain liquid at a lower temperature as the core solidified. Then, as the pressure on these pockets grew, the molten metal would squeeze out through the thick mantle, making vents, leaking pools onto the surface. No standard silicate granite here, only iron and nickel.

In the future, when all the bustle of creation settled, the asteroid would look more unnaturally smooth with its metal sheen. People flying by would wonder—was it core (as he thought at first) or mantle with a fine glaze of iron. Or maybe they'd think it was artificial, a world surrounded by boilerplate.

Ranglen believed he'd find Muletti here. It was a good hiding place but also loaded with potential wealth. And he remembered Anne's pallasite meteor. Peridots could form in such a mantle and then travel to the surface in one of the eruptions.

He reconnoitered from a far orbit in his new ship he got from Hatch (a bit smaller than his own and not as advanced).

At first nothing showed, but then he found a small base. Not too big, not too obvious, not hidden either.

It didn't need to hide. Who would ever come out here, so far from the swollen birthing sun? It apparently had material from another star that had passed by. The Annulus system was part of a cluster of newly formed suns still relatively close to each other, and he guessed they had interacted, maybe more than once. This asteroid with its heavy iron content might not even be from the Annulus system, whose sun was high in heavy metals but not high enough for a world as rich as this.

Through magnification and radiation scans, he could see the structures of the base and several small ships. Maybe it was originally a scientific station.

Ranglen wondered if he could sneak a landing away from the spot and then move up surreptitiously in a spacesuit. But that would mean walking on unstable terrain that might be fluid and much too hot.

Or he could just announce his presence. He was Mykol Ranglen after all. His reputation had helped on Rimport 3. "Just passing by, saw the lights. What's up with you?"

He was still debating when the decision was made for him. The radio alerted him to an incoming message. He clicked receive.

"Unidentified spacer, you are intruding near a restricted scientific base. Please state your purpose." The voice spoke in a Homeworld accent.

After hesitation, he took the plunge. "This is Mykol Ranglen of Annulus." He gave the registration figures for his ship. "I seek permission to land. I represent a business holder who was asked to visit here." Which, after all, was true.

Long silence. "Asked by whom?"

He bet his only card. "Aarov Muletti."

A longer silence.

Ranglen trusted, yet often lamented, his hard-to-control audacity. They might let him land just because they were curious, especially if they came from Homeworld where they'd know him only by reputation. And Homeworld having a secret base in the Annulus system was not too surprising. The boundary between planetary and interstellar territories was extremely vague and couldn't be patrolled—and Homeworld "owned" Annulus, after all.

Or they might blast him out of the sky for the same reason of being so isolated. Who would notice? But he didn't think they would. They'd probably let him land and show him everything—or nothing.

And if, at that time, they felt he was a threat, *then* they'd kill him.

Maybe he should have given Tarakov this location and let Annulus Security come instead with an armed team. But given the nature of the asteroid, a scientific base here would make sense, especially knowing that Homeworld's sun was relatively metals-poor.

Besides, he wanted to avoid Tarakov.

The voice said, "You have permission to land."

Ranglen acknowledged, received an approach path and expressed gratitude.

The course included a near full orbit of the planet, so he managed to see the place. He wondered if this was to frighten him, since no other sign of habitation was found. He saw only dark hulking volcanoes with glowing throats and reddish floods of metallic luster. The planet was like a huge metallurgy factory where everything had melted, flowed and run, forming a brutal abstract art that, if polished, would shine like an ancient warrior's shield. It looked like a foundry or a coal furnace. Or Hell.

The base was makeshift and temporary. Not formidable but not fly-by-night either. It would have required a sizable investment. It was not some wretched pirates' den.

He landed by a small operations structure with a dome for communication and scanning. Nearby was a storage depot, then a type of bunkhouse or living quarters, and a relatively large hanger. Yet another hangar was being built. One small structure gave no sign of what it was used for, though it was yellow and looked specialized and unvisited. Behind the base ran a wall of what Ranglen assumed was bonded ceramic, not stone or metal. It protected the inhabited area from the trails of running lava beyond it that must threaten the base periodically. The land out there was all black and scarlet, alive with heat and bubbling alloy.

A second ship sat beside him, an old cargo freighter. It was certainly large enough to transport the supplies such a base would need. The insignia on the side was Homeworld's.

The radio said, "Our supervisor will meet you at your vessel. Please don a spacesuit and come outside." Still the Homeworld accent.

Ranglen already wore his suit so he clamped on a helmet and left his ship. Someone met him with a darkened faceplate, which struck Ranglen as odd. The sun from here could barely be seen, and only the spotlights of the landing field provided illumination, which hardly needed to be shielded against.

Ranglen heard through his intercom, "Welcome to our small base, Mr. Ranglen. This is an honor. I'm not really in charge but I'm the closest to a head of operations."

Ranglen found the tone ironic, like subtly false information that was assumed to be recognized as false by the listener. The accent was that of Annulus—and the voice was familiar.

"Quite a place you have here."

"We like it. Follow me inside, and I'll show you around."

The person led him to the large hangar. The wide front doors were closed, so they entered through an airlock on the side. Pressurization followed, and they emerged into a corridor. Then they proceeded through a door into what appeared to be a small meeting room with a central table and chairs around it. Otherwise, except for stands to hold served food or other necessities, the place was bare. A video screen covered the wall to his left, and another door led into what Ranglen assumed, given the layout of what he'd seen so far, was the interior of the hangar.

"We can talk more easily here," the supervisor said. Both of them sat and removed their helmets.

The man facing Ranglen had a short white beard.

Muletti.

Ranglen had recognized the voice. He didn't believe the man had seen him at Rimport 3, but to be safe, he didn't show recognition.

Muletti seemed calm and sure of himself, as if not bothered by Ranglen's arrival. Or else he covered his surprise well. Or maybe he was setting up Ranglen for some possible shock, one of his own.

Ranglen tried to remember why he had landed there.

"If you want to remove your spacesuit, you can."

Ranglen did not. It was lightweight and flexible, designed for short surface work and not burdened with the thrusters or heavy shielding needed for extended work in space. It was almost comfortable, and Ranglen felt more protected inside it—which he knew was a foolish notion.

Muletti didn't remove his either. He introduced himself and said, "What can I do for you?"

"First, my thanks for letting me land. I'm curious what this place is for."

"It began as a joint scientific venture of Annulus and Homeworld to study the geology of the asteroid, the volcanoes and such. We call the world Forge, for obvious reasons, but its actual title is 82A, the first three digits of the catalog number, and we use that more often."

"You're here because of the mineral contents?"

"Yes, of course. As much as we can learn. We've built up a good understanding of the chemistry. It's quite a valuable find." Muletti seemed to recognize Ranglen's assumption—that all the science here eventually would serve commercial mining, the justification for the investment in the first place.

"But you haven't started the mining yet, I presume." Based on the lack of activity and small size of the base.

"No, but we will. We'll need more housing, processing facilities, and a larger landing field before we do, as well as more vehicles for negotiating the terrain. Luckily, the operation is fully run by Annulus now. All the profit will go to the Ring."

"Homeworld gave up their interests? I'm surprised."

"It required some persuasion." Muletti didn't elaborate.

Ranglen pondered this as he studied the man. Muletti spoke with a dry unruffled authority, as if hiding a vague sarcasm—or following a script. The fierce certitude he had shown at the rimport seemed purposely hidden. The gray eyes had a secret playfulness, the mouth a sensitivity, and the scars and mottling of his face made for an appeal based on suggestive history. He didn't look like a kidnapper or possible murderer.

Ranglen could understand Anne's attraction.

"It's ours now," the man added.

Ranglen felt uncomfortable with the "ours," not wanting to be included. He looked around the Spartan meeting room but still found nothing significant. He took a chance. "Why is that hangar beside us so big?"

"Would you like to see its interior?"

Ranglen, astonished, said, "Of course," though he realized his answer might have been too quick.

"Glad to show you. But first…could I ask why you're here? I don't recall suggesting any 'business holder' to visit, as you claimed."

Ranglen tried to look sheepish. "The claim is true, but it's more complicated. I came specifically to see you, Mr. Muletti. I've been searching for you."

"Oh?"

"I'm a friend of Anne Montgomery. She asked me to find you. And she *is* a business holder, and you did ask her to come here once." By including that last point, Ranglen was playing—and maybe dangerously. But he couldn't help letting Muletti know that Anne had revealed something private about him. It was a cheap move, but he felt it necessary to give himself some leverage.

"Ah yes. Anne." Muletti said this regretfully. "I've been lax in speaking with her, badly neglecting her. I helped her with a cargo, but it's been lost. She does know about that, correct?"

"She assumed it was gone, but she expects your input as proof. And, based on what she said, I feel she deserves it."

"Then tell her, for me, that it *is* lost, that I'm very regretful, and that I apologize for not letting her know. It was a small load of valuables from space, but the prospector who discovered them did not deliver any more of them, and he then went off on his own. Nothing I could do. I promise I'll get her investment back to her, with profit thrown in. That's one reason why I've been busy lately. I wanted to have the payment ready for her before I saw her again."

"She would have preferred you to reach out to her directly, the message may be more important than the money."

Muletti evaded the accusation. "Was it Anne who told you I might be here? Is that how you found this place?"

Ranglen compromised. "She told me of a world you spoke of, but I learned of its location through other means."

Muletti looked at him more coldly. "Would your other means be Annulus Security?"

"No, not specifically." He left that hanging and moved his questions in a different direction. "You say you've been busy lately?"

The man nodded.

"On Rimport 3?"

"Ah…yes, I see now." Muletti must have remembered then the raid on his ship's computer files. But he said calmly, "So you happened to be there?"

Ranglen's bravado could take him only so far. He had brought a weapon with him this time, hidden in a pouch on the outside of his spacesuit, but it was small reassurance now. "Yes, checking on some other matters and talking with the head of security there. I saw the two fires, and then a ship take off quickly. Someone was shot, but she survived."

He said nothing of the kidnapped woman, but he wanted Muletti to know the other person had lived.

The man first showed no reaction. But then his derision grew less controlled. "Okay, Mr. Ranglen. I think that's enough of my answering your questions—which I've done openly. You've found me and you conveyed your message. You can tell Anne that her cargo is lost but that her money is safe and she will be reimbursed. Is there anything else I can do for you?"

"You were about to show me that hangar?"

"Oh, yes. Quite." He actually did seem to have forgotten. He stood up then. But, in the next instant, he got a call on his cellpad. "Excuse me." He held its extension to his ear and answered the call, keeping it private. He listened blankly, then muttered to the person, "Okay. I'll be there." He signed off and said to Ranglen, "I have to leave for a few moments. Could you remain here please?"

"Sure. No problem."

"I won't be long." Then he left.

Ranglen waited several minutes.

Then several more.

Then he tried the door that led to the corridor.

It was locked.

No big surprise, though maybe foolish of Muletti for being so obvious in restraining him.

He then tried the door on the opposite side of the room, the one he supposed led to the hangar. He found it also locked—but by a simple mechanical latch and not an electronic code-box, which would have been the case if the hangar beyond was not pressurized. So, the door did not lead to an airlock, and the hangar itself had atmosphere.

He pulled out his pocket knife and worked the connection until he broke through. It was easier than expected.

He opened the door and looked within.

The hangar was, as he guessed, large, and keeping it pressurized would be very expensive. It also was bigger than what would be needed for a scientific base—a story he hardly believed anyway, and this was proof. The place was mostly empty, the ships small and likely used by the people staying. They were similar to Hatch's rental, the kind Muletti had escaped in back at the rimport. Ranglen wouldn't be surprised if that ship were here so he started looking for it.

But what grabbed his attention was a larger vessel on the far side of the hangar. It was a huge wreck, and being cut into pieces.

He now knew the exact purpose of this "base"—

It received confiscated or pirated ships, removed their registrations, laundered their histories, and then resold them. Or they were just cut up into scrap.

Something straight out of Tarakov's litany of crimes in space.

He checked the labels on the equipment around him and the registrations of the small spaceships. The port of origin on all of them was Homeworld.

A noise from behind him. He turned quickly.

Muletti carried the semi-automatic he used at Rimport 3.

"Mr. Ranglen," he said, "you are not disappointing. I guessed you'd sneak in here the second I left. I had been hoping, though with little reason, that you were just an innocent explorer who had wandered off course, carrying a sad torch for Anne Montgomery, but I now have to assume otherwise."

Ranglen tried to say something, pointing to the wreck on the far side of the hangar.

But Muletti moved fast, rushed up to Ranglen and swung his arm at him.

The butt of the gun slammed against his face.

Ranglen felt intense pain, and the force of the strike knocked him to the floor.

Chapter 10: The Fixer

Ranglen was aware of being lifted by Muletti and dragged out of the hangar, back to the meeting room where he was set in a chair. A second person—apparently the one with the Homeworld accent who had been on the radio—attended to his face, tested his cheekbone and jaw for breaks. Ranglen was in pain but, apparently, no bones had been fractured. The blood was cleaned away, the cracked skin left to heal. Then the man left.

Muletti sat across from Ranglen, folded his arms, and stared at him for a long time.

Ranglen bent forward, worked his jaw to make sure it still functioned.

A scar, he thought, probably rectangular from the semi-automatic's grip. His face was taking on a history, like Muletti's. Maybe all space explorers got this way.

"Well," Muletti said, "you're the founder of big beautiful wonderful Annulus."

Ranglen managed to speak, though with strain. "The role's not as glamorous as it sounds."

Muletti looked sympathetic. "It seems illogical, but I admire you, you and your type. You're so naturally impulsive, so ready to act, so quickly supported by the society behind you. Yet, you know so little. This is where the real work is done. You're just cover. You get to look the part. While we get to *be* the part."

Ranglen maneuvered his way through the rhetoric. "Social stratification aside, as well as your anger about it, why did you strike me?" What he heard of Muletti made the reaction uncontrolled and rushed. Jealousy? Envy?

"It's taken us a long time to establish this base, and your word could mess up our plans drastically. You're the big Mykol Ranglen, and one comment from you could bring some stupid oversight committee swooping down on us. Which is not a good idea. Not *yet*. Maybe eventually but not until we're ready. And, do know, I almost released you. I thought you were just Anne's messenger, using your status, privilege, and insider information to track me down, just to ask about her cargo. She has a heavy claim on you, doesn't she? She tried the same with me but didn't succeed. And then, you just had to indulge yourself, had to go further. That big hangar was too inviting."

But something was off about all this, which made Ranglen forget his throbbing jaw and sore teeth. The jabs against Anne were too obvious, the "tough" tone too affected. This gangster style wasn't the Muletti he expected from Anne's impressions. "Do I rub you the wrong way?"

"At Rimport 3, did you ask the security chief about me?"

"I said no more to him than what I told you, that I searched for you because of Anne."

"And what did he say?"

"That you hadn't been seen for several weeks."

"Well, that's Tarakov for you. He doesn't say much, but he can become a real problem. What did you think of him?"

"Seems right for his position."

"Yes, I agree. But he's also part of Annulus Security, and people there get swelled heads. They start playing the role too seriously. I don't want him on my tail—and you don't want him on yours either."

Ranglen scowled—hard to do with his aching mouth. "Let's stop acting, which we're both doing. You lied when you said Annulus was in charge here."

"Why do you say that?"

"This is no scientific base. Where are the laboratories, the chemical supplies, the ground craft for exploring the landscape, the drilling equipment, the earth-movers and sampling rigs? All you've got is a small communications structure, a big hangar, and a bunkhouse for a working crew, none of whom I've seen yet. And the only other person who's spoken to me has a Homeworld accent. Where are the people who are supposedly from Annulus? And why is the equipment in the hangar all from Homeworld? Even the small ships there are Homeworld's, too."

Muletti looked smug. "Well, Mr. Ranglen, 'by the eyes,' you are observant."

"And why did you let me enter the hangar in the first place? That incoming call to you was too well timed. You *wanted* me to see what was in there—but secretly, as if I snuck in. Did it give you some excuse to act tough, to use your mobster move on me, to scare me? Is that why you did it? Or maybe just to establish some fake authority."

"What are you getting at?"

"I don't think you're in complete control here, not as much as you want me to believe. Or else your authority is threatened somehow. Which is it?"

Muletti sat back, looked pensive. "What do you believe is going on in that hangar?"

"Obviously, it's a 'chop-shop' for spaceships. You're taking pirated vehicles, refitting and then reselling them. Or you break them up for scrap which is also then sold. That's what you're doing to that big ship which is in there now."

Muletti maintained a self-satisfied expression. "Anne did say that you were good."

"Let's leave Anne out of this, all right? And don't give me your crap about losing her cargo. You probably never intended to give it to her anyway. You claimed it was on that ship because you knew it would be destroyed. The pod was probably empty or just filled with ballast. *That's* why you disappeared and never spoke to her."

Muletti remained silent even longer. But he seemed more sincere when he spoke. "I had every intention of bringing her what I promised her. Things got complicated."

"I'm sure they did. Why isn't the *Lochner* here and being cut up for profit? Why was it destroyed? Was it too big to fit inside the hanger? Is that why you're building another one? Better accommodations? Reselling it would have given you quite a bundle, even as scrap. So why pass up a chance to make so much money—and *not* for Annulus as you claimed."

"I said it's complicated."

"And don't tell me you kicked Homeworld out of this base. Homeworld would never give up a tie to such a metal-rich asteroid. They'd beg for a place like this. They either don't know about it yet, or else people on Homeworld are secretly supplying you, paying for all this in order to get a fortune in return from both the piracy and the metals. Are you covering for them?"

Muletti's arrogance was gone now, replaced with impatience. "That's enough, Mr. Ranglen. You're going too far."

"Then it's time to get deeper. What did Homeworld do to you—to *you*, specifically— when they captured you and put you on trial, when they threatened to hang you for that mutiny you committed in space and for killing a Homeworld captain and crew? Because that's exactly how they'd react to it. They'd chase you for years till they found you. And they *did* find you, didn't they?"

Dead silence. Muletti didn't move.

Ranglen had crossed yet another line. But his rage over the threat to Annulus, the bitterness with Tarakov's lists of crimes, the distress over Anne's sexual wanderings, and now getting pistol-whipped by someone he felt was just showing off, stormed up inside him and pushed him forward—

"Yeah, I heard that story, about your rebellion on a Homeworld ship. I bet you were caught, though not till you felt you were completely safe. Homeworld's like that. They'd play you for a while. And then they'd execute you. Don't they still do hangings there, especially for mutiny? (Or maybe that's Ventroni.) And yet, amazingly, you're *still here*, free, alive. You even managed to get a high position in Annulus government, the Import Regulations Commission, 'fixer' for the Board. So—hey, I'm just speculating here, throwing out ideas—but maybe, just maybe, Homeworld *turned* you. And then you made it *seem* you worked for Annulus, while, all the time, you really worked for *them*."

Muletti's restraint looked ready to crack.

Ranglen let him simmer.

Then he added, as precisely and carefully as he could—he wasn't ranting now but trying to sound compassionate, "Look, I sympathize with what Homeworld did to you. I know what it's like to be compromised. I'm not trying to accuse you of crimes now—not at the moment. I simply want to find out what's happening so that Annulus is not threatened. I assume this base was used for privateering, supported by Homeworld's government or a corporation there, all to further Homeworld's efforts to curtail shipping between Earth and Annulus. This base would provide a perfect spot to work from—it has isolation, secrecy, a big hangar and barracks. The metals would be even a bigger draw. Hell, maybe your Homeworld backers don't even know about the metals yet. Maybe you're keeping that in reserve—a big negotiating point for you. A present for your Homeworld masters, a little magic in your spying hat."

Muletti then seemed to deflate. He looked resigned, suddenly tired.

Ranglen continued, "Only a few on Homeworld must know about the operation—they'd want their secrecy. It might even be a neat set-up between a small group in government and independent investors, providing both political muscle and economic gain. Power and money. How very perfect."

Muletti turned away briefly, his eyes heavy. Then he spoke at last. "It's not what you think."

Ranglen expected that response, but he almost felt the man was sincere. "Then exactly what is it? You've got your chance here. Defend yourself, justify what you've done."

Muletti's tone was almost apologetic. "Homeworld did enlist me as one of their agents when they brought me to trial. It was the only way I could save myself. But all that I'm doing—all I've *ever* done—is for *Annulus*. I've been very careful. And someday this place will be exposed. Everyone in the Confederation will learn what Homeworld is really like—corrupt, illicit, immoral, criminal. The powers on that world will get what they deserve. Not just Earth but everyone will become angry at them. I've been working this set-up for years. And in time, all of it will be revealed, and everybody will know what they've done to me and what they've done to others."

Ranglen listened carefully. He had felt all along there was more to Muletti than what even Anne suspected, that more than privateering was going on. The man seemed fixated by his attack against Homeworld, which made Ranglen feel a grudging admiration. "You certainly hate Homeworld, don't you?"

"Yes, I hate them. But I don't like Earth much better. And the two of them are ready to kill each other. You might not believe me, but I'd rather avoid that."

"Why did you want me to sneak into the hangar? What was the real reason?"

"When you arrived here, I thought that maybe I could use you, that you might like to write about this place, expose it as a Homeworld operation and show people how they exploit and abuse Annulus. I figured you'd want to since you're the founder of Annulus. Homeworld is running privateers but not officially. Yet, once I finalize this place, their greed will take over. I'll pull in more support from them, that, once exposed, will incriminate them. I'll show it to everyone. I thought you could write it up for me. I was trying to make you part of all this—which is a lot better than you messing up my plans and my needing to silence you."

Despite the ominous final line, Ranglen still had questions. "I can understand you letting me see 'accidentally' what was happening in the hangar. But then why the sudden change of mind—why did you hit me?"

"I remembered something there I *didn't* want you to see."

Ranglen waited.

"We hadn't removed the insignia yet on that ship that was being broken up. It came from Earth."

"But the *Lochner* was from Earth. And other Earth ships have obviously been boarded."

"But no one was killed on those ships. The *Lochner* was completely destroyed."

It took a moment, but Ranglen suddenly understood. "You really *don't* want to start a war."

"Naturally I don't. It would be a disaster. I meant to publicize just the base itself and Homeworld's support of it. But I didn't want to give any hard evidence that they were killing and destroying Earth ships. That was never their intention and never mine. They've been careful not to leave any tangible proof or to hurt the crews, who often collude with them. I want to stop what Homeworld is doing, but through public pressure from the entire Confederation, not through war with a belligerent Earth that would just lead to more killing—and real evidence of destroying Earth property would cause that."

Ranglen slowly nodded. "I see."

"And I think now you do. Things could get out of hand fast."

"Did a Homeworld privateer bring that ship in, the one in the hangar?"

"Yes, the fools. The Earth crew 'renegotiated' the deal, took part of the cargo and abandoned the ship to the privateer, but it was too hot for them and they only wanted to get rid of it fast. We're not cutting it up for profit, we're destroying the evidence. Then a bigger mistake was made with the *Lochner*. That ship was too large to be confiscated and it had refugees on board. The privateers must have recognized they were in trouble—human trafficking makes the crime and its punishment a lot worse—so they blew up the whole vessel just to get rid of the evidence, along with the conspiring crew and anyone else who just happened to be there. Luckily for them, and for us, no evidence remains, for it surely would have led to armed conflict between Earth and Homeworld."

Ranglen wasn't sure how much to believe, but Muletti's desire to avoid war seemed valid, even though he claimed he didn't care about the main participants. And the need for Annulus not to be caught in the middle was real—and tallied with Ranglen's own concerns.

Muletti said, "Light raids to steal cargo is one thing, secretly supported by Homeworld and the Earth crews who were bribed. Rogue pirates and even Earth have done the same. But wholescale destruction and murder? That's something else."

Ranglen still was uncertain. "What happened on Rimport 3? You kidnapped one woman and shot at another. And I know there was one more person on board the ship you escaped in, who was sedated or wounded. What's behind all that?"

Muletti looked bitter. "I did see you jump out of my ship, by the way, and I would have captured you then, but I had to get out of there."

Ranglen felt angry over being seen.

"But everything that happened there is trivial. The woman I shot I meant only to wound. I just wanted her out of my way. The first woman on board is a friend of mine and she came willingly. She had been hurt, and I gave her a sedative to help her rest. The other woman, who I supposedly kidnapped, I didn't know at the time, but she had been trying to get onto the ship, like you, so I wanted to learn more about her. And I've since found out interesting things. She, like my friend, are survivors of the *Lochner*. And *that's* the reason why I'm keeping them here and away from attention."

Ranglen was surprised. Everyone had insisted there were no survivors.

"You see my point? The two of them can be used. Especially if they identify any of the attack ships as being from Homeworld. Their stories aren't as reliable as a piece of wrecked hull, but they'd still be convincing. But I have to be careful. This whole base is in danger now because of the *Lochner*. If the groups on Homeworld learn that such damning proof is here, the base might be destroyed. I'm also worried they might learn of my loyalty to Annulus. If they get too nervous, they suddenly could decide to cut their connection to this base entirely. Then it might become like the *Lochner*—totally destroyed, just to cover their tracks."

"But if you don't want evidence that Homeworld is destroying Earth ships, then why hold the witnesses? Couldn't their stories also lead to war?"

"That's why I'm keeping them isolated and quiet. I'll use them eventually. Their stories will be told. But not until we get past this crisis with the *Lochner* and it's more in the past. I want the entire Confederation to place blame, for it will blunt any direct retaliation from Earth."

Ranglen thought deeply. For all of Muletti's high motivation and claimed loyalty to Annulus, he still felt something was off. "What about the ship you rented through Anne from Hatch Banner?"

"I needed a craft that had more cargo space, to load up the valuables the prospector had found for her."

"And the additions, the racks on the outside?"

"To hold containers for cargo. I wasn't sure then how much room I'd need, or how I would gather what she wanted. These were sizable rocks floating in space, and I wanted a safe way to gather and hold them. She was footing the bill, so I got what I wanted."

"Then why did you change the registry?"

Muletti showed his frustration. "By the eyes, Ranglen, have you become Anne's private investigator?"

"No, but I'm trying not to be her jury—or a witness against her. Let's assume the question's just natural curiosity."

Muletti growled. "I didn't want to label that I was from Annulus in order to keep some anonymity for Anne. Doesn't that make sense? I first changed the insignia to that of Homeworld because I wanted to use their hangar to keep the ship hidden at Rimport 3. Security there is required to leave that hangar alone. But once I started using the ship, I removed the insignia altogether. I wanted no identification once I got her cargo. It could arouse suspicions from other marketers."

"Like Ventroni?"

"Yes, like Ventroni. I was doing my job of protecting Anne. Which, I presume, you're also doing."

Ranglen kept quiet.

"Maybe we're more alike than what you think."

"Did you get Anne's pallasite from here?"

"This place is great for such oddities. We'll mine it eventually, once Homeworld is thrown out. All sorts of metals lie over the surface. It's a fabulous find."

"You'll set up your own company?"

"Not me, but I'll invest in it. I thought at first Anne would like to run it, but she only wants her specialty items, things she can hold in her hand. She'd never deal with a board of directors. She likes explorers, thieves, smugglers who bring things secretly to her, stuff she can look at directly and touch. 'Pieces of light,' she once called them. 'The universe in tiny frames.' I think she was quoting you. She enjoyed my bringing her such trinkets."

Ranglen moved away from this topic but still tried to catch Muletti off guard. "Why did the woman you shot back at the rimport know your name? I heard her say it right before you shot her."

Muletti wasn't fazed. "I've encountered her there several times before, sneaking into the hangar and stealing things. She's a pest."

Ranglen, disappointed that Muletti seemed to have answers for everything, took a deep breath and asked his last question. "What do you intend to do with me?"

"I think you understand the situation enough that you won't compromise it. You don't want Annulus hurt any more than I do."

"You're letting me go?"

"Not yet. I might have an important task for you. I hope not, but I want to be prepared."

"It's not more writing, is it?"

"No, but when Homeworld is ultimately exposed, if you want to support the accusations against them in your essays, I'd be appreciative."

Ranglen neither agreed nor disagreed. "The two people you took on your spaceship. I want to see them, just to know they're all right."

"They're fine. I intended to show you. I haven't told them the full story as I told you, but I'm sure they'll agree to be part of it, to be witnesses for what happened on the *Lochner* if that turns out to be needed in time. The older woman—her name's Krin—I'm sure would do it, and the younger one is after revenge so I think she would, too."

Based on the brief glance he saw of her, Ranglen wasn't sure she would be so accommodating,

"Follow me," said Muletti, "I'll take you to them."

As they moved into the hallway, Muletti got another call on his cellpad.

Ranglen saw the self-assurance drain from Muletti's face as he listened. He said in response, "You're sure? Then…don't allow it to land. Don't even answer it! Tell the battery to shoot at it—now! Don't wait for it to hit us first!"

He started running and yelled for Ranglen to follow him. "It's happening, just like I feared. We don't have a chance."

At that moment, Braya and Krin sat together in a small locked room. It had two beds and a tiny lavatory. They had been confined there for nearly a day, left together after random separation aboard the *Prowler*. But talking with Krin was still difficult. She couldn't listen to Braya with attention. She'd respond with a torrent of contradictions on the Seekers, "Lihandro," the Airafane, Hideki, Muletti—especially Muletti, always Muletti—but she'd never reach any conclusions. For Braya, unraveling such endless speculation was agonizing.

In the middle of this, an individual with a Homeworld accent had brought them twice to Muletti, to "chat" with him, though they were not permitted to leave and all the questions came from him. He grilled Braya on what happened to her after the break-in on the *Lockner*—what she saw as she ran through the ship, the details of how she got to Annulus, Hideki's enlisting her to go to the rimport. He fished for clues to something he was after, but he also had moments of surprising doubt or introspection, giving blanket criticism of Homeworld and odd statements about "duty." Then Krin would break in as if to help him. "Your history has shaped you, Aarov. You're not at fault for all that you've done." He'd ignore her, or tell her to shut up, but a vague indecision kept showing in him.

It bothered Braya. On first seeing Muletti at the rimport, she had assumed he was the pilot of the *Prowler*, so she felt instantly she should attack him and make him suffer. But he now seemed different from what she expected. He was looking for something that evaded him. She was still committed to her revenge but she felt his uncertainty contaminating her drive. She couldn't allow that.

Braya and Krin were quiet now, thankfully, each sitting on her bed in her own isolation.

They felt a soft boom, followed by a shudder that flowed across the floor and shook the bed frames.

They stood up from their mattresses and glanced at each other. Braya wasn't worried yet. Ground tremors were common here given all the nearby volcanism. On this overly active world, the base had apparently been built near much activity. The few people in the installation—they hadn't seen many—stayed indoors, followed enclosed pathways to the other buildings and worked mainly in the large hangar. They avoided the dangerous exterior.

Another thud, deeper and heavier. It seemed to come from beneath the installation. Braya assumed that if the activity was volcanic, it might presage an eruption, a big one.

Then a louder crack, sharp, as if a wall had been blown through. The room shook, flung up dust and rattled objects. In the washroom enclosure, bottles fell and glass broke. The doors vibrated as the lights flickered.

An alarm sounded in the hallway, loud and persistent.

Krin screamed, "Decompression!"

"No," said Braya, relying on her spaceport experience. "The alarm would be different. This is internal."

More rumbling, followed by a cascade of sound, as if somewhere a ceiling fell.

Krin looked hysterical. "This isn't right, Braya. It could be the end. Who'll carry on and take over what I'm doing? It might have to be you."

"Stop it! We're getting out of here." She yanked at the door but only an electric code would open it. Even with all the shaking in the room, it didn't budge. Their first thought was to get into spacesuits—the natural reaction during an emergency on a world with no air. But none were in the room. Braya had checked.

She banged on the door and yelled for help.

More shattering. They could hear from outside debris sliding across the floor.

"This is no volcano," she declared.

The lights on the lock pad suddenly flashed. Someone outside was working it. Braya jumped back.

The door swung open, followed by a fast plume of dust.

Muletti stood there with another man, both in spacesuits but still carrying their helmets.

Braya had seen the second man before at Rimport 3. He'd jumped out of Muletti's ship during the second explosion and ran into another. She had watched his quickness and then, after he escaped, the tight stare from his chilly blue eyes.

Muletti handed them two spacesuits. They were lightweight for easy access and quick excursions. "Here, put these on. You're both getting out of here."

Krin almost cried. "Aarov, what's happening?"

"We're being attacked by Homeworld. They sent an armed fighter against us."

"But you—"

"*Put these on!* Bombs are falling!"

Other people ran up to Muletti—apparently the defenses already had failed. He said to them, "Board the cargo ship and fight to get away—or use any means you can, the lighter craft inside the hangar, but some of them might not get you off-planet." They ran away in different directions.

Braya threw on a spacesuit and then helped Krin with hers. The second man watched her with a close attention, said nothing.

Another explosion, farther away.

"No decompression in this area yet," Muletti said. He spoke to the second man, "Here's that job I had for you, Ranglen."

Braya caught the name. She had heard it associated with the building of Annulus and Krin had talked of a "Mykol Ranglen," apparently a rival for Muletti with another woman named Anne Montgomery—described in Krin's gossipy details.

Muletti said to Ranglen, "You're getting these two out of here. I have other things I need to take care of."

Krin was unconsolable. "No, Aarov. Please."

Braya said, "You're letting us leave?"

"I didn't intend to but I am now. If we stay here, we'll all be killed. The whole base is about to be destroyed. I'm not heroic. I'm getting out, too." He pulled them through the door and pushed them toward Ranglen.

Ranglen looked angry and suddenly suspicious. He snapped at Muletti, "You were about to throw me in here with them! You meant to imprison me!"

"Yes. Sorry. But everything's changed now. Hurry, all of you."

Krin squealed, "Aarov, please! It's not—"

"*Don't argue!*" He threw her at Ranglen.

In the passageway, a wall blew out and scattered large pieces of wreckage.

"Dammit, dammit—"

They ducked and scurried, kept on running.

Braya yelled at Muletti, "Where are you taking us?"

"Ranglen's flying you off this world to someplace safe." He said to Ranglen, "Then afterward, you have more to do. Here"— he handed him a small data chip. "This has the coordinates of a planet where you'll find all the answers you want, everything you tried to get out of me but that I didn't give you."

Ranglen said, proud of his insight, "I knew you weren't telling me everything."

"Just go there, and *soon!* It'll clear up this mess. And it won't be easy. But be careful when you get there."

Ranglen grumbled as he pocketed the chip. He looked at Muletti with both anger and reluctant gratefulness. Braya sensed unspoken communication between them. And Muletti said, "If you get to see Anne, tell her...never mind."

Then he made all of them put on their helmets and switch their radios to a common frequency. The helmet reminded Braya too much of her deadly plunge into Annulus.

Muletti said to Ranglen, "Now, get them out of here. The Homeworld ship will go after the wall, the armory, and the cargo ship."

Braya said, "Do *you* have a ship?" She wanted to know if he could survive and then she'd still be able to confront him.

"Don't worry about me." He pushed them toward an airlock that led outside, the same one through which Braya had been brought into the base.

Muletti ran back into the building and away from them.

Krin pleaded, "*Aarov,* don't leave us!"

Ranglen pulled at her. "We have to go."

Braya muttered, "She won't listen if she doesn't want to." They tried to drag her along.

Another explosion, back where Muletti disappeared. The ceiling, the walls, everything fell. Air rushed in that direction, followed by a storm of fragments and dust.

The outside wall of the building had been breached. The rush of atmosphere pulled them back. They fought to stay balanced and push themselves forward. Braya found the airlock, and they rushed inside it.

Krin screamed into the radio, "Aarov! Are you all right?"

No answer.

She ran back through the opening. "I'm not leaving you!"

Ranglen tried to stop her, but she was too fast. Braya joined him, but Krin disappeared into the blinding dust.

"Let her go!" Braya said. "She won't listen. She's devoted to him."

"They'll both be killed."

"She only wants to be with him." Braya could tell that Ranglen wouldn't desert her. But she guessed that Krin had used this disaster to make her decision for her, to devote herself wholly to Muletti.

A string of explosions—like a row of missiles dropped in a line and growing more intense, felt more than heard.

She yelled at Ranglen, "He told you to go! We have to get out of here!"

They fought their way back to the exit. Ranglen looked angry as he overrode the safely locks—the air pressure was almost gone now—and opened the door to the vacuum outside.

They emerged into chaos. Huge tumbled slabs of the hangar lay across the landing field, most of the ships inside it destroyed. The attack must have focused on the office complex and the hangar first, and only now were the buildings with living quarters hit.

They ran through the debris on the landing field. Even amid all the destruction, Braya felt a fierce excitement of liberation. She was leaving behind imprisonment and the weird uncertainty that possessed her because of Muletti. She looked skyward—

And saw the *Killer*.

"That's it! That's it!"

She moved away from Ranglen, abandoning him.

He looked up. "That's a Homeworld fighter."

"It's the same ship that blew up the *Lochner!* It's doing the same thing here!"

The oval in the fuselage shot out missiles that arced down to targets. Two bombs sat under its wings.

Braya, hating it, was overcome with a yearning to destroy it.

And still no insignia could be seen on its side.

A slab of wreckage fell near her.

Ranglen yelled, "We have to get out of here!"

She hesitated. Then self-preservation took over and she followed him, even as she demanded, "Once we get out of here, we're going after it!"

"That's impossible!"

"First we survive, then we destroy it. Where's your ship?" Fury guided her as she centered on her goal—escaping destruction and getting the *Killer*.

He pointed her to a craft that was similar to the *Prowler*. On its side was the ringed identifier of Annulus.

Another big explosion.

"The wall," Ranglen said. "They're hitting the barrier."

Braya had seen the protecting wall when Muletti took her from his ship. A high barricade, a dike against floods. It guarded the buildings from the melted turmoil of the volcanoes, one of which she saw was now active and not far away, billowing out smoke and fountains of sparks that pulsed red, pelting bombs of melted rock that tumbled and fell on this side of the barrier.

The *Killer* shot more missiles at the wall. Part of it toppled.

The bastards! The bastards!

A long trail of molten metal, shiny and exuding vapors, leaked onto the landing pads. It crept forward, unstoppable. A dark cloud of glowing ash swept in and obscured the whole field.

The base wouldn't just be destroyed but buried under molten rock, erasing everything.

Ranglen pulled at her.

They scrambled up the ramp to his ship. He opened the door and led her through, closed it behind them.

He rushed forward to the instrument panel, jumped into the pilot's seat, and directed her to take the one on the right. "Buckle in," he said.

She pulled the restraining harness around her as she removed her helmet. "We'll attack that ship, right?"

Ranglen yanked off his helmet and powered up the craft. "We can't. We haven't any weapons."

She seethed with frustration. "Dammit! Dammit!" Her main target was right before her, but she knew they had no way to destroy it. A ship this size didn't come with weapons—they'd need carrier racks with missiles inside them. She knew all this, but still…

"It's destroying everything," Ranglen said. "They want no evidence."

She watched the *Killer* through the observation ports. She sat motionless, filled with hate.

"We can't go after it," Ranglen repeated.

"I want it *destroyed!*"

"I want that, too. But first we survive—just like you said."

What she said before was no longer relevant. She wanted only what she wanted *now*.

He lifted ship. Other small vessels rose too, but the single, larger cargo craft had been damaged. Rubble lay smashed against its support fins, and the long shape now tilted dangerously. A nearby hit would make it fall, anyone inside it quickly killed.

She thought of Muletti. Did he get away? He surely had an escape vessel planted somewhere, maybe the *Prowler* itself. Would he have time to reach it? Would he welcome Krin and take her with him?

He better! She deserves to be saved after what he did to her.

She didn't know what to think of him now, after he helped them escape and Krin ran back to protect him.

The *Killer* rained destruction.

Ranglen and Braya rose into the sky.

Ranglen said, "Every bit of evidence will be lost now—no ghosts can rise from beneath solid iron."

"I want that ship."

The base fell away, shrinking beneath them. The volcano raged. Other eruptions joined the wrath.

She looked to see where the ship had gone. "Where's the *Killer*? Is it following us?"

"What's the '*Killer*'?"

"The Homeworld fighter. Where did it go?"

Ranglen checked. "It's destroying the cargo ship now, burying the base under a massive blanket of cover-up. But it's not following us."

He didn't look up at her as he asked, "So where do you want me to take you?"

"Excuse me?"

"Annulus? Earth? I can leave you anywhere before I'm on my way."

Braya was appalled. What could he be thinking? "Are you *serious*? I heard what Muletti said. He gave you directions to a place where he said you could 'solve' this mess? Aren't you going there?"

Ranglen stared at her. "Yes, I intended to."

"Then, I'm coming with you."

He took a while before responding, his face changing as he considered. "Are you sure about that?"

"*Damned* sure. And you're not stopping me. Let's go. Now!"

He remained still. But then he grinned, oddly appreciative of her choice, and turned to his controls.

The hell with it all. And the hell with you. I'm coming along.

Chapter 11: In Flight

As his ship departed the planetoid, Ranglen studied her for the first time.

Her eyes impressed first, dark gray and vaguely sinister, outlined in shadow not produced by makeup but a withdrawn sullenness that seemed almost physical. The brows above them tilted inward, in an apparent anger that might now be permanent, ingrained in her face. The shags of short black hair fell in unwashed blades to her eyes and over her ears. The small mouth radiated hostility.

And yet, for all the power in that face, her small body seemed almost fragile, too endangered, too reduced even in the spacesuit.

Her words both snapped and persuaded, as if negotiating with him from the start. "Krin talked of the planet that Muletti indicated. I can tell you about it."

"What's it like?"

"Sorry. Not yet. I say nothing until we get started. Once we're in light-space and on our way, once we're *committed*, I'll tell what I know."

Ranglen pulled out the databank-chip Muletti had given him. "What's to stop me from secretly putting in other coordinates and dropping you where you don't want to be?"

"You won't do that. You're Mykol Ranglen. I heard Muletti say your name, and even Krin talked about you. She said you were respectable, that you and Muletti both knew your friend Anne—she talked about the three of you. She liked to prove she was close with Muletti and that he told her private things. You'll want to hear about it."

He thought he shouldn't and yet he did. "Why should we trust Muletti?"

"You *can't* trust him. He's killed people. Yet Krin thought highly of him, and I think he was going through some strange transformation toward the end. It seemed that way anyhow. He eventually let Krin and me stay together when he at first kept us apart, and then he helped all of us escape. I didn't expect that. It bothers me. But I'm willing to believe in him for now if we can use what he gave us to our advantage."

Ranglen wouldn't have hesitated before but now with her, he oddly did.

"Mutual benefit," she argued. "I win, you win. Partners in crime."

He was reluctant, but there was no other choice. "All right," he said, finally.

"Good. Go for it."

He connected the chip with a lead to the computer and brought up the coordinates. The world was located outside Confederate territory. Far outside.

"You're still sure?" he said.

"Just do it, okay?"

He punched in the figures. They entered light-space.

Ranglen heard Braya take a deep breath.

"All right," he told her. "Now, talk."

"Sorry, not yet. We have two days before we get where we're going. There's plenty of time. First, I'm getting out of this spacesuit and then, I want something to eat. You've got food in here, don't you?"

Ranglen didn't know whether to laugh or be insulted. His normal ship was quite accommodating (though it still was no pleasure yacht), and Hatch had moved all his supplies over to this new one. Did she just want a touch of normality before she plunged into pursuing her *Killer*? "You can have the cabin in back on the right. It has its own bathroom and shower. Freshen up if you want. I'll fix something to eat."

She asked no questions and quickly left him.

A bit later and after she returned, they had a meal but said nothing to each other.

Then, without prompting, she stated, "You *are* Mykol Ranglen, correct? I just assumed that from what Muletti said."

"Yes. And you are?"

"Braya. No more. I've used only false last names so they mean nothing."

Ranglen felt a certain admiration. "Rough life?"

"Not like yours—founder of Annulus, big reputation, scholar, writer. What are you doing here?"

"I was helping a friend and trying to stop a war. Then things got complicated." He hoped that would get a laugh out of her, but it didn't. "Why are *you* here?"

"About the same. Personal reasons that got a lot bigger."

Without her spacesuit, and in her flimsy tight-fitting clothes that were getting ragged, her small form took on strength, looked held in, like a spring wound too tightly and ready to strike.

She spoke as if reciting a manifesto. "I want the people who destroyed the *Lochner*. Both Krin and I were on board when it was attacked. I assume Krin's dead now. And people will want *me* dead, too. I'm the only one who can describe what happened. But I'm not running away. I'm running *to*. I want *them*."

The tone struck Ranglen as overwrought, but looking at her made him believe her. It was hard to deny such clear determination. "So, what happened?"

"One assurance I need before we talk. I'm not here to speak for others or to avenge anybody except myself. I'm no representative, no hero. I'm here for *me*. You might be the great Mykol Ranglen, and I'm just an ex-spaceport-worker, but that means I don't have to fill anyone's role or be responsible to anyone but myself. Don't ask me to stop. I want what I want."

"But you said things became complicated."

"Yes, that's right. Know that Homeworld, Earth, and even Annulus mean little to me. Muletti babbled about those worlds as he sat there, about loyalty and doing the right thing. But he can have it, and *you* can have it. I just want those who did the killing and the reason why they gave in to it, what's *behind* them. People don't destroy like that, not even for money or power. They kill because something is driving them—because they have to. Don't you want to know what that is?"

"Of course I do, but I also want prevention. I don't want this happening again. You sound like you're after only revenge."

"Well, maybe I am. But if I get pay-back, then you get information. That's a good trade. Nothing wrong with that."

"Then you're as much a killer as they are."

"I'm only after three people and what's behind them. Once I have that, *I'll* decide what's right or wrong. Maybe I'll kill them and maybe I won't. Look what happened with Muletti. Things didn't work out the way I planned with him."

"What do you mean?"

"He was one of those who boarded the *Lochner*. I saw him. He beat Krin and almost killed her. But now I can't figure him out. Krin said he has events in his past that still haunt him, that he's trying to atone for. She even said he saved her life. You saw how she sacrificed herself and ran back to help him, even after all that happened on the *Lochner*. I didn't like Krin, but her feelings for Muletti were genuine. What's it all mean? The boarders on the ship even shot at each other. Then there's something about a man named Lihandro."

"Lihandro? Who's that?"

"See! I do know things you don't. But let's be clear, Mr. Mykol Ranglen. You're not dumping me on some asteroid or shooting me into space like a stowaway. I know that's happened. I hear the stories. You're not selling me to some colony world for your own profit."

"Braya, for god's sake, I'd never—"

"No! Wrong line. It's all 'for the Mountain's sake' now. And there, too, what about the Seekers? They're somehow connected to all this. Krin and Hideki did everything for them. You see how much we can learn from each other? Are we still agreed? You won't throw me off the ship?"

"I already said I'd take you with me."

"But I'm often lied to and I won't be again. Krin called me an 'avenging soul.' I think I scared her. Do I scare you? Maybe I should. Because I'm telling you—I won't be held back."

Ranglen wasn't sure what to say. He did want information, especially since it sounded different from what Muletti said—was Muletti present at the *Lochner* disaster? He never admitted that. But, at the same time, Ranglen had his limits. "I won't desert you and I agree to work together with you. But I won't help you kill anyone. If you try, I'll do all I can to stop you. Our goal is to find what's behind all this, the cause of the destruction, not to bring about more. If you try to do that, then we don't work together at all."

He saw something deeper in her eyes, an unwilling exposure. Not soft, but not vicious either. She said at last, "Fair enough. If I go after anyone it'll be on my own. Is that all right?"

"If I see it happening, I'll still try to stop you."

"You're welcome to try. I can't promise how I'll react."

"I won't let you kill."

"As I said, you can try. But we can save that argument for later."

Ranglen said nothing.

"Let's get started."

She spoke of all that happened involving the cargo ship—the events in the spaceport back on Earth, meeting Krin and boarding the craft, Muletti attacking them, the raiders firing on each other, the dead crew, the three ships directly responsible for the destruction and the names she gave them—she insisted he remember them—the *Killer*, the *Prowler*, and the *Spy*. She described her escape from the *Lochner* and her fall to Annulus, meeting Hideki and what the woman said to her, the use of the Seekers, the planned break-in at Rimport 3, Muletti abducting her, talking with Krin while they both were imprisoned, and listening to Muletti when he spoke to them.

Ranglen stopped her there. "Tell me more what the two of them said to you."

"I never was sure about Krin. I don't think she was lying—not like Hideki."

"Hideki was the one shot at Rimport 3?"

She nodded. "Krin seemed genuine but Hideki a fake. Before we got to the planetoid—Muletti called it '82A'—he couldn't decide whether it was better to keep Krin and I together or apart. I think he was concerned we'd get too lonely, or maybe he thought we'd reveal something by talking together. For all he had done, he was getting strange. He'd throw me a lot of hard questions but then seem almost embarrassed by them. And yet nothing stopped him from continuing with his plans, whatever they were, and you could tell he had many. I wondered if something less destructive had been intended with the *Lochner* but then it somehow got out of hand. He'd bring Krin and me together and interrogate me, but he'd also rant about Homeworld and sometimes Earth. He never said anything negative about Annulus. He seemed somehow compromised. He'd suddenly get a far-away look as if he wanted to confess something about himself or even Homeworld. But he was unable to. Krin told me a little of what happened to him, that he once led a mutiny against a terrible Homeworld captain. To her, Muletti was a born-again saint. 'Eye of my affection,' she said, making stupid puns with words from the Seekers—they covered her insecurities, and she had plenty. The Seekers were her crutch. She even sounded happy when I told her Muletti tried to kill Hideki back at the rimport. She admired Hideki but she also despised her."

"Muletti said he only wanted to stop her, not kill her."

"Maybe, but he knew exactly what he was doing. Even if he did show a kind of warped hesitation in his talks with us, I still would have attacked him if I had the chance."

But you didn't. "What else did Krin tell you?"

"That she and Muletti knew each other for years and always helped each other. He saved her life on board the Homeworld ship where he led the mutiny and killed the captain. Krin loved him for it. They stayed in contact afterward for years. It was all hero worship from her and long-running victim-protection from him. But the memory of the event seemed to wear on him, as it obviously did for Krin."

Anne suggested the same when she described the incident.

"Krin returned to Earth after the mutiny, joined the Seekers, and became friends with some old man named Lihandro, who apparently found something valuable in space. She didn't say what it was, and I don't think he told her. He needed help to get it and bring it back to Earth. She told Muletti about it, and Muletti met the old man—on Ventroni of all places. They made an agreement. But then this Lihandro went off on his own to get whatever he found, by himself, which apparently changed his mind. He told Krin he would give to *her* what he discovered and not Muletti, so she could pass it on to the Seekers to bring them importance and prestige. She was supposed to take it to Hideki, who's an important person in the Seekers."

Was this Lihandro the same prospector that Muletti mentioned? But that man found only diamonds, according to him, not some strange unknown object.

"Lihandro never brought what he found to Krin. She went to meet him but he never arrived to give her anything. Then she said she learned he was murdered. I assume Muletti killed him because the old man betrayed him. But this put *her* in danger, too, or so she believed. She became desperate to get away from Earth, so she joined the same colony ship that I was on. That's how I met her."

"What did the man find? An Airafane Clip?"

"I thought that at first. What else could produce so much violence? But she was unclear. It somehow involved the Seekers. It wasn't just an object but some kind of new discovery that would change history, that might validate the beliefs of the Seekers—or destroy them. That's what he told her. But she didn't want to talk about it. It frightened her, though she also wanted it. And she became scared of Muletti, and yet also scared *for* him."

"For him? Why?"

"When he found her on the *Lochner*, he kicked her around but didn't kill her, which I didn't know until I saw her alive again on his ship. And when she talked to me, she said she was surprised he *didn't* kill her. It worried her. She'd get hysterical, leaping between fear of him and fear he might get hurt himself, that he wasn't sure about what he was doing—that everyone would be after him for destroying the ship and that Earth would arrest him, and that then he'd be exposed as the leader of the mutiny and given back to Homeworld so they could punish him. In both cases, she feared he'd be executed. That's what made her so protective of him."

Ranglen tried to keep up with all she said, to connect the many loose parts.

"But then things got more peculiar. Hideki was on Annulus because Annulus is supposed to be some strong hotbed for the Seekers. They've infiltrated the people under the Ring. I saw it myself. The *Lochner* was near Annulus when it was destroyed, and some cargo that Krin heard about from Muletti was supposed to be dropped there for your friend Anne—Krin talked about her because Muletti liked her and Krin was jealous. But she believed this Anne was using him, taking advantage of his contacts and experience. Krin also thought that she herself might be dropped on Annulus when the *Lochner* got there, that she had been intended to get there all along. But that was impossible—I could see when I reached the port that only cargo was deposited there, not passengers. And yet Annulus is where *I* landed—and it was Hideki who found me. Was that just coincidence? I wind up hitting the Ring near the very person Krin was supposed to meet? It doesn't make sense."

"Did Krin give you anything to carry for her, to pass on if she got hurt?"

"No, nothing. I wondered about that, too. Hideki went through my clothes when I was unconscious. I'm sure she also found nothing. And then there's this weird similarity between Krin and Hideki. It drove me nuts. They dressed like each other, looked like each other. Krin called Hideki her mirror self, her follower, even her fan. But Hideki called Krin a mental cripple, a 'cosmic accident'—I'm not exaggerating. This is what I lived with. I couldn't understand it and I didn't want to. I asked Krin why she dressed the way she did, and she claimed the Airafane looked that way. What in hell would make her say that? Did they have pink hair and decorated overalls? She also claimed they were priest-astronomers who spread through the stars and built Stonehenge. This is one of the reasons why I focused on just finding those ships. It made more sense than the insanity around me."

"Braya, you can't—"

"Don't tell me what I can't do, Mykol. Too many people have done that already. You can't stop me or what's happening—people getting killed, people bought and sold, people abandoning their children to look for stupid Clips. I've seen all this. I've been in camps. Krin told me that Lihandro deserted his own family to go into space, but it's just an excuse, a means to justify self-indulgence. Krin even argued that abandonment was a reason why the Seekers arose, to provide a community for those left behind. And they also wanted ties with all the 'underlings' of society—the refugees from Earth, colony transients, those 'under the Ring' on Annulus. But I can't see how worshipping a mountain with eyes helps anyone. For that matter, what good are the Clips that we all fight over? Where's the so-called progress they bring? They provide only means for more exploitation, excuses for using other people and profiting from them. They justify greed. Have they improved us? Are we any happier?"

Ranglen was overwhelmed by all of this. He felt he teetered on the edge of a cliff, that he was about to throw away his own restraint and join her in the strength of her outlandish, yet perceptive, beliefs.

"Don't look at me like that! You *wanted* me to talk. Maybe you should be more aware of what you ask for."

On and on. Two days of that. Hours of silence and then a sudden avalanche of words. Ranglen, at times, desperately wanted to get away from her, even when he agreed with her and knew exactly what she meant. He'd occupy himself with ship chores or else stay in his cabin. But people can't hide from each other inside a spaceship. The company of two can become a crowd, confining and cloying. He wondered if she felt the same.

But Ranglen noticed that for all her talk she said little of herself—and if she did, it came in hammerlike outbursts (like her sudden assertion about how much she'd "seen"). On other subjects, she'd give long critiques, as if declaring, "Take what you want from this. I don't have time to be selective." But in terms of herself, she'd get evasive, look cornered, then become angry for showing any anger—like an animal in a cage trying to be calm, maintaining cover but all the while plotting an escape.

He was fascinated, yet very careful. On their first night when he slept in his cabin, he locked his door.

Then, as they neared the end of their flight, they returned to the topic of where they were going. It had gotten lost behind all the other things said. "Did Krin describe the planet ahead of us?"

"Its unofficial name is 'Highland,' or 'Fell.' But Krin called it 'Hell' instead. She didn't say why."

"A 'fell' could be a high moorland…or 'highland.' Any idea what she meant?"

"No, and you have to understand that Krin wandered everywhere when she talked. She loved *stories,* the 'legends of space'—planets as temples, mountains as shrines, cosmic gods and wrecked spaceships. She would talk of caves as borderlines, of intrusions from other worlds, of horrors and Moyocks lurking on planets or inside nebulae—behind walls, even mirrors. 'Demons of hate.' You couldn't spend much time with her. She was a bottomless pit, and she kept trying to suck you into it. But she did say at one time this planet was Hell, and that deep inside it lived the Devil, but a devil we can never understand, a devil that's beyond *being* the Devil. I remember that. But I have no idea what she meant."

"What about the exact place where we're going, not the planet itself but what Muletti wants us to find?"

"Well, at one time, she did use a phrase for it, but I didn't pay much attention. I thought it was Krin just being Krin."

"And the phrase?"

"She called it, 'the Depot of the Dead.'"

It was one of the few lines Braya didn't elaborate.

Chapter 12: Cloud Forest

The planet seemed made of mountains and mist.

Great arcs of peaks corrugated its surface. Signs of plate tectonics shone everywhere, the crust broken into a hundred pieces that jostled and collided with each other. In the small seas, deep-water trenches ran beside the mountains. Sea-floor spreading provided heat from subduction—hot plumes rose, volcanoes spouted in the heights and beneath the water. The surface of the world was a confused labyrinth of rupture and uplift, landforms bent and sliding over and beneath each other, a jigsaw puzzle where the junctures crinkled into lines of crests.

But from space, it all looked delicate and serene. A smooth, white-swirled globe like churned milk, with traces and bands of gray waters, gray mountains, dark green slopes, basins with brown threads of rivers, pale green savanna. A tinted world, whose shapes and colors were blurred by mist.

It didn't look like Hell. "It's beautiful," Ranglen said, eager to prove Krin wrong.

But some continents appeared barren, the inner regions walled off from the wet air-currents coming from the seas. Deserts lay in rain shadows. Any moisture from the tiny oceans rose into the mountains on the shores and dumped snow on the tall crags, making rivers and waterfalls, high jungles in the vertical topography, the water soaked up by abundant growth and never reaching the badlands beyond—the ocean coasts laced with fog, the mountain tops snagged by cloud, the inner reaches of continents flat, stark, featureless, dead.

The world's gravity was the same as Earth's but the planet's size was smaller. Maybe the core with its heavier materials swelled into the mantle, making it hotter and more plastic, leading to busier plate tectonics and smaller convention currents but greater in number.

An odd world to house a base, like the ferro-volcanic planetoid. But 82A at least had been in the Annulus system. This world lay outside the limits of exploration. And it still was undergoing birth pangs, was overly active and a threat to safety.

Ranglen wondered if it held Clips. It had the right geology, the churning of the underworld that would bring a Clip buried in the mantle millions of years ago back to the surface. That would explain why the base was here, that it had been established in high hopes for finding a Clip. Ranglen thought of pulling out his Clip-finding shard of "fluorite," or Clip stasis material, and looking through it in order to check—the procedure being his great dark secret, the one that afflicted him in the middle of the night with responsibility and heavy guilt. His strictly private and exclusive way of finding Clips.

But Braya was near, so he didn't dare. And he could check only a hemisphere at a time.

He asked, "Why did Krin call this world 'Hell'?"

"Maybe because it has a place named 'Depot of the Dead.'"

Ranglen said nothing, focused on their approach.

They glided down without staying long in orbit, wanting to avoid possible surveillance, though he didn't believe there would be much. No one would come here except on known and accepted business. The world had to be listed in Confederation records, if only by long-range astronomical detection, surely labeled for "possible settlement," its atmosphere breathable according to Ranglen's instruments, its life most likely carbon-based. But other planets stood closer and thus were more financially viable.

Making it a good hiding spot for a secret and illegal base.

"Where will we land?" Braya asked.

"I'm checking Muletti's coordinates. They suggest we touchdown not near the base—its location is included in the data. He must want us to avoid detection, to come in carefully or to see something along the way. We'll need to walk. I'll have a better idea once we get closer."

They descended between loops of clouds, saw clear deserts, shorelines in fog, mountains sloped with banks of vapor. High plateaus looked bleak, some crags lifting into the cold of the stratosphere, saw-toothed ridges in aprons of haze. Glaciers crept downslope in search of oceans or deserts, to break off into floating icebergs or be lost in melted pools of color on the open ground—green, amber, red, black. Some clear, some maybe poisonous.

The eyes of the earth, Ranglen called them—they watched him in return.

The ship approached a coastline softened by low stratus clouds, desert backed by mountains. "We're in the rain shadow, which is odd, the wind patterns reversed. That's why nothing's growing. All the moisture must drain on the other side of the peaks. The fog that's here comes from cold offshore currents."

"Any landing spot yet?"

"The computer's programmed an approach to the top of those mountains, to the start of a foot trail I guess we're supposed to follow to the base."

"You're very trusting of Muletti's suggestions."

"I'm just going with the knowledge we have. What else can we do? You wanted to come here, remember?"

She stayed quiet.

Scanner beams bounced off the ground, and the ship took readings, a full breakdown of heights and slopes. The radar cut through the mist to the landscape. Nothing was seen through the forward ports, only fog. They flew strictly by programmed instruments.

"I don't like this," Braya said.

The ship's guidance controls took them up a valley and into a thicker bank of mist. According to the graphic visualization, they crossed a pass into the wetter opposite slopes, which were overgrown. They approached a high plateau and the marked location of the base, but they were taken to a spot kilometers away, on a shelf along the outside slant of the mountain.

The ship slowed and hovered, came down gingerly in thick fog.

This part was unnerving.

The computer spoke in dry tones, "Thirty meters…twenty-five…"

"It might not be a solid landing," Ranglen said. "The scanners say the ground is soft, under a lot of vegetation."

Braya looked tense but she didn't comment.

The ship rocked—made a loud noise as if scraping a wall.

"What—?"

It banked off course. Then staggered back. Pushed loudly again to the side. The lights flickered.

Ranglen fought for control. "Something's pulling at us." He compensated with steering jets. He couldn't see the ground but he tried to drop faster—to avoid whatever was yanking at them.

The ship slammed to the side, jerking them in their seats. The power went out and then returned. Ranglen thrust the ship back into position.

The landing jets howled, the computer droned, "Fifteen…ten…eight…"

Alarms sounded. A contact light flashed, flickered—a bad sign. They were being dragged across the ground.

Then the movement slowed, the mushy foundation or thickets of plants stopping them.

They came to a halt. The landing supports sank deeper, gripping the earth.

The ship settled but it was canted to the side, the exit door and airlock now closer to the ground.

Ranglen and Braya didn't move.

"What the hell was that?"

"At first, I thought it was atmospheric," Ranglen said, "like an air pocket. But it was electrical too. We briefly lost power." He looked for answers in his instruments.

"Is the ship damaged?"

"We didn't land well but we're stable now, and the systems check shows nothing bad. We'll have a rocky lift-off but that's not a problem."

Braya frowned. "This reminds me too much of Krin's stories—tractor beams, sudden shipwrecks, creatures reaching up and pulling you from the sky. She believed all that."

"I wonder if this is why Muletti had us land away from the base. If we'd gone there, maybe the ship would have been taken over completely, and we'd be captured or killed. But we made it in safely. I'm willing to believe it was a smart move."

"How far is the base?"

"About fifteen kilometers."

They first freed themselves from the harnesses and then checked if they could get through the hatch, that it wasn't buried in growth.

They slid into the tilted airlock, surveyed the atmospherics for toxicity and found nothing. Then they pushed the outside door open.

They had to press hard against branches and vines, a pack of dirt thrown up by their slide. They broke through—

And saw only featureless mist, felt an overwhelming dampness. The air was cool but very wet, filled with sounds of dripping water and strong odors—moist bark, damp soil, mold, fungus, and squashed plants.

"Dismal place," Braya said.

"The sun should come out soon. Let's map our path and get supplies."

They returned inside and pulled the door closed. Ranglen opened his cellpad and showed Braya the intended trail defined by Muletti. It was mainly flat except for an uphill climb in the middle, which would take them onto the plateau where the base was located.

"About a half-day's walk," he estimated, given the topography.

"You thought he wanted us to see something?"

"There's an area up ahead where the path kinks a little, swings around an obstacle before it continues to the uphill climb." Neither of them speculated on what it might be. "According to the figures for the world's rotation, we still have a full day of light, and the day's long here. We'll get to the base well before darkness. And if we run into trouble, we can come back here."

"I don't have clothes or shoes for hiking."

"I have some you can use."

Ranglen often landed on planets and explored, so his own ship was well supplied, and Hatch had moved everything over from it. Clothing for cold and warm climates, portable shelters, packs, provisions, medical supplies, tracking equipment, sunscreen and hats. He even had clothes that should fit Braya—intended for someone smaller than Ranglen.

"Who were these for?"

"A friend of mine." He once had taken Anne on a trip with him. It hadn't gone well.

"Muletti's pal? Sweet little Anne?"

Ranglen just continued to pack.

"Do we need all this?" She held up a tube of moisturizer.

"It'll be cold on the plateau. Windy, dry. Your skin and lips might crack."

She looked impatient. He often overpacked.

"The weather should be better by now."

Wearing backpacks and light jackets with thermal lining and heaters, they re-emerged and pushed aside the growth.

Sunlight shone in low beams, the mist thinner.

Hints of vegetation lurked around them, vines, flowers, still with that feeling of abundant moisture. Sharp aromas saturated the air, as if water pooled in flowers and intensified their scent. The altitude made the temperature cool but the mist was like insulation, wooly and damp. The sun awoke glowing spots.

Ranglen smiled. He felt he was inside a smoky gem, gold amid gray. Womblike.

Braya taunted. "You're enjoying this, aren't you?"

"Aren't you?"

"It's too alien for me."

"That's the whole point. You're out of your environment. Places like this still exist on Earth but you'd never see them."

"Oh, I saw them. While I was in a concentration camp in Ecuador and then Brazil. But most of the jungle had been cleared. It was all barren, cold, or hot. I hated those places. What's the attraction?"

Ranglen tried to describe what he felt—the mystery of new exploration, of open wandering and being adrift, of becoming a new person in a new world.

She wasn't impressed. "You sound like a priest or a Seeker. Or maybe a stalker."

"Only of landscapes."

She groaned.

"So, you said you were a refugee?"

"It doesn't define me so don't call me that."

Ranglen kept quiet.

They moved away from the ship and then looked back to get a good view of it. It had been dragged across the ground where it had torn up a mass of brushy mud and shredded plants, but it looked unhurt. The cause of the disturbance could not be seen. Ranglen checked the ship more closely and confirmed what his instruments had said—there was no great damage and the ship would still fly.

He returned to his cellpad and found the trail. They moved off along it and into a dense world of growth.

A sea of leaves, where pockets of mist glowed yellow-green and seemed like drifting living creatures. Trees stood on enormous brace roots like supporting legs. Festoons of translucent purplish-blue growth dangled from the forest's ceiling in narrow organic stalactites. Limbs dripped with bromeliads, epiphytes, air plants, parasites, in many different colors and shapes, some with petals like drooping tongues, some with flat distended bladders or misshapen balloons. Diaphanous insects flitted in busy crystalline clouds, and the high canopy buzzed with noise—flittering, rustling, squeaks and chirps. Branches swayed or snapped above their heads where monkey-like or spidery creatures used long limbs to scurry about, seen only briefly, more suggested than real.

"It's a cloud forest," Ranglen said, "which is not your typical tropical forest or jungle. Those are denser and lower in altitude. Cloud forests are found in the heights. The undergrowth is thicker because sunlight penetrates more—when there's no fog, which is seldom. But this trail looks easy."

Braya scoffed. "The smells remind me of a swamp city, where the water levels have invaded. Places in Florida were like this—without the growth but with all the smells of muck and filth."

The vegetation opened in places to show further slopes, where clouds slid up from the depths below, like gray claws clutching at the mountain. Bigger clumps moved more sluggishly. The sun, higher now, lost itself behind drifting vapors like prowling ghosts communing in the sky. Ranglen remembered Anne saying she wanted her office to be among the clouds. He didn't think she'd want it in this way.

As they walked on, everything was soft, lush, and damp, the fat leaves leathery and shiny, always wet, always dripping. Noise amplified when the mists closed in and the forest darkened. Ground squished beneath their feet and resembled skin. One shrub had big green leaves with burgundy veins that looked like wine. Or blood. Falling branches cracked on impact like rifle-shots. A tree stump, where it had broken, was coated with a vivid reddish sap—as if it were bleeding.

Then came a loud sound behind them—an upturning of earth, a churning of breaking branches or trees.

Ranglen looked back down the trail. *"The ship!"*

He ran. Braya followed.

They reached the spot where they'd landed. The ship had disappeared. All that was left was a hole in the ground filled with brush where the vessel had sat.

Then the ship heaved up again, pushed violently from below on a mound of dirt so covered with branches that what caused the lift could not be seen.

It rose higher, stood almost erect. Then the nose tilted and the whole vessel fell back into the ground, plummeted below into the earth.

The craft disappeared in a vast roar, as if sucked into a pit or a large tunnel beneath the surface. The mound sank too and filled up the opening.

Then, just for a second, Ranglen thought he saw, in the crushed dirt and sinking mess, a shudder of strangely organized movement, like the flexing of a muscle, or the stirring flank of a breathing creature.

A glossy, palm-sized eye glanced at him.

Then all fell below.

They walked to the pit. Clouds of dust and leaves swirled. They looked down into it but could see nothing, only packed dirt and torn plants. Whatever hole had swallowed the ship was now fully covered over and blocked.

Ranglen and Braya stood motionless, too astounded to react.

She spoke first, in a drained voice, "So, we're stranded?"

"I have a communicator that can reach that base, but I don't think we should use it yet, not until we know what we're getting into."

"Then we stay with the plan and walk there first?"

"Seems best. We can ditch the com or say it didn't work depending on what we find there."

They were still in shock and reluctant to start out. They adjusted their packs but only as an activity that might distract them.

Braya said, "I hope this wasn't planned by Muletti."

"I can't believe he brought us here just to have this happen. Maybe we should have landed even farther away."

"Or maybe this is what Krin meant when she called the place 'Hell.'"

Ranglen was still too troubled by it all—the suddenness, the muscle-like movement, and then, at the end, the parting "eye."

He forced himself to put it behind him. "Let's get started. It's better than just standing here. They should know at the base what caused this and have the equipment to dig us out."

He gave one last stare at the mound, not admitting that he looked for an eye that might look back.

Then, neither of them saying any more, they walked off down the trail again, now their only direction of hope.

An hour or so later, they heard a waterfall grow louder as they neared it. The howling inspired thoughts of inundation, drowning. But when they glimpsed it in a chasm below, they were surprised by how small it was.

The cloaking mist encouraged such deceptions, the humidity even affecting sound.

Ranglen tried to be practical. "Later, we might have to wring out our clothes and dry our boots."

They lost sense of time. They felt too enclosed, absorbed in a rotting half-world that lay indistinct behind gray veils. There was no horizon and little sense of depth, just claustrophobic layers of mist.

"What made this trail? Animals?"

"I assume."

"How big would they be?"

"Big enough." At another time Ranglen might have tried not to be ominous, but after the loss of the ship it didn't seem necessary.

Then a large animal *did* pass near them, cracking branches and jostling the leaves. They saw vaguely a low body on short legs, a fat neck, two tusks on a warthog snout.

Ranglen's hand moved slowly toward his pistol, carried now on the outside of his clothes in an accessible holster.

The beast prowled away into the mist.

They moved on, quieter than before.

"We're coming to the 'kink' in the trail," Ranglen said.

Before them lay a set of ruins.

It, at first, looked like Airafane ruins, the stone structures that were exactly the same on every planet where they were found. Ranglen was surprised and nervous. He once had much to do with such ruins, involving his past trip to Alchera, the experience of which, though dim to him now, was still associated with dark emotions. He had visited many such places on different planets so he knew their layout.

But he saw immediately that these were not genuine, just clever imitations. The stonework was not as advanced, the construction crude. The rocks didn't fit together precisely, the outlines of the top walls varied, and the rooms were not as big as they should be. These structures were made only to *mimic* Airafane ruins.

But why? Were they part of some primitive rite? Religious symbolism?

And if they stood here, then genuine ruins from the Airafane must exist somewhere on the planet (how else would pre-spaceflight natives, even if present, know of them and how they appeared in order to imitate them). Or maybe the locals—whether natives or human visitors—knew of interstellar transport and had seen an Airafane site off-world. When approaching the planet, Ranglen saw no signs of intelligent indigenous life, the night hemisphere being fully dark, so he wasn't convinced the structure was built by unseen natives.

Were people from the base then responsible? But again, why?

"They look too recent," Braya said.

"They're just an imitation of Airafane ruins, and they apparently weren't meant to be exact—they're *intentionally* crude, and erected quickly." Ranglen then wondered, "If the Seekers of the Mountain are supposed to worship the Airafane and their Clips, maybe this is some kind of temple for them."

"I never heard of them having 'temples.' And we're still far from the base, right?"

"Maybe that's the point. An isolated and secluded spot. A retreat."

"But who would want to retreat all the way to here?"

Ranglen didn't answer. He walked into the stone structure.

Braya stayed where she was. "The trail winds around. We can just keep following it."

Ranglen felt she didn't want to delay by visiting the place. "I need to see what's in here, maybe find why they were built."

She followed reluctantly.

Ranglen walked farther into the structure, then stopped in front of what looked like a shrine—an archway built from stone, a frame for a flat rock table that sat underneath. But this was not present in other Airafane ruins. And hanging from the top of the arch was a platter with the stonework above it darkened by stains—as if the dish held a fire whose smoke had blackened it. The table inside the arch was also discolored. Beside it stood two metal staffs set in the ground, their tops bent into hooks. And a small bundle, no bigger than a fist, dangled from each of them.

Braya moved up behind Ranglen and said quietly, "I know what this is."

"An altar stone? For ritual sacrifice?"

"Yes, I believe."

"But what, or who, was being sacrificed?"

"I heard stories at the Ecuador spaceport about workers on Ventroni, those who labor under dangerous conditions at mining camps in remote mountains. One method the companies use to keep them working is to make them believe in blood sacrifices—a ritual to provide protection in the mines. They generally use animals, but they also entice innocent workers with promises of money. The ritual supposedly provides immunity from death…at least for a while."

Dark uneasiness stirred in Ranglen. "That's probably why the people who built this place didn't care if it was artificial. It was only meant to frighten and coerce. Maybe they use just animals, since there seem to be no local 'innocents.'"

"Is this what Muletti intended us to see? Did he mean to scare us, make us turn back?"

"Or is it a warning to show us what we're getting into?"

Then Ranglen looked more closely at the bundles hanging from the hooks.

They were shrunken heads.

Like the one he saw in Anne's office. She, too, had claimed they were only animals. Good-luck charms. Holy relics.

"Let's go," he said. "We still have a climb to make." He hurried out of the ruins and onto the trail.

Braya followed.

He glanced at the stone walls as they passed them on the trail. They seemed outlandish now, cheap, overdone, an infestation brought into the peace (or gloom) of the forest—whose natural life around them continued, certain, persistent, uncaring.

Ranglen wanted to enter that realm, become absorbed by it.

Braya intruded. "Krin loved her stories, and she told me how legends built up around the Airafane."

"What do you mean? And how does that relate to what we just saw?"

"No one understands the Airafane, of course, so people have to make up explanations for them. Thus, all we get is what we imagine. And that was enough for her—the stories

130

didn't need to be true, they could *become* true if we believed in them enough. Like Airafane at Stonehenge. Weren't there blood sacrifices there?"

"That's never been proven."

"But, you see, it doesn't matter. These ruins are fake, but they can still be a temple. Everything's just a story, she argued, and all we eventually find is ourselves. I'm sure that's how the name 'Depot of the Dead' got started. Krin, or some other Seeker, made it up and now it's real. We see only what we want to see, find only what we intend to find."

"So what's your point?"

"The universe isn't haunted by the Airafane. It's haunted by us. *We* are all we'll ever encounter."

Ranglen knew what she meant, but he didn't agree. "We mix our imagination with the new. We become inspired by what we find. We combine what we are with it, our ideas stirred by the discoveries. We make more than the sum of the parts."

Braya snorted. "Look around you, Mykol. We come to a new planet—which you called 'beautiful' when we first arrived. And what do we find?"

He didn't answer.

"Shrunken heads."

After his continued silence, she added, in sympathy, "What did you expect me to say?"

Chapter 13: On the Plateau

Braya was tired.

Ranglen, no brutal taskmaster, allowed for plenty of stops and rests. But she was unused to steady physical activity. It had been too long since she worked at a spaceport, and her legs and feet grew sore. She became overheated as they hiked but then chilled when they stopped.

And she found nothing appealing about a landscape which Ranglen seemed to love. Did he forget they were stranded here? She couldn't understand him. He walked through horrors down in the ruins, yet still saw beauty as he moved on.

They trudged up a narrow passage between huge rocks for over an hour. It wasn't too difficult—they found enough handholds and the foot-path was manageable—but she still breathed heavily and her heart hammered. She neared the edge of her endurance.

Then the rocks grew smaller, the path leveled, and, at last, they emerged onto the open plateau. And there, in one burst, she could see for miles.

The land rolled and swayed before her in thin elevations, looked barren. It swept to either side of her and appeared stained and corroded, creased with wrinkles as if showing its age, maybe left out in the sun too long with its skin cracked, blistered and dry. A few plants grew, low and in scattered clumps, pale green, silver, beige. Swaths of yellowish grass encircled small lakes, more like puddles nested in slopes. Everything looked worn or smoothed out, crusty, old.

Braya's mind, at first, retreated as it had so often in the jungle. She wasn't used to such wealth of detail, and the forest below had been too intense, cloying, close, and what she saw there often repelled her—like walking through an urban sewer. But now, here, everything spread out into an open map. The colors were not intense but gentle. The cold was harsh and the air bitter, but the vastness made her feel alive again, opened her to what lay outside her.

She was reminded of looking at Annulus with Hideki.

And she suddenly became eager to move forward, to enter this wide, unframed picture. Was this what Ranglen normally felt?

"Volcanoes," he said, pointing ahead.

Slopes reached up to peaks with plumes of white.

"Probably steam from fumaroles, hot water pushed up through the earth. Expect to feel tremors now and then."

This darkened her enthusiasm.

A huge bird, or maybe a reptile, passed above them, with a two-meter wingspan, red face, wrinkled neck, and yellow beak like a curved knife.

It paid no attention to them, rose and faded in the high haze.

"We're exposed here," she said. "We need cover."

"We'll stick to the rocks."

"Are we totally above the clouds now?"

"The moisture from the oceans doesn't reach this high. That's why the plants are so small. Colder temperatures are an influence, too. The plants stay low to protect themselves from the wind."

Mossy clumps close to the ground had tiny red and white flowers.

Ranglen pulled out gloves for both of them and switched on heaters in their jackets. "The air is thin and doesn't hold warmth for long. The nights could be rough. The air will swoop down from the mountain slopes into the low pressure above the plateau. We shouldn't be here that long, though."

She tried to take a deep breath, strained to do so.

"I should have mentioned the elevation. If you feel light-headed, you might be close to fainting. Don't wait to tell me, just get close to the ground so you don't fall and break an ankle. If you feel nauseated, then definitely sit."

This didn't reassure her.

He kept them away from the low plain and stayed to the rocks on the plateau's edge, which was slightly higher. The wind sometimes blew strongly, raised plumes of dust. "It's just the daily transfer of air between plains and slopes," Ranglen explained, "not a sign of coming bad weather."

Braya watched him as they walked, as the wind obscured him or rendered him clear. She didn't think he noticed her watching him, but maybe he did.

He noticed a lot.

She appreciated his calm efficiency, his ability to know and use what he learned. But she wouldn't let him be aware of this, even if he likely guessed. And she didn't appreciate his unstated assumption that she didn't understand things or lacked education (she felt she knew quite a lot but it had been gained strictly on her own, in the off moments during her jobs). He was patronizing and didn't recognize it—which made it worse.

What scared her, though, and what she often resented, was his analyzing her, or what she saw as analysis—breaking her down, opening her up, making her believe more in *his* knowledge than her own. She wouldn't allow it. She knew what she wanted or at least assumed she did. And since she didn't know what *he* wanted, she refused to let his goals entice her and pull her away from her own. And he didn't seem to know what he sought, anyway. He looked at this landscape as if he'd longed for it—not to possess it but to know it fully, to somehow join with it. To become something other than himself.

Well, good luck with that. And let me know if it works. I'm more worried about getting off this planet.

When Ranglen found a natural shelter and wind-screen among the boulders, he paused and let her sit and eat. She didn't want to stop walking but he insisted. Energy bars, heated mush, tea—they needed it.

"Rest for a while. I want to look ahead, check Muletti's route. There's no trail now so we need to be careful."

Then he left her.

She grew suspicious. But she also was tired. If she shut her eyes briefly she'd be instantly asleep.

Ranglen had moved out of sight, beyond the rocks around her, apparently searching for a position where he could see ahead—and where, she felt, he wouldn't be seen by her.

She fought to keep herself awake. And after a few moments, she followed him.

She stayed hidden and reached a point where she could see where he was sitting. He did have a good view of the distance before them.

But he seemed to be looking through something he held in his hand, something small and thin, transparent, like a piece of glass or plastic. She couldn't make it out.

He quickly placed the object back in a container and hid it away. Whatever he had been looking for he apparently didn't find—his expression stayed blank. He started to turn, maybe to check if he was being watched. She quickly moved behind the rocks, sure he hadn't seen her.

She always suspected Ranglen had secrets. Now she was sure. But she didn't know what.

She stepped openly from her hiding spot and joined him, sat beside him as if she'd seen nothing.

"Feeling better?" he asked.

"I wanted to know what you were doing."

"Afraid I'd leave you?"

"Why would you leave me?"

"No reason. I didn't intend to."

"Then why ask?"

He shrugged. "Never mind."

They stared at the landscape's stark reality and grandeur. She was beginning to appreciate it, see it through his eyes. She liked that it didn't deceive, that after all the hypocrisy, greed, and lies she encountered, she now could admire its flat honesty.

She said, "You don't talk much, do you?"

He smiled disparagingly, did not answer.

"I bet your ideal for conversation is two learned and wise people, very knowledgeable, talking elegantly to each other...maybe in poetry."

A small laugh. "No. Not poetry. That would be difficult. And they don't have to be 'learned' at all. But I would want them to be *sensitive*, so we could talk in lines filled with special clarity and feeling, with shared delights—easy, unforced, and unusually free."

"You'll never have that."

"I can long for it."

"It's impossible. No one is like that. You just want an image of yourself back."

"Then why would I be here talking with you? You have a no-lie directness I appreciate. You're like this landscape—hard, uncompromising."

But this was exactly what she feared, his attempt to understand her, to summarize her. "Let's go," she said, before she grew angry.

They returned to the shelter and then quickly moved on.

For another hour, they weaved through the rocks and negotiated the distance before them. At times, the trail opened to strange sights, like plumes of steam from nearby geysers, which they could hear gurgling when they stopped walking. They passed close to one and saw a raised mound with bubbling water in a terraced pool. Streams of red-brown, orange, and green emerged from it, vivid in this drab, whitened setting.

"The terraces build up from minerals in solution. The colors come from algae that flourish in warm water."

A strong smell of rotten eggs. And when they moved on, a taint of burning lingered in the air. "More sulfur, from volcanoes. It can sting the nostrils."

134

"Are you sure no eruptions are likely?"

"I doubt it. I don't see signs of old lava flows, like the kinds of eruptions we saw on the planetoid. The outbursts here must be in clouds of steam and gas, which eventually cool and fall as ash. Pumice, it's called, with a lot of air bubbles, like a hot froth that solidifies."

"Is it dangerous?"

"Very much so. The clouds can move fast, become a wall of searing ash that crushes the land and burns up everything. And I do see signs of that, like those round pancake rocks over there. They come from lava bombs, melted chunks of flying stone that's still fluid when it hits the ground. Some of those small hills"—he pointed—"are really spatter cones made of cinders."

"Are you trying to scare me?"

"I'm trying to stay sharp and be observant."

"It makes me wonder—why are these camps built in such dangerous places?"

"Something must attract them, like the metals on 82A. I, at first, thought the ruins might be the draw for this world, but they're fake. Still, something's here they must want...whoever 'they' are. I'm mighty curious to know what it is."

"Maybe it's whatever swallowed our ship."

Ranglen only grunted.

The last of the haze above them disappeared. The sun came out and glowed fiercely. The beige of the landscape burned whiter, painfully bright, and its yellow deposits—of sulfur, Ranglen said—glowed like fire. The sky away from the sun was dark blue, almost indigo. He brought out sunglasses for both of them.

Braya looked at the sky through the lenses—and saw a tiny moving object. "Is that a ship?"

"Get down! Quick!"

They dropped to the earth and hid behind rocks.

The object passed over them at a high distance and moved in the direction where they were headed.

After a time, and feeling relatively safe, they stood back up.

"A ship from the base?"

"I assume. Probably an atmospheric craft. It wasn't following a surveillance pattern, and it would have come back if it saw us. We were lucky."

Braya wasn't sure about his identification. It looked like a small spaceship to her... maybe even...

They continued on, not speaking.

Ranglen said they were nearing the base.

But before they reached it, an incident delayed them. And after it occurred, Braya felt she had a better understanding of Ranglen.

They came up over a rise, and what they saw from there impressed both of them. They stood in mutual silence and stillness.

Spread across the flat plain below was a field of huge white spikes, like a regiment of tall soldiers in white uniforms. They were wide at the bottom but narrowed upward to a knife's edge. The tallest of them, in the middle of the field, stood about seven meters high. And they all leaned in the same direction.

Braya said, astounded, "They can't be natural."

"But they are." Ranglen's voice filled with awe.

She glanced at him. His face was almost childish with admiration, the blue eyes keen and alive. "They're called 'penitent formations,' and they're a purely logical scientific phenomenon. They're made by dense snow which has sublimated, not melted. This once had to be a huge field of snow that was very deep. But indentations in the surface caused it to sublimate into the air. The grooves got deeper till they reached the ground, leaving these shapes, like religious figures leaning forward and praying—hence the name."

She confessed to herself that she was impressed.

"Let's go down among them," he said with eagerness. "I've never been close to formations this big, or so many of them."

He didn't wait for a response. He hurried between the smaller spikes into the center of the field, where huge claws rose above them, the snow dirty and very hard. The objects were like wedges struck into the earth, or sharpened stalagmites meant to impale flying creatures, like a huge grater rising up through the ground.

She watched Ranglen speak—he was in his glory. "On very cold planets where the ice is like rock, you can find these same objects, but much bigger, overlapping on top of each other. They can make a whole landscape of fat swords. They were discovered on Pluto, but I've seen them elsewhere."

She had to ask, "You love this, don't you?"

"Of course I do—and, incidentally, this proves you wrong, what you claimed back at the ruins. This is *not* a reflection of just ourselves. It comes from outside us. We didn't make it. It's purely natural—part of the 'newness' you said didn't exist."

Braya didn't argue, but she didn't let herself be convinced by him either. She had seen too much the opposite of what he said.

They didn't stay long. Ranglen led them back to the trail—where she couldn't help muttering, "We still bring ourselves."

"But if we're open to the new, if we don't try to conquer what we find, if we *savor* it instead of consuming it, then we can be changed by what we encounter. The universe can be left pristine, and we can become its consciousness."

"That sounds too much like religion to me. Maybe you should join the Seekers."

"All I say is just humanism meeting materialism, the belief we are best when we're aware and open, when we recognize what's outside of ourselves."

"It sounds too lonely, Mykol. These places aren't very friendly, you know. You won't be kept warm by your 'penitents' out there. They're hard to cuddle up to."

He still smiled, untouched and serene. But to her, he was caught up in superior understanding, feeling only a gracious tolerance for those who can't comprehend.

Still, she wouldn't criticize him to his face—though that hadn't stopped her before. She only said, "Do you think the Airafane felt the same way?"

"I hope they did. I'd ask them if I could."

"Would you like to meet them?"

"I'd give everything in my life for it."

Braya was struck. Ranglen was usually evasive and ironic when talking of himself. This was a sudden revelation.

But she thought no more of it. They walked on in silence.

An elevated ridge formed a rocky path that led them farther upward. As they neared the crest, Ranglen made them both lie down so they could crawl to the edge and look over without being sighted.

The base lay before them.

It was larger than Braya expected. It had a medium-sized barracks or bunkhouse that could hold workers, then two larger buildings that resembled dormitories. They would accommodate a lot of people, but no one seemed around to inhabit them yet. One was still under construction, its framework exposed, and the other seemed only recently completed since building material still lay around it. Smaller storehouses sat scattered about beside a landing field with a sizable hangar on its far side. Only a few ships sat there now, none of them large, one a light transport and a few smaller craft probably used to survey the planet and limited to only atmospheric travel.

Then Braya thought she saw, inside the open bay-door of the hangar and mostly in shadow, a wasp-like Homeworld military fighter.

The *Killer*.

"That's it!" she almost screamed.

"What? What is?"

"Inside that hangar! The fighter that destroyed the *Lochner* and the base on 82A. Can't you see it? It's partially hidden but still there."

Ranglen looked where she pointed. "I'm not sure that's it."

"*I'm* sure! Let's get closer just to be certain." She was so excited she couldn't stop herself. She leapt up and started down the slope, not caring who might be watching.

"No! Wait!" Ranglen ran after her, pulled her back to their viewpoint in the rocks.

She fought against him. He pushed her to the ground. She tried to kick him, but he held her with his weight. "We have no cover. We need to stay here."

"You're not stopping me!"

"We *will* go down there but not yet."

"I'm not waiting, not till you feel things are perfect. We're stranded, remember? That ship must have flown here right after destroying the other base. That's why Muletti made us take the long way—so it wouldn't see us. But we managed to get here, and we need to act while we have the chance. We—" She knew she wasn't making sense, just pushing against his restraint and trying to *do* something.

"Braya, please. Those two bigger buildings are meant to house a lot of people. I don't know what's happening here."

"They look empty now. No one's around."

"And that's the problem. There's a whole landing field out there and at least one transport ship, so there has to be people."

"I'll go down on my own if you don't want to come."

"I promise we'll get there. Just let me—"

Then came the sound of another vessel, the low whine of an approaching ship.

They both tried to blend into the rocks and remain still.

This ship was tiny, and it looked old, appropriate for the thin drone it made. It seemed to descend with almost hesitation onto the landing field.

Braya writhed, again wanted to yell. "That's the *third* ship, the small one, the *Spy!*"

"How can you tell?"

"I saw it! I'd know it! They're *both* here now. Muletti was right. This place has the answers. Everything we want to know is here."

She raised her head to look more closely—but this time she also tried to stay hidden.

A wave of satisfaction struck her. She had *arrived*. She'd now reached where she'd wanted to go, but she also achieved what she wanted to *be*—a directed force, a means to an end. Her moment of Krin-like hysteria was past. The goals of her actions were confirmed now, so she could plan more carefully. Maybe only impulse had gotten her here but this was bigger, better—*hers*.

Ranglen moved close beside her and looked down to the installation. "I think you're right. Muletti did us well." He added, "It's a good thing you didn't kill him."

She didn't respond, for at that moment the hatch in the small ship opened.

And Braya recognized who emerged—the crazy hair, the bizarre outfit.

Hideki.

Chapter 14: Basecamp

Ranglen was afraid Braya would go wild.

She almost cried, "Why the hell would she be here?"

"Are you sure it's her? Maybe it's Krin. They look alike."

"No. She walks with Hideki's determination. It stands out more. Krin's not as confident. It's her all right."

Hideki entered the building that resembled a barracks. No one else came out of the ship.

"If that's the *Spy*," Ranglen said, "the ship used in the attack, then how did Hideki get it? You said she was on Annulus when she found you."

"That's what she *said*. But it might not be true. She could have been sent in to get me after I was found—maybe by the Seekers under the Ring, who then told her. But it doesn't matter. We need to get on board—*that* ship, specifically, more so than the other one."

"Why not the fighter?"

"Because Muletti's ship didn't have anything significant. I kept my eyes open when I was there. And I bet the *Killer* will have only weapons. But this last ship is too peculiar. It's *old*. Just look at it! It doesn't fit the other crafts at all. There has to be a reason why it was used, and I'm sure we'll learn that by going inside—and why Hideki is connected to it."

Ranglen nodded but he was unconvinced.

"Come on, Mykol. I'm ready now. Let's get going."

He examined the slope between them and the base. A gulley led toward the half-constructed dorm, the building closest to them. It wasn't much cover but at least they'd be partially out of sight.

"You know what we need?" she said. "A good diversion, like what they did back at Rimport 3."

"Sorry, I'm not like the Seekers—I don't carry explosives."

Braya grunted.

Ranglen stared at the base with a fierce longing to know what was going on. The gulley didn't seem as safe now.

But they started out anyway. He set aside the packs they had carried and hid them in the rocks, taking nothing except their cellpad communicators and small hand weapons.

They went only a short way before they got the diversion they needed—but it was more peculiar than what they would have asked for.

A roar, followed by a deep-throated wail, rolled across the landscape, strangely and frightfully alien. Huge, cavernous, like a fog horn being slowly strangled, or the dying scream of a crushed bull.

Behind the base and off to the right rose a line of barren hills, and the sound came from that direction. A wide walking trail, not artificial but made by many feet over time, led from the barracks and beside the hangar to a dark opening at the top of a slope, possibly a cave, which might be where the howl emerged—followed now by spastic cries and whining screams.

It was a call for attention, a plea, a labor.

People emerged from the barracks and the other small buildings, the spaceships, too. Not many, skeleton crews. And this crowd moved up the trail toward the cave.

They didn't hurry but they seemed transfixed, all walking at the same pace with their heads forward in bizarre silence, stepping in the same determined direction toward the cave. They didn't resemble brainwashed zombies—their postures were relaxed and they didn't move in lockstep—but they walked with obvious shared purpose. And the wailing seemed almost a known signal for everyone to stop what they were doing and join in this communal gathering, leading to the cave.

Ranglen looked for Hideki in the columns but couldn't find her. "They all seem to be leaving."

"Good! It's our chance."

He agreed, but he was suspicious of the whole situation, the strangeness of it, how suddenly odd everything had become.

They edged downslope, following the gulley of the old stream bed. At the end of it, they'd have to cross open ground, but Ranglen hoped by then that most people would have left the camp.

The two spaceships, the transport carrier that had been here when they arrived and the small ship that just landed and contained Hideki, as well as several hovercraft, sat on the far side of the base, in front of the low hangar where the *Killer* was held. Ranglen, like Braya, assumed that's what the vehicle was, since such discarded fighters would be extremely rare. The two of them would have to pass most of the buildings before reaching the small ship. This included the semi-finished dormitories, the barracks, and a few smaller structures of uncertain purpose.

As they drew close, they could see no one roaming about. Everyone apparently had moved up the hill to the cave entrance and then down into it. The strong animal calls had stopped, but strange noises still came from there—high-pitched whistles like that of birds, the piping of a primitive musical instrument, group chants, rhythmic pulses deep and earthy as if from a throat far underground, even an occasional, if half-hearted, scream.

These were disturbing and made Ranglen feel fragile, on the edge of a mystery he wasn't sure he wanted to uncover—which only made him more desirous to know it.

And, as if reading his mind, Braya said, "We're not going up there."

Was she growing more cautious? Or maybe she didn't want the cave competing with her fixation on the ship.

He nodded at the cave on the hill. "I think we've found the source of the Seekers, maybe even the 'Mountain' they're after."

Braya didn't comment.

They passed the large building that was still being constructed, made of the light but strong composite that replaced wood—though wood would be plentiful on this world. It showed how quickly the base had been built.

The exterior walls weren't fitted yet, and they could see the lay-out of the rooms—a large number of them identical and set around a huge central area. It did look like a dormitory, as they had guessed, but it would be cramped and was cheaply planned. If meant to hold a lot of people, it would be crowded.

The next building looked the same, completed but maybe only recently used. Signs of one-time habitation showed in the graffiti splashed on the exterior—unknown shapes and diagrams, undefined figures wielding weapons, a few scrawled phrases like "bottomless hell," "Moyocks of hate," "Little Redemption."

And many eyes.

"The Seekers, like I said."

Braya still didn't comment. But she looked angry as she stared at the dorm.

"What's wrong?" he asked her.

"I know what this building was made for. Refugees. I've lived in places like this. A lot of the people would be held in only the central opening, all packed together. I bet this is where the people from the *Lochner* would have been brought and then sold— where *I* would have been brought—if they hadn't been killed. And that's why Krin called this place Hell. It's for human trafficking."

She walked on. She did not look again at the building.

Then, before they reached the landing field, they passed a smaller structure painted dull yellow. It apparently had come pre-fabricated and was built here from a purchased plan. It looked simple but solid enough. The door was reinforced, locked with complicated security mechanisms. The place must hold important supplies.

Ranglen believed it was an armory. He had seen a similar one at Muletti's camp on 82A. It would hold weapons—explosives, armament, missiles, guns—to supply pirates or privateers. The heavy bombs required to break up the *Lochner* would be too big so they must be kept in the hangar (such weapons were rare and expensive—Ranglen still wondered how they were obtained), but a lot of firearms could be stored here.

They moved on, still saw no one. The noise from the cave had diminished but a deep-throated thunder sometimes emerged.

They reached the landing field and passed the cargo transport, ideal for supplying a base like this with stores or personnel. It also could be used as the kind of mobile armory that Tarakov had spoken of. Or as transport for refugees from dying ships.

After passing the hovercraft used for local scouting, they came to the small roustabout, the ship they had watched land.

It was in no great shape. It needed a power-wash to clean away the dirt and then a good paint job. Some patchwork was obvious. Ranglen's semi-trained eye felt it was still functional at least, and a few recent upgrades were obvious, like the sensor array and the shell for the pilot's canopy. He waited for Braya to confirm his thoughts with her own experience—but her attention focused on only one thing.

"The hatch is closed but not locked. I can tell from here."

Ranglen also noticed. The security lights beside the door were deactivated.

No ramp was necessary to reach the entrance. The ship was low enough that a dropped step was enough for access.

Ranglen didn't trust such invitations. They were getting too common. "This smells like a trap, like at Rimport 3."

"The ship just landed. Maybe the door's not locked for more unloading."

"Or maybe someone's inside."

"It would be cramped for more than one person. If we don't try it, why did we come here? I say we go for it."

Ranglen sighed.

They approached slowly, looking for signs of activity inside or out. They saw none. They reached the step that led to the door.

But they didn't get to make any more choices.

Hideki stepped up behind them, holding a gun. She apparently had been hiding within the entranceway to the barracks, the door left open by the people who exited for the mountain. "I've been waiting for you," she said, with an unctuous sweetness.

Three workers followed behind her. They also had guns, and they spread out to form a partial circle about the two of them. It happened so quickly neither Ranglen nor Braya had a chance to react.

Hideki gestured to the three guards. "They'll do what I tell them. You're better off being compliant."

As one guard took their weapons, Ranglen realized he had seen the other two before—they were the Seekers who had been waiting at Tarakov's office. He recognized their threatening stare, and he had no doubt they'd obey Hideki.

Braya apparently recognized them, too.

"Yes," Hideki said to her, "they were with us when we went to Rimport 3. They're Mountain Seekers, but they're more than that too."

Ranglen had a guess about what she meant.

She lowered her pistol, allowed the three workers to keep their eyes on the captives. She didn't act now like the eccentric that Braya described, and she had changed clothes since emerging from the small spaceship. She had donned more functional overalls that were not spattered with decorations and pins. She had cleaned her face and pulled back her hair into a careful gray tail, and she now wore walking boots instead of sandals.

"You two can try running if you want, but you won't get far. If my three helpers here don't stop you, then a few others who are watching you will. Not everyone went up to the cave. I saw you coming when I flew over the plateau, but I knew already you would make it here."

She spoke serenely, not with Braya's claimed outbursts.

"And, by the way," she said to Braya, "you wanted to know who piloted the ships that attacked the *Lochner*. Well, for this small one—the *Spy* you called it—I'll freely tell you. *I* was the pilot."

Ranglen wondered how Braya would react, now knowing another of the pilots. She didn't change her outward expression but her stare became more intense and piercing.

"You're not surprised? You should be. I felt I played a very good part in fooling you."

Braya still remained controlled. "So you weren't there when I landed on Annulus."

"The Seekers let me know what happened. I came and used one of their huts, with my own additions. We were all quite surprised about a survivor so we had to take advantage of it."

Ranglen asked, "Then you're not one of the Seekers after all? You were just copying Krin?"

"Oh no, I'm *more* than a member. You could even say I'm their *founder*. We've encouraged rumors it began on Annulus or Earth, but it really started here on this world. Precisely, in that cave up the hill. From this very spot, it spread across space, though we helped it along, 'aimed it,' so to speak, created its philosophy and its worship of the Airafane. I was first to see the advantage of people's believing in it."

Ranglen could tell from Braya's fists that she was seething.

Hideki went on. "I've *seen* what's in that cave. It doesn't need to be exaggerated. It's no myth or fictionalized story for people like Krin. It's *real*. And, by the way, I did imitate Krin. I wanted the right look for someone deluded and a little crazy. It worked perfectly."

"What's in the cave?" Ranglen asked.

"It's not easy to describe. A huge component life-form, part of this system's deep past. I wouldn't have believed it was real if I hadn't seen it. It might have been present even when the Airafane and Moyocks were around, though we'd never know what form it took then. I wonder if either race created it, maybe in order to frighten, or devour, the other. It undergoes different manifestations—starfish, squid, crustacean, worm—but, of course, these are just human filters. It has nothing to do with the words we impose on it. We don't know what it is but it makes quite an impression. All the stories that leak out about it, like a 'Mountain with Eyes,' have been useful to us, justifying the Seekers. When you get close to it, you'll understand what I'm talking about. It's life-changing. It changed *me*."

Ranglen's curiosity fought with his fear.

"I'm taking you up to see it—to our little 'Mountain,' the watcher of us all. This is the real goal of the Seekers. We say they worship the Airafane but it's really this, though only a few of us know of it directly. It might even have been *meant* to create a cult, to keep people stunned and obedient. It doesn't seem to have any other function—beyond surviving and proliferating. It's only *inspiring*, hugely impressive, just there to make you feel small. A typical characteristic of a dark god, to be inscrutable yet powerful, to push you to your knees, make you ready for more worship. Look at Krin. Look at *them*." She indicated the three guards.

Ranglen asked, "Those three, they're from Ventroni?"

"Oh, yes. You're perceptive. They speak their own language, a dialect of one of the clans there, which luckily I know—I came from Ventroni originally. They understand us but they choose not to talk to us, and I wouldn't try to oppose them. They can be nasty though they keep to themselves. They built those ruins you passed in the forest, just so they'd have a special place for their rites and practices, which you don't want to see. You'd be terrified at what people still do in our day and age. It's hard to imagine."

"You knew we'd pass the ruins?"

"I knew the path you'd take and I knew what the creature in the mountain did to your ship. It *was* the same creature, by the way, though we call it the 'Mountain with Eyes,' creeping through the veins of this hill we're on. The creature hadn't spread that far yet when Muletti was here. You're lucky you survived. I could have met you along the trail but I thought it'd be good to wear you down a little, let you travel a long road to your final conclusion, which you're very near. Nothing will be the same for you after the cave."

"You worship it yourself?"

"Let's say I'm ultra impressed. It's spreading through the continent, maybe someday the whole planet, like some huge branching system with limbs and eyes. They really aren't eyes but small life forms in symbiosis with it, cysts or tumors, but they sure look like eyes. It even can warp nearby space, reach out to ships and pull them in. The power's not based on magnetism but gravity itself, a focused squeeze of space-time, as if it can tap the mass of the planet. That's how we found it. We wrecked here, like you, though we now get along with it. We provide it with our own sacrifices. You'll want to see that. You can even be a part of it. You'll want that, won't you?"

Ranglen glanced at the guards—their blankness was terrifying.

"You better not look at them. They'll never let you go. They have their own good luck charms, habits that started in the mines of Ventroni. You saw samples down in the ruins. But *my* charm is bigger. It fills the whole mountain. I'm not sure its victims even die. Maybe they're absorbed into the creature and turn into the 'eyes.' When I'm dying, that's where I want to go, up into the cave to be taken and absorbed by it, to find if it's true. So many people will come here in time, just to do the same."

Braya finally spoke, moved by her anger and not Hideki's self-serving mythology. "You take refugees here and then market them to colonies, right? That's the point of this place—to make more money for corporate or political lords. And you want your product to be pliable and easy to sell. That's what your creature *really* does. There's no worship or religion involved. It exists just to serve your greed."

The three guards moved closer. Even if they didn't want to understand Braya's words, they could sense her growing hate.

Hideki looked at her. "Ah, yes, Krin's little flame. You deserved that title. Yes, maybe you're right, the creature provides us with money or power, whichever you prefer. You can have religion or you can have an army. Refugees to sell or refugees to mold."

Braya spat at her.

A guard clutched Braya's arm and locked it behind her, pulled her away.

Hideki said something that made them unhand her, but they stayed near. "Be careful what you say, Braya. They'll turn you into one of their holy relics. You don't want that. And as for what you said, I'll be honest. I don't care about economics or politics. I just focus on the creature. You'll see what it's like. It will measure and define you, stare at you, discover what you are. You can call it transcendent or call it sublime. Or say it's just a real kick to your soul. It reaches inside you and squeezes you dry."

Ranglen almost yelled, "What do you want from us? Just tell us what it is and skip all these threats."

"I need to soften you, use what I have to make you my tool, my bargaining chip." She glanced at Braya. "You see, I *know* what you really have."

Braya screamed, "You don't know anything! You're insane!"

"Let's go for a walk."

She led both of them up the hill, followed closely by the three brutish guards.

"Or maybe it's *the* walk, the best and only walk. Everyone's in the cavern now enjoying their daily call and outing. You came just in time. Meet the 'God in the Cave'—it's the kind of story that Krin loved. You'll beg for my help. I'll even be kind to you. And then you'll tell me about being on the *Lochner*. You'll tell me what I want, what you saw. And then, of course, you'll tell me what you *have*."

Braya leapt for Hideki and tried to strike her. The two guards slammed her aside and threw her to the ground. The third guard grabbed Ranglen and prevented him from reacting.

"No!" Hideki stopped them. "Not yet! Not until she talks!" She coaxed the guards away and told Braya to stand up again. "Let's continue now, walk a little farther. We're almost there."

The foreboding in Ranglen grew unbearable. As they neared the cave, even the grass and small shrubs seemed to become vaguely sinister, as if an unknown life-force had invaded them, something dark and uncanny. The plants looked like coverings for mouths, vines seemed to crawl or expand, stones resembled internal organs. And everything turned to follow them. All this he knew he must be imagining, but the resulting sensations seemed real, as if something horrible stirred beneath the ground and affected the growth, saturated it, saturated *him*.

Hideki's words added to the effect. "The boundaries get weak as we approach. You can feel it, can't you? Borderlines turn into cross-overs. The first people who landed here thought the place was haunted, that the mountain contained a gateway through which alien life leaked into the world and spread through its caves, down its slopes. But I think it comes up out of the planet itself. It's *all* the mountain, oozing its way throughout the ground and, in time, becoming the world itself, spreading into it with outstretched fingers."

People emerged now from the cave, lazily returning to the camp, to chores, routine—after their daily break with a god of horror.

Ranglen tried to fight the mood, the sense of hugeness bearing down on him, the weight of incomprehensible force.

The entrance to the cave resembled a mouth, the tunnel leading down into a ribbed throat.

Hideki droned on. "People are gullible. They choose to believe what they want, what's most self-serving for them. They come here and find only a creature, but they think it's a god, or something built by the Airafane or the Moyocks. It makes no difference. It's superior to either race. It's left their memories far behind."

They heard a rasping from the cave, a strange fluting, clogged breaths.

"We encountered rumors about the mountain even before we got here, from superstitious space crews spreading stories. Such wild tales start in myth but end in reality, an actual hill inside a legend. Believers gathered to it, and then the Seekers sustained it and made it even greater. In a cave yet, an interior world. I don't think it's intelligent. It doesn't talk or build anything. It's just very large, very engrossed, very unknowable. You only have to feed it a body now and then."

Closer now, the air from the opening flowed warm and turgid.

"Some workers on Ventroni believe that a sacrificed victim unleashes an 'avenging soul,' which will attack the people who killed it. So to stop that spirit, it needs to be contained—as in, get this, a severed head. It doesn't have to be the victim's *actual* head. They use animals that look vaguely human when they're sealed and baked. Those creatures live in the jungle below, running through the trees. You probably heard them in the branches above you. I say this because I've often wondered if you, Braya, were an 'avenging soul' yourself, released after the killing of the *Lochner*. Krin probably called you that—saw you as some vague arm of vengeance. She loved those stories."

Braya swore at her.

They reached the cave. People walked past in the opposite direction, looked at them indifferently as if they were expected. Ranglen wondered if outsiders came here often. Tourists? Pilgrims?

The ceiling of the cave was wrinkled like the roof of a human mouth. It echoed with the noise of labored breathing—broken, gargling, like phlegm in lungs, or shredded logs in crowded rivers. Fires and torches lit the darkness.

"Better talk soon. It gets hungry. You'll become mesmerized and walk right into it. You're feeling it now. Better assure me you're about to speak. It's time to bargain."

Braya screamed, *"What the hell are you after?"*

"Oh, you'll tell me. In just a moment, you'll beg to talk."

The air was hot, the walls like skin, wet and glossy. The cave opened into a chamber with a huge pit inside. People stood around its rim. They all looked down into the wide hole.

Inside the pit stirred a round flattened eye, an emotionless orb, with concentric patterns of light and dark, an obsidian dome with dull golden nerves around it. Outside that dome stretched extended arms or tentacles, not like those of a starfish because there were too many and they weren't uniform, each one moving with a life of its own, with its separate mouths and tiny limbs. Some had lizard-like scales, some were encrusted in the plates of crabs, some glistened like raw flesh with the skin ripped off—all in an ugly cave pallor, as if the creature had never left this spot.

And, impossibly, it seemed to watch Ranglen directly, hypnotically, drawing him forward. Surely everyone there felt the same, the desire to be seen by the enormous 'Eye,' to understand it, to become part of it.

"Make your choice now," Hideki said. "Me, or that."

Braya leapt at her again, breaking the spell falling over Ranglen, and this time his Ventroni guard was distracted by the huge eye—as all of them were. Ranglen attacked him and reached for his gun.

Hideki yelled. Guards closed around Braya.

Ranglen wrestled the pistol away and then shoved his guard down the slope, toward the creature. A limb or tentacle covered with small openings—lathered mouths or wet suckers—wrapped around him and pulled him away. The guard screamed.

Braya kicked at another guard, and he tumbled down the slope.

Hideki lifted the last guard's arm that held his weapon and pointed it at both of them.

Ranglen fired. The guard bounced back, tripped, fell.

Hideki screamed.

Ranglen grabbed Braya and pulled her away. She kept trying to get at Hideki. Ranglen pushed her toward the entrance of the cave.

A gun fired behind them. Bullets struck the wall.

Ranglen and Braya ran into the open—where a high-pitched whine came from above, a hard drone that grew louder, fast.

Ranglen knew what it was. "Run! Run!"

He and Braya scrambled away from the cave's opening.

Ranglen looked back and saw Hideki emerge with her single guard. She looked upward—and, in her arrogance, she didn't move as the incoming missile sped down.

Ranglen pulled Braya among nearby rocks.

An explosion followed, but it was small, maybe just a warning. It did nothing to break the cave entrance and threw up only a cloud of dust from which pieces of broken rock fell.

Hideki staggered from the blast but still stood firmly. She even walked forward, looking indomitable and staring skyward with her anger.

Ranglen and Braya, under loose stones and earth covering them from the explosion, stood to see what was happening.

A large ship descended tail-first, making a controlled and accurate landing with loud steering jets. It was the same size as the cargo carrier but more sleek, almost military.

And this one did *not* have its insignia removed. It shone brightly on the side of the hull. Annulus Security.

Ranglen almost smiled. The cavalry, here to their rescue. They wouldn't be sacrificed after all, or tortured by the followers of an alien god.

"I think we've just been saved," he said to Braya.

She grumbled, looked annoyed and vicious.

And then, for some lurking, hidden reason, he didn't feel as relieved as he should.

Chapter 15: The Interrogator

The ship had grounded outside the landing field, as if, Ranglen thought, it didn't want to claim a connection to the base.

Hideki, still standing, looked more insulted than frightened. But the guard who followed her, and the other guard who managed to survive and now emerged (the third never appeared), walked away from her, abandoned her and mingled with the other people heading back to the base.

They wanted to fade away quickly, it seemed, as if the first sign of law-enforcement led immediately to running for cover. Ventroni tradition.

Four Annulus-Security officers, in light armor over their uniforms, emerged from the ship and ran up the slope to encircle Hideki, Braya, and Ranglen.

Hideki glared at the officers, stood her ground with proud defiance. Ranglen and Braya came up to them and remained stoic.

The officers were armed. They effectively surrounded the three of them but stayed at a distance. Ranglen noticed they seemed more intent on watching Hideki than him or Braya.

They listened to commands on their helmet communicators and responded quietly into their mics, obviously getting orders.

Two moved closer to Hideki, but the next officer said to all of them, "Please come with us. You're to be questioned."

Hideki still looked furious.

They moved toward the ship. Ranglen stayed vigilant but he was clearly glad for the interference from this substitute for an Annulus army. He never believed Hideki would have actually thrown them to the creature, but the situation had become too dangerous and, as was proven, accidents happened—he wondered about the guard who fell into the pit. The compelling nature of the whole scene, the gradual loss of self-control in him and others, was deeply alarming.

He looked at Braya, who now showed little outward expression. He envied how she could appear so withdrawn. But he assumed she was as attentive and vigilant as he was. Their glances at each other were quick and furtive, with no secret indicators or messages passed. She, like him, seemed to want to avoid attention and just learn what was happening.

When they reached the Annulus Security ship, they were joined by a tall figure who marched down the ramp, heavy-set but powerful, with a stern face and fringe of pale hair on a large and commanding head.

Tarakov.

Ranglen was not surprised.

The officer said, almost cheerily, "Hello, Mr. Ranglen. You have a way of getting into trouble, don't you?"

"No more than usual," Ranglen said. "You're a little out of your jurisdiction here, aren't you?"

Tarakov looked almost embarrassed. "Well, I have a bit more authority than what I led you to believe—I'm not just a security chief for Rimport 3."

Ranglen gave him a conspiratorial look. "I wondered about that."

"Really? I thought I covered it well."

"Just my supposition. Not only are you a member of Annulus Security, but I wonder if you also work for the Bureau of Intelligence. Were you undercover at the port? Your being here suggests that you're part of an unfolding investigation, and it now just might be coming to an end. Am I correct?"

Ranglen wasn't certain of any of this but he hoped it was true. They would need authority a lot higher than that of a rimport security director to clear up this mess.

"What makes you think that?"

"You wouldn't have access to a ship like this if you didn't."

Tarakov glanced up at the smooth lines of the formidable craft. He nodded, and again seemed embarrassed. "I guess I shouldn't be surprised. I underestimated you before. But I hope you're grateful for my presence. If my information about that cave is accurate, and my spies are good, then I just saved you from a gruesome fate."

"I thank you, profoundly."

Tarakov then turned to Braya. "And you were with Hideki back at Rimport 3. You broke into the Homeworld hangar, and then you left with Muletti in a spaceship after being abducted. Isn't that true?"

Braya said nothing, stayed rigid and stubborn.

Tarakov smiled. "Okay. I intended to let you two relax a bit, but maybe we should start the questioning immediately."

Hideki barked, "What about *me?*"

Tarakov turned to her with flat authority and said, "You're being taken into custody for questioning, prior to possible arrest."

"You are full of so much *shit!*"

He ignored her, said to the two guards who stayed close to her, "Take her inside to the holding cell. Keep her under watch."

She was led away, fuming.

He said to the last guard. "And put this one"—he indicated Braya—"into the waiting room by my office. Keep her comfortable, and if she wants anything, please get it for her."

Ranglen protested, but Tarakov said quietly and convincingly to him, "Neither of you are under arrest. I just need to question you separately. It's protocol."

Ranglen grunted, showed his displeasure.

"Just doing my job, Mr. Ranglen. And I'd like to question you first, if that's all right. I think you'll understand."

Ranglen wasn't sure if he "understood" anything but he said no more as Braya was taken away. She showed no reaction and didn't look at him.

"Let's go inside." Tarakov led Ranglen up the ramp into his spaceship and to a small meeting room, apparently used for such interviews. It was clean and functional, with a table, chairs, and nondescript cameras and screens, though they didn't look active.

There was even a mirror, which made Ranglen snicker a little—was a two-way mirror an interrogation mainstay?

Tarakov sat behind the table and let Ranglen perch across from him, a reversal on normal questioning procedures—*he* should be the one behind the table and facing the two-way mirror instead of Tarakov.

"Please know, our meeting is completely private. None of this is being recorded, and no one's standing behind that mirror. We're alone."

"You're the ranking officer on this ship?"

Tarakov nodded.

"Then tell me, is the young woman I was with under some kind of suspicion?"

"I just need to learn from her more about a number of matters. Would you like a drink of water?"

Ranglen nodded. He very much needed one, and he trusted Tarakov enough to believe it wouldn't be drugged.

Tarakov got him a bottle from a small refrigerator. Ranglen drank half of it in one gulp.

"Long day?"

"Very much so."

Tarakov began in a tone of formality but tried to be pleasant. "The last I saw of you was after the events on Rimport 3. I questioned you about what happened in the hangar and why your ship was defaced by the Mountain Seekers. Your answers were vague and incomplete, but I let you go, intending to follow up after I knew more. Then you left Annulus, which I expressly asked you not to do. And now, oddly, you turn up here. Could you explain how and why?"

"Is this preparation for something more official, an accusation of some kind?"

"Not necessarily, but I do expect you to cooperate."

For a host of reasons, Ranglen didn't want to be too revealing. "I was helping someone."

"Do you mean Anne Montgomery, the one who knew Aarov Muletti? Or do you mean the woman I just found you with, this 'Braya.'"

How did he learn Braya's name? But Ranglen wasn't surprised he knew about Anne. "Both, actually."

"Please elaborate."

"I already told you of the possible connection between a friend of mine and Muletti. That was Anne."

"So the story you told about writing a book was all a lie."

"No. I'm always writing books, and I'm always collecting information for them."

Tarakov nodded, though he looked unconvinced. "And this Braya?"

"Her situation is complicated, and I frankly know less than what you think I do. But I can say that both she and I are ignorant of what's going on here, that we were both captives and about to be fed to whatever creature—or natural force, or whatever it is—that lurks in the mountain, which was when you showed up."

Tarakov looked pensive. "I know a little about that creature…and also a little about what's going on here."

"Then you realize we have nothing to do with it. We're just visitors."

"But *why* you're visitors is the major question. Getting back to Braya—was she a refugee on board the cargo ship that was destroyed, the *Lochner*?"

Ranglen lied, remembering why Muletti wanted her. "I know she was a refugee, but I don't know for sure if she was on that ship. I heard everyone was killed. She heard rumors of other refugees turning up here. That's why we came. We both wanted to see what was happening to them."

"Seems like a foolish thing to do."

"I agree. And that's exactly what it turned out to be."

Tarakov pondered, and Ranglen waited.

He knew it all depended on Tarakov's reactions now. Ranglen wanted the formal help of Annulus Security but not until he could learn more. He was maneuvering for mutual gain, that both he and the law could support each other. But if Tarakov wanted to, he obviously could force information out of him.

And the officer took on a more threatening tone. "Frankly, Mr. Ranglen, you're in a very compromised position, and you have a lot of explaining to do. But you're not what I'm after right now. I came here because of a hunch, and I think I'm about to hit pay-dirt—in terms of finding out about piracy, human trafficking, sabotage, and all sorts of recent illegalities."

He let what he said sink in before he continued. "In the midst of all that, your own criminal acts—and I think there are several—don't concern me much. I'm almost willing to look aside, especially because your presence here can harm my investigation. But it also can help me, if in a way that might surprise you, and might even be to your benefit. So, I'm waiting before I 'come down' on you. And, in the end, I even might have a favor to ask. You'll not get off free, but if you can convince me that you've just been reckless, I might be understanding."

Ranglen knew not to say anything. A deal had been offered and it sounded generous. But he still wanted to be clear on which one of them was bargaining more.

And he guessed where Tarakov would lead next.

"The person I'm most interested in is Braya."

Ranglen didn't nod, said nothing.

"Shall we bring her in now for questioning?"

Ranglen was shocked. That Tarakov would go after Braya didn't surprise him, but that Ranglen would be allowed to be present was extraordinary. "You mean I can stay here while she's being interrogated?"

"Let's pretend, just for appearances, that you're her 'legal adviser.' She might be more open with you around. Besides, I want you to know what I'm after. I don't think you'd be happy if I was hiding anything."

Ranglen was still baffled, but also, maybe, beginning to comprehend. "All right," he said, though he wanted it to sound tentative.

"Good." Tarakov motioned to the outside guard to get Braya. And he said casually to Ranglen while they waited, in a guise of shared confidence, "I was joking about the legal advice. If you try to stop the questioning, I'll have you removed. But I really don't mind if you listen."

Ranglen then saw another point behind the permission to stay. Tarakov wanted to frighten him, to show that Ranglen was ultimately helpless before him.

Braya was ushered into the room and placed in another chair facing Tarakov. Ranglen's chair was pushed back a little.

Braya's look was hard and defiant. She stared at both of them but didn't seem surprised that Ranglen was present.

Tarakov started immediately. "Hideki once told me you were aboard the *Lochner*, the cargo ship that was destroyed."

Ranglen assumed Hideki had said this back at Rimport 3 after she had been wounded.

Braya didn't hesitate. "That's correct."

Maybe Ranglen's presence did made a difference.

"As far as we know, you were the only survivor."

"I saw no one else escape."

"You then fled the ship's destruction and crashed into Annulus, where you were found by Hideki and the Seekers of the Mountain. And then you and a few other Seekers raided Rimport 3. For what reason?"

"I was in search of the ships that destroyed the *Lochner*. I saw those that did it and I believed one was at the rimport."

Tarakov tried to hide his excitement. "Can you describe the ships to me?"

"One was medium sized, a standard rental, type-2 engines, normally four cabins."

"And you knew this how?"

"I've worked at spaceports on Earth. I'm familiar with the makes of various spaceships."

Tarakov looked down at his cellpad as if to confirm the claim, then told her to continue.

"It had carrier racks on both sides, holding short-range detonation missiles. These were used to break up the *Lochner*. It had no identification or registration. Both had been removed. But my inspection of the ship on Rimport 3 suggested it was the rental."

"Your 'inspection'?"

"I walked around outside the craft and then I went inside. I looked with open eyes."

She said nothing of Muletti's kidnapping, though Tarakov would know of it.

He didn't pursue the point but made a note on his pad. "Continue."

"A second ship was small, comfortable for just one person. It was old and patched-up, in a state of disrepair. A simple roustabout, maybe a prospector's craft, well-used. It didn't appear till the end of the destruction. It seemed to be looking out for the other two ships, like a spy. That's what I called it. I felt it was as responsible as the other ships for the killings, though it didn't participate as much. Missiles were shot from carrier racks on its sides, too."

She didn't say this ship was currently sitting near them on the landing field.

Then Braya described the last ship, the *Killer*, and Tarakov's interest grew even more. "The last one was the most destructive. It resembled a Homeworld military cruiser, small in size but very deadly, almost a fighter or attack craft. It looked like a hawk. It was brutally effective in slicing apart the ship with programmed missiles. The weapons were held in an interior pod under the fuselage with an opening in front. It also carried large, self-guiding bombs, four of them, big enough to completely destroy the *Lochner*."

Tarakov's attention was fully alert. "And there was no insignia on this ship either?"

"Nothing I could see."

"Have you encountered this vessel anywhere else?"

"It's sitting inside the hangar right here."

"*Here?* At this base?"

"I caught a glimpse of it. I'm sure it's the same one. Check yourself—you might have seen it on landing."

"We were focused on the cave." Tarakov glanced at Ranglen for confirmation.

Ranglen nodded. "I saw it, too, though not well."

Tarakov turned back to Braya. "But are you sure that's the one?"

"I haven't been able to get close to examine it. But how many military Homeworld fighters can be out there in free use? Chances are that's it. And I'll bet you'll find enough evidence in its computers and in residue of explosives on the hull, to establish a connection. Should be easy. All part of your job."

"Yes, yes..." Tarakov looked distracted, as if maybe lavishing in visions of future glory. "My people have been busy rounding up the workers here, confining them and questioning them, all routine. We haven't had a chance to search all the buildings. But what you say is...very interesting."

Ranglen wondered why Braya had pointed out that the *Killer* was here but not the *Spy*. Did she still have hopes of getting on board?

Tarakov closed up his cellpad and seemed quite pleased with the interview. "All right, that's enough for now. Braya, I thank you. This is a big help. I'll have more questions but I've gotten basically what I need. I have a room for you, and this guard will take you there." He gestured for the attendant. He also gave some further instructions to another officer, which Ranglen was sure sent him to the hangar to check out the claim about the fighter.

Braya was led away, and as she left she remained expressionless. She sent no glance to Ranglen, no secret look, which was either careful of her or subtly dismissive. Maybe she thought he now worked with Tarakov.

After she was gone, Tarakov looked preoccupied. So Ranglen asked, "The three ships and their pilots who attacked the *Lochner*...what will happen now?"

"The people who did this will be punished. And the information from Braya is perfect. Having a witness changes everything. We'll blow this case wide open."

He seemed eager to explain himself, so Ranglen waited for him to say more.

"That fighter was a Homeworld ship—the description fits precisely. And if it's the one that's here now, then we can prove it. We'll have clear evidence for another friend of yours, Aarov Muletti, and his connections to Homeworld. I know he's working for them. And the tie to them will be fully exposed. So that, ultimately, this will be a chance to make public just what Homeworld has been doing to us. It's perfect."

Ranglen added, suspiciously, "Perfect for whom?"

Tarakov was too excited to note Ranglen's dryness. "We've been trying for months to find a means of accusing Homeworld of its illegalities. The tariffs, the embargoes, all the troubles with Earth. This is finally our chance—the chance for *Annulus*, for us to stand on our own. If the politicians work this correctly, it will be our means of becoming independent. We all want it, but now the Confederation will support us, too. I'm thrilled by this, Ranglen. And you can help us."

"What? Me?"

"You can write about it, popularize it, present our side and show our cause to the whole Confederation. It's for Annulus, *your* world, remember? If more people get behind the effort then we can break from Homeworld and, at last, go on our own."

"You're talking about rebellion."

"No, of course not! I'm talking legal separation. This gives us the bargaining points we need, the political power. Homeworld going after an Earth ship in Annulus space— it's just the kind of crucial and wild event that can change history."

"But Homeworld will fight it. Earth might, too."

"Homeworld certainly, but we've got evidence. Even this base. It's obviously a Muletti operation. He and Hideki worked together on this. Muletti made a deal with Ventroni to raid spaceships and take away refugees, making tons of money by trafficking them to corporate colonies. This 'depot' was set up as a clearing house, a full market and stage for such people—refugees like Braya. The general public on Homeworld knows nothing about it, but their intelligence agencies would, and important people in the government. Their agent, Muletti, ran it all along. Even the Seekers—they originated with Hideki and were part of the plan. None of this is accidental. They've been in total charge since the start."

"You say even the Seekers was used by them? Or *created* by them?" Ranglen wanted Tarakov's version as well as Hideki's.

155

"Our intelligence has put the story together. Muletti liked to listen to old prospectors' tales, anyone who explored out along the fringe. Most of the stories are absurd but he, at least, listened. There was a legend about *this* world, where a huge creature dwelled in a mountain. I knew Hideki at the time. She was a pilot who landed occasionally at Rimport 3. She knew Muletti, and he hired her to take him to this planet. They found the creature, and *that's* when the Seekers of the Mountain originated. A 'Mountain with Eyes.' They encouraged the story by taking advantage of the people under the Ring on Annulus, too, who all along have been innocent and didn't want to bother anyone. Hideki was careful never to act as the 'leader' of the Seekers—they always claim they don't have any. But she was at the center of every development. The movement spread throughout space. 'Worship the Airafane, the wonderful Airafane.' Like a private, if very disorganized, army that could be used—for sabotage, piracy—and run by Muletti, agent of Homeworld."

"I'm finding all this hard to believe."

"Trust me, Ranglen. It's real. When Muletti and Hideki arrived here and found whatever was lurking in that cave, they adapted stories about it to their advantage, transformed an unknown natural force into an Airafane god. They threw in animal— and even human—sacrifices from Ventroni to make a grisly and exotic scenario. We have evidence for that. It was all brilliant. Any unemployed or orphaned person or victim of a disaster who felt left out, like a refugee suffering from social neglect and poverty, especially on Earth, would love the idea—a unifying myth, a promise of ultimate Airafane power. We've had strong hints about all of this, especially the smuggling and trafficking of people, and we were moving in and learning more, but we needed *evidence*. And this wreck of the *Lochner* is just what we can use. With Braya's accounts and the presence of this base, we'll expose the villains to everyone. And then, in the end…we'll get freedom for Annulus!"

Ranglen couldn't help feeling excited by Tarakov's vision of future independence, but he remained skeptical. "What led you to this base?"

"The incident on Rimport 3, the one you were involved in. From surveillance cameras in the hangar—Homeworld doesn't allow them, but we had them there anyway—we could see it was Muletti who boarded the rental and kidnapped Braya. Based on that evidence—I left out your involvement—I persuaded my superiors to give me this ship so I could come here. They were reluctant. The *Lochner* made everyone nervous. I knew about this base already and assumed Muletti would show up here. He hasn't yet, but it's just a matter of time before he does, and then I will have him, too. We've got Hideki already—and she'll break under the weight of the evidence from Braya. We can corner and arrest all of them."

Did Tarakov not know of the destruction on 82A, that Muletti might be dead?

Ranglen didn't tell him.

"I'm asking you for your help now, Ranglen. Like I said, all of this is for Annulus. We'll need to approach the story in just the right way. The case against Homeworld must be perfect, presented in clear detail. I'll need your support and I'm sure I can count on you. We'll talk of this later. But, believe me, I'm certain we can work this out and that you'll want to do it—for the good of all that Annulus believes in, for all *you* believe in."

He gestured to a guard before Ranglen could respond, then added, "I need to attend to several matters now, like finding out more about that fighter, but I'll get back to you. I'm convinced we can make this happen, together."

Ranglen had little chance to speak before he was led away—or rather, he decided *not* to speak, to make it look like he was swept along by what Tarakov had said.

He was taken to a small room and told to remain there. The guard sat just beyond the open door.

Ranglen felt he was in jail, though the room was comfortable.

Tarakov impressed him, in the same way he had done back at Rimport 3—his skill, confidence, foresight, action.

But his story?

Ranglen didn't believe it.

Braya sat in her own room, filled with apprehension. The guard remained indifferent to her, but her tension grew. She hadn't moved since she sat down.

She didn't know where she stood with all that was happening. The clarity of revenge she had set for herself had kept her focused, moving toward her own special goal. But things had changed—Muletti was gone, Hideki detained (though Braya still wanted her punished), and the *Killer* sat in a nearby hangar and was soon to be overtaken by others. She was still determined to get aboard the *Spy*, and for that reason she had said nothing about it to Tarakov, but that too was becoming unlikely.

Then there was Ranglen. She didn't agree with him and knew just how different he was from her—he came from a world nothing like her own. Privileged, educated, overly cultured, a way she felt she didn't want to be. To everyone else, she was just a refugee, an outcast. But that wasn't the way she saw herself, and, to her, the label was no tragedy. She welcomed the role, used it, was proud of it, and didn't care what anyone thought of her. Unlike the others, she was still on her own, even as Ranglen worked with her, and she knew she could handle herself well enough with or without him. She often felt more decisive than him, more resourceful and even more empowered.

The guard opened the door, said she was needed now for more questioning.

She was led back to the interrogation room. Tarakov still sat where he did, but Ranglen was gone.

She immediately felt disturbed by his absence.

The guard pushed her into the same chair as before. But this time he was joined by another guard. They stood beside her, quiet, waiting.

Tarakov stared at Braya. She frowned back at him.

He nodded at the two guards.

They grabbed her wrists and tied her with zip-ties to the chair. Then they did the same with her ankles. She tried to fight back, but the chair had been fastened to the floor since she left, and they came at her much too quickly and forcibly. She almost screamed, but one guard rammed his open hand against her mouth.

Tarakov stepped around the desk and leaned now against its near side, stood in front of her, tilted forward. "Settle down. You don't want to hurt yourself."

Braya's head was thrust back as the guard took his hand away, leaving her mouth open to answer questions.

"Now tell me," Tarakov said, "where did you *first* meet your friend, Krin?"

She said nothing, scowled at him.

Tarakov slapped her.

Incredible pain—the left side of her face felt scorched with fire.

"Talk to me!"

Tears ran from Braya's eyes. She knew now she would be beaten. So, she gathered her facts, told him her story. "I met her…right before getting on the cargo ship."

"How did this happen? Did she speak to you?"

The pain burned in her cheek and mouth. "It was right after some crazy guy in the spaceport approached me…grabbed me and yelled at me."

"What happened to him, the man who approached you?"

"A security officer pulled him off me. Then he was beaten unconscious. I think he was killed. Krin came over and pulled me away, asked if I was all right. After that, she stuck with me as we boarded."

"Did you meet her before?"

"No. Never. And I tried to stay away from her. I didn't like her."

"What else did she say to you?"

"All stupid stuff about the Mountain Seekers. She was one of them. But I wanted no part of them. She was a colonist, too, so she followed me and tried to stay with me. I pushed her away and she left me alone. I told her I didn't like her."

"Do you know of a man named Lihandro?"

Braya hesitated. "No."

He slapped her again.

This pain was worse, a fierce agony on already tortured skin. She felt blood drip from her nose and mouth. Her eyes flowed with unstoppable tears, her vision blurred, her head leaned forward in torment. "You bastard!" she squealed.

"Stop lying to me!"

"I *don't* know him!"

"He's the man who approached you at the spaceport, the one who yelled at you, who tried to talk to you and who was beaten into silence."

This surprised her, but it didn't change what she said. "I *still* don't know him!"

"He had a partnership with both Krin and Muletti. A deal was made among the three of them. Muletti got a spaceship through Ranglen's friend, Anne Montgomery, a ship for a secret mission they planned. I want to know where that mission went—what Lihandro told you, what the arrangement was about."

"*How the hell should I know?*"

"What did he say to you at the spaceport?"

"He was crazy, yelling. People looked at him like he was out of his mind. They all moved away from us. He yelled at me about the Airafane, that they were 'near,' that I would 'meet them,' that history would change and everything would be different. And stuff about eyes. It was all crazy. Seeker stuff."

"You're *lying!*"

"*I don't know what you're talking about!*"

He slapped her once more, but with the back of his hand on the other side of her face. The new direction gave her time to cringe—which made it worse. Strings of saliva tumbled from her mouth, reached down to the floor. Drops of blood followed.

She said nothing.

"Your friend Ranglen has been lying, too."

"I never saw him before Rimport 3, not until Muletti took me away from there—and I don't know why he did."

"I know *exactly* why. What I don't understand is why *you* don't know."

"*Then you've got more information than I do*. Why the hell are you asking me?"

"Because..." and he paused here, wanting the effect, "because you, my dear, my 'little flame' as Hideki called you...*you*...are Lihandro's daughter."

A long silence filled the room. This revelation cut through all the pain she felt. She hadn't known. But, at the same time, she didn't believe it, *couldn't* believe it. "I never knew my father. My parents abandoned me when I was small, first him and then my mother. And he wouldn't know me. I've never seen him and I've had no connection to either of them. All my records were lost in floods back on Earth. I have no papers or data from them. All my documents I've had to get new."

"You're just a little refugee, eh? Kicked here, kicked there."

In all her pain, she felt a fury she couldn't express.

"Well," Tarakov said, "*I* tracked you down. So, he must have been able to do it, too. He even got to you before I did. I was on my way to the Brazilian spaceport, all ready to grab you. But then he showed up. I didn't get to see him meeting you. I wasn't there yet, but my agent was. And the old man went to only you. That was his mistake. He should have gone to Krin. He *knew* her and had promised Krin he'd do so. But, instead, he ran up to you. And *that's* what I want to know about. I want to know *why!* And, be aware, I'll keep slapping you—and then I'll kick you, and then do worse—until you *do* tell me. Or I'll dangle you over one of the thousand mouths that creature has up in the cave. Do you want that? Huh?"

"I can't tell you anything. I don't *know* anything."

"What did he give you?"

"He gave me *nothing, nothing!*"

"Then, what did *Krin* give you?"

"She gave me nothing…I don't know what you want."

"She came to you for a reason after Lihandro was pulled away but not to help you. She maybe said she did, but it's too much of a coincidence for her to turn up right after Lihandro spoke to you. Krin knew Lihandro and Muletti. And then, on board the *Lochner*, when Muletti attacked you—what happened?"

"He broke in to where the colonists were housed. He had people with guns."

"And who did he go after—go after first?"

Braya realized what he meant. "He went after Krin, but only because she stood up to him. She was blocking his way."

"No. That's not true. Muletti went after her because he wanted something from her."

"He grabbed her and beat her. I didn't see him take anything."

"Lihandro had something that he gave to her or else he gave it to *you*. Muletti wanted it."

"Then ask *Muletti!* Or ask Krin!"

"Krin's dead. Muletti's dead. They were killed at a secret Homeworld base that was blasted apart…by a Homeworld ship, that must have been covering its tracks after attacking the *Lochner*. Yes, that ship in the hangar outside. But I think you know all that already. I'm sure your friend Ranglen knows. I even think he was there at that base when it was destroyed."

"Then ask *him!*"

"I'm saving him for something else. I have *you* now."

"Then go to hell! Get fed to that monster in the mountain yourself. I think it's coming for you. I think it *wants* you!"

Tarakov laughed. "Getting desperate, eh? But if anyone gets fed to the creature, it'll be you. Just not until I get what I want. Come on, 'flame.' Let's work that mouth of yours. I know you like to talk. Tell me now what I want to hear. Tell me where you hid what you have."

"I have nothing…nothing…"

He raised his hand to strike her again.

Ranglen waited alone in his room. The longer he paced the more nervous he became. He realized Tarakov might be interrogating Braya. The officer had wanted Ranglen present, at first, but then, just as emphatically, didn't want him there. What was he doing to her?

The guard who stood in the open doorway prevented Ranglen from leaving, and she didn't look very talkative.

Then, into the silence came a fiercely loud crack, like a nearby strike of lightning, hurting the eardrums. The floor shuddered, and pieces of debris could be heard pummeling the side of the ship.

A big explosion right outside.

Ranglen wondered if the Seekers were up to their old tricks, part of a relentless trail of destruction that ran from the *Lochner* to Rimport 3 to 82A and then to here, catching up with them and trying to kill them.

The guard fingered the receiver in her head-com, getting a message and saying something back.

Then, she took off and left Ranglen alone.

He didn't wait. He ran out of the room and down a ladder to get back to where he had been questioned.

As he exited the shaft, he saw Tarakov and two other guards running to the lower level of the ship and the exit ramp. The door to the interrogation room was open.

Ranglen raced into it—and stopped, appalled.

Braya was bound to a chair, her ankles and wrists held with zip-ties to the legs and arms. Her face was covered with bruises and cuts. Blood ran from her nose. Purple splotches covered her cheeks, forehead, chin.

He ran over to her, pulled out a handkerchief and wiped at the wounds on her face, scraped away blood. "What the hell did he do to you?"

Her eyes moved until she was aware of him. "The bastard," she muttered.

She turned her face, was able to open and close her mouth. Since she could do that, if painfully, he assumed no bones had been broken.

"He hit me, Mykol. Over and over. But he got nothing from me. I told him *nothing.*"

Ranglen realized they had left her bound to the chair so no one would be required to watch her—which was good for him. No guard had stayed.

He ran behind the desk and pulled out drawers. He still had his pocket knife but he knew that wouldn't be strong enough to sever the ties, so he searched until he found a pair of cutting pliers, maybe left there for just this function—he used them to break the bonds holding her.

He massaged her wrists and then helped her stand up. "We're getting out of here."

She staggered after him. "I heard an explosion."

"I think I know what it was. Let's go."

He led her into the hallway, trying to be gentle and yet rushing her at the same time.

They raced down one level and reached the exit ramp, hurrying onto it before looking around. When they got to the bottom, Ranglen pointed.

Where the yellow shack had stood, the one they had passed when they snuck into the camp, a plume of fire poured upward through billows of smoke. Pieces of metal had tumbled down around it to form an apron of wreckage. Tarakov's four-person crew hurried amongst it, looking for a way to fight the fire.

Tarakov himself ran in a different direction, toward the hangar.

"It was an armory filled with weapons." Ranglen pulled Braya across the landing platform. "There was one just like it on 82A—to supply the pirates so they wouldn't have to go into a port. Whoever torched it here knew what they were doing."

A spaceship passed overhead with carrier racks holding missiles. It looked like Hatch's rental, the *Prowler*.

Braya said, "That must be Muletti. I thought he was dead."

"Maybe he had an escape route back on the planetoid. I didn't see the ship on the field there so it must have been hidden. Maybe he saved Krin."

Muletti's craft made a sweeping pass. The racks could carry only four missiles and three were left.

Then, one of them shot toward the hangar.

The explosion struck the bay doors and broke them open, tearing down a part of the roof but leaving most of the structure intact.

"Muletti's smart," said Ranglen. "First the armory, now the hangar where the *Killer* is housed. He's on a mission. *Your* mission, Braya."

"We have to get out of here."

"We don't have a ship."

"We're taking *that* one." She indicated the *Spy*.

Ranglen didn't like how decrepit it looked but he overcame his reluctance.

Braya rushed toward it, hardly slowed by the wounds from Tarakov. Ranglen ran beside her.

They came to the one-step stool beside the entrance.

The door was still closed, but this time the security lights showed it was locked.

Ranglen swore.

"Wait. I can do this." Braya flipped open the security box and worked the keys.

"It's hopeless! The code will be personal. You'll never get it."

Braya kept working.

Muletti's ship swung in an arc across the flatlands, swooping about for another attack. The fire from the armory spread now to the new dorms, especially the one only half-constructed—burning debris had landed on it. People hurried out of the barracks, those seen walking to the cave. But they were less concerned about stopping the fires than in getting away. They ran across the plateau and moved as far from the buildings as they could—which seemed foolish. They must know something Ranglen didn't.

Hideki rushed out of the barracks with a group of her Ventroni thugs, heavily armed. She apparently had broken away from her guards with their help. The gang raced for Tarakov's ship.

Ranglen guessed she would try to board her and steal it. But she couldn't liftoff without Annulus Security's formal codes that only the pilot and Tarakov would know.

The Annulus officers must have seen her, for they ran back to the ramp and shot at her and her followers, trying to stop them from getting onboard.

People ran for cover. Bullets flew.

"I'm in," Braya yelled. "Ha! So easy!" She yanked open the hatch and jumped inside.

Ranglen was astounded as he hurried in after her. "How did you—?"

"Never mind. Can you pilot this?"

He said, "I'll learn." He ran to the front and sat in the control seat. Thankfully, a startup code was not required. He powered the engine and opened the screens.

Through the forward port, he saw the wrecked front of the hangar.

And emerging from its smoke and debris, like a primitive beast rising from the ruins of an ancient world, a delta-winged feral spaceship glided upward, took to the air.

Braya's *Killer*.

"Tarakov," Ranglen said, remembering him running for the hangar.

The Homeworld fighter lifted into the sky, gathered speed, likely in search of Muletti's ship to blast it out of existence.

And Muletti's craft, at that moment completing its wide attack swoop, released a third missile—leaving only one in its racks. The missile wasn't aimed at the *Killer*. It fell in a vapor-line to the top of the mountain and there—with pinpoint accuracy—entered the cave.

"Braya, we need to go!"

She wasn't in the chair beside him but doing something in the back of the ship.

A dull boom from the heart of the mountain, a shaking of dirt and loose rock that disturbed the ground. But nothing spectacular. No visual damage.

Why shoot one of the missiles there? To kill the creature?

Then, the whole top of the hill thrust upward and cracked open. Two slabs of earth slid away in either direction, like the breaking in half of a swollen abscess.

And up through the chasm squeezed an enormous, salmon-colored, gelatinous mass with pink-white cords wrapped around it. It howled in fury from an unseen mouth and pushed both upward and forward. The land rocked as if from an earthquake.

The creature—or whatever it was—*oozed* down the slope, its fat starfish-like tentacles made of wet skin, like internal organs never before exposed to daylight, covered with veins filled with milk. And eyes, hundreds of them—black, clear, concentric, or slits, huge spheres of murky depth, some grouped together in heaps like soap bubbles in foaming suds, some gold and white like shreds or lumps on a gilded fabric. Mouths, too, opening gaps, with teeth or bared purplish gums swollen inside them. It was many life-forms cut into fragments and piled together, multiplied into a colossal indiscriminate bulk, creeping downward, getting closer.

"*Braya!*"

"Take off! Don't worry about me!"

He turned and saw her inside the small washroom looking for something. "You have to get up here and strap in! The acceleration—you'll be knocked against the wall!"

"Just go!"

"What are you—"

"*Go!*"

Ranglen lifted ship. It moved slowly at first, the engines taking long to react.

Outside, he saw Tarakov's vessel chasing Muletti's, shooting particle-beams and lasers. But Muletti evaded him and came around for one more pass—firing his last missile.

But it flew on its line of gentle steam straight for the Annulus Security ship still on the pad.

The craft blew apart in a vast fireball, burying in wreckage the gunfight that still had been battling between Hideki's gang and the officers.

Ranglen then realized Muletti's plan. He had hit four specific targets—the armory, the hangar, the cave, and the ship. But if his purpose had also been to take out the fighter, he failed in doing so. And Ranglen still questioned hitting the mountain—except maybe to arouse the creature and let it finish the job of destruction.

And the creature might be doing just that as it flowed around the hangar and onto the landing field—like a huge faded Klimt garment filled with wet orifices and eyes. No wonder people had tried to run away.

Ranglen's ship rose higher and gained speed. "You okay back there?" he shouted to Braya.

A quick, "Yes."

But the whole landscape was coming alive. As people ran across it, the plateau cracked in different spots like breaks in a frozen lake, the fissures widening and unleashing more animal or crustaceal forms. Tentacles, limbs, eyes, mouths—squeezed out like awakened organs in a fossilized corpse, taking on life as they pushed aside the plates of earth. Fractures grew, spread apart. In the distance, even volcanoes erupted, shooting columns of fire upward as if the interior of the continent were rousing itself, breaking free, an underworld uprising that churned apart the countryside.

And in one horrifying bout of paranoia, Ranglen saw a fat, fleshy, roiling tumescence form an arm that reached up out of the earth for *him*—to grab him! take him! pull him down into it!

"Braya, we're leaving *now*." He slapped in as much acceleration as he could.

Pressed into his seat, he heard her tumbling on the deck in back. "Tell me you're okay!"

No response.

He couldn't stop. He had to keep going.

Then, he heard her mutter, "I'm fine…fine."

The sky turned dark. The horizon curved. He didn't want to look back at the plateau but he caught a glimpse of the two ships, tiny now, still chasing each other.

Braya staggered forward and dumped herself into the second seat, her face still showing its bruises and cuts, but her expression untouched by the pain. She looked ecstatic, with a smile he had never seen on her before. "I got it! I found it!"

"Found *what?*"

She threw a strip of duct tape onto the instrument panel. "What every damned one of them has been looking for."

Stuck to the adhesive side of the tape was a small wafer of dark metal, narrow and featureless.

Ranglen groaned.

Braya laughed hysterically.

"It's a fucking Clip. A goddamned Airafane Clip. And *we*, dear Mykol, *we're* the ones who now have it!"

Chapter 16: Long Night

Ranglen felt a strange despair.

Braya almost squealed, "That's what everyone was after. And it's *ours*. What do you think of that?"

"I knew there had to be more to it than piracy," Ranglen said, but not ecstatically. "Why else would they destroy a whole cargo ship—and then a basecamp afterward. It makes more sense now."

"*This* is why Muletti beat Krin onboard the *Lochner* and took her. Why he wanted *me*. He thought one of us had it. But neither of us did. Yet, here we are, and *we're* the ones who finally got it. We're off to see the Airafane, Mykol. How do you like that?"

"Braya, settle down."

"Are we being followed?"

He checked his instruments and saw nothing. "They must still be preoccupied."

"Muletti and Tarakov killing each other. Maybe Hideki, too. Or that monster from the mountain eating all of them. But not you and me—oh, what we've done, Mykol, where we're going!"

"Where *are* we going?"

"Here, I'll show you." She typed a list of numbers on the screen in front of her.

"Coordinates?"

"I assume."

"Are they Earth-based?" He needed the zero settings that defined the system.

"How the hell should I know? That's all I was given."

"But who gave that to you?"

"Long story, can't tell it now. We need to get out of here."

Ranglen agreed. If he assumed the coordinate system used was centered on Earth's Sol, then the numbers defined a location outside Confederate space. "I'm trusting you, Braya."

She laughed, wildly. "Shouldn't do that. Too much happening. Not many left alive. Just you and me—and we're almost there."

"Almost *where,* goddammit?"

"Where all this started. Where the Airafane and the Clip want us to go. And we'll be the ones who finally arrive."

"But we might not be the *only* ones."

"Then, we'll have to get there first. Go! Go! Come on, Mykol. Do your stuff."

Ranglen entered the coordinates and kicked in the drive for light-space.

The stars vanished. They left their known universe behind. They wouldn't return to time-space for 2 days, 3 hours, 46 minutes, and 7.85 seconds.

It brought to Ranglen a sense of foreboding.

Braya looked around, disappointed. "This ship is cramped. Your ship was roomier. Too bad we lost it—I hope the creature enjoyed swallowing it, if that's what happened. Yet, *this* is the ship with all the answers, not the base back there. Muletti was wrong, though he was close to being right. It's our means of finding what everyone wanted. And it's ours, *ours!*"

Ranglen had never seen Braya like this. She'd been quiet on the walk through the jungle and across the mountain, tight-lipped, bitter—unless she unleashed one of her tirades. But now she seemed manic. "What's happening to you? You sound obsessed."

"No, no, Mykol. This is science, realism, not the crazy stories of the Seekers. But we have to be careful—and we've got to be quick. I'm sure they put a tracker on us."

Ranglen assumed the same, which didn't help. They should have checked the outside hull for messenger drones that could return data on their location once the ship left light-space, but there had been no time.

He said, "We've got over two days before we emerge. That won't make any difference to a follower, but you and I have some time now. So, tell me, how did you know about this Clip—and how did you *find* it?"

"I wasn't after it. You have to understand that. I wanted revenge. The *Killer,* the *Prowler,* the *Spy,* and their pilots. I wanted them to suffer. But here we wind up with *this* instead. Ha! Do you like it?" She lifted the duct tape and the Clip that adhered to it, then threw it down as if trying to show her lack of concern, how cheap it was compared to her ambitions. "Pretty lucky, eh? But it explains why everyone was acting so crazy. A Clip! Do you believe it?"

"*Answer my question!*"

"Okay, okay. But I can't help thinking how it turned up with us, became ours. *We* get to open it. You and me, Mykol. 'You'll see the Airafane.' That's what he said. You've wanted that all along, didn't you? I know what you're after. Tarakov wanted it just for the money. He tried to get it out of me but I said nothing. Yet, he told me who the old man was. I didn't believe him. I didn't *know*. But Tarakov won't stop us from getting to where we're going."

"Braya, *please!* How did you get this?"

"Remember the man I said came up to me at the Brazilian spaceport? He grabbed me and yelled at me, like he had a lot to say but didn't have the time. Tarakov told me *I was his daughter*. But I ignored the old man, thought he was stupid. I forgot all about it till Tarakov threw it at me. I didn't know his name was Lihandro. Remember the guy Krin talked about? The one she tied up with Muletti?"

Ranglen realized this had to be the old prospector, the one with the diamonds Muletti spoke of.

"When he came up to me at the spaceport, he said he had something for me. But he kept looking around like someone was after him, that he was running out of time. He said he wanted to 'make amends.' I remember that because it sounded ridiculous. He shoved a brochure for the Seekers at me, which I didn't notice had something written on it. And what he said to me made no sense. I thought he was crazy. I yelled for help. A security guard grabbed him, dragged him away and started beating him—I think he killed him. I got out of there. I didn't want any police getting me. Then, Krin showed up, and I used her for cover. We went on board the *Lochner* together, though I couldn't stand her."

"The brochure, what was written on it?"

"I didn't pay attention to it and almost threw it away. But I later saw three lines. First, a row of numbers. That's what I just gave you, coordinates. Then, a phrase with both numbers and letters, which I assumed was a password. And, finally, a sentence, 'On the Airafane City, above the sink.' And *that's* where I found the Clip, under a lot of duct tape above the spigot, right here on board this ship, the *Airafane City*—that's the name of it. The tape sealed a connection in a pipe over the sink. A crude repair job. No one would look there."

Ranglen knew that no Airafane "city" existed, even in ruins, so the title was purely fanciful. He couldn't help admiring its originality. "But how did you know that? The registry on the side was removed."

"You'll like this, Mykol. When Hideki found me after I crashed into Annulus, she had a coffee mug with words on it—'Airafane City.' When I saw it, I remembered the line from the brochure. I had thrown it away by then—a good thing, since she searched my clothes—but I memorized what was on it before I did, just in case, since it was all so weird. And when I saw that cup, I knew Hideki was lying. I asked her about it, and she said she stole it from a spaceship. I assumed it belonged to the old man who met me. I didn't know his name was Lihandro yet, so when Krin talked about her friend, I didn't see the connection. But, apparently, he wanted to give the Clip to the Seekers, through Krin taking it to Hideki. But he *didn't* give it to her. He put it on *this* ship, the one we're on, the one which Hideki flew and where she found the cup. He hid it, but he let me know where it was. That's what he was telling me in that third line. 'On the Airafane City, above the sink.' I pulled up the duct tape and—would you believe?—there it was!"

Ranglen remembered Tarakov saying how a ship's identity could be changed, but that simple objects could give it away—a jacket, a t-shirt, or a monogrammed coffee cup.

Braya's face was filled with excitement, which made the abrasions more obvious. But a quick sorrow suddenly possessed her. "He was my father, Mykol, and I laughed in his face, thought he was stupid. He was telling me how to find a Clip, a pure treasure, and I never understood. That's how I got us on board through the locked door. I took a chance. I typed in my name, just my name, and the door opened. How did he find it? How did he find *me*? No wonder Krin wouldn't leave my side. He was her friend but he didn't give it to her, so she must have thought I had it all along. Then Muletti thought *she* had it, and that's why he attacked her on board the *Lochner*. But I didn't know and I just ran. So, when those ships destroyed everything, I ran after *them*. I wanted to kill them. And now I'm on one of those very ships. With our *own* Clip. How did all that happen?"

"Braya, your face is bleeding. Let me treat it."

"Later. I don't feel it. And I still don't see the connection to Homeworld, why they attacked the *Lochner* and how Muletti got involved—Krin said he hated Homeworld."

Ranglen murmured, "I think I can answer that."

This caught her look. "Are you holding out on me? I told you what *I* know. What about you?"

Ranglen sat back, readied himself to tell all he guessed. "I think Homeworld had nothing to do with destroying the *Lochner*. The action was all a smear campaign against Homeworld—that's why one of their fighters was used to attack the cargo ship, making it seem like a military operation and government approved. The ship must have been decommissioned and restored with a false registration. That's illegal but, if you have the right connections, you can do it. You also need a place where it can be done. Like the planetoid 82A."

"Muletti did all that?"

"Muletti was involved, but someone higher up was needed, someone with ties to Annulus Security, the Bureau of Intelligence, and to people willing to follow him, people both inside and outside government, plus some help from a place like Ventroni."

"You mean…Tarakov?"

"Yes. I've heard that within Security there are groups with their own agendas. I'm sure they're small and mostly ineffectual, but if they have the right connections, they can take advantage of other movements, like the Seekers and the people under the Ring. I don't know all the details for certain, but after what we've seen, I'm convinced he's behind it."

Braya didn't answer, maybe thinking of how Tarakov treated her.

"I suspected him at first because he was lax when you and Hideki raided the rimport, as if knowing the operation was coming and allowing it to take place, keeping his people occupied with the fire. The point was to get you to follow along with Hideki's 'illegal' act of breaking in so he'd have the excuse to arrest you, and then use you as a witness to prove that Homeworld destroyed the *Lochner*. He admitted he knew Hideki, and she probably was his agent in the Seekers, so when he first heard from her that you survived, he must have been thrilled. An actual witness. He'd want you badly."

Ranglen let Braya stomach the idea and to feel the danger that had been around her for so long. "But then, the discovery of the Clip changed everything. I assume Muletti was supposed to stay hidden at the rimport after the *Lochner* was destroyed, but he took matters into his own hands by abducting you and throwing you and Krin together. He thought he'd learn where the Clip was located. I don't think Tarakov was prepared for all that. He came to 82A maybe to deal with Muletti, but Muletti attacked him so he fought back and destroyed the base, which he probably intended to do anyway, erasing evidence of his set-up against Homeworld. He did this in the same fighter that destroyed the *Lochner*—to argue that Homeworld was still the villain. Then, when he came to Highland, maybe to do the same, his claim that he brought an intelligence force to take over the base was a clear lie. He'd have more than one ship with a whole detachment of enforcement officers, not just four, who were probably only followers in his private cabal."

"But how could he get away with all that?"

"There's been too much resentment on Annulus over the tariffs and threatened blockades from Homeworld, the fear of trade becoming stymied and preventing all growth. Tarakov's plans probably started small, maybe with help even from corporate supporters on Earth. Annulus is a big growing market, and war can be profitable. He might have begun with just small raids on insignificant ships and claimed he was only evading the tariffs, while setting up 82A as his supply base, where confiscated vessels could be refitted and registrations quickly changed. The damage to shipping would still be small and not troubling enough to start an interstellar furor.

"But then the *Lochner* was to be the big event, the final way to push tensions to a head—a direct assault against Homeworld's reputation. Eventually, all the media would learn of it. Tarakov even wanted me to write copy for him. You said you saw one of the ships picking up pieces after the wreck? I'll bet those were the surveillance cameras (they have radio beacons so they can be found after a crash), to be used for his propaganda. It might have led to armed retaliation or open rebellion, Annulus against Homeworld with help from an angered Earth, exactly what he and his cabal wanted. 'Power for Annulus,' but really power for *him*."

"But why didn't it work? Didn't people just say the ship hit an asteroid?"

"Tarakov must have expected Earth to scream over the loss, but Earth went quiet, maybe because they believed the phony story of the asteroid and wanted to protect their own pilots or they didn't want to admit that an Earth crew could have plotted with a raider—you said they didn't resist. But the real point is that, after a time, people wouldn't have followed Tarakov's plan anyway. Though Earth might support our economic ventures against Homeworld, it would not get behind a *military* move. Earth won't be led by a small and undeveloped colony—it's beneath their pride. They might even fight *for* Homeworld against us, especially once they learned that Ventroni was involved. Earth and a lot of other worlds oppose Ventroni joining the Confederation. And here's Tarakov negotiating with them, which would have been seen as far too dangerous. I believe in Annulus breaking ties with Homeworld. And it *will* happen. All of Annulus is for it. But if we have to rely on Earth or, worse, Ventroni to do that, then Annulus would wind up being subservient to them, not free at all. Tarakov was lying to himself, and he was being used by a bomb-providing cartel on Ventroni and probably by private corporations on Earth who were not above smuggling humans. His plot became murderous. And instead of gaining freedom, Annulus would have lost more of it, their new masters being much more repressive than Homeworld."

Braya said scornfully. "No one would want to be ruled by Earth. I've lived there. I know."

"And then Tarakov was blinded by making too much money. Through Ventroni's influence, his raids were taking *people* as well as merchandise. The selling of colonists would be very profitable. Sure, he could blame all of it on Homeworld, but it's backed by *Ventroni*, and once you let Ventroni in, they'll just take over. The 'depot' on Highland was designed to hold refugees (plus, I'm sure, disobedient crews who didn't take bribes), and they would be sold to the corporate colonies run mostly by Earth. That was the point of the dorms we saw there, just as you said.

"Tarakov maybe could have convinced the public that the base on 82A was Homeworld's doing—it was designed that way, with Muletti's guidance—but arguing the same would have been impossible on Highland, which clearly was for holding and moving people, and dependent on Hideki's thugs from Ventroni. Even the creature there in the mountain was part of the scheme. With Hideki's help, Tarakov must have believed it would provide more control over the captives, make them submissive. And, with its reality, the Seekers could infiltrate more areas of society and provide even greater means of control. Maybe he thought they'd build an army for him, using religion, terror, and alien fascination—'the eyes are watching you, so do as I say'—making Annulus into a breeding ground for a horde of zombies."

Ranglen stopped to breathe, to let the enormity of the plot sink in. "And all of that was getting out of control and probably would have exploded in Tarakov's face. Then, on top of that, the Clip came along, and with it, things changed drastically. Tarakov had put his scheme with the *Lochner* into operation. But now he heard through Hideki of a possible Clip, supposedly coming from an old man to be given eventually through Krin to the Seekers. And he knew that Muletti had ties with Krin. So he must have tried to muscle Muletti, already involved through his work on the planetoid, intending to get him to pressure Krin before hitting the *Lochner*. But Krin boarded the *Lochner* instead. Muletti reached it first and thus got to Krin, but she had no Clip. So Tarakov, now afflicted with Clip fever and angry that he lost it, must have gone wild and destroyed the whole ship, the refugees, and even the base on 82A, since, by then, he no longer trusted Muletti and would want to stop him.

"He likely meant to destroy Highland's base too, to wipe out Hideki and cut all his losses. But the Clip fever hit him once more when he found you, the person he had wanted all along. Surely, you knew where it was, so he tried to beat it out of you, reducing everything to one crucial and all-consuming asset—the Clip."

He paused again, this break more significant. "Or, in other words, I'm sure he's still after us."

"Could Muletti have killed him back on Highland?"

"I doubt it, given the difference in the two ships. And Tarakov's certainly tracking *you*. At first, you were just an accidental witness to the *Lochner*, to be kept in reserve. But the plan to get you at Rimport 3 turned into a disaster. And he would have been suspicious then because of what Hideki was saying, that you had some connection to the Clip through being with Krin, and from Lihandro approaching you at the spaceport. Muletti must have suspected that Tarakov was behind Lihandro's death—maybe an accident of excessive force by one of his own security guards who didn't know Lihandro had important information. So, Muletti, after working with Tarakov, went rogue on Rimport 3 and grabbed you for his own. He already must have felt cheated by Lihandro when, as Krin implied, the old man acted on his own and got the Clip for himself—intending to give it to the Seekers, which I'm sure made Muletti furious. So, when he left the rimport, he must have felt he needed to cut his own losses, too, take his friend Krin and get away from Tarakov.

"But finding you was too good to ignore—so he took you too, the Clip obsession now ruling him again. He got nothing out of you, and Krin got nothing, which I'm sure is why he put you two together. So, maybe after that, in the long run, he was starting to have second thoughts, maybe appalled over what Tarakov had done—and what *he* had done. He truly wanted to embarrass Homeworld—he hated the place—but he claimed he didn't want to start a war, which is exactly what Tarakov *did* want. I agree he seemed changed on 82A, even repentant, reluctant to squeeze you for any more information about the Clip. And since he apparently survived the attack there, he went after Tarakov on Highland, the two of them shooting it out."

He stopped again, looked away and pondered. "What amazes me most about all of this, based on what you're saying, is how much the independence of your father was so important. Tarakov's elaborate plot, which he saw at first as a noble venture, had slowly become a tawdry, money-making scheme and a brutal push for political power—which would have been a disaster for Annulus. But, then, Lihandro throws his Clip into the pot, making the whole conspiracy boil, first saying he'll give it to the Seekers through Krin but instead hiding it, all to bestow it on only one person, the individual he must have felt he neglected most…his own daughter. It's incredible. I wish I could have met him."

Braya said nothing, looked wistful.

"And that's why Krin followed you on board the *Lochner*. She must have been at the spaceport to meet Lihandro and get the Clip, but she probably saw you talking to him and assumed he gave it to you before he was pulled away. She obviously didn't know the *Lochner* would be destroyed. Maybe Muletti, when he boarded the ship near Annulus, was trying to save her as much as beat information out of her."

Ranglen stopped, then added sadly, "We so believe in the Clips and how valuable they are to civilization, and yet…look what they do to us."

Braya asked, "Who were the pilots of the three ships?"

"As we guessed, Muletti flew the *Prowler*, with its weapon racks already added, either to fight Tarakov or to add to the destruction of the *Lochner*, which he did go along with. Muletti's resolve must have swung back and forth. And the pilot for the *Spy*—or the *Airafane City*—was Hideki, as you assumed and she admitted. She was Tarakov's friend and his link to Ventroni. And finally, for the *Killer*, Tarakov himself—he went for that ship and flew it on Highland so he must have known it from before. Having lost the Clip with Lihandro's death and, then, Muletti not finding it with Krin must have driven him wild, even turning against some of his own raiders. The torment of knowing the Clip existed but was just out of reach would have justified him doing anything."

"So, two of them might be dead, and the last is chasing us."

"I'm sure he won the dogfight with Muletti, so Muletti's probably killed. Let us hope Tarakov is at least detained. But he *will* come. He missed you at Rimport 3—the point of Hideki's 'raid' was to bring you to him. He missed you again at 82A where he used his fighter to shift blame and conveniently kill Muletti—he probably didn't know you were there. So, he must have been ecstatic when he found you on Highland, a very lucky break. And Hideki had been trying to soften you up with her creature theatrics to make you into a better gift for him. No wonder she was angry when he arrested her. She felt betrayed, enough to turn on him, even though he just might have been faking it for our sake. He wouldn't inspire the kind of loyalty that Krin felt for Muletti. And now you're here, getting away from Tarakov once more. So, yes, I'm sure he's after us…unless the creature got him. We can hope."

"It's all madness."

"But a cold logic sews it all together. The plan was brilliant. An Earth ship in near Annulus space attacked by a Homeworld military craft, all to start dissention and maybe rebellion. But the plan used murder, the selling of refugees, Ventroni gangsters, corporate greed, a phony cult, and so many lies that it's hard to keep track of them."

The silence this time went on for a while.

Then Braya spoke, in a tone that did not include regret. "And yet…Mykol, *we've* got the Clip. It is *ours*. I don't care about Tarakov now. I'm too excited."

Ranglen felt his eagerness growing too, though dismay also touched him. He remembered, briefly, the actual fourth Clip, the one he had discovered and eventually destroyed. He recalled the feeling—the thrill, the adventure, then the pain and loss.

He also remembered a mountain with eyes.

But he let it all go. This was a new "fourth Clip"—with its own story.

"What'll we do, Mykol? You're the expert."

He despised that role.

"Come on, spaceman. Super 'Clip Finder.' It's time to open it and see what it does. We're the only ones here. Aren't you ready ato jump into the brink?"

"Just you and me and the universe, eh? Out here alone in the middle of nowhere."

"That's right! Just us. But *we* made it here and *we* found it. It's *ours.* "

"Okay then. Let's do it."

He placed the Clip on a metal table, explaining how it would absorb the metal and produce nanobots that would make a machine to provide instructions. These could be complicated or very simple. The response varied as well as the time it took. They would have to wait.

They sat there and watched.

Nothing happened.

They *continued* to watch.

But while they waited, Braya let Ranglen finally use his medical supplies to clean her face, spread disinfectant, use a bandage where necessary. He tried to give her a sedative but she refused.

They checked the Clip again. Nothing had changed.

They grew tired and hungry. They gobbled down dried food, trail rations they found in cupboards, drank fruit juice from a small refrigerator—all Hideki's stuff.

They looked at the Clip again. Still nothing.

Ranglen told Braya to sleep on the pull-down bed across from the table. He would use a portable mattress he found in the cargo hold.

But they were too restless, too eager. They soon gave up and returned to the Clip. No change.

"When does it start?"

"Should be anytime. Usually there's something by now. At least the Clip should've attached itself to the metal of the table." He nudged it to see if it would move.

It did.

He picked it up. "Dammit! It should have connected by now."

He examined it closely. No change in the surface.

He swore again.

"So, this isn't expected?"

"We have only a few samples for comparison. But the Airafane knew we'd be ignorant of how to proceed so they provided guidelines. All four of the other Clips had them."

"Four?"

"Three. Sorry, too anxious. But this one I just don't understand."

"It isn't 'dead,' is it?"

"I didn't say that." But he was beginning to wonder.

Then he noticed… "Wait. This wasn't here before."

On the side of the Clip that had faced the table, a shape had risen slightly above the surface, like an arrowhead, pointing toward one end of the rectangle.

He showed it to Braya. "I'm sure this wasn't on it before."

Ranglen didn't know what it meant. Should the Clip be placed in a particular direction? Inserted somewhere with the arrow pointing forward?

Frustration and doubt surged in him. Why did each Clip have to be so different—and so damned obscure?

Braya reminded him, "Lihandro said we would 'meet' the Airafane."

"And how the hell would he know that?"

"Maybe he did what we're doing now."

"Then the arrow already would have been on the Clip."

"But maybe he took it to where it was supposed to go."

"Always 'maybe.' We have to find out." He seethed with impatience. "Wait, maybe there are records on board. It's Lihandro's ship, after all."

"A journal? But wouldn't Muletti or Hideki have found it?"

"Maybe they weren't looking." And Ranglen knew tricks that Hatch had shown him on how to open ship's data, though private records would still be locked by private means. "You said there was another line in the message he gave you, the one you thought was a password."

"Yes! Let's try that."

They opened the computer's storage files and saw two folders named "Log" and "Journal."

But the password opened neither of them.

They tried to open other folders using the same key.

Still no response.

They applied it to as many places as they could. Still nothing.

Then they came to a folder buried deeply inside other maintenance files, called simply, "Chance."

The password opened it.

It contained only one document, unnamed. And in it was only a bulleted list of statements on a single page.

But when they read the list, they felt it had to be Lihandro's summary of what happened to him.

A passage of time apparently existed between each item in the list, making the document like a series of comments in a diary:

- Diamonds. And a round asteroid, *perfectly* round.
- Fled in terror. Ashamed of myself. A planet with an eye. A structure, a door. I know I'll need help. I'll talk to Krin.
- Met Muletti on Ventroni. Hate that world! Said he would get me a new ship.
- I now doubt Muletti. And my own ship has one more flight in it.
- Returned alone and entered the door. Found the Clip. Reinserted it and saw the message. But I won't do it. I'm not the one. Not anymore. I'll give it to the Seekers through Krin.
- *Not* through Krin. Muletti would get it. Have to find my daughter and give it to her.

That was it, except for a row of numerical commands that, Ranglen assumed, would tell the ship's computer's where to find the original landing site.

Ranglen and Braya looked at each other. The lines said both too little and too much. "Diamonds?"

Ranglen explained that Lihandro's first visit must have found diamonds—big ones, since a larger ship was needed to carry them. But when the Clip was discovered, they apparently became unimportant.

"A perfectly round asteroid, which he fled 'in terror'?"

Ranglen couldn't answer that one. He added his own question, "A planet with an eye?"

"What would he 'not do' about the Clip?"

"He said, 'reinsert' it. Did he have to pull it out of something?"

"So there *was* a message associated with the Clip...but what did it say?"

"And how did he go about finding you, his daughter? When all the while Muletti—and Tarakov—would have been after him. He was in danger for all that time."

Their comments seemed ineffectual, guesses in the face of growing mystery.

"So, the Clip worked after all," Braya said. "It *is* alive."

Ranglen held it up. He noticed the arrow was more prominent now. The Clip was changing.

Pointing the way?

Their enthusiasm burned strongly, but their nerves were too strained, their bodies exhausted. Ranglen knew they'd have to pull back and relax a little. "We need to stop and rest now, Braya. Get some sleep. Then we can plan after we get up."

She didn't seem to hear him. "He said we'd meet the Airafane. Yet, he didn't refer to that in these 'notes.' But that's what he said. 'Meet the Airafane.' I remember those words."

"You told me Krin talked about the same thing, so maybe he told her about it too."

"And she and Hideki both called me 'little flame'—some secret code, as if they knew. But I got so tired of that. I preferred Krin calling me the 'avenging soul,' her Ventroni idea about sacrificed animals. It's how I felt when I wanted revenge—the determination that got me here. I loved that feeling."

"Braya, don't over-react to the Clip. It's better we settle down. Everyone who finds one gets this way. It's not good."

"But *you* don't react, Mykol. You're calm. You're always the rationalist. I'm not like that. I've been in flooded cities on Earth and camps where children played in barbed wire. People despised me even when they tried to use me. And what I say comes from *me*—not the Clip. I'm the one justified in acting this way."

"People who've found a Clip often get touched by a strange hysteria. Don't give in to it. It's dangerous."

"But I've been buried for too long—under Krin's babblings, Hideki's nonsense, Tarakov's beatings, and at last learning about Lihandro. I can't call him my 'father' yet. Fathers don't trade their children for a Clip, for a *gamble* on a Clip. He deserted me and got what he wanted, what everyone wanted. But we have his Clip now, even if we did get it because of him. We'll make it real. We'll get there first and then we can become our own 'flames,' little or big—we can burn up planets!"

"Braya, please! What you're doing is predictable. People lose their control. Look at Tarakov, even Muletti. You have to hold yourself back."

"But I feel *alive!* This is my moment. I was asleep when the Clip woke me up. And the Clip's alive as much as we are. I'm touching something bigger than myself. Does this happen to you when you're out there exploring your alien landscapes, your 'penitent formations'? Is this what you feel? Aren't we just trying to be bigger than we are?"

Ranglen didn't know how to answer her—or how to stop her. And a rogue rebellious part of him didn't want to, the frenzy of the Clip touching him, too. He longed to jump right in after her, follow her to wherever she was going.

"I've got to leave everything behind me now, destroy my past. I won't be cheap labor anymore. I don't trust anyone. We're all just users and victims, you know. Even when you took me to Highland, to the jungle and the mountains, I found nothing different there. I saw only ourselves. We're too self-centered to be anything else. We bring our own greed, cults, conspiracies."

"Braya, stop this."

"*No*, not for where we are. There's no authority on knowledge here. You're the patron saint of bright-colored Annulus, of a supposedly beautiful world that still has an *under*world. It looks good from the top but there's sorrow on the bottom. Or maybe it's the other way around. That would shock you. But you'd rather be out in space anyway than on your nice habitat. And maybe that's selfishness, too. In the end, don't we all just want our own story? And where do refugees go on *your* world? Are they swept under the Ring? Do they contaminate your readership so much that you have to get rid of them?"

"That's enough."

"Face it, Mykol. I'm *here* now. I'm enjoying myself. No one's stopping me. How often do I get to talk like this? How often does *anyone*? We've got the Clip so we can say whatever we want. And Tarakov beating me gives me the *right!*"

"Tomorrow we plan. But now we can't indulge in—"

"*Indulge?* What do you mean? If a mountain has eyes then I can have a mouth. I'm an avenging soul, remember? I can be part of your Annulus revolution, or maybe you'd just toss me under the Ring? But you'll be there yourself in time. It's only your money that keeps you out. You don't fit that bright surface, you know. You've got more of *my* attitude. I'm the flame, and you're 'the man who loves alien landscapes'—Krin called you that. So of course we don't belong on that world. It's too bright and cheery."

"That's enough, Braya. You have to stop this." But as he tried to fight her, he grew too fascinated, too absorbed by her.

"Krin told me about your Anne, more than I said to you earlier, everything she heard from Muletti. He liked to talk of her. He *wanted* her. I bet that bothers you. Maybe she and Muletti were becoming too close. Is that why you're here? Chasing down a rival? Did you feel a touch of vengeance yourself? I was ready to kill him. Would you have stopped me? Do you ever wonder?"

"That's *enough!* Just shut up now!"

"Ah, finally, I've gotten to you. I see you now—the quiet expert of the stars, the high adventurer. High *privilege* is more like it. Don't kid yourself. None of what I say is coming from the Clip. This is just you and me out here alone—riding humanity's wave of exploitation. I have an excuse. I'm a refugee. But what about you? What's *your* story? Who discarded you?"

"Stop it! Stop it!"

"Oh, come on, Mykol, what are you running from? It's not the same as me. I come from a city that turned into a swamp but you're from that bright ribbon in space. Something must have ruined your dreams. Did you abandon someone? Hurt someone? Any lost children? Are you like me after all? Would that embarrass you?"

"Braya, we haven't time for this."

"And what will you say to the Airafane when we meet them? I'm the vagrant, but you're the scholar, the learned, the wise. What will *your* chosen words be, your message and greeting, your big secret? Your outright *lie*? What false claims will you give to them—that we're innocent, orderly, sweet, 'nice'? You're the chosen emissary, the appointed one. So, how will you explain us and show them what we are?"

"Shut up, shut up!"

"You have to think about it. You've got a job now. And I'm just passing on to you what Tarakov gave to me, his little torture—preparation for what's coming. We've got to be ready. Big meeting ahead. Peak of human history. And you're the one, Mykol. So, you need to get your pride in order. We're about to be measured, pulled forward or thrown a thousand years into the past. What will we do with it? Have you decided? Don't you think you should know more about yourself? Do you prefer empty planets over people? What do you really want after all? Is it your Anne? If you like her so much then maybe I should get her for you. Bring her as my own private gift to you, in a belt of stars and a necklace of diamonds. I'll bring her on a platter—with an apple in her mouth!"

"Shut up! Shut up! Shut up! Shut up!"

It was night. "Night" of course being irrelevant on a spaceship, but Ranglen followed a standard 24-hour cycle, and he dimmed the lights while he was sleeping. So…it was night.

His door was closed but not locked. He lay on the mattress in the cargo hold with a sheet and thin cover over him. He had insisted she use the pull-down bed across from the kitchen. It was a tighter fit but more comfortable.

He couldn't sleep. Early "tomorrow" they'd come out of light-space in Lihandro's star system, and Ranglen was too filled with expectation, dread, longing, and outright fear.

The talk between him and Braya finally settled. When he left her, he was still in a rage, but she became quiet. They ate together, exchanging small gestures and comments. Simple attempts at a simple bond. It helped to soften the verbal spectacle that had blown-up between them. They soon parted and went to bed.

Then, after hours of his sleeplessness, the door opened, emitted a glow from the dim running lights along the floor outside. Braya entered, in her dark slacks and loose undergarment with thin straps (they had no change of clothes, all had been abandoned in their packs left behind). She was barefoot, her hair uncombed.

She didn't say anything. She closed the door behind her and sat on the deck, her back against the wall. He could barely see her. Only the light from the figures on his portable clock and other instruments made any illumination.

She sat motionless for a long time, her arms on her knees. She held something in her hand he couldn't see well enough to identify.

They said nothing.

Then she stood up and crossed to his mattress. What she carried was a candle.

Where did she get it? Maybe Lihandro had a stock somewhere. Ranglen kept some on his own ship, for "moods," nights like this. She must have secretly searched for them.

She struck a match—of all things—and lit the candle. Then she leaned over the floor beside his bed, tilted the candle so that its wax fell onto a deck panel. She stood it in the wax and let the bond harden so it would stand.

He wondered if the wax would stain the floor. Silly thought. Everything in the ship was worn and dirty.

She pulled back his sheet and cover. She slipped in beside him. She didn't ask, just assumed they'd want to be together. Or maybe it had nothing to do with him and it was all her, responding to some need that, surprising her, came unawares.

Or maybe not. She *had* searched for the candle.

They didn't touch. Her joining him was not romantic, not sexual. He didn't feel encouraged to touch her. Maybe for both of them it was more an agreement, a permission given to an impersonal human gravity, allowing it to act on them, pull them together. They were the only two people in this light-space universe, so maybe a natural and instinctive attraction drew them toward each other. Maybe neither one of them chose it. It was easier to assume that it chose them.

Ranglen stared at her, but she didn't look back at him. She gazed at the blanket, the sheet, the buttons on his shirt. Not at his face. Anything but him.

They still said nothing.

Then, after this careful lack of regard, this sensitive, yet impersonal separation, he finally reached over, as if crossing a profound depth, and touched the strap of cloth on her shoulder.

She stopped him, pushed his hand away.

Then, she sat up and crossed her arms, not looking at him, and dropped both straps from her bare shoulders. She held the bottom of the cloth and pulled it over her head, exposing her slim body and small breasts. She still didn't look at him. She didn't rearrange her tousled hair. She didn't seem eager, yet not resistant either. Resigned, but not so much resigned to him, nor to any attraction to him, but to some larger force that seemed deciding for both of them.

He opened and removed his shirt. She peeled down her black tights, he the rest of his underclothes.

They lay back beside each other. They still didn't touch.

She looked at him furtively, as if afraid of desiring him. He did desire her, but as much because of what they'd soon encounter. To face each other was more comfortable, more necessary at that moment than facing where they might be going—or, for that matter, what might follow them.

He waited until, hesitantly, she touched his arm, slid her fingers back and forth.

And then, at last, they explored each other, both of them tender, never straining, never demanding. Fingertips gave way to open palms, hands offered back as much as they took. Attraction became silently acknowledged, the unhurried caresses almost luxuriant. Their breathing never grew intense, but it came to them long, deep, and satisfying.

Arousal moved them like a rising tide, not some spurious agitated wave.

Their bodies intertwined, twisted over each other, aligned, melded. They eliminated any space between. They entered each other gently, tentatively, and not as clinging survivors of a disaster, not declaring "We're alive!" Their coupling was subtle, pre-event instead of post-crisis. They knew what they faced soon could be drastic, so they needed to express basic life before it.

They made no sounds, no moans, no sudden exclamations of passion. The climax for both of them seemed almost incidental, inevitable, part of some larger natural script. And yet, in its very impersonality, what they did was richly meaningful, profound, grand. They weren't just the only life in their universe, they were the *best* life. And their act thus contained all its universal wonder.

And too, maybe, like all humans, they felt they were being used—by evolution, by survival. But it didn't matter. They were as much taking advantage of *it* as it was taking advantage of them. Theirs was a quiet shared celebration, no loud call, no intensifying for effect.

All very real. All very needed.

They lay there together for a long time afterward, in sustained enjoyment of each other's touch, movements, tastes, small looks of close attention. An awareness of detail.

They were only people, but they felt, tomorrow, they might meet gods.

At last, she stood up from his bed and re-entered her clothes. Not one word had been said. She blew out the candle, which seemed to extinguish more than just flame.

She walked to the door and opened it. The low light came in once more.

But before she left, she looked back at him. And then, slowly, she returned to the mattress. She leaned over his face and kissed his forehead.

She said, "You be nice to them, Mykol....And you be nice to *us*."

Then, just as slowly, she walked out and closed the door behind her.

He thought about what happened for a long time after.

But it was not the kind of thinking that led to a conclusion. His thoughts were like wanderers in an ill-lit city, where people moved without direction and would never find their proper home.

There was no home.

Chapter 17: Eye

The blood star.

Copper in tint, mainly white with a tinge of brass. Nothing special. Still a bright and fierce sun.

The ship emerged but far out on the edge of the system. No worlds yet could be seen.

"Where are the diamonds?"

For all the morning, Braya had been brutally silent. Typical of her. Wild mood swings, manic to depressive. Shutting down after saying too much or doing too much. Supernova becomes black hole.

Ranglen realized he was becoming like her—thinking in her own spastic sentences.

He didn't know what she'd do when they got there. How they would negotiate the Clip, what it did, where they might go.

He was over-reacting but he had to fight thinking like her, feeling for her and feeling *like* her. They had gone from tirade to making love to dark silence and now back to speech. What would be next?

"I assume we'll see them," he said, about the diamonds.

"And we'll meet the Airafane."

"We can't, Braya. They're extinct."

"But it's what he said, 'meet the Airafane.'"

"There's no trace of them being alive."

"You said this Clip is different."

"They're *all* different, unique in each way."

"But you're feeling something, Mykol. I can tell. A longing. So am I. We're not here to find some grubby new technology to sell to people and make a lot of money. That's what *they* wanted, Muletti, Tarakov. That's not what *we* want. And not diamonds either."

"Braya, please."

"You want to *touch* the Airafane. To walk right up to them and show them who we are."

"I want to find what this is all about."

"Yet, you'll be good for meeting with them, showing them who we are. Forget that I criticized you. I can't help it. You've got your learning, your books, your art. You're the one. I know you want it. The chance to be at the front of humanity."

"Of course I want it."

"You're good, Mykol. I believe in you. Why else are you here with me in all this desolation? What can my life offer? You've been primed. I can imagine you talking with them, joining with them. If anyone gets to meet them I'm glad it's you."

"Just let me pilot."

And he did need to focus. The stellar system was cluttered with debris even to a range above the ecliptic, reminding him of the Annulus star that was much lower in the HR diagram and just coming into existence. But this star stood at the end of its lifetime, bloating out, causing destruction. Its large planets were gone, maybe broken up by other passing stars, leaving a sheet of tumbling stone, waves of disturbance, rock strays.

The spot they wanted was halfway in toward the sun, within a circular area that was relatively clear.

"Where would diamonds come from?" Braya asked.

"White dwarf stars. As the sun dies, the pressure builds until the carbon crystallizes. But you can't land on a white dwarf. You'd be squashed by gravity. There can be diamond planets, too—maybe expectable for a carbon star like this one—but they'd be unreachable. High gravity again, with probably an atmosphere of carbon dioxide and soot, thick smog, ground blackened from graphite, lakes and rain of hydrocarbons, oil. But the volcanoes might spit out diamonds."

She stayed quiet. He felt she was accusing him of showing off his knowledge.

He added, "If a white dwarf accompanied this star and got struck by another star, torn-off pieces could form the clutter. That would explain the jumbled-up orbits. Maybe they're all diamonds."

"That's hard to believe."

"They wouldn't be worth much. Over-abundance kills the market."

He thought of Anne, of value coming from constructed stories, the universe made into merchandise. Was he becoming as cynical as Braya? "The blood in your veins is composed of iron, made in rare exploding stars, supernovae. It's the only place where iron comes from. Even all of it that was on 82A—it came from inside a special type of star."

She looked unimpressed.

He focused on piloting. "So, we're in search of a world with an eye?"

"Should be easy to find."

"If partially diamond, the gravity would be too high for survival. You need a lot of compression to make diamond."

"He said he landed on it, that he found a structure there."

Ranglen didn't expect Airafane ruins like those that came on other worlds, imitated by the fake structures on Highland. He knew all about those kinds of places but he didn't expect the same thing here. He wasn't sure why.

They moved forward through tumbling rocks, dark and unimpressive. Probably covered with graphite.

An alarm sounded and warning lights flashed.

"We're being followed."

He checked radar and scanning returns. "Just one ship, could be either the *Prowler* or the Homeworld fighter. The instruments here can't tell me if it has missile tubes or not."

"Assume the worst. So a tracer *was* left on our ship."

"I ran a number of scans to find anything after we came out of light-space, but we don't have the best programs."

She fell quiet.

"It's keeping its distance. If it's the fighter, it certainly could move faster than us, but it's following the same path we are. If it stays back, we'll have some time when we reach the world before it catches up. I'll go a bit faster to see if it also changes speed—but we can't go too fast, given all the clutter around us."

He accelerated briefly, then continued at a higher velocity.

"It did the same, matched our speed."

He brought the ship back to its original pace. "And it *still* did the same. It's following exactly what we're doing but staying back as far as before."

"They want us to go in first, encounter any danger, find what they want, and then move in and take it away from us."

He agreed.

He assumed it was Tarakov, but anyone could have survived the battle, even Hideki.

In short time, Lihandro's coordinates brought them to an asteroid over 300 kilometers in diameter, smaller than a white dwarf but bigger than a neutron star. The gravity was wrong, reading too light for the apparent density, which was high. But it'd be good for walking, he noted. And the orb had many rocks encircling it in highly stable and organized orbits that made no sense, the objects aligned like the spokes of a wheel.

The world was a yellowish crescent at first. Ranglen normally would use several orbits to examine the place but he didn't have time. He approached the dark side, intending to move to the sunlit part and then descend quickly, landing at the spot where the ship had arrived before, indicated by the data in Lihandro's list. It was located on the illuminated half.

"We'll approach in shadow and decelerate quickly. We won't get a high view of the landing area. This'll be hard on the ship, but I think it can take it. The gravity-plates are working well." Airafane components always survived while those made by humans did not.

As they neared, they could see swirls on the saffron crescent, reds and browns, swaths of white, a fuzzy rim of air.

"The atmosphere's impossible," he said. "Too dense for such a small world and near Earthlike in composition. Nitrogen-oxygen. We could even breathe it."

"Lihandro said nothing about needing a spacesuit."

"He also said the world had an eye."

Braya went quiet.

They passed over the dark side, dumping speed. Phosphorescent patterns gleamed below, vague in the blackness. They formed no recognizable shapes, no paths or designs, no messages in the night.

A glow spread across the horizon, a golden scimitar with an orange sun rising in the middle.

Beneath it, the landscape widened and spread.

Trees stood everywhere, in delicate shapes and warm colors, in patterns and sweeps and trails and curves—scarlet, cinnamon, snowy bluish-white (how could there be blue under this rusty sun?), all on a background of soft yellow-ochre. The trees waved like living fronds at the bottom of an ocean, the winds lively and yet benign.

The planet seemed to breathe, or the movement of its growth like long fur waving in choreographed dance. A small paradise. You wanted to step out and enjoy it, take in the air. The gravity just right—even if wrong.

"Is this a diamond planet?"

"The density's right, but the gravity isn't."

"Where's the smog, the lakes of oil?"

"I have no idea."

"It has to be artificial."

"Yes, of course." Ranglen couldn't help feeling rapture. Even Braya looked impressed. Airafane wonders. The presence of gods.

Down, down, till they skimmed the tops of the feathery boughs, lacey and soft—at least they looked that way.

A wedge valley opened before them, spreading equally to either side, the walls creeping apart from each other and forming a symmetric arrowhead.

He understood. It had to be part of the eye. What Lihandro had seen. What they, too, would have seen if they had looked from a higher orbit.

They flew between the open lids, above a dull whitish ground.

Then a curved wall rose before them—the edge of a structure, or the edge of the iris, hard and steep. Above the wall that leaned inward was a flattish dome of dark gray, riddled with cords and nerve-like structures. The color of Braya's—and Muletti's—eyes.

They could just see the black cornea on top.

Ranglen wanted to view the object from space. It would resemble the Red Spot on the face of Jupiter if smaller in comparison to the planet. But, instead, it'd be an eye.

And it frightened him. Maybe it was better not to see it, not to tempt a reaction to something so inexplicable, so overwhelming—dead matter enacting form, order, purpose…uncanny as hell. A planet staring at you.

Though not as dramatic here in close-up, which made him glad.

The ship hovered, tilted upward, landed on struts that emerged unevenly.

The engines stopped. Everything settled.

"It doesn't look too scary," Braya said, peering outside.

"It's not the best view."

"Where's the ship that followed us?"

"Still approaching at the same speed. When it gets here, we'll be easy to find. We have about thirty minutes before it arrives."

She moved toward the airlock. "The air's breathable?"

"I need to test it."

"No, we can't wait. Lihandro was here. He can be our test."

She opened the outer hatch. Orange-tinted light flowed in around her.

Ranglen followed, running analysis on his cellpad but not waiting for answers. He wanted a pistol, something protective, but they had found no weapons on the little ship.

He suddenly put his cellpad away. Caution didn't matter now. He was about to meet the Airafane.

He made sure he had the Clip. Braya had trusted him to bring it.

They hurried across the whitish surface. The ground was solid and very hard, mottled, dirty, light and dark. It had no growth. Ranglen reached down and touched the surface. He scraped away any blackness and saw white translucence beneath.

Diamond?

But the cliffs forming the "eyelids" looked like normal silicate and soil. Maybe part of a crust over a diamond mantle, a thin covering in which the trees grew.

The world was *designed*—with unseen gravity-plates to allow people to visit and walk, maybe a whole shell of them, like an iron glove warding off the pull of degenerate matter.

The idea was staggering.

All that the Airafane did was like that.

The eye must be there to get people's attention. *Come and visit. Everyone welcome. We've made it safe for you.*

A trap?

"The doorway. It's open."

Ranglen's nerves were frayed and trembling. He couldn't turn away. He ran to the door as fast as Braya did.

She stared into the opening. Maybe there never had been a door, just this huge vertical slot, rectangular, big and inviting.

She ran her fingers along one edge—almost fondling it, caressing it. "You have the Clip?"

"Yes. We need to hurry."

They moved into the passage and emerged from the corridor into a wide chamber. Enough light came in through the door and reflected off the far wall—where another scored rectangle stood, in the same outline as the entranceway. Beside it was a smaller inlaid square. In the middle of it, a slot.

Obviously, where the Clip was supposed to go.

"Do it," she said.

He brought out the Clip.

She stopped him. "Which end?"

He almost laughed. "The arrow points the way."

Then he inserted it.

It stopped halfway in.

They both waited.

Vague memories stirred in Ranglen. Somewhere he had done this same thing before. And it must have gone badly for his mind had buried it and almost erased the memory.

In the air before them, small lights appeared, hovered in front of the large rectangle. Ranglen couldn't find from where they were projected. Maybe microscopic nano-drones came out of the walls and ignited.

They formed patterns.

A figure took shape, human in appearance, standing before the door-like outline. It was just a pale glittering frame, a suggestion of a person—but Ranglen could swear it looked like a combination of him and Braya, a fuzzy overlap. You could see through it.

This figure pulled another glowing framework from the wall, small and rectangular, like a Clip. This object was then placed back into the slot—and the "person" was pulled into the rectangle, drawn right through it.

And there the figure seemed to glide beyond the wall—where it met other figures, more projections that hovered inside the stone, indistinct, vaguely human but with less detail.

They moved off together.

The images vanished.

"*That's* the instruction," Braya said. "Remove the Clip and then reinsert it."

Ranglen nodded, a bit more warily.

"I know now what happened." Braya's eyes glowed like flames. "Lihandro took out the Clip when he found it and then inserted it, like we did now. But when he followed the instructions and pulled out the Clip again, he *didn't* put it back. He, too, must have seen the figures but he didn't follow through with the directions and insert it a second time. That's what he meant when he said, 'I won't do it. I'm not the one.' He's not the one to go through that doorway and meet the Airafane. That's what happens when you're pulled through. You *meet* them. The Clip is a transport device, bringing someone from now back to *them*."

Ranglen was unconvinced. This was just speculation. "But it would have to be time travel back to when they lived. That's impossible."

"We can't assume things, and I don't want to guess. Maybe they are extinct now, but they want one of us, want to meet us. That's what the figures show."

Then another projected image came up, moving from the opposite side of the room to the rectangle on the wall. This figure pulled out the wire-frame Clip and inserted it.

Nothing happened.

The projection turned around and walked away.

"You see?" said Braya. "Only one person gets through. The Clip must work only once. No wonder Lihandro wouldn't do it. It was too monumental, too important. Only one person from the entire race is taken back to them."

Anticipation flowed through Ranglen, a sudden overpowering wonder.

She pleaded with him. "This is why you're here, Mykol. Don't be like Lihandro. You *have* to go."

"Why not *you*?"

"Be serious! You know more about this than I do. I got you here, but you're the one to take the leap. You have the learning. You'll know what to say. You were *made* to do this. Probably everything you've done up until now has led to this moment—the writing, the exploring, all your time alone. No wonder you and Anne never worked out. You were meant for something bigger. Just *do* it. Reinsert the Clip. Don't wait. There might be a time limit—that's why it went through the instructions again when we got here. The Clip had been away too long or it might have pulled one of us through already."

Ranglen forced himself to move. He pulled the Clip out of the wall, held it in his hand, felt its strange tantalizing appeal.

The Airafane. The Airafane.

"It's your task," she said, "your 'destiny.' You should see it that way. And if they send you back here, you can write about it, make it into history, poetry, a masterpiece. You like alien landscapes, don't you? You'll get to see the best of them now, a million years of them. Lihandro gave the Clip to me but *I* give it to you. It's *my* gift. My claim for the future. I know who deserves it the most. You made Annulus but you're set for something greater than that. You be the envoy, the voice, *our* voice. You have to do this."

Ranglen inched forward.

"Tell them our stories, Mykol. Make us look good."

"Maybe they just want a specimen, something to examine—even to dissect."

"That's nonsense! They'd learn *nothing* from that. Why take a body when they can have a mind, a living being. It's *my* Clip, remember? And I get to use it in the way I choose. I know you want it and that you'll be the best. You'll do fine. You'll do *us* fine."

"Don't you want to go?"

"Of course, I want to go! I'd *love* to see their world. But I'm filled with too much anger and loss. I would have killed three people if I had the chance. Do you want to give them that? No, it's meant for you. It always was for you."

He held up the Clip, stared at the slot.

"Lihandro called his folder 'Chance.' This is *your* chance."

It really was all he ever wanted.

"Dammit, Mykol, do I have to kick you on your way? Go! Go!"

"No one's going anywhere!"

This shout came from outside. The light in the doorway suddenly blocked out. Someone stood there.

Tarakov.

Even in silhouette, he was recognizable. He held an assault rifle aimed at them.

"Don't move," he said, "not the slightest. You obviously have something I want."

He stepped farther into the room.

Ranglen fought a devastating sense of loss, the slap in the face of his own desire. He tried to think, find a way out. "You got here sooner than expected."

"I let you believe you had more time. But I just waited long enough to learn your destination. I had a tracker on this ship all along—on *every* ship back at the camp. No one could escape. And so…I'm here. Now, give me the Clip."

"You're not interested in your plot anymore? The rebellion against Homeworld?" Ranglen said anything just to delay him.

"It'll still work, or another variation of it. But *this* is for me. And with it, I'll be able to do whatever I want."

"Did you kill everyone back on Highland?"

"No, but most of them are dead anyway. Some might have outrun the creature from the mountain but they won't live long. Hideki's dead—I saw her get it."

"And your dogfight with Muletti—who won that?"

"Obviously, me. He crashed and took Krin with him. I heard her whimpering when he tried to radio me."

Braya snapped, "I don't believe you!"

Tarakov looked surprised she spoke at all. "I don't care what you believe. Maybe it's possible they survived the crash. But I'm sure you won't see them again. Let's move along here. I want the Clip."

Ranglen said, remembering Annulus, "You ruined everything by bringing in Ventroni."

"That was Hideki's idea. She's tied to them. And I needed the firepower—I couldn't have blown up the *Lochner* without it. And you forget, Ranglen, once I have the Clip, I can do anything I want. I won't need Ventroni anymore. I'll get independence for Annulus my way. And I'll be in control of it afterward."

"This Clip will surprise you. It won't give you anything."

"It doesn't matter. Just *owning* it is enough. It doesn't need to do anything at all. It's a bargaining tool, the best tool anyone can have. So, just hand it over. I don't want to kill you—I still might use you in the way I said before. But *her* I'd kill in a second. So let's have it now."

No one moved.

"This gun fires a stream of bullets. But it also has finesse. There's a laser on its side that can drill a hole right through your hand—the one holding the Clip. You'll *have* to let go of it. And, by the way, isn't that your writing hand?"

Still no movement.

A roar of spaceships came from outside.

Tarakov spun around, saw something beyond the doorway. He fired his gun at it, spewing bullets.

The sound of another blast came in return.

Tarakov's head snapped around, and blood splattered from his face. He fell backward to the ground.

Ranglen heard people running up to the door, the thunder of more spaceships landing.

Braya yelled at Ranglen, "Use the Clip! Go! Insert it now!"

He stared at her.

"Please, Mykol! Do it!

Then he smiled. "No, Braya....It's you. You're the one."

He flicked his thumb—the Clip flew to her like a cheap spinning coin through the air.

She caught it, looked at him.

"Go for it," he said.

Shouts from outside. "*You, in there! Come out now, slowly, with your hands up!*"

Her eyes looked vivid, so alive.

With no glance back, she inserted the Clip and pushed against the marked section of wall.

She slipped through it. She disappeared.

Another shout, "*NOW!*"

Ranglen touched the wall where Braya had vanished.

Hard as rock. It *was* rock.

He pulled out the Clip and inserted it again.

Still solid. It allowed only one to enter.

A bullet struck beside him on the floor. "*You! Turn around! Take your time about it!*"

He raised his hands. He spun about slowly.

Three officers stood there before him, with rifles similar to Tarakov's. They wore the uniforms not of Annulus but of the Federal Investigators from Earth.

More soldiers hurried in behind them.

Chapter 18: The Obligation

Ranglen expected whips and chains.

But the officers said, "We have more subtle ways now."

He assumed they were joking. They probably weren't.

Muletti had called in the cavalry, in the form of Earth's Federal Investigators. He apparently did survive his dogfight with Tarakov and sent off a messenger drone to Earth—or maybe he had done that before the dogfight. He must have been fed up with Tarakov and the whole operation by then and wanted to bring a stop to it. Maybe he and Krin did manage to escape. But according to what Ranglen eventually heard, the wreckage of the *Prowler* was absorbed by the creature.

So, no one knew now for sure. Ranglen hoped they did get away—and that no one would ever see them again, since only in that way could they remain safe.

Muletti chose Earth to inform because Earth still had the most power. He must have felt it would be needed. And the *Lochner*, after all, had belonged to them, so they should be interested. As it turned out, Hideki also got independent herself, and had put a tracker on Tarakov's ship, the one he used to follow Ranglen and Braya to the eye asteroid. So the Earth ships after arriving on Highland quickly found their means to reach it. The gap in time-space (normal space) being instantaneous during such travel helped them to arrive quickly—the one advantage for any rescuing force in this future world.

Of course, Ranglen had to give up the Clip. The government agents would have killed him as easily as Tarakov would have done—a sad fact of modern day prerogatives. With a show of defeat he didn't feel, he handed it over. Which was easy, because he was certain it would never work again and was now worthless. (They too inserted it into the wall—several times, over and over—but nothing happened.)

Maybe Braya was laughing somewhere. Maybe a million years ago.

Ranglen got a good look at the "eye" when the Federal Investigators' ship went into orbit (they dragged him quickly from the Clip chamber so they could learn as much about it as they could). After all he had been through, the eye, seen from above, looked rather tame, obviously artificial. He felt no horror, no fear it might "blink" or follow his movement as it stared at him.

Until the iris turned blue.

The color of *his* eyes.

This disturbed the hell out of him.

And then the *real* threat of the world grew apparent.

Soon after the ship reached an orbit in space, he heard an officer report, "The gravity on that world is increasing, and incredibly fast."

Ranglen guessed that the gravity-plates were shutting down, unleashing the held-in attraction of the original orb.

The world was turning into a small white dwarf star—what it apparently started as.

Ranglen almost chuckled. When the Airafane indicated the Clip could be used only once, they really meant it.

All people and their spaceships had to leave, and very quickly. Emergency evacuation brought everyone to the edge of the system's disk, where they soon ducked into light-space. Nothing of the Airafane structure would survive, and eventually the system's orbits would develop different and complicated dynamics. Even the blood star would lose some of its plasma, running and bleeding into the new bottomless pit of the crushed star.

Maybe a good indication the Airafane got what they wanted.

And he hoped Braya got what *she* wanted. He had to fight down the envy he felt. He had little doubt she was enjoying herself now.

"Now" of course being wholly relative.

The white dwarf also would swallow all those diamonds. He felt bad for Anne, but at least the market wouldn't be flooded now.

The Federal Investigators kept the Clip, though Ranglen assumed they'd learn nothing from it. He felt they'd eventually put it into hiding, in a deep vault somewhere, after becoming so frustrated in studying it and getting nothing in return. Then they'd start a rumor that it held the secret to a vast "power" that was still being studied, something that could be used as a bogus threat.

After all that happened, as they "traveled" in light-space, came the long rounds of interrogation.

He made no claim to the Clip at all, which helped him. He declared ignorance about its function, saying it was sitting in the slot when he got there and that nothing happened when he reinserted it. He described the chamber in detail and how he was attacked by Tarakov at the end. He said nothing of Braya's use of the Clip and her disappearance, only that she had been shot by Tarakov before they reached the eye and that her body had been left among the trees. He could say pretty much anything about what happened since all evidence to the contrary was now squashed out of existence.

As for the rest, he told it all. The long and ugly story of Tarakov, the human trafficking, the exploitation of refugees, the secret cabal in Annulus Security, the use of the not-so-innocent Seekers (the officers were happy the eye on the asteroid no longer existed—best to keep such tangibles out of reach of fanatic believers), the political maneuverings, the base on 82A and the sordid function of the "Depot of the Dead," even Tarakov's dream of rebellion against Homeworld—he told it all.

And he had his reasons. Frankness bred their trust, and he didn't want to see such events happening again. He wanted *all* of Annulus behind any declaration of independence, not to be led by the obsession and trickery of only one man. And he felt that Homeworld, if it ever got wind of what happened (and not even Earth could cover up everything), might now think twice about its own heavy-handed treatment of Annulus. Some attitudes could change for the better. They might even feel independence was not a bad idea, a good way to keep both Earth and Ventroni out of the Ring.

They grilled him without mercy, but they never got to being physical or biologically "persuasive," though he felt some of them wanted to do that. Except for a few minor details (mainly dealing with Braya and Anne) he told the full truth, and he knew the story would find enough evidence for corroboration. Besides, they ultimately had what they wanted, which was the Clip, and they had a ready group of people to blame for the *Lochner* being destroyed, and those people most responsible were now conveniently dead. So, there was a sense of case closed, supported by expedience. No need to go further.

Annulus Security would be informed, which certainly would lead to a major shake-up within their ranks. People across the political spectrum could show how appalled they were and thus gain points, but even they too might find support shifting into new directions. Ranglen secretly welcomed this. Annulus needed self-examination.

They let him get tired and hungry and sore as the grilling went on. They weren't above testing his endurance by stretching out his agony. But Ranglen knew they couldn't do much to him. It was mainly bluster. They just wanted to make sure he squirmed a little, to reassert their superiority.

Besides, he guessed, the *real* confrontation hadn't come yet. This was just build-up. And he was sure the final blow would not be physical.

He waited for that. He grew rather nervous. And, finally, it came.

One last person came to speak with him.

This individual resembled a congenial grandfather. Tall, a bit weighty, with restrained gestures—he seemed almost embarrassed by his size and authority. He walked gently into the room as if not wanting to knock over anything. He wore a drab civilian suit suggesting he was no great dresser. His graying hair was indiscriminately cut. His eyes looked rheumy, his lips thin, his skin dry. But his hands moved with a flawless grace. And his voice...oh, how it impressed Ranglen. It would have been perfect in recording his poetry. It was slow, deep, exact, pure, with no accent at all, no trace of contaminating social history or locale, utterly assured in its lucid depth. It was like the sound between the stars—if you could hear that sound—the voice of millennia, cold yet mellow, beyond mere empathy, on a cosmic scale that transcended feeling.

Probably what Braya was hearing right now.

Though the man's appearance was that of a minor if efficient civil servant, his voice put him in touch with the universe.

He sat across from Ranglen and smiled at him gently, attentive and polite, all his actions so obviously likable.

But the wet pale eyes in their fans of wrinkles surely missed nothing.

Ranglen felt a panicky unease.

"Good morning, Mr. Ranglen."

Morning? Though the near-military craft did not follow a day-night cycle, this man apparently did.

His tone made you feel privileged to hear him, as if he spoke in a church hall especially for you.

His handshake was firm but not over-powering—kindly, reserved.

"My name is Burrowcliff. I'm the head of Earth's Federal Investigators."

Ranglen trembled all the way to his toes. He was being met by the most powerful spy-master in human space.

"Don't let my title frighten you," he said reassuringly. "When I heard you were involved I couldn't help meeting you. You've always impressed me."

Ranglen trusted none of this. But it had to be genuine because, if otherwise, it would be so obvious a lie as to be absurd.

Then Burrowcliff talked of Ranglen's essays, Ranglen's ideas, Ranglen's stand on exploration and society, even Ranglen's poetry—some of which the man knew quite well, though he obviously was more interested in the social than the personal topics.

"This is all fascinating, Mr. Ranglen—can I call you Mykol?—and I hope we can talk again about it soon. We have a long two days together. But I do have some business that needs to be enacted, and maybe we should clear that up first."

"Mykol" tried not to cringe.

"I want you to know immediately that your welfare is my real concern. I'm not exaggerating when I say that several members of my team recommended I be extremely harsh with you. They suggested body scans, memory probes, drug therapy, even physical and mental…'reconditioning.' All of which I'm sure you'd find intrusive and probably quite painful."

I'm sure.

"To be frank, they wanted to probe every inch of your body, outside and inside, and then try to unravel your brain, lay it out for examination and reconstruct every thought."

Ranglen did his best to show no reaction.

"We'll all after Clips, you understand. The recognized and unrecognized powers of today, of space, governments, corporations, everything. We can't help it. It's a product of our time, the only way of keeping control of historical change, and thus of the future, the future of our lives. And my team believes you carry major secrets on you…or even *in* you…that can lead to the finding of yet more Clips."

Ranglen swallowed. "I've just been lucky."

"I tend to agree, but you really are quite exceptional, you know."

A long pause.

"You've found not only the third Clip, the one that built Annulus, but you now also have found the fourth. That's two in a row…which is *half* the number of *all* Clips that have been found.…Those are damned good odds."

Ranglen tried to stop his lower lip from trembling. "I didn't find this last one."

"But you had it when we arrived. That says enough. That says quite a lot."

Ranglen moved his legs and tried to get more comfortable. It didn't work. He hadn't slept well lately, his meals had been sporadic and hurried, but he couldn't allow his thinking to become clouded. "What are you getting at, Mr. Burrowcliff?"

The man smiled, just slightly. "To be accurate, that's *Secretary* Burrowcliff."

He said this as if it were a small joke, but it expressed serious volumes.

Ranglen argued, "I'm an Annulus citizen. For all your forces here, you have no legal jurisdiction over me."

The Secretary showed no impatience or ire. "You do have rights as an Annulus citizen, but several matters supersede those rights. We're quite far from Annulus at the moment, not just in the 'high seas' of space but also another physical universe, where jurisdiction, it goes without saying, can be hard to determine. And the laws involving Clips—what few laws have been established—transcend both planetary and interstellar boundaries. I could read to you several regulations now, Confederation decrees you don't know even exist, that come into effect when it's convenient for them to do so. Frankly, I have enough means to convince any judge—even on Annulus—to imprison you for some time, possibly the rest of your life. Some of my colleagues want to do just that…and more."

He let Ranglen simmer for a bit.

"But I think that would be foolish. *I* want you untouched, completely free. *I* want you to be able to go anywhere and do what you want."

Ranglen could hear the emphasis on "I."

The man leaned forward and said, in his precise, clear, and near galactic voice, "From now on, I want you working exclusively for *us*, for the Federal Investigators of Earth."

He gave time for Ranglen to stomach the idea.

"Why would I do that?"

"Because all of this, especially if made public, would be very embarrassing for your world of Annulus. It would be humiliating for Homeworld too, but ultimately—and this really would hurt you—it could be a political victory for them. Think of the impact of the story told: rogue officials on Annulus trying to make Homeworld look bad, through the use of piracy, human trafficking, and murder. That leaves the door open for all kinds of recriminations, restrictions, confinements…exactly what your world is trying to avoid. And Annulus then would look very foolish in the eyes of the Confederation. I think you'd agree that none of this would be good for your delightful ring in space."

Ranglen understood now.

They wanted him to be a spy.

"If you agree to this, all the matters dealing with Tarakov, Muletti, the murdered refugees, the destruction of the *Lochner*, even the two illegal bases, all of that will be kept private and not reach the Confederation. Furthermore, the trade war between Earth and Homeworld will also stop. Everybody concerned will understand that one crisis was quite enough—and our holding the Clip will give us the strength to enforce what changes will be needed. No more tariffs growing out of control, no more privateering, and, to be frank, no more Seekers. We'll clean them out too. Annulus will help us in each of these concerns, especially after we give them the details about Tarakov and his cabal, their own agents of law-enforcement breaking the laws they're supposed to enforce. All very embarrassing."

Ranglen just listened.

"We understand that differences are growing between Annulus and Homeworld, and we're not averse to Annulus independence. Indeed, we'd welcome it, for our own reasons. But there's a distinction between us taking over Annulus and *enforcing* a break with Homeworld, or us standing back and allowing you to build a more solid base of approval in the Confederation, for allowing you to do this on your own, which you well might be capable of after the extremes of Tarakov are dealt with, and once you—and Homeworld—accept what can happen when real dissatisfactions are not addressed. An alliance between Annulus and Earth could be very helpful here, one that respects both of our interests. The other side, however, is that of a pure take-over by us, something our military could easily do, and thus leave you no freedom of choice at all. I don't think you want that. But which of the two possibilities occurs depends a lot on *you*…on exactly what you decide to say to me…here, and now."

Ranglen delayed. "Why end the Seekers?"

"We don't think they're sincere or genuinely dedicated. They only lasted this long because Tarakov was using them for his own partisan ends. Hideki's dead, so her influence is gone too, and she had little interest beyond personal gain. She also had far too many ties with Ventroni, a world we're keeping well out of all this."

"What about the creature on Highland?"

"That too will be dealt with."

Goodbye, creature. "I hope it will be studied at least. It's more than what we think. Maybe a direct Airafane product."

"Studied…and yet confined."

Ranglen felt regret. Nothing learned would be shared. The creature's existence might as well be over.

Unless it took over the universe someday.

"What's your answer, Mr. Ranglen?"

He couldn't help thinking, *what other answer is there?*

"Please understand," Burrowcliff went on, "we're most interested in future Clips. And since you seem to have found more than one (we won't advertise that you discovered this recent Clip too), we want to stay close to you. But we don't want to *follow* you. We don't want you limited in what you choose to do. We will not spy on you. What we want is, if, under any circumstances, you find information about the possible whereabouts of new Clips, then you let us know *immediately*. We'll provide you with a secret means, a small and undetectable communication satellite in the Annulus system. Control of that satellite will be solely yours. Only you will be able to access it. To us and to others, your cover will be so deep that no one but myself and one or two of my colleagues will know what you're doing. You won't technically be a spy since we'll never communicate with you, never pass you messages, never send secret orders. You will tell us only what you learn about *one specific subject*...the location of Clips."

Ranglen couldn't stop himself from saying, "So I won't be your agent or your spy, but I will be...'yours.'"

Burrowcliff looked appreciative. "I admire the way you said that."

Ranglen wasn't complimented.

The great spy-master of Earth continued. "And, in the interest of interstellar cooperation, which I know means a lot to you, you can tell anyone about any Clip you find *after* you speak to us about it first. Annulus, Homeworld, the Confederation, anyone. All can still share in the discovery. We will not monopolize it. But the *first* people you tell will be exclusively us."

Then came a pause.

"And you know how hard things will be for Annulus if you don't do this."

Ranglen knew. If he wanted to keep his world free and untouched, he would have to surrender. He frankly didn't feel Earth cared that much about Annulus one way or the other, but Earth cared about Clips. And if he had to negotiate to get a positive forward path for Annulus, he would do so.

And he rather liked the idea of his own private communication satellite. Maybe he could use it to *his* benefit. Fool even Earth.

He said, as if openly pondering, or as just an afterthought, "You're assuming, by the way, that the finding of Clips really is good for humanity, that it's what we *should* do."

The man looked meditative. "I understand your point, and I share your concern. As I said, I've read your essays. But that's also why we insist on control. You might not believe me, but we're not doing this for money or political gain. We're doing it for the survival of the human race. History is ultimately out of one's control, but there can be varying levels of management, and we prefer to at least make an attempt. And don't think we're fooled. We're fully aware that Clips can destroy as well as liberate."

Ranglen tried to look as contemplative himself.

And then, as if Burrowcliff felt that one more threat might be needed to bring the negotiations home, he added, "And I'm fully aware, Mr. Ranglen, that you might be more…interesting…and that you might have more resources at your disposal, than even my own colleagues suspect."

Alarm flowed through Ranglen. How much did the man know?

"I won't say anything more, but I think you understand."

Burrowcliff then stood up slowly, with no superfluous motion or gesture. "And I believe I have your agreement, am I correct?"

Ranglen nodded. It caused no more pain than he expected it to.

Then he asked, "Did you save the ship that brought me to the asteroid?"

"Yes. It was small enough for us to bring it on board."

"Can it be taken to Annulus?"

"Do you intend to give it to Anne Montgomery, so she can use it to make up for the loss of the rental?"

He of course was not surprised that Burrowcliff knew about Anne's renting a ship. But still, he'd admit nothing about her.

"Yes, you can have it," Burrowcliff said, "and Anne Montgomery will not be implicated in any of this."

"Thank you."

The man with his velvety style and iron content opened the door and said behind him as he left, "Good day, Mr. Ranglen." The door closed.

Silence.

Ranglen looked down at his hands. He was embarrassed to see how much they were shaking.

And of all the sad thoughts he encountered this day, the saddest was this…

He knew his future would never be the same.

After returning to Annulus, Ranglen contacted Anne and said he wanted to see her.

She told him to come to her office after working hours, as if sneaking him in.

He brought a box with him. It was solidly made and very heavy. He wheeled it to her on a portable dolly he got from a storage unit in the entrance to her building.

He said, as he came into her room, "I have a gift for you."

She eyed the box critically. "Really?"

"It's a substitute for the cargo you lost. I couldn't retrieve the cargo itself, which I frankly believe didn't exist anyway, but I did find this. I felt you were owed it."

He discovered the box in a hidden locker beneath the main engine on Lihandro's ship. He always had a feeling something more was on board after the Clip had been found there. He assumed Burrowcliff had discovered the locker too and its contents, but chose to ignore it. A kind of payment to Ranglen, a gratuity. No Clips were there and that's the only thing Earth wanted. The pilot who delivered the ship to him on Annulus said nothing about it. And Ranglen gave the craft directly to Hatch, which wouldn't make up for the loss of the two rentals but Hatch would find a good use for it.

Anne opened the box. It was full of dirty blackish rocks of various size.

Ranglen wouldn't prolong the suspense. "They're diamonds. Not gem quality, I assume. But I'm sure you'll spin something from them and manage a most sizable profit."

Lihandro apparently had stashed away the rocks on one of his expeditions, maybe before he found the Clip. He kept them on his vessel, and he either wanted them for himself or Braya. Or the Seekers. Or even Muletti. Who could say? Braya wasn't around now, and the others…"But please be careful. You know Ventroni still controls the diamond market."

Anne sat down as if her legs had weakened. She looked incredulous. "Mykol, you do take your assignments seriously. I'm very impressed. After all that happened, I never expected you to find anything."

"Neither did I. You're also lucky that all possible incriminations against you have been dropped. I won't go into details. Let's just say the interested parties no longer have interest."

Anne looked at him strangely, as if acknowledging that quite a lot was not being said.

"I can't know for sure," he went on, "but I don't think Ventroni will want to pursue any leads to what happened involving the cargo ship. It would be embarrassing even for them, so I think you're free for now. You've also lost the rental ship you got from Hatch. I made up a part of that, but it would be best to pay what's left of the penalty, plus any back payments, and not try to fight it. Making any kind of case would be impossible, and it would dig up matters you want to remain buried." Ranglen already had negotiated with Hatch over the rental *he* lost on Highland.

She nodded, back in the real world again. But the box was still there, and she intentionally backed a little away from it. "I can't examine them now," she said about the rocks, "or I'll get too preoccupied and stay with them for hours. Let me build up to it."

"A wise move. They should provide you with quite enough to start up your business."

"More than enough. I can pay for the new building now."

"You could make it even higher, so your office can really be in the clouds."

She smiled, appreciating the idea.

Ranglen let her dwell in her imagination for a while, before he punctured it. "By the way, I think the restrictions on your type of imports will become tighter. If you sneak anything in now, you might pay highly for it."

She looked defensive but said nothing.

"What Muletti was doing was illegal and dangerous. Luckily, your name won't be associated with it. But his operations have become known. They won't be made public, but they will change things. So expect some new laws. You might need to re-examine what 'legit' really means, and maybe consider different types of imports." All this, Ranglen assumed, would result from Burrowcliff's talks with Annulus, however private.

"Thank you for the warning."

"It'll help you in the long run. You've been maneuvering too close to the edge."

Ranglen didn't expect it but an odd tenderness crept into her face. "I have a lot to thank you for, don't I?"

"I'm just fulfilling part of the assignment."

"I'm assuming it became more 'complicated' than enjoyable."

"It was quite an experience. I didn't enjoy it, but…it was an experience."

She pointed at the box with her chin. "Did you keep one for yourself?"

"Yes," he admitted, not showing guilt. "A small one, a souvenir."

"You're welcome to more."

"No. It'll do."

He sat down then, close to her. And he said, gently. "I think you've guessed already that Muletti is probably dead. And even if he's not, which is unlikely, I'm certain that none of us will see him again."

Her face softened more, but she didn't look surprised. "I did guess." She turned slightly away. "At one point I really liked him. As I said, I knew he had gone through a lot by how much he wouldn't talk about it. I think he meant well. But I knew that more was going on with him. And when he didn't turn up, I suspected he was in deep trouble, life-threatening trouble."

The silence stretched then, as if they waited for each other to say something significant.

She spoke first. "You look sad, Mykol. But I know you won't tell me what happened out there….or what happened to *you*."

"No, not now. Maybe someday."

"Are you aware you always say things like that?"

"This time I mean it. And you frankly might not want to know."

If she asked specifically about Muletti's death, or disappearance, he would have said more, if only in general and vague terms.

But she didn't ask.

And for his part, for all his silence, he didn't know how to say to anyone that he just passed up an invitation to meet the Airafane—to see another world, to see *all* worlds.

Assuming that's what it was. And the uncertainty in knowing was almost as bad.

Braya…where was she now? In the birthing light of the galaxy? What would they think of her? What would they think of humans?

And if *he* had gone, would they think any differently?

Did it even matter?

Well, it did, if only in one way—in how much he wished that *he* were there, seeing what she was seeing.

"What are you thinking, Mykol?"

"Nothing. I better go. Enjoy those rocks." He stood up then.

"Do give me the details behind them someday—the astronomical facts if not the illegalities. It'll help me to tell stories about them. They'll sell better."

"Next time. I promise."

But she stopped him before he reached the door. "A question for you, unrelated to all this. Will you start giving your lecture tour again?"

Ranglen hadn't thought of that, but doing so now suddenly was appealing. He had given lectures before about how the experience of other worlds and alien landscapes could change people, their impressions of art, their impressions of themselves. "That's a good idea. It'll keep me occupied. For a while at least."

"I ask because I recommended you to some student friends at the university. They might want to attend your talks."

"Sure. Send them by."

"There's one named Mileen Oltrepi who might consult with you directly. She's an e-artist who's quite good. And she's interested in painting alien landscapes."

"Tell her to see me. I'll talk with her." A number of people after those lectures often came to him for such information.

"Mykol, for all that you did for me, thank you again. I think I understand how much you made sure I can remain independent, and out of prison."

"No problem. My pleasure."

She laughed. "Didn't you say once, 'To be good for someone, just to be good'?"

"I did write that."

"It describes *you*."

Ranglen was touched, yet he felt his sensitivity was too fragile at the moment to take any compliments. "Thank you, Anne. But I'm so tired now, I don't think I could be good for anyone."

"You don't have to choose to be. You just are."

Now he surely had to leave, and he quickly said goodbye.

As he walked through the deserted building, he smiled as he thought of Anne recommending him to students. He'd make sure he was nice to them.

The name "Mileen" reminded him of something, something that hovered on the edge of his memory but would not take form.

Another name, perhaps…like a chime, in snow.

But it didn't come back to him.

He emerged from the building to find this portion of Annulus in night-phase. The dark sky and shallow atmosphere made the stars clear and brilliant, even in the light from the far side of the Ring.

He could see the Milky Way.

Diamonds.

Acknowledgments

This was a Covid novel, so the "usual suspects" of supporters, the wonderful students and faculty of Seton Hill's MFA in Writing Popular Fiction (which I've been a part of since its beginning), were limited in being as influential as they usually are. But their inspiration still transcended pandemic limits (through the filter of Zoom), and I thank them again and as much as always. I'm also grateful to two works which were very helpful, *The Outlaw Ocean* by Ian Urbin and *A Practical Guide to the Law of the Sea* by James P. Benoit (and thanks to Abby Gallagher for sharing with me her copy of the latter). Appreciation too to Aiden Beck, who graciously answered questions about customs procedures (and I wish I had known him when I first conceived the novel because many fruitless starts might have been avoided). Thanks also to my tireless editors, Jennifer Barnes and Heidi Ruby Miller, and the wonderful institution of Raw Dog Screaming Press and Dog Star Books, which they represent. And a special thanks to Heidi for the delightful introduction. Many thanks also to Bradley Sharp for the fabulous cover (I'm not exaggerating when I say I write these books just to see the art he'll provide). Last and especially, much gratitude goes to Carol—partner, friend, companion, wife—who put up with my writing preoccupations even during the larger social isolation. Much love and appreciation to all, but especially to the last, my other player in our long-running romantic/screwball comedy. (She puts everything into perspective by laughing at my recent editing lamentation, "*Why* did I put in *so many* commas?")

About the Author

An early interest in astronomy, DC science-fiction comics, and the Sunday Flash Gordon adventure strip led Albert Wendland to a life-long fascination with science fiction. He wrote one of the earliest dissertations on science fiction, and even his drawings and paintings had SF themes. He's taught literature, fiction-writing, and often SF at Seton Hill University, where he co-created the MFA program in Writing Popular Fiction, which emphasizes genre fiction exclusively—an emphasis rare in graduate writing programs. His SF novel, *The Man Who Loved Alien Landscapes*, a starred pick-of-the-week by *Publisher's Weekly*, was released by Dog Star Books and became the first installment in his "Mykol Ranglen" series (described by readers as "space noir"). It was followed by a prequel, *In a Suspect Universe*, and then by a collection of poems, *Temporary Planets for Transitory Days*, which supposedly were written by the protagonist of the first two books. The current novel, Haunted Stars, takes place between the two earlier stories, and Wendland currently is working on more novels that will be sequels to the first one. (He's described his series more as a spiral than a straight line.) His other interests are geology, astronomy, landscape photography (see his pictures on Facebook and Instagram), graphic novels, film, and the "sublime" in prose, art, nature, and outer space.